LEGENDS
Of The 6ix

DEVANSH GUPTA

BlueRose Publishers

First Published in February 2021

ISBN: 978-93-5427-399-5

BLUEROSE PUBLISHERS

www.bluerosepublishers.com

info@bluerosepublishers.com

+91 8882 898 898

Cover Design:

Inderjeet

Typographic Design:

Namrata Saini

Distributed by: BlueRose, Amazon, Flipkart, Shopclues

About the Author

'Inexperience should be treated as a premium because someone who lacks experience does not know what cant be done and finds a way to do it'. This is one of the guiding mantras of Devansh Gupta, who is a young and dynamic entrepreneur and a prolific writer. As a student, Devansh wrote avidly about the verdant forests, the picturesque mountain hamlets and the streamy rivers during his visits to his father's tea gardens in Dooars. After finishing his high school, he went to pursue further studies at the University of Toronto in Canada, which is one of the most prestigious universities in the world. It was his experiences at the University of Toronto which inspired him to write this book with such intense emotions, powerful characters and unexpected twists.

Devansh went on to pursue post graduate studies at the London School of Economics and Political Science which further honed his writing skills. He believes in using language that can be easily understood by a beginner reader, but would also pique the interest of voracious readers and fans of fiction.

Acknowledgements

Foremost, I would like to express my sincere gratitude and thanks to my parents for their continuous support, allowing me to follow my dreams. They have financially helped me throughout my education abroad, where I realized how people way more talented than me lost out on opportunities due to a lack of resources. Their patience, encouragement, motivation and enthusiasm throughout this journey played a great role in the culmination of this book.

Besides my parents, I would like to thank my awesome friends who have unknowingly inspired me to write this book. Their good characteristics and flaws have helped me mold many of the characters in this book. To Andre, who was my roommate and my first friend in university, who logically reasoned with me whenever I acted on misguided preconceived notions. To Ryan, who I have spent a lot of time studying, partying and making memories. Also, I would like to thank Megha, who proofread the first draft and suggested valuable changes.

The people of Canada, in particular Toronto, where I spent the most amazing years and the University of Toronto for swallowing a boy and spitting out a man who can think more critically.

To some of the world's best dating coaches whom I have had the privilege to learn from and the filmmakers who approach me to write scripts. I am very grateful for your love and confidence in me.

Lastly, I would like to thank my publisher Bluerose for enabling me to take my work to readers across the globe.

Contents

The Reunion

It was 7:10 pm when my flight from London, England, touched base at the Toronto Pearson International Airport in Canada. I had just landed in my favorite city after being in the air for eight hours with roughly five hundred other strangers who had flown with me from the Heathrow Airport in London. Even though I was in a different continent, a different country, and in a different city, the queen that signed a bill in this country and made it the law was the same lady who lived in the Buckingham Palace in London. Canada, once a part of the mighty British Empire, followed some age-old traditions until today, even after achieving its independence. Even after 150 years of gaining freedom from the British rule, the effects of colonization were visible and reinforced in its traditions, language, and the systematic disenfranchisement and impoverished conditions of the Aboriginals. The reason these features crossed my mind was because I was born and brought up in India which was also a former British colony, and it was fascinating to see how the influence of a colonizing power affected a country's culture on a macro and micro scale. Moreover, I had a penchant for understanding the power structures and the underlying reasons of why society evolves the way it does, and it was probably why I had chosen sociology as one of my majors in university. As I looked outside the plane's window, the smell of familiarity seized me. It was bright outside, as the sun sets late in the summers. The city's skyline looked as beautiful as ever, basking in its glory, unaltered in its tryst with the thousands of people who are in awe of it from the moment they arrive in Toronto. I sat impatiently on my seat waiting for the cabin crew to begin deplaning the passengers, because I couldn't wait to be back to my stomping grounds. I had flown back for the annual reunion at the University of Toronto, which had been my home for four years, and I was stoked to meet my friends who had made it feel like home.

I cleared customs, collected my luggage, and caught a cab outside the airport. 'Where do you want to go, sir?' asked the chauffeur.

I gave him the address of the Airbnb that I had booked near my university downtown. 'It would cost you 55$, sir,' he said. I was pleasantly surprised as I vividly remembered that the standard rate for a cab from the airport to downtown was 55$ even six years ago when I had come to Toronto for the first time in 2013 as a student. The driver asked me if he could play music in his car, to which I gave a passive nod, as I was lost in my thoughts about the chain of events that would unfold the next day. I would be meeting some of my most treasured people in the world. I couldn't believe I was finally back in Toronto after two years, because it felt like convocation was yesterday and the whole ceremony played in my mind. I was distracted from my thoughts as the driver changed the track to Drake's *God's Plan*, which was the biggest hit from the artist's album last year. As the car drove into downtown Toronto, I could feel the vibe of the city settling in as I was listening to Drake who coincidentally was also from Toronto and the semi-Torontonian in me felt very proud of his achievements of putting Toronto on the global map through not only music but also through his other endeavors that he constantly undertook to represent the city. If there was one god I believed in, it was the '6ix God' – a terminology used to refer to Drake – and maybe it was some God's plan that I was back for this long awaited reunion after taking a week's leave from work, for which I had applied three months in advance.

I was welcomed warmly by my host Alyssa who was a tall thirty-year young Caucasian lady with blonde hair and a nose ring that gave her somewhat of a hipster look. She worked in homeless shelters as a social worker. She had a dog named Tequila, which piqued my interest, as I liked both dogs and alcohol.

'This is your room. Feel free to eat or use anything that I have in the kitchen. Treat it like your own house,' said Alyssa with a big smile on her face. 'Knock on my door or shoot me a text if you need anything.'

'Thank you so much, Alyssa. I am pretty tired, as I have had a long flight and have an early start tomorrow. I reckon I will eat some food and go to bed. I have some home cooked Indian food with me. You could try some if you like,' I said, offering to share my dinner with her.

'I love curry. I have eaten dinner, but I can always make some space for your curry,' she replied.

Living in the West had made me habituated to experiencing stereotypes or outright ignorance about my culture from the average White man (or in this case woman) who brushed the cuisine of a country as diverse as India down to curry. At this hour, I thought it would be pointless to get into a geography lesson about the richness, multiculturalism, and diversity of a country where the local cuisine, language, and dialect changed every 100 km. I couldn't be less lackadaisical even if she was one of those people who believed India was worth visiting only if one wanted to see the Taj Mahal or snake charmers. The color of my skin has evoked subtler comments in the West by White folks who have complimented me for speaking fluent English. I have always returned those compliments with a tinge of innocence and sarcasm by saying that they spoke fluent English too.

'I don't have curry with me, Alyssa, I have a dish of potato and cauliflowers with some Indian bread (*rotis*). I am a good cook. You can trust me.' To which, she coyly replied, 'Sure.'

The next morning, I woke up at 8:40 am because I had to pack my bags for the weekend getaway that we had planned after the reunion event. The reunion event was a BBQ lunch organized by UofT[1] at the front campus at King's College Circle. After packing my bag, I had a jentacular cup of coffee with an avocado sandwich before going for a shower so that I could reach the campus by 10:30 am, two and a half hours before the event started. The reason I wanted to reach the campus much before the

[1] University of Toronto

scheduled time was so that I could go down memory lane once again and cherish every spot on campus that I had a history with and be one with nature's mesmerizing beauty that adorned one of the prettiest and biggest campuses situated in the heart of the city as busy as Toronto. Deep within, I was still pining after my bright university years as the eighteen-year-old who was excited to be living far away from the gaze of his parents, a time where you find yourself staring into the vast ocean of possibilities, looking forward to summer vacations that last four months, or ordering pitchers at the bar with your friends until the last call because the next day didn't have a morning lecture. I wanted to escape the daily grind of adulthood, and the only way to flee the rut was to reminisce the good old days of university.

I entered the campus through St. Mary's street right through Gate House, a student residence that is divided into two sections by a huge gate in the middle. The grey stone walls covered by ivy were a classic feature of the Neo-Gothic architectural style, and the residences at Victoria College (UofT was divided into seven different colleges, and every student was affiliated to one of the colleges unless you had an engineering major) had gargoyles, turrets, and battlements which added a *Hogwarts* feel to its ancient look. Gate House had been notoriously infamous for some of the most outlandish traditions, hosting crazy toga parties, and rituals like 'stirring the chicken' which involved underage drinking, partying, and sculpting a penis from snow. The walls were partially covered with green branches and leaves which have several benefits like controlling the pollution, reducing carbon dioxide levels, protecting the students from UV rays, and contributing to the natural beauty of the campus. The first thing I did upon returning back to campus was swoon over the lush green grass at the Victoria quad while the sun was shining brightly down and the atmosphere of campus life seduced me.

I lay down sideways on my back and observed my surroundings to notice how nothing had changed. A group of students was playing pass with the soccer ball, another student was sitting on the grass and reading a novel while a young couple who looked like they were in their first year were making out on the bench which had the bronze statue of Northrop Frye, the same bench which had featured in the movie *Almost Adults*. I could see myself in these students, as it wasn't very long back when I was doing these same things. Except that the bench where I took my dates was down the steps from the Victoria quad, behind the EJ Pratt Library, as one could see a small artificial waterfall from that bench and that spot made a more picturesque setting for a romantic smooch.

I moved in the direction of Queen's Park towards the Philosopher's Walk which had been one of our favorite spots for intense group discussions. On my way, I crossed the Old Vic building which in my opinion was the most visually appealing building on campus embodying the best form of Richardsonian Romanesque architecture. The Philosopher's Walk, as its name aptly implies, was a scenic leafy footpath used by most students and professors to commute from one end of the campus to the other while others used it to stroll, think, and contemplate. It was a quiet reprieve from the bustling campus life of downtown Toronto and right at its epicentre had an amphitheater which was barely used for plays but had a precious place in my heart, as this is where our friends' group often met to unwind, rejuvenate, and reconnect with nature, as our well sequestered, urban living, binge-drinking and pizza-eating lifestyle needed some fresh air and natural light to sustain itself. After all, as university students, we knew that even the most processed of food products traces its root to something grown in soil. As urban dwellers, human beings have internalized their urban lifestyles to such an extent that many of us don't realize that we have spent an entire day without touching the soil or watching a wild animal. An eminent author called Kahn coined a phrase called 'environmental generational amnesia' to describe this phenomenon where every generation creates a new explanation of what is environmentally natural based on how one is brought up.

I sat down on one of the benches of the Philosopher's Walk to deconstruct my emotions, and this was the first time

I was sitting there without my friends. The silence felt comforting as I heard the rustling of the leaves that quivered in the tepid breeze; the lush moist grass seemed to be oozing out its green as it was kempt and healthy. The stone pathway of the Philosopher's Walk that people used to commute from Hoskin Avenue to Bloor Street had a rusty grey texture that shone brightly in the morning sun as a raccoon swiftly strode across it to hide in one of the bushes. There was no one around me other than an old couple who looked like they were in their sixties, sitting on an adjacent bench and quietly munching their hotdogs. They seemed like they had attended one of the alumni lecture events, as they both were carrying their nametags that were hanging from their necks. University of Toronto had many alumni events throughout the reunion week on all three of its campuses. The couple seemed to be contently enjoying their hotdogs after scavenging out a quiet refuge from the din of the city. I thought how different the campus must have been when they were students. Firstly, technology was not ubiquitous, and they didn't have the luxury to take notes on their laptops, view missed lectures online, or find love on their phones. The university had evolved drastically with many new residences and departments focusing on innovation, engineering, and campus life. I wondered if they were university sweethearts and met while studying here, as universities are statistically one of the biggest marriage markets in the world. With the onslaught of technology, would I feel outdated on this campus when I turn their age and come back for a reunion? Or would I be a busy grandparent who no longer feels wistful about his college years and has stopped going for reunions?

I heard a distant clamor and saw a group of school children being guided by their teachers, just like a herd of cattle running amok is guided by its owners, who try to make them follow a particular path and discipline their movements. They had probably come on a school visit to either the Royal Ontario Museum or the Bata Shoe Museum, which was the largest shoe museum in the world, both of which were at a walking distance from the Philosopher's Walk. In fact, the Bata Shoe Museum was situated right on campus. It was 11:30 am, and I had half an hour to myself before Andre and Sam reached the university. They were reaching an hour before the event started, as I had informed them that I would be arriving on campus early. I knew exactly the place I had to visit before they came, as both of them weren't at all nostalgic about going to this place and, if anything, fretted at the thought of entering it. We had spent countless nights in that place and raked up bills of hundreds of dollars, sipping caffeine while pulling off all-night study sessions. In my final year of university, I had spent more time there than in my own room or lecture halls. This place was called the Robarts Library. Therefore, I decided to follow the herd of the two-legged cattle out of the Philosopher's Walk.

I entered Robarts Library through its revolving doors, which was one of the forty-four libraries at the University of Toronto, but what made it unique was the fact that Robarts was the largest of them all. The University of Toronto has the third largest academic collection in North America after Harvard and Yale, and it took immense pride in the systematic organization and operations of all its libraries. The first floor of Robarts had a cluster of about 50 computers that were accessible to the current students and alumni. I could blindly navigate my way around this floor, as I had spent innumerable hours typing essays on these computers. Every monitor, keyboard, and mouse on this floor could recognize me by the touch of my fingers. I steadily made my way towards the escalator and went up to the first floor where the cafeteria and Starbucks was located. I felt delighted, but that delightfulness was mixed with a bit of spite on seeing the students eat their meals while they laughed with their friends or spoke on video call or listened to music on their phone while some Asian whizz kids were multi-tasking their food with complex math topics like integration. Even though I worked as a digital strategy and fintech analyst at JP Morgan in London and no longer had to live within a student budget, I longed for these student meals because they were shared with people whom I cared for and who cared for me. If I didn't have the reunion lunch, I would have definitely bought myself a subway sandwich from the cafeteria or noodles from one of the many Chinese food trucks that were right outside the library on St. George Street. Nonetheless, I decided to queue up in a long serpentine line like my former days for the ever-reliable Starbucks that had kept us awake and full of energy through countless midterms and exams. Considering the weather outside, I decided to go for the tall iced caramel macchiato with whipped cream instead of my usual venti soy green tea latte. One of my courses at university called Sociology of Food had included a case study on Starbucks through the lens of cultural imperialism, which is a very important framework for analysis. I had learnt how Starbucks had especially conceived its complex terminology as it gave its customers a sense of importance while ordering coffee, which was not possible in a local café where one had to order a 'medium green tea'. It also drew on its origins of America and the superiority of the Western culture and lifestyle to make significant inroads in Asia and Africa as well as in the minds of hundreds of students who come from these continents to study in the West.

When you have an Indian name that isn't as simple as Raj, chances are that the Starbucks personnel in the West are not only going to misspell it but also embarrass you when they call out the most creative form of your misspelled name in front of strangers when the order was ready. Therefore, I always went with Dave instead of Devansh whenever I ordered a drink at Starbucks. After collecting my order, I went to examine the quiet study spaces to see if they had renovated or changed the furniture during the two years of my absence. Sipping my drink and looking at the students who would rather be enjoying their summers than taking extra credits in summer school, I thought how most of them would eventually be longing for this time when life hits them with a shovel and they will wish they had savored more of these carefree days. Hoping that my thoughts weren't audible, I heard the sound of a text notification on my phone. It was 11:58 am, and I had just received a text from Andre which read:

Sam and I have reached and are at the Fung. Where you at, nigga?

Fung was short for Howard Ferguson dining hall, which was located inside Morrison Hall, a residence hall at University College (one of the seven colleges). It is a huge dining hall that is finely paneled in wood with several long tables and wooden chairs, ideal for living out your *Harry Potter* fantasies or fantasies about studying in an institution that conflated modern thoughts with old interiors. Fung rang a lot of bells because we had eaten countless meals and held all possible kinds of conversations that ranged from intense, meaningless, and lighthearted to general chit chat inside it during our time at university. There was so much history, drama, effervescence, criticism, and gossip embedded in that room. The Fung was a short walk across the street from Robarts. I replied to Andre's message:

I will be there in two minutes.

I was filled with excitement and enthusiasm as I entered Morrison Hall; adrenaline rushing through my veins as I briskly walked past its patrons with a confident smile on my face. The first one to spot me was Sam, and he stood up with zeal to walk towards me as I entered the Fung. Andre screamed, 'My boy is finally back,' as he turned his head and saw me after Sam had sprung out of his chair with great vigor. Sam shook my hands, and we hugged each other like brothers hug when they meet after a long time.

'Devansh, I can't believe you are actually back in Toronto,' said Sam. 'Man, you seem to be in good shape, been hitting the gym lately, eh?'

'Yeah, you know how work life is, man. Sitting at the desk for eight hours a day. Need some physical activity going on to de-stress after a long day,' I replied.

'Are you sure that is the reason or have you found a new bird in London whom you want to impress?' he said with a wry smile on his face.

'You seem to have gained more than what I have lost,' I said looking at his small beer belly. 'Your millionaire lifestyle is getting to you, I guess. Remember? The rich man suffers from the gout,' I quoted Shakespeare in the last sentence, though I doubt he got the reference. Sam was one of those millennial millionaires who had made his fortune in cryptocurrencies. Buying and selling Bitcoin at the right time had thrust him into the club of elites, and he spent his newly acquired wealth travelling and partying all over North America from the high-end hotels that resonated with opulence and luxury in Las Vegas to the sunny beach resorts in Cancun that had overflowing tapas bars. His Instagram, Facebook, and Snapchat stories were a testimony to the king-size life that he was leading. If I were sitting on a pile of cash like him, I would have had a pot-size belly by now. He was still doing better. The brands on his outfit complemented his luxury lifestyle. He was sporting a casual light pink crew top from Valentino with a pair of white jeans and high-top sneakers from Ylati, which is an expensive Italian brand. His outfit was supported with a belt from Hermes and Louis Vuitton sunglasses which looked slick for the summers.

On the contrary, Andre was wearing his regular Hollister full sleeve t-shirt with dark denim jeans and a pair of suede loafers that matched the color of his denims. Andre was six feet tall, slightly muscular, strong, and a light-skinned Black Canadian, who was born to Jamaican parents. The only person I knew who was capable of looking suave in any outfit was Andre. Even though he wasn't wearing any flashy brands like Sam, he looked sharp and well-groomed. Andre shook my hands and said, 'We missed you, man. It is so good to have you back. We have so much to catch up on. London! Your job and also the girl whom you told me about at your office. What was her name, Adrianna?'

'London has been amazing, but I miss you guys a lot. The six o'clock pub rush in London is the best atmosphere ever when everyone gets out of their offices and rushes straight to the pub to grab a few pints. It seems like the whole city descends down to get wellied after a long day's work with some pockets in central London like Soho, Shoreditch, and Leceister Square being the liveliest places on Earth'.

'Lucky bastard. I want to live in Europe one day. You didn't say anything about Adrianna though. Did you hit a homerun with her?' (An American expression that meant whether I had slept with her or not.)

'She is super hot, but I am not planning on fooling around now. Those days are behind me, mate. But I hear you have been hitting a lot of homeruns at your work and new gym.'

Andre glanced at Sam as soon as I said this, who coyly looked away with a slight grin on his face. He was guilty of ratting out Andre's sexual conquests to me and, in the process, stealing the pride that Andre would have experienced had he narrated anecdotes from his promiscuous lifestyle to me. Sam was fully aware of the miniscule details that pertained to Andre's life, as Andre was living in Sam's penthouse apartment in downtown Toronto that Sam had bought last year. Even though Andre was drawing a handsome pay cheque as an investment banker, Sam insisted that he live with him, as his place had two bedrooms and he wanted a trusted cohost for the parties that he threw at his place. Sam had graduated from university a semester later than us, but the frat boy inside him that loved playing beer pong had not. Furthermore, Sam had outright refused taking even a single dollar in rent from Andre, even though Andre had been persistent in his efforts that Sam accept a meagre amount at least. Sam's only condition was that Andre used his rent money on partying with him, to which Andre gladly agreed. Moreover, Scotiabank, where Andre worked, was a short distance from the penthouse, so the arrangement worked out well for both of them.

The three of us sat down at Fung and carried on our banter while I attempted to catch up with their lives in detail.

'How are things at work?' I asked Andre.

'Just the usual. Long hours and lots of meetings.'

'And for you, Sam?' I asked vehemently even though I knew it was mostly play for him. Sam didn't have and did not need a full-time job like us and was only managing his personal portfolio of cryptocurrencies. Yet, he earned way more than both of us combined. He had sold 500 Bitcoins at their peak price of 18,500$ to rake up a fortune worth 9 million dollars. Very few people would have the motivation to do a full-time job when they have made so much money at such a young age. Whenever asked about work, whether it was coursework at university or his investments in cryptocurrency, Sam had a patent answer that he gave everyone, 'Work is unbelievable.' The irony of his statement was that you never knew what to expect of it or what exactly he means. One could never know if things were going good or bad. We were always left confused whenever anyone of us asked him about his essays or assignments. Maybe that was his way of dealing with pressure. He never got tensed about the hardest of exams or the lengthiest of essays. He never talked business with or without pleasure. Considering the position he had reached, one needed to possess a calm mind as well as a sharp acumen for dealing with people, and he had both.

The BBQ lunch was about to start soon, so we headed out to King's College Circle from the back exit of Morrison Hall to collect our nametags and food coupons, thereby crossing the beautiful quad of university college. We were in the queue waiting for our turns when I felt a tap on my shoulder. I turned around only to receive the warmest and the longest hug I had received in a while.

'You haven't changed a bit. You looked so different when you had last spoken to me on Skype from London. I could notice your fade from a distance,' said Sonia with a loud display of alacrity.

'You shocked me. But I always missed your hugs in London. They were like morning coffee to me in university. There is something magical in them, you know? I felt so much more energetic the whole day after receiving them. Where is Nigel?' I asked because they were supposed to come together. She pointed behind her. He was walking at a distance, waving his hand in our direction. I guess he dropped Sonia first and then went to park the car, which probably explained why he was strolling behind her.

Nigel and Sonia were total opposites when it came to dressing up for an occasion. Sonia was wearing a pink floral, backless maxi dress with a sexy plunging neckline, a thigh split, and Laela heels in black micro. Moreover, she had the perfect blend of foundation, natural mineral mascara, and lipstick that complemented her skin tone. She had brown skin and came from a mixed heritage, as her father was a Pakistani and her mother came from Saudi Arabia. On the contrary, Nigel was a Caucasian male with long blond hair which he kept tied. He was wearing a simple short-sleeve grey t-shirt with black pants and running shoes. Nigel had an athletic physique, as he had been playing American football from a young age and even represented our university at the varsity level. He was consistent with working out and practicing kickboxing as well.

We collected our nametags and lunch coupons and headed straight towards the food counters to avoid the long queues later. Lydia was the only one missing. She had informed Sonia that her train from Hamilton was leaving around noon, so she would be a bit late. Considering how expensive education at UofT is, I felt the university should hold more of these events. There was a wide array of food options at this BBQ luncheon. The first counter had choices between (vegetarian, chicken, and beef) burgers or hotdogs where one could then choose the toppings that ranged from red onions, pickles, sautéed mushrooms to lettuce and tomatoes. I chose the vegetarian burger and added some horse-radish mayo and ketchup in it. The next counter had boiled potatoes, coleslaw salad, roasted asparagus, cheese pasta, and an endless supply of soft drinks. The event was very well organized and King's College Circle had tables and benches laid out for everyone to sit. There was even a temporary shelter constructed which housed round tables for more seating and an alumni photo booth with fancy props and juice counters. People of all ages, sizes, and races soon descended upon the beautiful front campus and the huge ground was full of cheer, fun, and frolic. An onlooker would reckon it to be a busy beehive. There were scenes of merriment, friends catching up, children lining up outside the ice cream trucks, and old and young members meeting their friends and batch mates after a long duration.

Andre and Sam had found us a table, and the rest of us were heading towards them with plates of food in our hands. We sat around the table with our food, and this brought back so many memories. Life on campus involved hundreds of breakfasts, lunches, and dinners with friends, because when a person is living in university dorms, friends play the role of family. All moments of joy, excitement, sorrow, and stress are shared with friends. They become your support system when you need someone to be around you physically. Parents can emotionally support you only to a certain extent, as they are far away and can't partake in one's daily struggles.

'How is your Airbnb?' Nigel asked me as he manducated his chicken burger. 'This burger is so juicy and sumptuous,' he added with the look of contentment in his eyes.

'My accommodation is pretty comfortable, and the hostess seems like a nice lady. Also, I was lucky to find a reasonable place close to campus considering how expensive Toronto has become. The real estate market is only going to go up. It is a very good time to invest in the GTA. Tell me about the house you guys have booked for our weekend getaway. I haven't got any pictures yet.'

Sonia replied, 'I wanted our holiday villa to be kept a surprise. The pictures will spoil all the fun. You guys should see and judge our taste. Lydia and I took a lot of time to zero in on this one. All I can tell you for now is that it has a big swimming pool and the interiors are plush.'

'Whether we like it or not, Nigel would definitely have to appreciate your taste,' said Sam with a naughty smirk on his face. Nigel and Sonia were in a relationship, and Sam had always enjoyed taking an occasional stab at Nigel even in his former relationship by mocking how henpecked he was. Well, Sonia and Nigel were still our favorite interracial couple.

'Stop being a douche,' replied Nigel.

'He has a point though. That booty has you like...Damn! Hot girl, two o'clock,' said Andre, pulling Nigel's leg further.

All of us turned our heads in the northeast direction from where Andre was sitting since that is the direction where two o'clock would fall on a watch. He was correct. The prettiest girl in the reunion had finally arrived with a carryon luggage for our weekend retreat.

'I am so sorry guys for being late. The best train that I could catch left at 12:30. The other train would have gotten me two hours early for this event. Devaaaaansh...' she rushed to hug me. 'How are you? It is so good to see you. You forgot me after going to London. You barely call or WhatsApp.'

'You know how work is. Plus, I am in a different time zone. By the time I get done, you guys are still working here.'

'Hello, Lydia. We exist too. You are seeing us after a long time as well, even though Hamilton is barely two hours away. The last time we met you was New Year's. By the way Sonia, did you notice how Nigel's head turned when I said hot girl at two o'clock?' said Andre.

'Yes, I did. Someone is in trouble, I guess,' said Sonia, trying to join in on the fun.

For a moment I felt like I was dreaming. I had been envisioning this reunion for months, and now it felt like time had come to a stop. Other than Ryan, everyone was here. Even though my stomach was still half empty, my heart was finally full. This moment was priceless, and even a three-course meal at a Michelin-starred restaurant in Toronto could not compensate for this company.

'There is very long queue for the food now. I will eat something at Maddy's. Let me grab a pop from the ice boxes,' said Lydia.

The Madison Avenue pub or Maddy's as it was popularly known among the student population of Toronto is a mega pub that was built by connecting three Victorian mansions and was a five minute walk from campus. It was hugely popular with the locals for its convivial setting and weekly specials for students who are always broke. It comprised of several floors with six British style bars as well as darts and a pool table for people who get fiercely competitive after a few drinks. We had planned to go to the Madison to grab a few suds before heading to our weekend getaway home.

By the time Lydia returned with a coke, we had almost finished our meals. We decided to get some pictures at the photo booth inside the marquee before heading to Maddy's. I took the cliché moustache photo prop while the others took boards which had some text written on them. Sam held the prop which read 'Still a troublemaker' while Andre sported the 'When did we get so old?' prop. Sonia held 'We are still together' and pointed it at Nigel. Lydia made an expression of guilt and slightly raised the prop of 'Came for the gossip'. Nigel couldn't find anything interesting to hold, so he just held Sonia by the waist. After collecting six copies of the picture, so that everyone gets to keep one, we headed towards the Madison pub.

The six of us entered the Madison and got a table upstairs on the patio. Emily, a server who had started working at Madison when we began university, instantly recognized us, as we were regulars and generously tipped her. She greeted us with a lot of enthusiasm and gusto, 'Madison has not been the same without you guys. All of you have grown up now. Lydia, I still can't forget the party at your sorority that you had invited me to. Guys, I am going to get you the menus even though I don't think you all would need it. As my favorite customers, your first round will be on me,' said Emily.

'Thank you so much, Emily, we all appreciate your gesture,' Lydia told her.

'She is such a sweetheart,' said Sonia after Emily had gone to get our drinks. 'The best part about this place has been its excellent customer service. No wonder, in the neighborhood that has so vibrantly evolved over the years, the Madison continues to stay and make business.'

'That is true. They have always had excellent deals for students too. At this time, we would get the appetizers at half price. Should we order what we always get?' I asked.

'Yes! I am craving their voodoo chicken fingers. Let us get two of those and one nachos supreme. That would be enough for the six of us. Since I will be driving the car after we are done here, I will just be having one beer,' said Andre. Voodoo chicken fingers was the best-selling item at Maddy's.

'Me too. I am driving the other car, so I won't be drinking at all. I will just have some food,' said Sonia.

I was surprised to hear that Sonia was abstaining from liquor, as she could xertz beer quicker than any of us. Even though she came from a strict Muslim family, she had indulged in everything that her parents had always asked her to refrain from like drugs, alcohol, and premarital sex. She aptly embodied the saying 'Halal on the streets, haram in the sheets'.

'Okay. Let us order two pitchers of beer and one wine sangria. How about Molson and Bavarian? The Bavarian beer at Maddy's is something that was on my to-do list in Toronto.'

'I think our order is perfect. Just like the good old times,' said Nigel.

By then, Emily had arrived with the first round of drinks and was ready to take our order. She repeated it just to make sure that she had it right.

'Suds on a Friday afternoon at Maddy's! Sonia, I will have your beer, since you aren't drinking anything,' chuckled Sam, to which Sonia gladly agreed.

I wouldn't be bragging if I said that there were some of the heaviest male and female drinkers on our table in Toronto. The drinks and the food came. We drank and laughed and talked as the sun gradually lowered over the horizon. Three pitchers among four people is not something that even the students who occupied the tables around us would dare to order.

After his fifth or sixth glass, Sam drooled over the table and said, 'I wish Ryan was here right now. He is missing out on everything. Let me Snapchat a groufie to him.'

Ryan was the only one who couldn't make it to this reunion. He was busy with an article of clerkship in the United States, and it wasn't possible for him to fly back. I knew for a fact that the picture that Sam was about to send him would result in him having more FOMO. I am sure he would regret not being able to make it. As soon as Sam mentioned Ryan, I sensed Lydia feeling a bit uneasy. Her face suddenly grew smaller, and she put her hand behind her neck as if to scratch it. As close friends, we all knew each other so well that I could easily tell that scratching her neck was a sign which meant Lydia wasn't comfortable. Although the cause of this uneasiness was related to an incident that happened two years ago, Ryan and Lydia had barely spoken after that and had only shown the courtesy of wishing each other on birthdays (that too on Facebook). I was the only one whom Ryan had confided in. Lydia had expressed feelings for Ryan a month after the convocation and had wanted to date him, but Ryan could never reciprocate those feelings because he didn't feel the same way about her after all these years of friendship. Also, he was leaving for law school to Yale and did not see himself dealing with a long-distance relationship.

'How are things with you and Luke?' I asked Lydia in order to change the topic and distract her from her current emotions.

'We are going to live together once I move to Australia for work. My job at ABC News starts in September. Can't wait to flaunt my bikini on the beaches there. We are getting a place near the beach.'

Lydia had gone to intern at the Australia Broadcasting Corporation in January and managed to secure a full-time job offer at the same company. During her stay in Sydney, she met a guy called Luke Rigo at one of the media events that Luke was organizing. Apparently, the bloke was pretty famous in the event management industry and had pictures with 50 Cent, Rihanna, and Shawn Mendes. I knew this, as I had stalked him online after Lydia had shared the news with me in March. I was happy for her. Also, she had escaped the harsh Canadian winters and was enjoying the warm Australian summers.

'I need to take a leak. God! I have drank too much,' said Nigel after his fifth drink.

I turned to Andre in my semi-drunk condition and put a 5$ bill on the table. 'I bet you five bucks to get that brawd's number who is standing by the bar,' I said. When we were students, we played this game amongst ourselves where we would bet each other a dollar or two to talk to attractive women especially when we saw them in the library or a bar, as they were not in a rush then. This game served two primary purposes. One of them was to push each other to talk to attractive girls, because as freshmen we were nervous about approaching girls randomly. Secondly, it was a fun exercise for the whole group and a good way to improve our social skills. The only condition was that one couldn't refuse the bet. The only thing that changed from our university days was probably the amount of money that I was ready to gamble, as I could easily afford losing five bucks now.

Andre was stoked for the challenge. He got up with an air of confidence and walked towards the girl with a smile and looked sharply at her, trying to find contact with her eyes.

'Hi! I am Andre. Do you believe in magic?' he asked the brawd.

'No, I don't,' she replied.

'What if I told you I could read your mind? I like to break people's beliefs. If I fail to read your mind, I will buy you any drink in this bar, and if I read it correctly, you don't have to give me anything,' he said making her an offer that she would never refuse.

'Sure. Let's see what you got,' she replied.

'Okay, think of any number between one and nine. Don't tell me. Just type it on my phone without showing it to me. I will guess your number accurately,' said Andre, taking out his huge iPhone 7 Plus from his pocket.

The girl took his phone and typed a digit into it. Sam and I already knew where this was going, as all of us had learnt this trick and used it a thousand times from the same book which was called *The Game* by Neil Strauss. Neil Straus is considered one of the greatest pick-up artists (PUA) in the world and very few people could claim to be better with women than he was. The trick of this game was that most people choose seven when they are asked to pick a random number between one and nine. The reason Andre used his phone for this trick was to confirm whether the girl actually chose seven or some other number by seeing which part of the screen she touched. If she touched the lower left side, it was a seven. In the rare case where she would have touched something on the right side it would be either a 3, 6, or 9. In this case, the girl had chosen a seven, and Andre could see her finger press something on the lower left side. However, just to double check and pretend that he was a good magician, he said, 'Is your number between five and nine?' while maintaining eye contact.

Sometimes, it is possible to mistake a four for a seven, as four is just above the seven on the keypad. If the girl had said no to Andre's question, he would have gone with four.

She replied 'Yes' with a slight nod, looking down at the screen.

After pretending to read her mind for ten more seconds, Andre said, 'The number you chose is seven.'

'How! How did you do that? You have to tell me,' she exclaimed in disbelief.

'Only on one condition that you send me a good review on Instagram so that I can use it as a testimonial for the website I am going to create to promote myself as a magician,' Andre said. The bastard was not creating any website nor was he a magician. He was slyly sliding into her DM by taking her Instagram account.

'Here, take my phone. You can add yourself here,' she said.

Andre made up a false explanation for the trick by saying that her eyes moved in the upper left direction which is the creative side of the brain. He told her that this narrowed his options down to a four or a seven, and he took a stab at seven when she said that her number was between five and nine. This left the girl in awe. He had already validated himself in her eyes, and he leveraged this to continue the conversation, flaunt another NLP trick, and take her phone number. After a while, he returned to our table with the look of victory in his eyes and grabbed the 5$ bill from the table where I had put it.

'I may not be playing the game so often, but I haven't forgotten it,' said a rodomontading Andre. Meanwhile, Sonia had called for the cheque. We paid off the bill and tipped Emily generously before we drove off to our luxury villa in Richmond Hill only stopping at my Airbnb to collect my bag. Andre drove Sam's SUV while Sonia, Lydia, and Nigel took the other car which Sonia was driving. Richmond Hill was an hour's drive from downtown Toronto, so by the time we reached the house, it was already 9:15 pm.

Our house in Richmond Hill was a manifestation of ultra-rich luxury and modern architecture. The house was made completely of glass and stone and consisted of five bedrooms, five and a half baths, a swimming pool that had an adjacent cocktail bar, a cinema lounge, a huge kitchen, and a living room. The living room had a St. James' solid Apalasian white oak table that had seating for eight with velvet chairs. The kitchen was slightly separate from the main living area and had an oversized sub-zero integrated refrigerator, custom designed cabinets, polished mercury black marble on the island, a six-burner gas cooktop, and even a distinct wine refrigerator. The bedrooms had vinyl flooring with a queen-size bed in every room (other than the master suite which had a king-size bed) that was padded with a cushiony leather background and a wooden chair in the shape of an arm that was made from a single big piece of wood. The bathroom had ivory white marble floors that were radiant, heated for the cold Canadian winters, and porcelain sinks that added a feeling of richness to the guest experience.

We decided it would be best if Nigel and Sonia took the master bedroom, as they would be sleeping together. The rest of us would get a room to ourselves.

'Wow! I am in love with this house already. I can't wait to dive into that pool tomorrow morning,' I said.

'Glad you liked our choice,' said Sonia.

'Since we are all exhausted, why don't we go to bed soon and start the day early with a swim?' said Lydia.

So we all decided to head to our rooms, change our clothes, and go to sleep. The following day all of us were in the swimming pool by 8:00 am. Sam had gotten up early to stock up the house with all the party paraphernalia that he purchased on his personal expense and was carrying it in his SUV car. Even after we all insisted, he refused to let us contribute any money towards his purchases, even though some of the alcohol was very expensive. He had bought everything that one needed to party under this roof. The alcohol ranged from Carbonadi vodka, Stroh rum from Austria, Chardonnay ice wine, twenty-five-year-old Bowmore scotch, a two-four (which is Canadian slang for 24 bottles or cans of beer), 20 grams of cannabis (which included some pre-rolled joints)to chocolate cigars that he had picked up from a Cuban shop on his recent trip to Miami and solo cups. Partying was serious business for Sam, and I could see that he had spent a lot. Ice wine, a very sweet wine which is widely popular and grown largely in Canada, is made through a very labor-intensive process. The bottle of Chardonnay ice wine alone cost Sam 1,000$.

Sam had made us all an orange Stroh cocktail before joining us in the pool with his own drink. Relaxing in the pool under the morning sun with a cocktail that had 80% alcohol in it was the perfect way to start a Saturday morning.

Moreover, the blaring music on Nigel's speakers added to the vibe of a pool party. The pool party transitioned into a beer pong game where Sam, Lydia, and I were in one team and Sonia, Nigel, and Andre in the other. We obviously won because Sam was so good at this game that he could score with his eyes closed. After four years of being a member of a fraternity at UofT and roughly 220,000 CAD later, he had championed the art of beer pong and making cocktails. Beer pong gradually gave way to slap cup, flip cup, and *Cards Against Humanity*, all of which involved drinking alcohol. We were beginning to get hungry by lunch time, so Andre ordered pizza from Papa John's for all of us and poutine from Big Smoke Burger. We decided to eat our food in the cinema lounge while watching *The Sound of Music* that featured Julie Andrews in the lead role. By the time the movie finished, it was 3:00 pm.

'It is time to get high now,' said Sam, pulling out his packet containing marijuana, a grinder, and paper rolls.

'This stuff is blessed, man. Don't roll anything for me. I am going to smoke the pre-rolled Casablanca,' I said. This was the first time I was smoking weed ever since it was made legal in Canada. It is a strange feeling when you don't have to sneak away in a public park or make sure that the smoke goes outside the window of your college dormitory so that your neighboring students don't complain. Now, it seems that half the fun of smoking it was in the secrecy that one had to maintain. However, since marijuana became legal, one could buy pre-rolled joints as well as be assured of the authenticity of the marijuana, which wasn't possible when buying weed from a sketchy dealer on the street. Casablanca was the right fit for me. Not too strong but got the job done. The next few hours were spent under the influence of legal drugs as we had a good laugh discussing our adventures from the past. Sam was the only one who was smoking his chocolate cohibas, as he planned to smoke pot later.

At 7:00 pm., the boys left to sleep for two hours while the girls took a shower and started to dress up for the night. I had always wondered why girls took so much time to dress up before clubbing. As boys, we needed fifteen minutes for a shower and another fifteen to get ready. Eventually, I understood how society requires us all to play gender roles, and in the case of girls, it requires them to look pretty, apply make-up, do their hair, wear heels, etc. All of this systematically evolved over hundreds of years to restrict their movement and make them behave and think in a certain way with the goal to sustain a patriarchal society. Sam had also booked a party limousine and a VIP booth with bottle service at the Uniun night club in downtown Toronto. The party limousine arrived sharply at ten o'clock, and we were greeted professionally by a suited chauffeur who opened the door for us.

The limousine had leather seats, multiple panel TVs with USB ports, complimentary Wi-Fi, electric plugs, and a top-notch sound system. The interiors bedazzled with fiber optic lighting, mirrored ceilings, buttons to control the climate, and an inbuilt bar with glasses, ice chests, and stemware. We were carrying pizza and a bottle each of whiskey and ice wine with us to stay hydrated in the hour-long drive. Sam was smoking his weed while enjoying the city views from inside. This level of comfort and style could only be achieved in a limousine where everyone had enough space to themselves and we could still accommodate more people. We reached Uniun at 10:57 pm. Booking a VIP table with drinks allowed us to skip the queue, and we only had Sam to thank for that. The night was young and so were we. Looking at the crowd where people were flaunting their sexiest outfits and the cocktail waitresses were wearing short black mini-skirts while revealing their cleavage as much as they could made me feel how this city just gets younger with each passing day, until you start feeling too old to enjoy some of its nocturnal gems like Uniun. Well, at least today was not that day for me.

We danced and drank as the club started to pick up and the DJ dropped some crazy tunes that were popular among the locals. Gradually, as more alcohol flowed into our systems, we let loose and the group began to split. Sonia and Nigel were lost in each other's eyes as they held each other on the dance floor and locked lips. Lydia started getting approached by random guys who gyrated around her, most of whom were Black men wearing bling. Andre approached a set of two girls and developed a great rapport with one of them. Sam, inebriated and high under the influence of marijuana, was trying to find an easy target for the night, as he was not in his senses to hold a decent conversation. Lydia, who had exceptional skills as a wingwoman, had gone to rescue Sam. A hot wingwoman like Lydia immediately put the whole girl gang's defense system to rest. No wingman could do the job that she did. She helped Sam with a drunk girl that he was planning to approach. Lydia befriended the girl group and introduced Sam to his target. After fifteen minutes of getting comfortable with Lydia, the group started opening up to Sam. He eventually started grinding his crotch against his target's ass which was cue for Lydia to leave, as her job was done.

Lydia came back to me and started twerking against me, as I was the most sober of the lot and was dancing by myself. As she twerked against me, I held her waist with both my hands in the most platonic way I could. The best part about our friendship was that we never got carried away. We could enjoy doing the dirtiest of dances without actually feeling any attraction or crossing the line. Lydia and I were now facing each other and dancing while I noticed Sam get a sloppy make out from the girl he was dancing with. I think she was too drunk to know what she was doing. Andre was playing his cards right, as he had already attracted the blonde to himself. She was giving him a lap dance in our private booth while he was motorboating her boobs. Andre had prurient cravings to validate himself by approaching women in bars and clubs.

At 3:00 am, all the lights of the club were switched on, and the music stopped. It was time to leave when I saw Sam walking back with a look of disappointment in his eyes. 'Her friends cockblocked me. Damn those bitches. She had agreed to come back home with me when her friends came out of nowhere,' he said. I doubted how consensual that agreement was. Her friends would not be able to cockblock Sam had she said yes in her senses. We left the club, and all of us were waiting in the limousine for Andre. He finally arrived with a stranger whom I recognized as the girl from the lap dance. She introduced herself as Clara and sat down with Andre while we offered her drinks out of courtesy. Most of us were exhausted on our ride back home except Andre and Clara who were passionately and physically esurient to know each other in the spacious limo. I wasn't surprised about Andre's behavior, but I expected the girl to show some restraint since she didn't know any of us. Maybe she had never made out or got her boobs pressed in a party limousine before and was living one of her fantasies.

The next morning, I woke up at 11:00 am. Andre and Sam were already downstairs by the BBQ grill, preparing hotdogs for all of us. 'Where is your nocturnal friend or is it too late to ask?' I asked, assuming he had already gotten rid of her. 'No, I think she is a really nice girl. We exchanged numbers before I booked an Uber for her. The only reason I didn't want her to stay is because I thought she would be intruding on our reunion,' said Andre. At this point, I looked at Nigel who was trying really hard to control his laughter while flipping his Polish sausage, because he knew what a snollygoster Andre was.

'Oh! Come on guys. I am going to hit her up again and take her out on a date. What is so funny?' said Andre.

'And the next time I watch a porn video, I am actually going to believe that the plumber has come to the girl's house with the intention of fixing the pipe in the washroom. Anyway, I am kind of hungover. I am going inside the pool,' I retorted and went upstairs to fetch my swimming shorts.

In half an hour, I was joined by Sam, Lydia, and Sonia in the pool. Sam got the pack of beer from the fridge that we were consuming in the pool. The afternoon was spent munching hotdogs, drinking booze, and relaxing in the water while the music system played the latest collection of rap songs. It was 4:00 pm, and we had two hours to pack our stuff and bid adieu to the house before we went our separate ways. I was meeting all of them again for dinner on Friday before I flew back to London on Saturday. During the week,

I had scheduled to meet Karan, Pukhraj, Vibhuti, and Nitya who were some of my Indian friends from university. I was sitting beside the pool and checking my email to see if I received any important updates from work when I got a message on my phone from Afifah that read:

Devansh, I need your help. Please meet me on Wednesday. It is very important, and I feel you are the only person who can help me now...

For a moment, I was staring at the screen without an iota of clue as to what this meant. I knew something was very offbeat. Afifah knew that I was in the city for a week, as I had come back for the reunion. I had casually messaged her while in London to know whether she was attending any alumni events. I pondered over the sudden nature and the urgent texture of the message that was sent without any context. Why would she send me such a message? What could I do for her that her family or friends in Toronto could not?

NOTE TO THE READER: At this point, you must be wondering who Afifah is. In order to find out, I will have to take you back to my freshman year where all this began before I tell you what happened after I received that text.

Year 1 Semester I

I moved into my room at the St. Hilda's residence at Trinity College. It was 5th September, 2013, and it was my first day at university and my second day in Canada. I had landed the day before and had spent the night at a hotel near the airport. Trinity College was considered the most prestigious college at the University of Toronto, and a large proportion of students who were children of Trinity alumni, if admitted to UofT, were allotted Trinity College. I was among the exceptions. Being a part of Trinity was a matter of pride in its own way with Trinity having special dinners, customs, and traditions that no other college at UofT had. Some of the most distinguished alumni of UofT have been known to come out of Trinity. Before coming to Canada, the university had sent me an email with the name and email address of my roommate Andre Cadore. We had connected on Facebook and chatted briefly there. After unpacking my suitcase and finding something to eat, I decided to knock on Andre's door which was connected to my room through a common washroom in between. Even though we had private single rooms, we were still called roommates by the university, as we shared a common washroom that was in between both the rooms and had one door opening in my room and the other in Andre's room.

Andre opened the door in his ultra-soft coral fleece bathrobe with sleep still in his eyes. 'Hey, you are Devansh, right? I came back at 4:00 am from the Toga party. That is why I am so sleepy. But it is a good thing you knocked, or I would have missed the fresher's event today.'

'No worries. Why don't you get ready while I unpack my suitcases and setup my room? Then we could leave together for the tri-campus parade,' I said.

'Sounds good. By the way, I met this really cool guy from India. His name is Samreed. I will introduce you to him. He lives down the hall and belongs from New Delhi,' said Andre.

We met after an hour and decided to go to Strachan Hall to grab breakfast before going to the event. 'Hey Samreed, I was just telling Devansh about you. He is from India too,' said Andre, introducing an Indian guy to me who was just walking out of Strachan Hall.

'*Tum India mein kaha se ho?*' said Samridh, which means 'Where in India are you from?'

'*Calcutta se* (From Calcutta),' I replied.

'*Bhai, in Canadians ne toh mere naam ki maa-behen kar di, yeh bhi mujhe Samreed bulata hai. Mera naam Samridh Lakhanpal hai,*' said Samridh.(Brother, these Canadians find my name to be a tongue twister. Even this guy calls me Samreed. It is S-A-M-R-I-D-H Lakhanpal.)

I guess when someone from Delhi uses a native slang that is referencing a female relative, anyone from India who watches Hindi films can connect to him or her.

'Why don't you go by the nickname Sam? It will save you and everyone here a lot of trouble,' I said casually, but he took my suggestion very seriously.

After we finished breakfast, we headed to King's College Circle to join other froshies and frosh leaders. At UofT, a freshman is called a froshie and freshmen week is called frosh week. Soon, the ground was filled with thousands of froshies from all three campuses of UofT for the tri-campus parade which was to be followed by a Lupe Fiasco concert. The frosh leaders of all the seven colleges of UofT St. George, UofT Mississauga, and UofT Scarborough started organizing the freshmen behind them as different colleges took on one another in the cheer off.

UofT Mississauga took a potshot at the St. George students to start the cheer off:

I'm an ArtSci,

I'm an ArtSci,

I'm an ArtSci drinking beer

But I'd rather be an ArtSci than

A FUCKING ENGINEER (middle finger in the air).

The Engineering students wearing their yellow hardhats countered this with:

St. George rejects,

St. George rejects.

To which UofT Mississauga replied:

Get the best sex!

The froshies and upper-year frosh leaders at Woodsworth took a jibe at Victoria and Trinity students:

Deep in the heart of the Woodsworth jungle, you can hear the wolf pack rumble

Ooh ah ooh ah, ooh ah ooh ah

This cheer was followed by another yell:

We out here dripping in finesse

Cause Woodsworth is the best

Out here dripping in finesse,

Trin knows, Vic Knows.

In response, Victoria and Trinity did the yells that we were taught to counter Woodsworth in the orientation cheer booklet that we received in the frosh kit:

Your wood's worth nothing.

Your wood's worth nothing.

Your wood's worth nothing.

University College decided to take a potshot specifically at Trin, hinting at the elitist culture that prevailed at Trin, which I had mentioned earlier:

Trin, trin!

Your parents got you in.

Trin, trin!

Your parents got you in.

One girl from University College who specifically caught the attention of the crowd as she sprayed a water gun on the Trin students was narrating a University College cheer which was as follows:

We will, we will

Grab you, slam you, hit you up, and ram you...

Your mama,

Your papa,

Your greasy, greasy grandma,

Got a hole in her panty,

Got a big behind like a Frankenstein,

Going beep-beep-beep down Sesame Street.

After the cheer off ended, I walked up to her, as I was really curious to know who she was. She looked so pretty. Probably the prettiest girl I had seen in Canada ever since I came. She was 5'5" and had beautiful child-like eyes which reeked of mischief. Her body had the perfect curves with a slim waist. She was a brunette and her hair tumbled over her shoulders. She seemed to have sugar sweet lips which were lilac soft and slender eyebrows. She had a cheerful and bubbly character which made her easy to approach. Also, White girls like her were naturally more appealing to me, because I grew up around people who were brown-skinned like me and fairer skin was considered more desirable. I found myself fascinated by White girls and their culture already. Western culture allowed them to express their sexuality freely, whether it was wearing skinny shorts or shouting cheer slogans that included words like 'pussy', 'cock', etc., which I could not imagine girls doing publicly back in India.

'Hi, what is your name?' I asked her.

'My name is Lydia. What is yours?' she asked.

'My name is Devansh. I really liked how you did the greasy grandma cheer. Where are you from, by the way?' I said.

'I am from Paris,' she replied.

'Wow! Even you are an international student like me. Paris is such an iconic city,' I said in amazement.

'No, no, I am not from France. I am from Paris, Ontario. It is a small town. We even have a London in Ontario which is a two-hour drive from Toronto. The British couldn't come up with original names when they ruled Canada so...' said Lydia.

'Well, you seem like a cool person. Let me introduce you to my friends,' I said and called out to Sam and Andre. Before we knew it, we were all walking together in the tri-campus parade where thousands of students walk all the way from UofT down Bloor Street and then go into Yonge Street which is the longest street in the world. All of us were cheering, talking, and bonding during the two-hour long parade before we reached back to King's College Circle for the Lupe Fiasco concert that was organized by the student union.

'I have been looking for you this whole while. Where were you?' said a brown-skinned girl catching Lydia unexpectedly with us.

'I was walking the parade with Trinity. I met some really nice guys. We had so much fun. By the way, guys, this is my over-possessive roommate Sonia. Sonia, this is Sam, he is Andre, and this is Devansh,' said Lydia.

'Nice to meet you all. Where do you guys live?' asked Sonia shortly.

'We live at St. Hilda's at Trinity. And you?' inquired Andre.

'Lydia and I share a double room at Whitney Hall. And this is Nigel. He is also from University College. We met him at one of the cruise parties organized by our college. We have heard so many fancy stories about Trinity and your legacies and were actually eager to meet people from Trin,' said Sonia.

'Hey, I am Nigel. I live at Morrison, so I guess all of us live close by. We can host dorm parties together,' said Nigel and came forward to shake Sam's, Andre's, and my hand.

'I just got a text from my roommate Ryan. He missed the parade today, as he overslept after yesterday's Toga party. I will tell him to reach the concert, as it is going to start soon,' said Sam who had just introduced himself as Sam to Sonia and Nigel instead of Samridh.

All of us were very stoked to see Lupe Fiasco live. Hundreds of girls were giggling like lovesick teens, and the boys were impatiently shouting for him to come on stage. The electricity in the crowd and on stage brought the students together. Most of these students would behave like complete strangers inside an elevator and avoid eye contact, but these same students were now a melting pot of people from around the world, singing out loud. There were new friendships being formed as people could let themselves loose while not being afraid of being judged by others for freely expressing themselves. That is why music is considered one of the greatest unifiers, and these concerts find a place for themselves during frosh week. You could sing a song to three thousand students, and they would sing it back to you for three thousand different reasons.

Sam's roommate had arrived just in time for the concert. A slim, tall Caucasian male with long brown hair that was exactly the way how Brad Pitt had it in the movie *Troy*. He was wearing a thin, white polo shirt with a buttonless, half-sleeve, yellow shirt on top that was very thin too. On top of that, he was wearing a thin, dark blue sleeveless jacket that had orange trumpets designed all over them. This was contrasted with grey pants and a blue Jays cap which showed his love for the city's baseball team. The cap served as a good conversation starter.

'Yo man, you reached just on time. Everyone, this is my roommate Ryan,' said Sam.

'I am a Jays fan too,' said Nigel, pointing at Ryan's cap.

'I guess we will get along just fine then. Forgive me if I take time to remember all your names,' said Ryan as he met all of us individually.

I overheard Lydia whispering to Sonia that she found him cute. The crowd was like a congress of baboons when Lupe Fiasco came on stage. As we were not in the front rows, Sonia went on top of Nigel's shoulders to watch Fiasco. Lydia asked Ryan if she could sit on his shoulders, as he was tall. I wondered if she actually wanted a better view or was doing this because she thought Ryan was a snoutfair! Ryan obviously obliged. Who wouldn't when you get an opportunity to have someone as beautiful as Lydia piggybacking on your shoulders? I could sense a lot of guys staring at the two beautiful girls sitting on top of Nigel's and Ryan's shoulders rather than looking at the stage. Those looks had envy, awe, and 'I want some hot girl on my shoulder too' kind of feeling in them. The crowd seemed to know the lyrics of every song, every drum beat, and the exact moment when Fiasco would rock his solo. The concert ended on a high note, and everyone dispersed for three hours to come back for the final event of frosh week at 9:00 pm. UofT had several buses leaving from King's College Circle at 9:00 pm for Guvernment, which was Canada's largest nightclub.

This break of three hours before the buses departed for Guvernment gave the seven of us more time to solder our friendship. Andre had made a fake ID for buying alcohol at university, as he refused to go through freshman year without being able to purchase liquor or drink at bars. His fake ID was a boon to all of us, as we needed someone to abet us in buying alcohol. The legal drinking age in Ontario was 19, and none of us were 19 yet. I hadn't even been in this country for 24 hours, and I was already breaking the law. In my defense, I needed to get ready to enjoy my first night out in Canada.

The buses left King's College circle for Guvernment at 9:00 pm on the nose. I came from a city in India where the biggest nightclub was probably 5,000-8,000 square feet. The Guvernment complex sprawled over an area that was 60,000 square feet and had eight different rooms excluding a rooftop patio that offered a panoramic view of Lake Ontario. The club had hosted some of the biggest names in the music industry like Coldplay, Oasis, David Guetta, and Toronto's very own DeadMau5. It was featured among the top five nightclubs in the world with huge LED screens, numerous bars, and tight security as some of its distinct features. Tonight, it was booked completely by UofT for all its frosh students. We had a long queue ahead of us, and it took us an hour to get inside the club.

What I saw going on inside completely blew my mind away. There were so many freshman students making out. Girls and boys grabbing each other by the waist and locking their lips to the EDM tunes. In another room, I saw scores of tall Black boys with their backs pressed against the wall whereas the girls shook their asses against their crotch. In one of the booths, a girl whose boobs were the size of a durian was giving a lap dance to a huge African student. In another booth, one of the frosh leaders was spanking the ass of a petite Asian girl. I couldn't get my head around what was going on. I had been to nightclubs back home in Kolkata, but I found myself totally lost here, unable to relate to how people behave inside clubs. I thought to myself, 'This country has a strong dating culture. So many people are in a relationship here. These people must be dating since high school. Probably that is why they chose to apply to the same university. If dating is given so much importance here, I must find someone too if I want to enjoy inside the clubs here. Every couple is busy satisfying their physical needs. The single people seem to be dancing in groups or getting bored.' A lot of different thoughts ran through my head. In order to clear my head, I thought it would be fruitful to go to the rooftop patio to obambulate and catch some stellar views. As I entered the patio deck, I saw Nigel in the corner talking to a guy and smoking.

'Hey Nigel, you didn't like it down there?' I asked

'I have a girlfriend. There is a lot of distraction down there. I might end up doing something that I will regret later,' he said.

'Yeah, what is with couples going to the same university in Canada? So many people already know each other. All these couples are dancing...I wouldn't call that dancing though, but yeah, it is so different in India where people actually shake a leg inside clubs. Even if you go to the same university as your girlfriend, you wouldn't grab her boobs or put your crotch against her in public like people here are doing.'

'What the hell are you talking about, man? 95% of these students don't even know each other. They just met tonight. In clubs here, we like to grind and twerk. Also, once the girl is comfortable, you can easily proceed to make out, grab her tits...Welcome to North America, my friend,' he said with a laugh. 'Don't worry, give it some time. You'll learn how to roll here.'

'You seem to be fresh off the boat. Where are you from?' said the guy whom Nigel was smoking with. He was six feet tall, muscular with his biceps bulging from his arms, brown-skinned and had a sharp jawline. He had a Canadian accent and wore a black waist bag that had the initials ET.

'I am from India. How about you?' I asked.

'I thought so. You have a strong Brown accent. I am from Brampton. It is a town adjacent to Toronto where all the Brown people live. That is why everyone calls it the Brown Town.'

'So, are your parents from India or South Asia too?' I enquired.

'My mother is a Punjabi and my father is a Christian. They immigrated here from India, but I was born and bred in Brampton. I can barely speak Punjabi, but I understand the language,' he replied.

'Sorry, I never asked your name,' I said.

'My name is Emmanuel Teji. But I go by the name Manny. What is your name?'

'My name is Devansh Gupta,' I said.

'You want to smoke some?' asked Manny wanly.

'I don't smoke. But what is that you are smoking? It doesn't look like cigarettes,' I said.

'This is Kush,' said Manny, rolling a new joint, since the one Nigel was smoking was already over.

'What is Kush?' I was curious and unfamiliar with the terminology in Toronto.

'What! You have never smoked Kush before? Jeez! This shit is grown best in the hill stations of India. In Toronto, Kush is slang for weed,' said Manny with a look of disbelief.

'I know what weed is. But yeah, I have never smoked it before'.

'That is what university is meant for, Devansh. You are going to do a lot of things for the first time in your life here. You might question me now like you may question some of your professors in class, but trust me, you are going to thank me later. You will experience a slight trance, and all your senses will be enhanced. Even the music will seem to reverberate in your ears. Sometimes, I feel like I am in a lucid dream where I can control how the dream proceeds. Just trust, trust, trust,' said Manny, trying to give a convincing monologue.

'Alright, I will take a puff,' I said.

I inhaled the newly made joint, and before I could exhale, I started coughing.

'What the fuck is this?' I said.

'You are doing it wrong, Devansh. You need to inhale, keep it inside for a while like this and then slowly exhale. Don't mouth fag it,' demonstrated Manny.

'This stuff is not for me,' I said, passing it on to Nigel who was loving the free marijuana.

'I am glad you took your first puff though. It will take time, but you will learn it. Uni has just begun. By the time you graduate, you will be a professional at it,' said Manny.

'Manny, your stuff is really great. Thanks for sharing it. The next time I will treat you to some Kush. Give me your number. We need to start chilling,' Nigel said while enjoying his high.

'I would love to hang out with you guys. People at St. Mikes College are so boring. It is so catholic with all their catholic values and traditions. Fuck them. I need better people to socialize with. My number is 6477784294,' said Manny. It was evident that Manny was an iconoclast after seeing his disdain for Christian values and traditions.

'Talking about parties, there are a lot of frat parties for freshers during the first two weeks. We could all go to them,' I said.

'Hit me up, you guys, and we are gonna have this thing on lock,' said Manny.

Although lectures had begun, we were still not dedicated to our weekly readings at school. Everything was so new, including the newly found independence that we were bound to misuse. The euphoria from frosh week continued as we found ourselves attending frat parties, dorm parties, visiting clubs like Gravity and Fiction (that allowed students over the age of eighteen instead of other clubs in Toronto that required one to be nineteen) and drinking different kinds of alcohol purchased with Andre's fake ID. Instead of burning the midnight oil, we were burning the midnight joints, something I soon realized was not viable at one of the most difficult academic universities in North America. Someone who wants to graduate on time needs to take a five-course load per semester whereas undergraduates at even Harvard took four courses per semester. Also, unlike students in the UK, we didn't get a month's break before final exams. It was just a week's break at UofT. Therefore, I refrained from joining a fraternity. However, Sam and Andre were rushing Lambda Chi Alpha, one of the fraternities on campus, while Lydia was rushing Alpha Gamma Delta.

Rushing is a process where students who are interested in joining a fraternity or a sorority voice their interest, and the existing members organize social events to get to know if prospective candidates should be given a bid or not. Once you accept a bid, you become a pledge. Seeing the intensive coursework ahead of me, I decided to join something less demanding, so I joined the Hart House Debating Society at UofT, which is one of the most prestigious debating societies in the world.

It was the fourth week of university, and I had taken an astronomy course to fulfill my science credit requirement along with Lydia, Ryan, and Manny. Astronomy 101 was a first-year course, and there was a huge demand for it by students who wanted to finish their science credit requirement. There were around fifteen hundred students in the course. That is why the lectures took place at the Convocation Hall. The Convocation Hall was shaped like a domed rotunda and was built solely for holding convocation ceremonies, but during the year, it was used for academic and social functions. This was the same convocation hall where the Illinois High School Mathletes States Championship scene from the iconic chick flick *Mean Girls* was shot. The class was taught by Dr Michael Reed who was regarded as one of the best professors at university. Andre and Sam had informed me that they would be doing something funny during the lecture and wanted me to shoot their video, as the video clip would need to be produced as evidence in their fraternity. It was probably one of the requirements for initiation, a practice involving humiliation, embarrassment, or abuse used by fraternities to include a pledge as a member. Neither did I ask anything more nor were they supposed to talk about their initiations with me.

Midway through the lecture, I saw Andre and Sam run into the Convocation Hall wearing only their underwear and t-shirts. They both had two oranges inside their t-shirts, to give the impression of possessing female boobs. They ran around the whole Convocation Hall shouting slogans from Lambda Chi while the whole classroom cheered them further and boosted their morale. Luckily for them, the professor stopped in the middle of Einstein's theory of relativity and watched with amusement rather than taking any offence. After completing two circles of the lecture room, they stood in front of the whole class and opened their t-shirts, waving them in circles. By then, all the oranges had fallen on the floor. After getting everyone's attention, Andre stopped waving his t-shirt, looked at the students sitting on the upper deck and then at the ones on lower deck in front of him, and started his speech:

Hello everyone,

*I am Andre and this is my friend Sam. We are here to give you all our official proposal for love making. We are on the market. Yes, you heard that right. We are on the market. However, there are some conditions that you need to adhere to if you want to apply for any of us. Girls, you need to be at least 5 feet 5 inches tall. Secondly, we like to Netflix and Chill all the time, even during the day, so you need to be prepared to miss your lectures. Lastly, you need to have good looks, so don't bother applying if you aren't an 8 out of 10. Alright, we will accept 7.5's but nothing less than that. Since we are too busy to screen all the applicants, you can send your applications to our secretary *pause* Professor Michael Reid. He will let you know if you have been selected or not.*

At this point, he had got the whole room laughing to his tunes. Even the professor couldn't resist giving an applause. They waved to the whole class and signaled me to send them the video before leaving the Convocation Hall.

Fall was coming to an end as the trees withered off their red, orange, and yellow leaves to make way for winter. I was on my way to Hart House to play the weekly chess society drop-in games that were held on Mondays from 6:00 pm. It was the first time in my life when I had actually witnessed snowflakes falling from the sky. The first snowfall of the season was a visual delight for international students like me who had never witnessed snow falling from the sky. I had seen snow many times before in Switzerland, New Zealand, and Kashmir, but I had never seen fresh snowfall. Fascinated and pondering over the wonders of nature, I was mesmerized when I saw Afifah dart towards Hart House, wearing a bright orange fur coat. I could feel her without feeling her, inhale her without breathing, and hear her just by looking at her eyes. She had stunning, innocent eyes that I believe were a reflection of her pure heart and vivacious curves that made her look ravishing. She was a regular like me in the weekly chess drop-in games. Normally, she came with her friends and played with them, but today she was alone.

I entered the room behind her. She went and sat on one of the tables and opened her fur coat to hang it on the chair. I was mesmerized by her beauty and wanted to speak with her since the first day I had seen her, but I could never muster up the courage. She was always with her group of Brown girls. I knew that if I approached her randomly, her friends would make me feel conscious by dropping in on every word I said and later tease her. Brown girls have this innate talent, where they can sense when a boy takes a shine on one of their friends. I felt today was my chance. If I don't go up and talk to her today, I won't ever be able to talk to her again, and the chances of finding someone at a big campus like UofT St. George are slim. Therefore, I went up to her and asked her, 'May I play a game with you?'

'Sure, I was looking for someone to play with too. Unfortunately, my friends couldn't make it, as they have a midterm tomorrow,' she said.

'What is your name?' I asked even though I knew it.

'Afifah. What is yours?' she asked.

'My name is Devansh. Should we start?' I said nervously without looking at her. I couldn't believe that I was playing a game with Afifah. Ever since I saw her, I was desperate to speak with her. Now that I was playing chess with her, I was at a loss of words. I perceived that she would sense my nervousness. I didn't want to ruin my impression by saying something silly or be caught staring at her face without saying anything.

'Sure, let's begin,' she said and moved her pawn, as she had the white pieces and white plays first in chess.

'Oh! So you like to play the Sicilian open,' she said as I moved the black pawn in front of the black bishop instead of going with a conventional opening.

'Yes, I like to play Sicilian. I find it to be a stronger defense,' I said looking down.

For the next thirty minutes, none of us spoke as the game continued. She was a clever player, and I started getting offensive with my moves.

'You really are after my queen, aren't you?' she said as she moved her queen away. I smiled in response because she had not noticed that my knight had a fork. In chess, a fork is a tactic when a single piece is in a position to attack two or more pieces of the opponent.

'Check mate,' I said, killing her elephant with my knight, and this was the first time I looked up at her. I wish I could tell her that I had no interest in her queen but wanted to make her my queen in real life. She was looking at the chess board with a look of surprise that slowly became disappointment.

'Damn! I didn't see that coming. You are a great player. This was a nice game. I am normally used to winning, as my friends aren't that good. What do you study?' she said.

'I am doing a double major in sociology and management. How about you?' I asked.

'I am studying digital enterprise management at UofT Mississauga. On Mondays, I take the inter-campus shuttle to come play chess because I love chess a lot,' she said.

'We should play again sometime. Let us connect on Facebook,' I stuttered, as I thought it might be too early to ask for her social media profile. But then again, I couldn't bear the thought of losing the opportunity to connect, especially after knowing that she was from a different UofT campus.

'That is a good idea. Give me your phone. I will add myself. There are two Afifah Javaids that come up. This is me.' I was elated, and my happiness grew manifolds on the inside just like a dog with two tails. I believe that a recipe for a happy life has two ingredients - something to keep you busy and someone to love. University was already keeping me busy. Today, I had found my second ingredient. The whole room seemed to be redolent with her fragrance.

Robarts Library

11:05 pm

Our final exams were starting in a week's time. Robarts Library was open 24/7 until the end of exams. We had just ordered pizzas from Pizza Pizza and were sitting in the cafeteria, taking a break from studies.

'There is no way I am going to pass economics, and I need it to get into Rotman next year,' said Sam.

'ECO100 is too damn hard. We got past exams from our brothers who took it out from the frat's repository of past exams, but I just can't figure out the math,' said Andre.

'You guys are lucky that you have such a strong support system because of your fraternity. But UofT is hard as fuck,' I said, referring to the group study sessions that Lambda Chi held for its members so that its new members can benefit from the advice of the seniors as well as push each other to study. Contrary to popular belief, fraternities are not all about getting laid. They organize study sessions for their members when there is a demand for it.

'I am sorted with political science. But Virginia Woolf is going over my head. Some authors are really tough to critique,' said Lydia, as she was doing a double major in English and political science.

'Fuck, I regret partying so much. Pretty much all I did this semester was drink, smoke, and party,' said Sam.

'And boink the occasional sorority girls in our mixers. I can never forget Ashley. I lost my virginity to her,' said Andre.

'Man! I can't forget that either. I had gone to use the washroom when I heard these loud moans from a girl. I was wondering why Andre was watching porn so loudly. Then, after some time, I heard his door open. So I opened the door of my room and saw this Asian girl looking at me with embarrassment. Then she giggled slightly before pacing down the hallway. Then I was like, "Oh fuck, Andre just got laid."'

'The next time I am doing it, I will hang a tie on my washroom door,' said Andre, referring to a North American signal that roommates use when one of them is getting laid. 'Man, UofT is capable of kicking the "wis" out of wisdom, and I feel so dumb at this school. Everyone around me seems to be fucking smart. Especially these Asians. I bombed my midterms. I am really depending on my final exams to pull up my grades,' said Nigel, reaching out for another slice of cheese pizza. He was doing a specialization in computer science and a minor in geographic information systems.

'I am looking forward to Christmas. Just want these exams to get over now,' said Ryan who seemed confident with his study material. Ryan and Sonia had stellar grades, and they both wanted to go to a good law school which required them to have a high GPA.

'This semester just flew by. Manny, could you please explain the Facebook case study? Like how does Facebook make money without selling any products? The only case study that I found interesting in Swanston's class was that of Bitcoin. I invested all my savings of 7,500$ and bought 625 Bitcoins with one Bitcoin at the price of 12$. After the professor's lecture, I did my research and believe that Bitcoin has a lot of investment potential in the future,' said Sam.

'What most people don't know is that Facebook actually has the best product. In fact, you are the product. Yes, all of us. Facebook is selling us to advertisers. Our personal data including our age, where we live, things we 'LIKE' on Facebook, celebrities we follow...everything. Facebook is collecting all this data and selling it to advertisers who can target specific advertisements to us. Data is the new oil, my friend,' said Manny.

Sam still looked flustered.

'Okay, let me make it simpler. I will try to explain it in a way that is easier for you to understand. Now, you know there are many clubs that allow ladies for free before a certain time but only charge men for entry, right? That is because these clubs use a somewhat similar model. They allow the girls for free and charge boys who want access to these girls. You see, a nightclub is very similar to a multisided platform like Facebook or YouTube.'

'Now I get it,' said Sam with a laugh.

The exams started. We found some to be easy, some to be moderate, and some to be tough. Sam was the only one who found everything to be tough. Unlike high school, I was never tensed or nervous before giving an exam or a midterm in university. In high school, good grades meant getting admitted into a good university. In university, I knew that even if my grades were average, a few internships and a UofT degree were sufficient for a good-paying job. Even my parents didn't care to ask me about my grades anymore as long as I was passing my courses. The experience of entering an examination hall and taking a seat with a blank booklet and unknown questions was no longer daunting. Since this was my first time away from home for such a long time, I was looking forward to going back home for the winter break. Canadian universities are known to give the smallest breaks in December that last only two weeks. Three weeks at the most if your exams get over early or if there is no final exam for some modules.

Sam and I flew back together to India for the Christmas vacations. He got off in New Delhi whereas I boarded another plane from New Delhi to Kolkata. Andre, Nigel, and Sonia were spending Christmas with their families in Toronto. As Sonia's parents were Muslims, Christmas was not a big affair in the Agha household. Therefore, she planned to make the most of the break to do everything recommended online for Torontonians in Christmas season.

Her plans ranged from ice skating in Nathan Philips Square to visiting the Christmas market in Distillery District and making the most of sales during the holiday season. Ryan went back home to St. Catherine's to spend Christmas with his mother and siblings. Manny drove down to Brampton and was very happy to spend time with his mother and twin sister. I was gutted when I found out that Manny and Ryan could not celebrate the biggest festival of the year with their parents under one roof. Ryan's parents were separated, and Manny's parents were divorced. Lydia was flying down to Miami to spend Christmas and New Year at her aunt's house. All her relatives and cousins from America and Europe were joining them there, as the Thomsons were having a big family reunion.

Year 1 Semester II

The next time we all met in January, it was a new semester, a new year, and winter had come in full swing.

Location: Andre's room

'God! I missed you guys so much. I didn't realize that I had gotten so used to living away from home. I missed our late night talks. Especially this residence,' Ryan said.

'Yeah, I missed the luxury of eating prepared food from the cafeteria which wasn't available at home. Getting a hot breakfast or lunch that is already prepared for you is the best thing ever. Also, Strachan Hall does have good food on some days,' said Andre.

'Well, then you should definitely visit me in India sometime. All our meals are prepared, and I get hot breakfast every day. I have never even had to wash dishes in my life. Labor is so cheap there. Like the first time I probably washed a dish after eating something was here in Canada,' I said.

'I missed Canada overall. Everything is centrally heated here. Back in Delhi where the temperature doesn't even hit negative, it is freezing as fuck,' said Sam. Sonia and Lydia were fascinated by the Indian handicrafts I had bought for them from Kolkata and were taking pictures with them. For the boys, I had bought a scarf that was on sale during Christmas.

'This scarf is so dope. I am wearing it to my lectures,' said Manny, trying out the scarf, and he was proficient at wearing them in multiple ways.

'The scarf reminds me, I was reading this book over the winter break called *The Game* by Neil Strauss. It has this theory about peacocking. Basically, boys should wear a good scarf when they go to sarge in nightclubs and bars. Peacocking is the practice of wearing a few garish, noticeable items which draw attention and could be a good conversation starter. It could be a bright scarf, a shiny watch, flamboyant clothing, men's jewelry, or a Krypto light glow in the dark necklace. The Krypto light necklace is also very good for peacocking. You can also use it for anchoring.'

'I am confused. What is "sarging" and "anchoring"? I am lost here,' Nigel butted in.

'This is the terminology that I learnt from the book. Sarging is the act of going out with or without other pick-up artists or wingmen with the intention of meeting women whom you want to seduce. The difference between going out and sarging is that when you are in a sarge session, you are actively seeking out other women. Anchoring, on the other hand, is the art of instilling feelings into a physical object so that the person receiving the object associates that feeling to the giver of the object and in the process remembers the giver. For example, placing a cheap pendant around a girl's neck is not only romantic, but the physical contact of the pendant with her skin as well as the optical stimuli of the pendant that she feels whenever she looks at it will subconsciously make her remember the person who gave it to her. The brain is a highly associative organ, and assuming that your interaction with her was very positive, the pendant will bring back pleasant memories of you to her mind. Therefore, the girl is less likely to bail on you. This book has some really powerful stuff. You guys need to read it,' explained Andre.

'Man, I am liking it already. Approaching women whom you don't meet organically in lectures or student societies is so difficult. I need to download this book right away,' I said.

'Yeah, all of us need to. Sonia and Lydia are the only ones who would never need this book because they are girls. They have pussies which is the best motivating factor that has ever existed since the birth of man. Pussies are the fuel that keeps the whole world running. Pussies are the reason why most men study, get up in the morning and go to work, hit the gym, or run for president. Bill Clinton wasn't happy with one pussy even after becoming president. That is why girls like to regulate the supply and make it difficult for us men to get pussy. Imagine a utopian world, where girls could just start slinging pussy without having any stigma attached to the act. All progress in society would come to a halt. That is why most hard drugs are banned too, because drugs make it easier to get pussy,' said Manny.

The whole room burst into laughter. 'Real talk though, this world of pick-up artists that you guys are about to enter is a multi-billion-dollar industry. There are many dating coaches that teach this stuff, though some of them suck. I found some genuine ones on YouTube who have good game, and many of them give free seminars online with a lot of useful stuff that we can learn from. I am following Mystery for now as he is the one who trained Neil Strauss. Mystery is from Toronto and is regarded as the greatest pick-up artist in the world,' said Andre, taking pride in his city.

'Let me look this guy up now. All of this sounds so intriguing,' said Sam as he fired up Andre's laptop.

'I really like this hanging wooden parrot that you got me from India, Devansh. Looks like you are *anchoring* me already,' said Lydia with a wink.

Sam looked at one of Mystery's interviews online and remarked, 'This guy dresses pretty obnoxious but is really confident. Everything that he wears or says seems to have a reason. Looks like he has broken down the whole process of seducing women down to a science. He knows what to say and when to say it.'

'Yeah, he is credited with bringing the world of pick-up artists on the global spectrum. By the way, I am using this game called The Lying Game that I saw Neil Strauss teach in one of his bootcamps online. It is very good game to get instant dates or coffee with a girl,' said Andre.

Nigel stood up to leave at this point, 'Yo! I am a relationship kind of guy. This shit is not for me,' he said. 'See you guys tomorrow'. Lydia and Sonia decided to leave with him too, as the room was starting to stink of toxic masculinity.

'Carry on. I am curious to know more about this,' said Ryan as Sam, Manny, and I keenly listened and took mental notes of everything he said.

Andre continued, 'Okay. So once you have built some rapport with a girl, you can challenge her to a quick game, but tell her that it has a wager involved. Girls love to be intellectually stimulated. In order to explain this game, I am going to demonstrate it with Ryan being the girl I am trying to take out on a date. Are you ready?'

'Yes,' said Ryan.

'Okay, so I am going to play a game with you. I call this The Lying Game. In this game, I am going to ask you five questions, and you need to lie to all those questions. If you tell me the truth, you lose. However, if you successfully lie to all five questions then you win the game. However, there is a wager attached. If I lose this game, you can ask for anything you want, but if I win this game, then you have to buy me a coffee. Is that fair?'

'Yes, but how would you know I am lying?' asked Ryan.

'I will. Trust me. Are you ready to play?'

'Yes'.

Andre: First question. Which city are we in?

Ryan: New York

Andre: What is the color of your t-shirt?

Ryan: Black

Andre: What is your name? Come on, you need to be quick!

Ryan: My name is Justin Bieber.

Andre: *pretending to think* Ummm, how many questions do I have left?

Ryan: Two

Andre: See, I got you. You told me the truth.

Ryan: Damn, fuck you. Fuck, fuck, fuck...how did I not see that?

Andre: In case someone is smart enough to lie in the fourth question, you can still get them in the fifth one. Just be like, 'Damn, you are too good. You have played this game before, haven't you?' and most people will say that they have not played the game before because they are too excited to win. That is when you tell them that they spoke the truth.

Sam, Manny, and I marveled at the creator's ingenuity. You can take a girl out for coffee without asking her out or opening yourself to rejection. Also, you aren't even the one paying for the coffee. Girls have this habit of politely refusing a coffee date by giving the excuse of their nonexistent boyfriend. However, they like being challenged. Attractive girls get hit on by guys like us on a daily basis. The chances of such a girl saying yes to anyone for a coffee are very slim. Everything valuable in life needs to be earned, and The Lying Game seemed like a good tool to setup dates.

During the next four weeks, we devoted as much time to reading *The Game* as we spent on our modules. We approached women wherever we could. Even when we studied in a group in the Robarts Library, we would often challenge each other to go speak with different girls. Whoever got anxious or wouldn't succeed in getting a number/Snapchat ID or a date would have to pay up a dollar for losing the challenge. Losing even a dollar can push you a lot. *The Game* had become an integral part of our lives. Once you start getting results, it becomes very addicting. Even the girls whom I found very challenging to speak with, I could confidently go up and talk to them because I possessed a set of tools that helped me choose the right words. There were less awkward pauses in conversations. I didn't feel nervous while talking to the most attractive girls in my lecture. My body language started to improve. Within a month, I could already notice a lot of change in me. All of us had finished reading the book and were now about to start another book by Neil Strauss called *Rules of the Game*.

'The Lying Game is doing wonders for me, mate. I had three coffee dates this past week. Do you know Alice Li? She is a residence peer assistant leader who lives on the floor below us. I went out with her on the weekend to a cute café in Chinatown,' I bragged to Andre.

'No way, you mean that hot Asian chic? She looks like a model, dude. I would give her a nine,' said Andre.

'Yeah, all the credit goes to you. Thanks for introducing us to this world of pick-up artists. I always believed that some guys are naturally good, and some people just have the gift of the gab. Or that one had to spend a lot of money or have a very good physique to go on dates with such women. I am glad I know now that seducing women is an art that can be learnt,' I said in an excited voice.

'Yes, it is truly an art that can be learnt through knowledge and practice. Unfortunately, a lot of people wouldn't be in serious relationships if they knew about this stuff. Especially the Asian and Brown kids, because all their parents make them do is study. They don't end up cultivating any social skills and are maladroit in social situations. Many times, they just creep the girl out,' said Andre.

'True, I used to find it very difficult to carry on conversations with girls. There used to be awkward pauses earlier, but now I feel that my conversation skills are improving,' I said.

Andre looked happy to hear that. 'But tell me, how did your date with Alice go?'

'It was good. We ordered drinks and spoke about academics and her life in China before she moved here as a child. She even told me that she is preparing a short dance for a talent show in UofT. Then we ordered some food...'

'So, you didn't even get to first base?' interrupted Andre carelessly.

'No...I mean this was the first date. Like, how could I? What would she think of me? She needs to trust me. We have to be friends before...' I couldn't complete my sentence before he raised his voice, 'Shut up, shut up, shut up...just zip it. That is not how you get laid, my friend. You aren't in India, and you don't have to run around trees and flowers with a girl to make her like you. This is not Bollywood. Remember one thing for the rest of your life if you want to be fucking your fair share of women which I know you do.'

Lesson 1: *The less fucks you give, the more fucks you get.*

I had just learnt my first big lesson at university, and it was from my roommate.

Andre plowed on, 'You need to stop being a pussy. If there is one thing that girls can sense from a distance is a lack of confidence. So, instead of switching from one random topic to another, try to use sexual innuendos in your conversation. Spice it up a bit. Like I do this one thing a lot – the brain, you know, processes images. Our mind thinks through images. As humans, we cannot filter out a negative action or not doing an action. For example, I often tease my dates by saying, "Don't worry, I am not going to take you to my room. I am not going to undress you and push you against the wall. I won't slowly penetrate you from behind as the stars light up at night." See, even though I said I won't or I am not going to do these things, the girl can only picture me doing sexual stuff with her because she thinks through images. Even though she knows that I won't be doing these things, her brain alludes a sexual scenario between her and me. Unless you want to be friends, you need to divert the direction of the conversation from platonic to sexual. Stop being so nice. Haven't you heard the saying "Nice guys finish last"?'

'Yeah, I have heard that', I said, though I knew he had asked me a rhetorical question.

'Remember, *The Game* mentions about using "Kino". Kino is the action of touching someone in order to build attraction and comfort. It is one of the fundamental elements of picking up a girl. This can prevent you from being friend zoned by her. The most sensitive areas of a woman's body are the ones that are least exposed to air and sunlight, like the inside of an elbow, inner thighs, and the place behind her ears. Kino, if done correctly, can arouse a girl and sexually stimulate her. But these are more advanced touches. You need to make sure that you start Kino early and establish touching as a normal conduit to your behavior. This will help you escalate progressively. After this, you can proceed to kissing her and then eventually taking her to your bedroom. Start with the simpler stuff. Like make sure that when you hug a girl, it feels natural to her and you. Palm reading is another easy Kino building technique. You don't need to learn palm reading. Just memorize four or five scripts that I give you and keep using them alternatively on all the girls. Make sure that Kino needs to be done often to set the right frame and get her comfortable with your presence around her. Don't be hesitant to take a girl's hand or pat her shoulder if you want to show her something on your phone. If you are nervous, both of you will be intensely aware of the contact which will hurt your chances with her. Practice it till you can do it naturally and playfully so that girls are chill about it and consider you a cool, physical, and sexual guy,' advised Andre.

'How do you know all this stuff? Did you learn it at the frat?' I asked.

'The fraternity does help a lot because I observe what other experienced brothers are doing with girls and ask them later why they spoke the way they did. Also, we share our experiences with girls and get constant feedback on how to proceed. Sometimes I have other experienced guys text girls on my behalf. I am learning a lot of text game at the moment. It is very important to be a good texter in today's world because I am communicating with many girls at the same time through my phone. However I learned most of it from YouTube, books, and online blogs of pick-up artists,' replied Andre.

'Wow, there is so much to learn in order to become a great pick-up artist,' I thought to myself.

As the winters got harsher in February, so did the coursework at school. The only respite that the university offered us amidst our intense coursework was a week's break called 'reading week'. The University of Toronto Student Union organizes a trip to Montreal every year during reading week. The eight of us had paid for the whole trip and had booked three rooms amongst us. During winters in Canada, hotel room rates fall quicker than the temperature. Sonia and Lydia were sharing one room. Nigel, Andre and I were sharing the second room whereas Ryan, Sam, and Manny took the third. This was our first vacation together, and we were all ecstatic about it. Nigel was the only one who had visited Montreal before. He had gone there with his girlfriend Hannah and told us about the places that we should definitely see and the restaurants he enjoyed eating at. The rest was taken care of by Google. The package for the trip included our ride to Montreal and back, our accommodation in Montreal for three nights and entry to a new club every night.

Several buses left from the Hart House bus stop in the morning. I sat by the window to get a view of the Canadian landscape. The bus driver and the tour guide were both eloquent orators and kept us entertained throughout the journey. The tour guide was an upper-year British student from University College who referred to all the students in the bus as 'You lovely lot' whenever he had to address us. The atmosphere in the bus was full of energy, as all the students were in the spirit of partying. I could feel the adrenaline rushing through my veins, which resonated with the vibes of my surroundings. A person's immediate environment has a lot of impact on his or her state of mind. Maybe there was some truth in the Chinese art feng shui that objects (or in this case people) in your surroundings do emit energy. In Montreal, the legal drinking age was eighteen which made Sam, Nigel, and Lydia very happy, as they were still eighteen and, for once, could drink without using their fake ID cards.

As the bus reached the outskirts of the city, I became lost in the scenic beauty outside. Vast stretches of land covered with snow marked the winter landscape. It appeared as if someone had covered the ground with a white table cloth. The Arctic air seemed to bring light snow showers as the snowflakes dropped slowly from the sky. We crossed several farms with protruding barns that looked desolate with vaulted, wood-beamed exteriors. Nothing could more aptly represent inclement weather, extreme winters, and holiday season than a snowman that was exquisitely built out of three stacked spheres of snow, which was provided a fitting climax by a semi-chewed carrot and a slick cap. Whoever built it had made an effort to depict a stumbling drunk, as the snowman carried a beer can in one of its arms. I noticed that Sonia, Manny, Nigel, and Ryan were playing cards on the backseats of the bus. Andre was trying to levitate a bottle, because Mystery often used this trick to impress women. Sam was religiously practicing some magic tricks with cards to improve his game in clubs. Lydia had dozed off on my shoulder. I tried to get some sleep before the bus reached our hotel in downtown Montreal so that I could stay fresh at night.

I woke up with a jerk, as the bus came to a screeching halt. We had reached hotel Gouverneur, and our tour guide asked us all to exit the bus and collect our luggage from the luggage compartment before assembling in the lobby. The Gouverneur was a four-star hotel, and we had been given rooms on the twentieth floor that had an awesome view of Montreal's skyline. Being centrally located, the Gouverneur was very close to the city's street festivals, shopping district, bars, and the Berri-UQAM subway station. Nigel and Manny were already hitting the pool and gym whereas the rest of us decided to get stogged at a Mexican restaurant called Three Amigos, which was suggested by Nigel. After lunch, all of us met to stock up on alcohol and explore the downtown core before heading back to the hotel for taking a shower and getting ready.

'Let us get our bombers out for the night,' said Nigel, as all the boys were going through an infatuation phase for leather jackets after watching Nigel look regularly dapper in his bomber. Nigel would sport his leather jacket every other day at university, and we all followed suit. Sam was the last one to purchase his. Now, we could officially call ourselves the bomber squad.

'Pass me that cologne. The first impression always needs to be on point,' said Manny, trimming his sideline. Manny was always groomed and had the sickest fades.

'I am all set to peacock tonight. I suggest all of you have your scarves on or at least one piece of attractive jewelry,' said Andre.

'I am wearing this bling golden necklace,' I said, putting on the cheap 20-dollar necklace that had a huge golden square pendant which was sparkling with a black circle in the centre. I was looking like a secret underground rapper. To cap it off, I put on an onyx ring that was emerald cut.

'Looks like the bus will come anytime now. Let us go to the lobby. The girls are waiting there for us,' said Sam in a semi-drunk state, as he was drinking since evening.

The buses dropped us off at the Ivy Nightclub, and all the students huddled against each other to stay warm as they waited for their turn to enter the club.

'I love the music in this club,' said Lydia.

'I feel I am still sober. Let's get some shots, Ryan. Who else wants to join us?' said Sonia.

'I am down,' said Sam.

Ryan went up to the bartender, 'Ten bubblegum shots please.' The bubble gum shots were a hot seller at the Ivy.

I looked at the menu and ordered three blowjob shots. Apparently, blowjob shots had baileys mixed with shooters, which made it taste sweet.

Meanwhile, Lydia was winging Manny on the dance floor. According to Neil Strauss, an alpha male had two main characteristics. He is a leader of men and is preselected by women. By having a glamorous diva like Lydia winging him, he already looked preselected by the most beautiful girl in the club. Meeting girls was not difficult now.

Andre asked me to wing him and at the same time watch and learn.

'Hi! I am Andre,' he said, spewing forth a plume of chutzpah as he introduced himself to a set of two girls. 'And this is my friend Devansh.'

'Hi! I am Nicole. Nice to meet you,' said the girl.

'You have a wonderful outfit, but it doesn't go well with your shoes. I think some silver Cinderella type shoes would go well with this dress,' Andre said, giving her a neg. In pick-up language, a neg is a backhanded compliment. The purpose of the neg was to distinguish himself from the other guys who had been hitting on her and to navigate her bitch shield. It helps a man demonstrate that he is not another guy who will place her on a high pedestal because she is pretty and has a good booty. It demonstrates a lack of interest in hooking up with her, even though hooking up is always the goal, but the neg gets her guard down.

'You think so?' she said surprisingly. 'I really like these shoes. I bought them from an upscale boutique in Yorkville,' she said.

'Will these shoes allow their owner to dance with the ugliest guy in the club?' chuckled Andre. He was trying to make her laugh by using self-deprecating humor and build a rapport. Most guys fail to do that. I was closely deconstructing every move he made, trying to learn his game.

'Oh, stop saying that. You are not ugly. You are a good-looking guy,' said Nicole, giving Andre her first indicator of interest.

'Really! Does that mean I won't have to make love to my girlfriend tonight?' Andre said, giving a demonstration of obnoxious humor while spinning her around with one hand.

'Hahahahaha, you are a really funny guy. What do you study at UofT?' she asked, placing her hands on his shoulder. Now she was the one asking him questions, which was an indication that she was taking an interest in him. By placing her hand on his shoulder, she had shown that the ice had broken and she was comfortable with him.

I started speaking to her friend and used a different neg from the list that I had prepared at the hotel and memorized on the bus ride. Soon, I was grinding her and she was vigorously twerking against me. This girl was an international student from America, and her name was Chantelle.

'You want some Tic Tacs?' I said, doing the Mystery routine.

'Sure,' she said as the DJ played a Punjabi tune, to which everyone raised their fingers in the air.

'Chantelle, if you didn't know, I am an Indian giver. I want my Tic Tacs back,' I said, sensually lowering my voice and making eye contact with her as I held her tightly by the waist. She understood where this was going and smiled back. Then she closed her eyes and gently moved her lips towards me under the frame of returning those Tic Tacs. I leaned in and kissed her for five minutes without unlocking my lips from her. We were both breathing through our noses as I grabbed her ass. I had my first make out in Canada. It took me a while to get the ball rolling, but the results were coming in good.

Manny leveraged Lydia's winging prowess and utilized some pick-up tricks to get with a Black girl who seemed to be head over heels for him. After setting him up with the girl, Lydia found a tall, white stallion for herself. Sonia was flirting with a guy whom I recognized from one of my lectures. Sam was wading through the crowd of grinding pairs of men and women, trying his game on women. After being in the frat and learning pick-up, his game had improved a lot, but he didn't find anyone yet. So he joined Ryan for drinks. As the night was coming to an end, I tried to seed ideas in Chantelle's mind about going back to my place. But her friends managed to cockblock me and whisked her away. Andre came up to me and told me that I had to work on overcoming obstacles. No matter how much the girl is into you, she will show some resistance before sleeping with you, or her friends might prove to be obstacles. Once the club closed for the night, Lydia went to the White dude's place in a cab while Sonia took the guy who was flirting with her back to her room. Andre and Manny were getting lucky as well, and they both took their one-night stands to our hotel rooms. Therefore, Sam, Nigel, Ryan, and I had to wait in the lobby until they were done as all three rooms were occupied.

The following night, the university took us to a club called Muzik, which was even bigger than Ivy. Andre had taught Sam a magic trick which was Mystery's favorite trick inside clubs and bars. Sam could now effortlessly levitate a bottle and captivate his audience of tipsy girls and guys. After getting no results the previous night, he practiced that trick the whole day until he could perform it smoothly inside the club. He was already the alpha in the club, as all the girls were fascinated by his bottle and card tricks. Therefore, today he locked in on a really pretty Albanian blonde whose boobs were semi-popping out of her dress, and her cleavage could be fully seen. Lydia and Sonia had no trouble finding someone new for themselves to go back home with again, which made us envy the privileges that attractive women enjoy. They could get laid whenever they wanted whereas we had to work on our game here to stand out. Once the party was over, Sam, Lydia, and Sonia went their ways to shag their transient partners while the rest of us went to McDonald's to buy cheap fries, wraps, and burgers. Also, McDonald's was the only savior for the students who partied until the wee hours of the morning. It was inexpensive and open 24 hours a day, 365 days a year.

After we ordered our meals, Andre started the perennial discussion that every meat lover has with a vegetarian. This was probably the twentieth time we were having this discussion, and I had become inured to being questioned and explaining myself to him and others.

'Devansh, you should really try eating chicken once. Trust me, you are going to like it,' said Andre.

'Bruh! I haven't been brought up that way. I don't understand how you are okay with eating another living thing. Don't you feel disgusted at the thought of eating flesh and tissues of an animal or bird?' I counter questioned him.

'It is not like I am having raw flesh and blood. The meat is always cooked and seasoned. In fact, it tastes so good. You wouldn't know unless you have tried it,' Andre said persuasively.

'And what the about the suffering? Have you ever been empathetic to the plight of these animals who are caged, tortured, and butchered to satisfy your hunger? Just because they are nicely packaged and displayed beautifully on the shelves of grocery stores doesn't mean that you can ignore the suffering that goes behind it. You vote with your dollar. I would suggest you should introspect and maybe try converting to a vegetarian,' I argued getting emotionally invested in the conversation. For the first time, I was trying to push Andre to give up meat rather than justifying my reasons for being a vegetarian.

'Stop trying to convince him, Andre. If he doesn't want to eat meat, it is his personal choice,' said Nigel who had just finished one of the two junior chickens he had ordered.

'I would stop convincing him if he could back his beliefs with logic. His reasoning is highly flawed and pure drivel. He is talking about killing living things. Devansh, you vegetarians eat plants. Those are living things too. Just because they don't have eyes and a face doesn't mean that they don't suffer or they don't die. One should always listen to their elders but at the same time critically think before blindly believing something. You are an obedient guy, but don't follow a hierarchy without questioning the underlying logic of things,' said Andre.

'I mean plants are the source of all life on Earth. They are at the bottom of the food chain. Life wouldn't exist without them. We would all die if it wasn't for plants. Even the animals you eat survive on grass or other animals who eat grass or grains. There is a reason why religion forbids eating meat. As a Hindu, I can't even think of eating steak, as we consider cow very sacred in our religion,' I said.

'That is exactly the problem. You are bogged down by a lot of hierarchies in your life. Religion being another one. Don't forget that God never made religion. People like us did. And everything that has been socially created has been created to serve an ulterior purpose. For example, in India, there was a time when it was considered preposterous if a woman did not burn herself with her husband's body after his death. The practice of *Sati* was fostered under the garb of religion to marginalize women and devoid them of their rights. A man on the other hand would not have to practice *Sati* if his wife died. This practice would still have continued if people didn't question it and stop it. Why do Hindus not refrain from eating other kinds of meat? I was researching about your city Kolkata the other day. People there seem to love fish and chicken, and Bengalis are Hindus too. How do you distinguish between a cow's meat and another animal's meat? It doesn't make sense,' said Andre.

'If it doesn't make sense, then why are so many people in India vegetarian? Also, why has the cow been considered sacred for centuries and why are people sticking to the religious belief of their ancestors if these things don't make sense?' I said, challenging his position.

'Well, if you are talking about numbers, then let me update you on some figures. India is just one country. There are around 200 countries in the world, majority of which are meat-eating nations. Look at China, the UK, Russia, America, Pakistan, Kenya, Brazil...If you believe what the majority of people do is right, then the majority of the people in the world are meat eaters. In fact, you vegetarians are the minority here. There is a reason why McDonald's in Canada doesn't have a single vegetarian burger on their menu. You are forced to eat a wrap or a salad every time, and that sucks. I am sure you would agree on this.'

'But why are so many people in the West converting to a vegetarian diet if eating meat was so much better? It's also proven that a vegetarian diet has much more health benefits,' I said as I could not bear the thought of being constantly questioned for being a vegetarian. I wanted to end this discussion once and for all.

'Human beings have existed from much before the advent of agriculture. As tribal men, we lived as hunter gatherers and procured food from hunting or gathering. Fire was discovered much later, and agriculture was discovered after fire was discovered. Until then, how do you think your ancestors lived? It's very easy to say now that religion forbids this, or that you cannot eat dead animals. But it has always been the survival of the fittest. How do you think humans thrived while so many species became extinct? Would it have been possible without getting our hands bloody? As a society, we have survived because we aren't just the fittest but also the brainiest. And how do you think our brains evolved to be so superior?' said Andre.

'How?' I asked.

'According to a lot of scientists, a gram of brain tissue takes twenty times more energy than tissues from the liver, heart, or kidney. The brain is a very nutritionally demanding organ and eating meat made it possible for the brains of our pre-human ancestors to grow dramatically over a span of thousands of years. Meat even enabled other functions like better thermoregulation and more mature speech organs,' answered Ryan before Andre could say anything. By now, the whole table seemed to become proactive in this conversation.

'Also, who says that only non-vegetarians have the blood of animals on their hands and are responsible for their death? You know, Devansh, the suppliers of top clothing brands that have factories in China like Adidas, Nike, Lacoste, H&M, and Calvin Klein discharge waste with poisonous, hormone-destroying chemicals. These facilities discharge toxic waste in rivers that kill marine life. Similarly, leather and textile industries in Bangladesh dispose plastics in water bodies and emit hazardous gases that result in the death of thousands of birds, fishes, and animals. Plastics are one of the most dangerous pollutants for water bodies, as they are non-biodegradable in nature. Don't we all purchase clothes from these brands or buy leather belts and wallets made in these factories? Crony capitalism exists on the blood of these creatures, and we all contribute towards it. Sure, as a vegetarian you might not be killing them directly for food, but you are killing them by voting with your dollars,' said Andre, borrowing my expression.

I didn't know how to respond because it didn't seem like he was indulging in conjecture. He had arguments backed by logic.

'Fine. I will try chicken today,' I whimpered, ending our strife.

'What? Is this actually happening?' said Manny as Andre stood up hastily to order a McChicken burger for me before I changed my mind. The look on their faces was priceless.

'That is my man,' said Andre as he gave the most excited order of his life. He could have paid 20$ for that burger if the attendant had asked him to.

Nigel and Ryan took out their phones to capture this moment.

'Sam, Lydia, and Sonia are missing out on this. I am going to be the one to Snapchat this to them,' said Nigel.

'Devansh, are you sure? Or are we dreaming? Andre, you should join the fucking debate team. I salute your convincing powers,' said Ryan.

I sat mute and tried to gather my thoughts together. What did I just say? Was I prepared for this? The thought of meat grossed me out. I could visualize the faces of my parents revolving in front of me. I didn't know what to say or how to react to Ryan's questions. My mother's advice echoed in my ears, 'Devansh, never do anything that will bring shame upon us. Always remember the values that we have brought you up with.' I was feeling guilty. Another voice played in my head that said 'Devansh, don't chicken out now. Just grow a pair and eat that chicken.' I was perspiring as the stress started to overcome me.

Andre had brought the McChicken burger to the table and unwrapped it like it was a ticking time bomb, slowly and cautiously.

'Devansh, just go for it, man. Trust me, you are going to keep on licking this chicken. Don't overthink this. You will never find out what you are missing in life if you don't try it now. Come on,' said Andre as the others joined in on the rooting by singing a modified version of Michael Jackson's song *Beat it* but keeping the same tune.

How come you're always such a fussy young man? (MUSIC)

Don't want no captain crunch

Don't want no raisin bran

Well, don't you know that other kids are starving in Iran?

So, eat it. Just eat it. Eat itttt.

I held the burger in my hands and stared at it. The thought of eating chicken overwhelmed my system. The smell of meat that I detested made me feel like I was about to eat the food that was rancid. I closed my eyes and took my first bite, masticating my food several times to experience what chicken tastes like.

'How was it?' said Manny with his eyes enlarged.

'Didn't think I would ever witness this,' said Andre as Ryan and Nigel took videos and pictures of this moment.

'It tastes like dry tofu. I don't understand why people love it so much. I feel like I am having tofu that is devoid of moisture and over-fried. It is just more filling than vegetarian burgers I suppose,' I said.

'McDonald's is basic. This isn't the best chicken you are going to eat. But I am glad that your mindset has altered. It was very important to clear your mental blockage. This experience will allow you to get out of your mental prison and try a lot of new things from which you were holding yourself back. People do a lot of things just because they are prisoners of their own identity,' said Andre.

'I guess so. I would be less worried about trying other kinds of meat or taking bolder decisions in life. I feel like I was carrying a lot of weight. Nothing seems to have changed after eating chicken. Looks like I was tensed for no reason about this whole episode,' I said.

Freshman year was coming to an end. We had finished our lectures and had a week's break before the final exams. Trinity College had organized the fresher's ball for its residents during this week, and it was a highly anticipated event. Trinity was known to spend lavishly on the fresher's annual ball and this event was the most popular event held at Trinity. According to customs, boys dressed in black whereas the girls wore red. The principal of Trinity College attended this event along with several resident staff members. There were different bar counters, and the finest meals were served in exquisite settings. Well-groomed, polished waiters wearing uniforms served delicious staples and multi-cuisine delicacies like foie grasparfait and goat cheese soufflés. Everyone at Trinity residences was offered a guest pass to bring along a date or a friend. So Andre decided to bring Sonia as his date whereas Ryan brought Lydia. I gave my pass to Manny, and Sam gave his to Nigel. Nigel paid extra to buy another pass so that he could bring his girlfriend Hannah as his date. This event was held at the Cassa Ricca banquet hall which had a capacity for 600 people.

The round tables could accommodate ten people easily, so we were all comfortably seated on one table. My date for the night was Adrianne, who was a resident student at Trinity College. I used The Lying Game to ask her out for the fresher's ball. She agreed, as she was fond of me and also because she lost the game. I helped her on some of her sociology assignments, and we had developed a strong camaraderie. I had taken a shine on her because she was pretty and White. The Brown man inside me was fascinated by White beauty, and she checked both the boxes. Since it was an open bar, we drank until we got hammered. The ballroom was probably accommodating its largest gathering of inebriated adults, as no college student abstains from free alcohol. The bars had to be closed early, as some students got really shit faced. Nigel's girlfriend Hannah had drank so much that she barfed in the ladies' room. Also, she was underage for drinking, which made Nigel nervous, as he didn't want to invite trouble for us from the security. Dinner was served as a live band played trance music. Instead of enjoying the intimate delicacies, we were eating out of hunger and the necessity for our body to soak up the alcohol. By now, I was eating more non-vegetarian dishes than anyone on the table. Not because I developed a strong inclination for meat, but I wanted to try everything, widening the horizons and breadths of my experience. Adrianne had finished her meal, so I took her to the dance floor. Ryan and Andre followed soon with Lydia and Sonia. Nigel was taking care of Hannah. I noticed that Sam and Manny were still at the table, and they seemed to be having what looked like a serious discussion.

Adrianne draped her hands on my shoulder while I swayed her to the tunes of sentimental ballads. She looked beautiful and wild. The slow dance gave way to Eminem's hit song *Shake that*, to which Lydia lost all her modesty and started twerking against Ryan. Andre and Sonia had gone to play poker, as the college had organized poker tables with professional dealers for us. As gambling was legal in Canada, the university didn't view it as a contradiction to the values it upheld and allowed the residence staff to arrange it. Sam and Manny still seemed to be having a heated discussion, which didn't look normal to me. I sent a text message to Sonia, Andre, Ryan, and Lydia that read:

Something doesn't seem right between Sam and Manny. We should check what is up with them.

Ryan glanced at me, and I signaled back at him to get Andre and Sonia from the poker table. Meanwhile, I asked Adrianne if she could check up on Nigel and Hannah, as I didn't want her to be present when we spoke to Sam and Manny. I told her that I would be back soon, as I had to take care of something. When I looked around, I saw Manny leaving the table miserably while Sam chased him outside the door to the smoking area. Ryan, Andre, Sonia, Lydia, and I followed.

'She is not agreeing. I don't care about anyone else, but I thought she would understand me,' vented Manny in an angry tone. Since we had just come out, we had no clue what the matter was.

'What is going on? You don't look fine,' Lydia said and put her hand on Manny's shoulder to comfort him.

'It's nothing. Don't spoil your fresher's ball. Go inside. I will join you soon,' said Manny.

'You can share everything with us. We are your friends. We want to know what is bothering you. Maybe we can help,' said Ryan.

'I will be fine. Seriously, it's nothing,' said Manny.

'Are you sure? Because you don't look okay,' asked Ryan.

Sam interrupted at this point, 'He wants to drop out of UofT. Sorry, I had to tell them because they need to know this.'

'Why? What! Are you for real? Your grades are decent. What happened?' asked Sonia.

Manny took a deep breath, looked at the ground, and then said, 'There is something I haven't told you guys before. Deep down I have always wanted to be an actor. I feel a sense of liberation whenever I go on stage but...My mother wanted me to pursue business at university. She came to Canada so that my sister and I could have a better life. My father left her for another woman. She doesn't want us to face the struggles she endured back in India. Her parents were not well off, so they couldn't send her to a good college. Moreover, her degree in India was not worth a lot in Canada, and she had to do odd jobs like working in restaurants or as an office clerk to bring us up. She wants a better life for me and my sister.'

'Since this is your internal family matter, I cannot tell you what you should do, but if I were to give you one advice, all I can tell you is that UofT is not a school where you can get away with studying something you don't like. You are not likely to graduate with good grades if you don't really enjoy what you are doing because things are going to get harder in the next three years,' I said.

'Yeah, but watching me graduate from the Rotman School of Management was her dream. I don't know how to convince her. She broke down on the phone last month when I told her that I wanted to quit and pursue acting,' said Manny.

On hearing this, Sam said, 'Tell her you are getting decent grades even after disliking what you do. Look at me, I am not getting into Rotman, even though I wanted to pursue commerce because all I have done this year is drink, smoke, and party. My grades have tanked, and the only way I can make it is if I nail all my final exams which is unlikely.'

We were all dumbstruck on hearing this. We knew he was a laggard, but the fact that he won't be meeting the cutoff for commerce was shocking news to us.

'So, what is your backup plan then?' asked Sonia.

'Don't have one,' said Sam, lighting up a cigarette as it started to rain. 'I don't know what I want to major in if I cannot get into commerce.'

I couldn't believe how calmly he said that. How could he maintain such a restful composure after seeing his plans dismantle in front of his eyes? Either he had a very thick skin or he didn't let things affect him. He always said that the biggest killer in the 21st century is not cancer but stress.

Manny took a cigarette from Sam and lit it up. For a moment, there was silence when Sam spoke the golden words which changed Manny's life forever, 'Manny, you are making it into Rotman, even though you didn't want to pursue management. I wasted my year and misused my independence, even though I don't regret it because life it too short for regrets. However, you, my friend, have the discipline in you to achieve every milestone that you have planned for yourself. I am not getting into Rotman, and I don't even have a backup plan, but you, you aced your backup plan! Just imagine your potential when you finally pursue what you love. We can achieve all our goals if we believe in them with a strong conviction. When you have achieved everything you have wanted and you are sitting on your rocking chair and contemplating life, the only thing that will matter to you then will be your family, your wife, your children and grandchildren. Nothing else will matter. No amount of money, fame, or success will bring you any happiness, and you can only be happy when your family around you is happy. Think of what kind of a role model you want to be for them. Someone who isn't happy with his work, or someone who loves his craft and comes back home with a smile on his face.'

On hearing that, Manny threw his cigarette on the floor and squashed it with his shoe to extinguish it. Then he took out his phone and typed a message to his mother:

I have given this a lot of thought. I gave my all to Rotman and UofT, but I don't belong here. My true calling is acting. So I am dropping out of school. Hope you will understand. XOXO

Dropping out from the most prestigious institution in Canada with a solid business school like Rotman was a tough decision. But I guess life is full of tough choices, and fulfilling one's dreams requires a lot of sacrifices. You win some, you lose some, you dim sum. Silence dawned upon all of us as we stood out in the cold and watched the rainfall. Everyone was lost in their own thoughts. I had just witnessed one of my friends drop out of university. Another didn't seem to be making the cut. As the rain slowly stopped, the banked-up remnants of the retreating rainclouds made me realize that spring had begun. Nature's law states that change is the only constant. Life, at that point, resembled the change in seasons as the sky above us and the mood around us looked gloomy. However, it also meant that the bright sunny days were about to come.

We finished our exams towards the end of April and went our separate ways for the summer break. This summer, everyone excluding Nigel, Sonia, and Lydia had tasked themselves with improving their game by learning new magic tricks, rune reading, NLP routines, how to text effectively, and basically anything that would enable us in the process of getting laid. While the others stayed back in Canada, Sam and I had gone back to India. I was doing a summer abroad at King's College, London, UK, and had plans to execute my pick-up skills in England. In India, Narendra Modi's Hindu nationalist party (BJP) was expected to form the new government with a full majority. The political landscape in India was highly charged with other countries closely following the largest democratic exercise in the world where 800 million voters would cast their votes. The BJP under the leadership of Narendra Modi seemed to dominate the national discourse with its promise of development that aligned with its hardline Hindutva agenda. His catchphrase slogan 'Good days are coming' aimed to remind people of the policy paralysis, nepotism, and corruption that had scathed the current UPA establishment. Modi's lucratively financed campaign was also an indication that the richest people in the country would get even richer and inequality would increase. Money is known to be the root of all evils. Just like the prime minister of a democratic country is undemocratically decided by the financial lobby behind him, similarly, the size of a parent's bank account could also decide if their children could get a bachelor's degree abroad. Coming back to India after finishing my first year had made me much more humble, more aware, and more grateful in life.

Year 2 Semester I

We were back to school for our second year. All of us were seeing each other after a wonderful summer that I wished had lasted longer. Now that we had cultivated strong ties of friendship, our living arrangements altered slightly because most of us decided to move out of our student residences. Andre and I had rented a two-bedroom apartment in a newly made condominium overlooking Yonge Street. Nigel, Ryan, and Manny were renting a private townhouse near campus. Lydia and Sonia were the only ones who continued to reside at Whitney Hall. Sam moved into the house of his fraternity, Lambda Chi Alpha, to live with other members in the spirit of brotherhood. After he failed to meet the minimum requirements for commerce at Rotman, he spent the summer pondering over what he wanted to pursue and decided to major in economics, as economics did not have a high cut off. Manny had enrolled himself in the Toronto Film School, which was also downtown and had a three-year course, so he would be graduating at the same time as us.

UofT was prepared to welcome its new batch of frosh students as well as upper-year students like us who were returning back to school for a new academic year. There were parties all over the campus, but we decided to try the bar hopping scene on Queen West, because now we all could legally drink and were excited to demonstrate new pick-up skills that each of us had acquired and honed over the summer. I had been following a pick-up artist called Madison, who was very good at crafting stories and keeping his targets engaged. He believed that people can deduce a lot from stories, and the best way to reveal your personality or character traits to others is by telling them a story about yourself. This theory goes back to our tribal ancestors who passed on lessons from one generation to the other through stories, because writing had not been discovered then. Stories played an important role in filling the silent gaps in the conversation, because a lot of girls lose interest when the conversation becomes mundane like an interview, where the guy is only asking them questions. One needs to know the art of talking and demonstrating higher value about oneself through short stories.

We had decided to go on a pub crawl at Queen Street West. Set against a background of historic city architecture, Queen Street West has one of the trendiest shops, restaurants, and bars in the city of Toronto. The bars play an array of music genres from roots to salsa and rock with many venues having live music. Located in the downtown core and easily accessible by public transit, Queen Street is popular for its pub crawls that happen throughout the year, which are organized by different event companies. As the bars are so close to one another, you can literally 'crawl' from one venue to the next if you are too drunk to walk. We decided to refrain from choosing an organized pub crawl because we wanted to drink and dance at our own leisure, without having to follow a guided group from one venue to the other. Sam came up with a list of six bars, and we decided to start the trek at the Friar and Firkin Pub and move to the other venues in logical order. The six pubs on our list were Friar and Firkin, Black Bull Tavern, The Rivoli, Horseshoe, Cameron, and Tequila Bookworm. Sam had suggested the Hideout instead of Tequila Bookworm, but I got the last one modified due to my former experience at Tequila Bookworm.

We started the night with a pint each at Friar and Firkin because their beer flight deals allowed us to purchase eight pints for 16$. Friar and Firkin was a stereotypical British pub with the usual pub grub and cozy surroundings.

'To our first drink as upper-year students now that everyone is 19. Cheers!' said Sam.

'Cheers,' we all said in unison as we touched glasses and spilt some foam.

'Guys! We are planning to have a housewarming soon. I cannot wait to throw our first party there,' said Nigel.

Andre took this opportunity to mention our apartment too, 'Yeah, that is going to be awesome. We have the perfect view to get drunk to. The view from our balcony on the 27th floor is breathtaking. You can see the whole stretch on Yonge up to Eaton Centre. Devansh, we should throw a housewarming party as well,' he said looking at me.

'First I need to warm my bed. I have learnt so much about pick-up over the summer. Feels like I can literally be one of those coaches though,' I retorted.

'He is right. Our cherry boy here needs to get laid,' said Ryan with a wink.

'There is a right time for everyone. You don't have to rush into anything. I lost my virginity at 16, but I have friends who were born in Canada and are my age, but they haven't even kissed yet. Don't listen to this idiot,' said Lydia.

'But I want to get laid now. I have learnt so much about pick-up and the art of seduction. Time to implement my study in the field,' I said.

'You and your pick-up world. That is all you guys are obsessed about,' said Sonia with a look of umbrage.

On hearing that, Sam confronted Sonia, 'You girls got your cherry popped early and have it easy in this feminist world that we live in. We guys require a lot of practice in order to be successful with women. Don't you see how these rich fat guys who drive swanky cars are shagging hot young girls all the time?'

'Bye, Felicia,' said Lydia using a White-girl expression which meant get-out-of-my-face in a polite way because she knew what Sam said was true.

We headed to the next bar called the Black Bull which was an old-school tavern located in the same place since the last two hundred years. The Black Bull had a laidback vibe, but it catered to a mixed crowd of young local professionals and hip out-of-towners. The murals on the wall portrayed a sense of how Toronto has evolved over the years, as some pictures dated back to a time when horse carriages dominated the streets of 'Toronto the Good', as Toronto was colloquially known. We ordered several rounds of tequila on shotskis. A shotski is a single wooden plank that has several shot glasses affixed to it by drilled holes that are equidistant from one another and allow several people to drink together. Our shotski had five glasses attached to it, which enabled five of us to drink at the same time. This technique for simultaneous alcohol consumption created epic Instagram and Snapchat moments for all of us.

After Black Bull, we hit The Rivoli. The Rivoli was a live music venue with a huge bar along most of its west wall. The east side of the venue had a huge space for dancing and socializing. Upstairs, there was a pool room with eleven antique tables and a small bar. There was also an outdoor patio, which was very popular with the loyal locals. We ordered eight whiskey sours as well as eight gin and tonics so that there was one of each drink for all of us. The booze was having a strong effect on us because we were mixing different types of alcohol at each bar. Mixing so many types of drinks in your stomach is not recommended unless you want to get drunk very quickly. In order to reduce the effect of the alcohol, we ordered the hot-selling sticky rice balls and pad thai that The Rivoli was known for. As we were grooving to the beats of the live musicians, Sonia was approached by a boy who looked biracial. He was white-skinned but had large lips and Afro hair.

'Can I buy you a drink?' he said using the cliché line that every guy who wants to get to know a girl in a social setting like this would use.

'Why would you want to do that?' said Sonia teasing him.

'Because I like what I see. By the way, I am Keanu,' said the biracial guy.

'Sonia,' she said shaking his hand, 'Sure, I don't mind a shot.' And they headed off to the bar.

That one shot became three before they knew it, and they made a smooth segue to the dance floor, going to the bar for the occasional shot that Keanu was buying Sonia.

'This guy seems loaded,' said Nigel.

'Looks like a student to me. Seems like his father is the one making bank,' said Manny.

I was easing up to a White blonde who was partying with her friends. Everyone in that group other than her seemed to be from an East Asian country because they all had slit eyes. Ryan and I slowly moved our way towards them with our backs turned so that they don't realize that we would be approaching them. I used an opener that I had conceived over the summer that followed the same rule as the openers that Neil Strauss used. It should be non-threatening and genuinely make the girl feel that you want her opinion by intellectually stimulating her. Lastly, one should always give a time constraint so that the girl does not feel that you are going to stay long because that might get her guard up.

'Hi there, I need your opinion on something real quick. My friend and I seem to be having this argument for quite a while, but we can't seem to settle it so I thought we should get a female opinion on it. That is why I wanted your help on this,' I said.

'What is it?' replied the blonde.

'Do you think that JLo will get married the fourth time? I think she will whereas my friend *pointing towards Ryan* thinks she won't, because after three divorces, he reckons her to be an unstable partner. Moreover, he thinks that she wouldn't believe in the institution of marriage anymore.'

'That is a tricky one. She might, I don't know. It all depends on whether she meets someone she considers very special. She still has those looks going for her,' said the blonde.

Our conversation continued steadily while Ryan took a shine on one of the Asian girls in the group who turned out to be from Kazakhstan. We managed to isolate the girls from their group and were dancing with them separately. Isolating the girl from her group is an essential rule for seducing her later. The fact that we could seamlessly isolate them in the bar was an indicator that they were interested, and our pick-up skills had substantially improved. I dropped one of the stories that I learnt from Madison in the middle of the dance to keep the rhythm going.

'You know Ivy, back in the day I used to be super introverted, like super shy, it just felt like life was literally passing me by. I used to be socially awkward in big groups when I was in high school, and I would see my friends going out on weekends and posting crazy stuff on social media, but I used to be afraid of going out socially with many people. As a result, every time they had crazy adventures on the weekend, I would get super jealous when I saw their posts on Facebook. Fuck! I am missing out on so much that life has to offer, and even if I reach the pinnacle of socially defined success, I am not going to be internally happy unless I have those same types of experiences in my life. At one point, I made this decision to actively seek out discomfort. I was scared of heights, so much so that I couldn't stand on top of a tall building and look outside the window. So, a female friend of mine and I, we finally did it. We decided to go skydiving, and it was the most emotionally exhilarating experience of my life. We jumped outside the plane, and it was indescribably amazing. The adrenaline rush was crazy, felt the fucking wind gush against my face. I can't even put it into words. But the craziest thing happened after that. Once we landed, we felt so much in control after taking this risk that we felt we could do anything. So what my friend decided to do was call up this guy whom she had had a crush on for like a year but never had the courage to say anything. She called him up and asked him out. He said yes, and after three years of being in a relationship, they are getting engaged next year. The implication of the story being, once you go against your conditioning, good things will happen,' I recited my fake story which was scripted to the last syllable.

This story helped to set the frame for the night. She would be more acceptable to the idea of sex than before (one should go against conditioning), and it also showed that I was an adventurous guy. Pick-up artists like Madison had been in the field for years, and their methods were tried and tested. One needs to be patient and believe in the system. Most of the failures in life happen when we lose patience or lose faith in ourselves.

Ivy and Bahtyzamal (Ryan's target) were students at York University who had come out for a girl's night with their gang. Ryan and I decided to proceed to the next bar with the girls in order to isolate them further from their friends. Keanu was grinding hard against Sonia by now, and they both seemed to be so lost in one another that they didn't care how others were looking at them. Keanu was passionately smooching her and pressing her boobs hard. They looked like two lovebirds who had found their cozy nest while grinding to the music. Manny gave me a wink and a thumbs up as Ryan and I left for the next pub with the girls. Pick-up artists profess that changing locations with a girl has two benefits. It gives an illusion of more time spent together than one does, which subconsciously helps a girl to trust the guy. When you frequently change a location, the girl is likely to have a new experience at every place which makes her think that she has known the guy for a longer time than the time she has actually spent with him. New experiences also give more stuff to talk about and changes the frame in the girl's head. Casinos use exactly the opposite psychology when they block out the light so that one does not realize the passage of time.

The next pub we went to was called the Horseshoe Tavern. The Horseshoe Tavern was a dive bar that could best be described as a microcosm of the indie, rock, and funk music that was available anywhere on Queen Street. This dive bar boasted a proud collection of local craft beers.

'Have you tried the Bavarian beer?' Ivy asked me.

'No. What kind of beer is that?' I replied brazenly.

'It's German beer that comes from the southeast portion of Germany. As a third generation Canadian German, I try to assimilate the German culture as much as I can. I like Bavarian beer a lot ever since my cousins in Germany made me try it. You should try it too,' she said. Ivy's family was settled in Calgary, Alberta, and she had moved across the country to pursue higher education in Toronto.

'Sure. Let me order two pints for the both of us,' I said and led her with my hand to the bar. I used Kino with her and made her comfortable with my touch without it looking awkward.

As the bar was busy, we were waiting for our turn to give the order. I turned around, looked into her eyes, and went in for a kiss. She followed my lead again, and we played tonsil hockey for a while until our turn to order drinks had come. While we were sipping our drinks and making small talk, Ryan came to us carrying Ivy's friend in his arms.

'I guess we are going to my place,' said Ryan.

Ivy's friend Bahtyzamal told Ivy that she would be fine and that she should not worry about her. Then they communicated with their eyes, and Bahtyzamal gave Ivy a hug while Ryan was still carrying her in his arms.

After they had left, Ivy told me, 'Don't take me wrong. Your friend looks good, but I never thought Bahtyzamal was the kind of girl who would sleep with someone on the first night. You should at least get to know the person. Right?' I thought to myself, 'Does this mean that she won't be sleeping with me tonight? 'Was she indirectly telling me that I shouldn't keep my hopes up or that she wasn't as easy as her friend?' This could also be a shit test. According to pick-up artists, girls continuously give shit tests to examine how the guy is affected by what they say. The rules of the game state that a pick-up artist should always believe in himself. The game is always on unless the girl has explicitly said no. My orbital frontal cortex whirred into action. Therefore, I smiled and changed the topic without getting nervous or showing a lack of interest on my face because girls are very quick to catch onto that. I behaved as if what she said did not affect me at all. That is how a shit test is passed.

'Let me try some NLP stuff with you. I want you to picture a screen between you and me. Now, picture a basic shape like a square on this screen but not exactly a square. Now, I want you to picture another basic shape around this shape. Did you do it?' I asked.

'Yeah,' she replied.

'So, inside this screen, you pictured a circle that is surrounded by a triangle. Am I right?' I asked.

'How did you know that?' she exclaimed.

'This is just the calibration key to real mind reading. There are many books on NLP, and I love reading this stuff, you know,' I said, demonstrating higher value.

Soon, Lydia arrived with two shots for the both of us, and I introduced Lydia to Ivy as a really good friend. Lydia and I were communicating telepathically, where she was helping me wing the girl by getting her a free shot and showing her that I was a decent guy who had attractive female friends. I was thanking her for showing me as a desirable person who hangs out with attractive girls. It goes back to the theory of an alpha male being preselected by women.

'My friends are going to continue bar hopping, as they have two more bars on the list, but I feel like sipping wine on my balcony. I just rented a new apartment on the St. Mary's and Yonge intersection. You would love the view from there. Let us grab the next drink on my balcony,' I said, planting the idea of moving her to my house.

'I don't know. My friends are still at the other bar. They would be waiting for me,' she said showing some resistance. I had to assume this was another shit test because she didn't want to come off as too easy.

'Don't worry, I will get an Uber for you from my house that will take you wherever you want. As long as you promise not to rob and kill me, I can promise you that we will have a good laugh and nothing else,' I said humorously while at the same time making it sound casual.

'Fine. I promise not to rob you or kill you,' she said as we proceeded towards the exit.

I booked an Uber to take me to 75 St. Nicholas Street Toronto, M4Y 0A5, which was saved as home on my Uber app. We went upstairs in the elevator, and I took Ivy to my balcony. After playing all my cards correctly and passing all her shit tests, the stellar view of the city from my place was like a cherry on top of the cake. I corked open a bottle of wine and brought it in two glasses to the balcony while we admired the engineering ingenuity that embodied downtown Toronto with numerous condominiums and tall offices of various shapes and sizes. The dazzling lights of the city against the backdrop of tall glass and steel structures were a manifestation of modern technology and innovation. As my sociology modules had made me aware of the politics behind how space is developed, I felt a sense of empathy for the squeegee men and panhandlers who face trouble with law enforcement officials to make way for these plush residential and commercial districts. At that point, all I could see was a smile on Ivy's face taking in the view, and all I could think of was how to get into her pants.

I got a text message from Sam which read:

Ask her if she would like to cuddle with you. That is how it begins, and then one thing will lead to another.

I wasn't sure what to do. I didn't want to fuck it up, but I knew that I had to stop giving a fuck if I wanted to fuck her. I was grappling with my thoughts when Ivy turned towards me and placed one hand on my cheek and moved in to kiss me. I kissed her back, and the moment played out like a romantic Hollywood movie where silence follows a kiss on the balcony or deck of a house.

'Did you like it?' I asked stupidly.

She nodded coquettishly.

'Let us cuddle in my bedroom,' I said, taking her by the hand. She readily obliged.

We lay there on my bed while I was spooning her. I had got hard out of excitement, and I was sure that she could feel my boner. I had borrowed Andre's music playlist for seduction, as he had taught me that music was necessary to set the mood.

'I want you to teach me some German. How do you say "inside" in German?' I asked as we listened to trance music in the background.

'*Innerhalb*,' she pronounced in a German accent.

'Do you want me *innerhalb* you?' I asked naughtily.

'Yes,' she squealed with laughter.

I turned her around by her waist so that we faced each other. With my hand still on her waist, I kissed her passionately. I gently moved my hand while still kissing her as I made my way on top of her. We were kissing passionately when I tugged her tube top in an effort to pull it off. She helped me remove it, and I stared at her thin lacy red bra and bare stomach. She looked gorgeous with her blue eyes anxiously waiting to see what I would do next. I unhooked her bra and threw it on the floor while gazing at her boobs with a look of hunger in my eyes. I started sucking one of her boobs while massaging the other. Her boobs were soft, supple yet big enough that I enjoyed cupping her left boob with my right hand. I was sucking her right boob and occasionally circling my tongue around her nipple. I could hear her breathe heavily as her nipples hardened. She gently stroked my hair as I continued to tease and taunt her nipples artfully. I removed my right hand from her boob and slowly moved it down her sternum while feeling every iota of it. I started moving my mouth in the same direction, pressing my lips against her torso as I made my way between her boobs. My mouth reached her belly, and I start tickling her navel with my tongue. She seemed to be a ticklish person. Suddenly, she sat up and fiercely pulled my shirt. I straightened my hands so that she could take my t-shirt off easily.

'I want to suck your dick,' she said while reaching for my denim's button.

I laid down on the bed as she unbuttoned my jeans and pulled my fly down. I helped her undress me with all the clothes that were south of my waistline. I lay there completely naked in front of her, feeling vulnerable, as the last time someone had seen me naked, I had been a child. She held my dick in her hand and started stroking it.

'Damn, you are so hard already,' she said playfully.

She started sucking my balls and I felt a tumultuous rush of adrenaline gushing through my veins. Then she was deep throating my cock with full vigor, and the skillful movement of her mouth was an indication that she had done it many times before. I was smiling profusely, as I received my first blowjob. My dick felt moist from her saliva, and my spirits were on cloud nine. However, I thought I should stop her before I ejaculated from the blowjob because oral sex, though new to me, was not the goal today. I wanted to fornicate the fuck out of her brains.

I grabbed her by her hair, 'Stop. Let me satisfy you now. I am from the land of the Kamasutra. I can satisfy your appetite for the whole night with my brown dynamite.'

We changed positions, as now she was the one lying on her back while I went down to do the work. I pulled her skirt down and repeated the same action with her panties. She didn't have a clean shave, because I don't think she was expecting to get laid tonight. But the grass on her hooch wasn't stopping me. I was still going to play ball. I slowly thrust two fingers inside her while I looked at her face. There was a look of contentment on her face. I vigorously started moving my fingers in a back and forth motion as she started to moan. Her moans started getting louder as I moved my fingers in full force. This was the first time I had my finger inside a vagina. My body started shaking, and I could feel my face turn red.

'You are shaking. Are you nervous?' she asked.

'No, I guess I am feeling cold without my clothes. That is all,' I lied.

I stopped fingering her to get my condom. Having put on the condom, I squirmed as I experienced euphoria that juxtaposed with feelings of nervousness, as I could feel the sensitive nerves on my dick. Without any preamble, I thrust myself inside her, making her scream. Lifting both her legs, I fiercely and laboriously impaled her again and again until we started feeling each other's frequency. I continued for two minutes as she moaned with her eyes closed as her back slightly arched. For some reason, I couldn't look at her eyes now. As it was my first time, I was very nervous about my performance in bed.

'I want you to ride me now,' I said.

We switched from missionary to cowboy as she went on top. Holding my penis in her hand, she eased it into her moist pussy. I grabbed her by her thighs as she moved up and down on my dick. I was more confident looking at her now, and she looked back at me. We had become one in the true sense. Her boobs bounced up and down with every stroke of my dick, so I placed both my hands on her boobs to stop them from oscillating. For the next eight minutes, she was riding me, and I could feel now that I was about to climax soon. I swiveled my hips to get a better grip and started going at it with all my strength and energy.

'Aaa aaa yes, fuck me, fuck me, fuck, fuck, fuckkkkk,' she moaned.

I tried to hold myself from bursting for as long as I could. Finally, I orgasmed, releasing my bodily fluids as my ardent self felt drained out, like someone had sucked a lot of energy and stress out of me. My head felt light, and my feet muscles convulsed. She realized I had cum as I lay still with a feeling of satisfaction on my face. My dick was still inside her. I indicated her to lie down beside me by tapping my mattress. What is it about orgasms that you suddenly feel gay after having them? I had this beautiful girl next to me, and all I wanted to do was clean myself and go to sleep. But I knew that she would want to finish as well. I started fingering her rapidly and played with her clitoris until she reached the zenith of her satisfaction and reveled in the sensation, finishing with a mind-blowing and bed-blowing orgasm.

The next day I woke up with a new identity. I felt the nineteen-year-old boy inside me had metamorphosed into a man. I felt too proud to be crawling on the ground like a caterpillar. I felt like I deserved to spread my wings like a butterfly and be on top of the world, because my spirits surely were there. Andre had already spread the news of my salacious escapade like wildfire among our friends. I learnt this from the blitz of messages that I received on WhatsApp, in the group that had the eight of us. Andre and I decided to invite everyone for drinks in the evening to show our new apartment and fulfill their curiosity as to what my experience had been like.

Location: Andre and my apartment at 75 Nicholas St.

'Congratulations on leaving the virgin club. You have finally grown. So, did my tip about cuddling help?' asked Sam.

'Yeah, she gave me a couple of shit tests. She was just checking how desperate I was to get laid. I behaved like I didn't care and was only there to have a good laugh. I kind of gave out that vibe like I get girls all the time. Girls are naturally more attracted to guys who have a lot of options and don't show that desperateness for sex. I learned that you should always let loose when she is most expecting you. I just kept her confused, never directly hinting at sex,' I said.

'Tell us about your experience. What does pussy feel like?' asked Ryan.

'I didn't last long, as I was pretty nervous. I guess it's a myth when they say that only girls get nervous on their first time. On the contrary, Ivy was way more confident than me, as she was definitely not a virgin. But getting inside that pussy was the best experience ever. It feels like you are entering something moist and squishy. Pussy feels lukewarm after you have spent some time inside it. But what changed the most after losing my virginity is the level of my confidence. I feel more independent now for some reason. I think I should take care of my own expenses and stop asking for money back home.'

Sam added with an unerring confidence, 'See, getting girls can be broken down to a system. It is a falsely perpetrated myth when people say that she is out of your league. There is no league, and no one is classifying girls in different leagues. If you follow the correct steps and learn from men who have been picking up women for years, you will naturally start to get results. I believe in the saying "Whatever you invest in, grows". For example, if you invest in stocks, mutual funds, or segregated funds, you will see your investments grow over time. Similarly, Nigel invested in American football since a young age and made it into the varsity team. Ryan invests a lot of time studying and has a perfect 4.0 GPA. Likewise, the more you invest in learning and practicing pick-up, the better you will get at it.'

'Yeah, but picking up includes a lot of deception though. I feel like there are many times I was tricking her rather than revealing my real self. I lied about being a part-time practicing magician after showing her a few card tricks in the Uber, who earns enough to afford living in this apartment. Isn't that wrong though?' I asked.

'Absolutely not. Compared to how much Andre, Manny, and I lie, you didn't do anything wrong. Pick-up is all about deception, and pick-up artists lie all the time. Why do you think they get laid the most? Because, when it comes to matters of physical or emotional intimacy, no one wants to hear the truth,' said Sam.

'What do you mean? I was attracted to the guys I have been with. I don't think they needed to lie to have sex with me,' Sonia interjected.

'You don't know that. Men directly or indirectly lie to women all the time. So do women. I mean a husband is forced to appreciate his wife's cooking even if he doesn't like it. There are so many men who cheat on their girlfriends all the time. I can open Tinder from your account and show you how many guys would be ready to come to your place within minutes, even though they have girlfriends. Do you think it is a coincidence that most people claim to fall in love with someone from their own religion and socioeconomic status? In public, even politicians denounce racial and religious hatred, but they are not always happy with the choice of partners that their sons or daughters have made. There are so many women who wouldn't be in a relationship if you took out the money from it. Expensive lawyers are hired to defend lies, rapists, and murderers, and they do this professionally without batting an eyelid. We are living in a system that has its roots entrenched in a bedrock of lies and deception. White privilege, racial profiling, gender wage gap – these are not lies, but every employer, police force, and government wants you to believe it does not exist under their jurisdiction. What are they doing to fix it? Are they even owning up to it?' said Sam.

He finished his speech with a self-invented captive slogan in Hindi, '*Chooth ke liye jhoot bolna padta hai*' which means one has to lie for pussy.

'I hope Keanu is not like that. I really like the guy, and I am going to continue to see him,' Sonia said, referring to the biracial guy she met last night.

'Seems like she is getting hit with the love bomb. How was your night, Sonia?' teased Ryan.

Sonia continued, 'We went back to his apartment, which is on Charles Street, very close to this place. I think it is 55 Charles. Turns out that he goes to St. Mikes. He is in second year like all of us. But seeing how big UofT is, I am not surprised we never met him before.'

'How is he in bed?' asked Nigel.

'The best I have had yet. We did it twice last night, and I came so hard that he had to double up on his bedsheets.'

'Where is he from and what does he study at UofT?' asked Andre.

'He is from Whitby. We have been texting each other ever since I left his place. He is studying philosophy at UofT but has no clue what to do with it. He loves gaming though. Seems to be obsessed with his PlayStation. He told me he had his boys coming over for playing Fifa on the PlayStation. Doesn't look like a party guy to me, which is fine. He is more of the type to call his friends over and chill with them. We are planning to make some challah bread next week at his apartment. Since he is Jewish, he knows how to make it really well and is going to teach it to me. I am thrilled about our next date. And before you guys judge me, yes, he is loaded, but that is not why I like him. Affording that apartment all by himself is not possible for a student unless his parents are making dough,' Sonia said.

'Next week reminds me, Ryan, Manny and I are hosting a housewarming party for our new house, and you all better mark the date on your calendar. Everyone needs to be present, and we will be inviting a lot of people,' said Nigel.

The next few weeks went by picking up different girls and having wild, hot sex. We would go on sarge sessions to the Eaton Centre, Ryerson University, King Street West, the nightclubs on Adelaide St. West, and the many dining halls at all the different colleges at UofT. Our lifestyles would probably put the lustful Roman emperor Caligula to shame. It was the middle of October, and I had arranged a lunch with Afifah at Nandos. We had constantly been in touch over phone or Skype ever since our chess game and had gotten to know each other better. She seemed to be the most benevolent and well-behaved girl on this planet. I had never even heard her use the 'f' word casually in a conversation. She had even sent me pictures of her trip back to Pakistan in the summer. Unlike us millennials who like to go to bars or party hard until dawn with their friends, she was the type of girl who would prefer to go for lunch with her cousins or a movie with her Pakistani friends. She didn't seem to have White, Black, or Asian friends and kept a very low profile on social media as well. Her Facebook profile didn't have a display picture, and her older pictures were from high school. Her social outings usually included family weddings or eating at restaurants. She was an avid lover of cricket and would always send me a picture of her wearing Pakistan's jersey. My infatuation with cricket had long gotten over with the dozens of match-fixing scandals that had come to light over the years. As I had gotten older and learnt about millions of dollars that are put on stake at every match and how some cricketers were in connivance with fixers to purposely perform badly, I couldn't really get back to watching cricket unless it was India playing its arch rival Pakistan.

Afifah was coming all the way from Mississauga to eat lunch with me at Nandos which was located on Bay Street in Toronto. I was feeling very special. So I decided to make her afternoon special too. I reached Bay Street two hours earlier than our scheduled time to wait in queue at Uncle Tetsu. Uncle Tetsu was known for making the best cheesecakes in Toronto, and it had opened its first location outside Asia in Toronto. Uncle Tetsu's website described its Japanase cheesecakes as being made with 'decadent cream cheese, premium butter, and the finest eggs'. The bakery had a policy of giving one cheesecake per person due to the limited capacity of the ovens, which created a long serpentine line outside its store. The minimum wait during rush hour was 1.5 to 2 hours. The long lines outside its stores were also a tacit way of advertising its brand. People who didn't know about the famous Japanese store were curious to visit it after seeing the long queue.

I bought the cheesecake that had a soft and airy texture. It felt like it would melt in my mouth without even biting into it. After entering Nandos, I was seated in one of those round leather sofas that had beaded Portuguese strings hanging on all its sides. The ambience injected pizzazz and grandiosity, even though the food was not pricey at all.

Afifah walked in wearing a traditional black Pakistani dress with floral imprints that was complemented with golden *jhumkas* (earrings) and golden high heeled shoes. She was looking like a trophy girlfriend any guy would be lucky to have. I was so mesmerized by her beauty that I forgot to wave my hand while she looked around for me. Eventually, she spotted me and waved. She came up to the table as I stood up to give her a hug. I had never been so elated to hug someone platonically. What is it with Pakistani women? They are some of the prettiest women on Earth.

'You look so pretty in this dress,' I said complimenting her for the first time.

'Thank you. I bought this from Pakistan when I went back in the summer. I really enjoy dressing up,' she replied.

'Look what I got you *showing her the cheesecake bag*. Uncle Tetsu's cheesecake is synonymous with Japanese cheesecakes worldwide. They opened their first location outside Asia in Toronto. My friend had tried it, and he loved its taste.'

'Oh my god, Devansh, you didn't have to do this. I have heard they have insanely long queues. Why did you take the trouble?'

'If you can come all the way from Mississauga on a weekend just to have lunch with me, this is the least I could do for you,' I said.

'All right, but you need to try it too,' she said.

'On one condition. Only if you feed me with your own hands,' I flirted. She blushed profusely. If she was a plant, she would definitely be a mimosa that closes up on the slightest of touch.

'Sure,' she said. 'But let us order first, or they might object to us eating something from outside over here.'

So we carefully perused the menu, and she decided to go for the legendary peri-peri chicken which is the most popular dish in Nandos. I went with the portobello mushroom with halloumi cheese and chili jam with peri-peri chips as a side. We both got a drink combo to go with it. After placing our orders and collecting our drinks and cutlery, we headed back to our table.

'You are going to like the food here. I ate at Nandos in London when I was there for my summer abroad. The food is delicious,' I said.

'I have eaten at Nandos before,' she replied.

'But you told me you have never been to a Nandos in Canada,' I asked surprisingly.

'We have Nandos in Karachi too!' she said.

'Really? It isn't there in India', I said surprisingly. I was shocked because I didn't expect an international food chain to open its branches in a country whose economy was in shambles before opening it in a country which was the fastest growing economy in the world.

She coyly said, 'Don't underestimate us. Pakistan is ahead of India in some respects.'

'Well, not in cricket. Just watch how India thrashes your team when we play in the world cup next year,' I mocked her.

The word cricket got her zealously engaged in the conversation.

'No, we are going to defeat you. Let us watch the match together. Come to UTM. There is a big Brown population on the Mississauga campus which adds to the clamor of the occasion. We are sure to get you guys this time.'

If Pakistan winning a cricket match brought a smile to her face, I would wish that her team wins every match that they didn't play against India. I wish I could tell her that. She looked so innocent, childish, and pretty. Not many people could maintain that innocence in this cruel world. Girls her age were busy shagging their boyfriends or strangers on a weekly basis. Everything about the way she spoke or the way she dressed or even argued had so much modesty in it.

Our food had arrived.

'Do you want to try some portobello mushroom?' I asked.

'Yes. You should also try some of this chicken.' If this offer would have been made to me a year ago, I would have politely refused, but now I found chicken delectable.

'So, what is up with your brother and younger sister these days?' I asked. She had a twin brother who went to the University of Waterloo to study computer science.

'My brother is keeping great. He is fascinated by his new car. My father recently purchased a Mercedes for him, and he is obsessed with it. He sends us videos of driving his friends around town. My sister is busy with one of her assignments. It is a film review on *Titanic*. Have you watched the film?'

'Yes, I have. In fact, I loved it,' I replied.

'I am trying to help her with it. I have a Microsoft word document on my phone. See if you can proofread it or add to it in any way,' she said, pulling up the document.

'There is a grammatical error in the very first line of this film review,' I said, skimming through the document.

'Really, what is it?'

'It says the movie talks about the sinking of the Titanic on its maiden voyage. It is wrong to say the movie talks about...or the article talks about, it is a common grammatical mistake that a lot of people make. Because a movie or an article never talks or speaks. You could use the word "depicts" instead. The movie depicts the sinking of the Titanic on its maiden voyage.'

'Thanks, I will remember to make that change. Carry on, you are doing a good job so far.'

'I had a look at the whole thing. It seems fine. You guys have done a great work explaining the plot, characters, direction, setting, and costumes, but I feel that your cinematography and photography section needs to be expanded. You need more matter, as the cinematography played a huge role in bringing the director's imagination to life.'

'Do you have any suggestions?' she asked.

'Hmm...let me think,' I said, picking up two pieces of the peri-peri fries. 'Give me your phone, let me type my thoughts to get a better flow.'

I typed the following into her document:

The beautifully illuminated ship in the vast majestic ocean is a sight worthy to behold, both during the day and night. When the ship strikes the iceberg, it is depicted so realistically that one can almost experience the colossal collision. The audiovisual effects are synchronized artistically to show the disaster in its magnificent and magnanimous proportions. The rescue operations rightly show the feverish urgency, which must have been required then.

She read what I had typed into her phone.

'I like the way you have written this. It really adds more substance to this review. You are a good writer. I am going to be pestering you with proofreading my essays. You mentioned you were into debating right? That must require you to come up with stuff very quickly,' she said.

'Yes, debating helps a lot. Also, sociology is one of my majors, and I need to write a lot of essays in that program, you see,' I replied.

We finished eating our meal. I was having the last few remaining pieces of chips when I thought of doing a pick-up routine with her that did not involve anything sexual, because I wasn't risking my friendship with her. Other than Sonia and Lydia, she was one girl I genuinely cared about, and I was okay with not trying to sleep with her.

'Afifah, what are two things about you that you haven't told me ever that would enable me to really know you? I mean like things that only your best friends or your family know about you. I would understand if you didn't want to share them with me.'

She said, 'That is really personal. Okay, but you go first, and then I will tell you.'

'I lost my virginity this year. I was a vegetarian until last year, and my family does not know I eat meat,' I said.

'What!' she exclaimed. 'Then how did you start eating meat? What changed?'

'That is a long story for some other day. Basically, my friends logically reasoned me into having meat, and I couldn't come up with any viable defense of why one should be a vegetarian. But now it is your turn to spill the beans,' I said.

'Damn, I don't know if my answers are going to be as interesting as yours, but let me try. Okay, once in school, I was stung by a bee on my tongue. Basically, I was drinking from a can of sprite, and I left it open because I had to go to the washroom. When I came back from the washroom and had my first sip, I felt that there was something big inside my mouth that I spat out immediately. By then, the bee had stung me on my tongue. I didn't realize that honeybees had entered the can of sprite while I was away and were on the inner walls of the can. That sting hurt me for an entire day, and I was crying. My parents had to come to school and take me home. Now, the second thing. I would like to choose the guy I want to marry, but my parents are strict Muslims. They only want me to marry a Muslim boy, and that boy should be someone they choose for me. They want me to get married right after I finish my degree at UTM,' she said.

'Do you want to get married so young though? You would only be 22 when you graduate,' I asked.

'No, I want to study more. I have always wanted to do a master's. Therefore, I want to study hard and prove myself to them. Maybe they might allow me to study further,' she said.

'And what if you want to marry someone who isn't a Muslim?' I prodded further.

'That is something they will never agree to. My parents are devout followers of Islam. Unless the boy takes up Islam, they won't agree, and I don't think I can protest against their decision,' she said.

I was grateful my parents were not like that. This was one aspect where I appreciated Indian parents more than Pakistani parents. Pakistani parents seemed to be getting their daughters married off young and sometimes to their cousins. I met several Pakistani students at UofT whose parents were cousins. That was weird to me. Since we had finished our meals, Afifah decided to try the cheesecake, making sure nobody was watching us, as the cheesecake did not belong to Nandos. She brought two spoons from the cutlery section and cut out a small piece from the cheesecake and put it on her plate. She had a small bite, and I saw her eyes roll upwards.

'This thing is heaven. I have never eaten such a scrumptious cheesecake before,' she said.

'Yeah. Cheesecakes are my favorite. The taste of cheesecake is to me what a serenade is to the ears of a musician,' I said.

Then she took the second spoon and dug into her plate. This time she moved the spoon towards me to feed me.

'You wanted me to feed you, right? Here you go,' she said as I opened my mouth to devour the dessert.

'I don't know what is sweeter. The cheesecake or your gesture of feeding me,' I said. There was an inherent softness in her which made me feel that she would be a loving girlfriend and a doting mother.

'Thank you. I will take the rest home with me,' she said.

We left the restaurant, and I decided to walk her back to the Hart House bus stop where she could get the inter-campus shuttle bus to UTM. Her mother was picking her up from there. She had told her mother that she was meeting a friend downtown to study for a group project. She couldn't tell them that she was meeting a guy and that too from India. As we left the restaurant, I felt so satisfied that I became oblivious to the fast paced and upbeat traffic of downtown Toronto. I had forgotten that I had hands and legs and a body that was perfectly functional. I was only looking at Afifah who was treading carefully through the busy streets of Toronto, which were very different from the quiet neighborhoods in Mississauga that she was habituated to. The smell of hotdogs and roasted peanuts hit her olfactory senses as she paused to gawp at the colorful stands of the street vendors. As people started leaving their tall office buildings and populating the streets, something emblematic of the urban life in Toronto which coincides with the lazy descent of the evening sun, I came out of trance and held Afifah's hand as we crossed a busy street. Initially, she raised a dubious eyebrow but allowed me to hold her until we had safely crossed the street. She told me that my gesture made her feel protected.

Year 2 Semester II

The second semester of second year had commenced. We had received our final grades for all our courses from the previous semester. Sam and Andre had incurred a further setback in their Grade Point Averages (GPA). Both their GPAs had fallen, which strained them emotionally. Andre realized that balancing fraternity life with academics was not sustainable for him in an academically challenging institution like UofT, so he decided to quit his membership before his grades deteriorated any further. Sam's GPA had fallen to a 2.1, and he had received an official warning from his fraternity. There was an annual inspection of grades at his fraternity, and he was required to have a minimum GPA of 2.5 in the following semester to avoid being suspended from his fraternity. Overall, his cumulative GPA (CGPA) could not be less than 2.3, which meant that he needed to work very hard to make up for repeatedly slacking in school. As friends, we were all very worried about his situation, as he had already failed to meet the cutoff for Rotman. The last thing we wanted for him was to get suspended from university for having a low GPA. Therefore, we thought of holding an intervention for him.

The stage was set. The intervention was to be in Nigel, Manny, and Ryan's living room, which was spacious and fully furnished by the landlord. Lydia and Sonia had decorated the entire living room with helium balloons and party alphabet balloons that spelled 'Intervention'. There was a bean bag on the floor where Sam would be seated whereas we all would occupy the sofas. Just like a school classroom, the position of people in a room determined the flow of power. Classrooms are designed to ensure that teachers are seated in a higher position, as a higher position legitimizes the flow of authority and enables the teacher to monitor everyone. Manny was prepared on a sofa chair with his guitar to play a tune as soon as Sam entered. Ryan and I had party blowout whistles to make the atmosphere as light as we could. Lydia was the master of ceremony and would decide on the chain of events and call upon different individuals to speak. Everyone other than Lydia had prepared a speech for Sam. We were holding this informal intervention to convey how his insincerity towards school was affecting us and hoped our words would have the same effect as pheromone, thereby inciting positive behavioral change in him before the school authorities formally sanctioned him. Andre was the only one who could not be physically present for the intervention, as his mother had sprained her ankle and he was helping her with household chores. He was commuting to attend lectures from his suburban home, as the doctor had advised her to rest. However, he wanted to be present virtually through Skype to attend the intervention. As a result, we had a laptop open on the table that enabled him to see us through the camera and vice versa.

The only predicament now was to get Sam over to the house without raising any suspicion. Knowing Sam, he would never come if he was even remotely skeptical that we had planned an intervention to address his low grades. He was not a confrontational person, and his strongest weapon was silence. He could use silence to dismember his critics in a better way than one could use a serrated knife. He would rather put up with a friend's irritable behavior than confront them in the fear of provoking an irreparable feud. He conveyed his feelings in a passive way rather than addressing a problem directly. He was more of the type to cancel plans last minute or refrain from replying on WhatsApp, even though you had sent him a flurry of messages that he had seen. He telegraphed his annoyance against a person passively and expected others to do the same. But one thing that he could not resist was missing a good soccer game, especially if his favorite club Arsenal was playing. So, we decided to hold the intervention on a day when Arsenal had a game. Nigel enticed him to come over to his place so that they could watch the game together. Also, Nigel had got a new PlayStation 4 for Christmas and had promised Sam that he would be playing Fifa with him after they had finished watching the game.

Location: Nigel, Manny, and Ryan's house

At 6:00 pm, the front door of the house opened with a jerk, and we could hear Nigel praise the graphics of the video game on his PlayStation 4. We could hear them open their shoes and proceed towards the living room where all of us and a virtual Andre waited impatiently for him. Ryan and I blew our party whistles whereas Sonia opened a beer for Sam to make him comfortable in this staged milieu. Sam was perplexed, as he could not process what was happening. When realization struck him, he turned around in an effort to scurry off, but Lydia made sure he didn't leave. In addition to being the emcee, she was also playing warden.

'We have ordered pizza from Cora. Don't worry, it is not going to be a tough intervention. You are not a drug addict. It is about your grades,' said Lydia, pushing him inside the living room and closing the door.

'There is no way I am sitting through this nonsense. Nigel, you cunt, thanks for tricking me,' raged Sam.

'Hey, it wasn't my idea. Everyone was of the opinion that you would never come if you got a hint about this,' said Nigel.

'Yeah, you are damn right. I would never have come to this intervention, and I don't intend on staying,' said Sam.

'This intervention is necessary. Friends are your only critics who would warn you about your mistakes and spot the red flags before it's too late. You know we have your best interests in mind,' said Lydia.

'I have already got a warning from my fraternity, and I plan on working very hard this semester. I won't be partying so frequently, and I am also cutting down on binge drinking, as it is having a chronic effect on my grades,' said Sam.

'So then there is no harm in listening to us. We are only here to catalyze the changes that you already plan to bring,' said Nigel persuasively.

I stepped into the heated argument, 'I guess it is settled then. Sam is going to sit down for half an hour and hear us all out. You will get your chance to speak and disagree with anything you feel is unfair.'

'All right,' said Sam reluctantly.

'No, don't sit there. You are going to be on the bean bag here,' said Lydia as she pointed at the grey bag on the floor while Manny started strumming his guitar to play a soft tune.

We all took out our letters that we had written for Sam on colored paper.

'Ryan, why don't you go first?' said Lydia.

Ryan had written his letter on a red paper and adjusted his spectacles before reading out loud. 'Sam, I feel that your approach towards academics is lackadaisical. Your dismissive attitude towards studying is reflecting in your grades. As a friend, I want you to graduate with us and maintain a GPA that you can be proud of. When you look for jobs in the future, I want you to walk in that interview room with an air of confidence and be proud of your achievements. I feel you are treating academics as something that is just a fleeting phase of your life that will end soon. Start caring about education because education does not end with school. Whatever you do in life, you will have to keep upgrading and educating yourself to stay relevant. CEOs, lawyers, and doctors read and consult a lot of books even after establishing their careers. Don't detach yourself from books but embrace them. Watch how things will get better.'

On hearing that Sam looked at Ryan and said, 'If anything, I am the complete opposite of a philomath, and I cannot stay in the company of books for long. I thought college would be easier than high school. That is how they show it in Indian movies, you know. Like college is meant to be all fun and games. But things here turned out to be so different. In order to do well, one actually has to put in five to six hours of work daily other than attending lectures. Also, it requires consistent effort. The system is so different in India. If you study a month before exams, you are good to go. But, over here, there are midterms or assignments on a weekly basis throughout the year. I am not accustomed to studying so much,' said Sam.

Lydia intervened at this point and asked me to read out what I had written for Sam. I opened my letter that was written on an orange piece of paper. 'Sam, I have seen so many students drop out of UofT. You know, we have one of the highest dropout rates in North America. Look at how many students from first year did not make it into second year. Continuous midterms and tough exams are synonymous with UofT. People who didn't get into Rotman ended up transferring to Ryerson or York because they couldn't pursue what they wanted at UofT. What happened to you, man? You had a 93.5% in grade 12, but you are throwing it all away. I am happy that you didn't drop out but chose to major in economics, but now that you have chosen economics, give it your best shot. You are studying at the most prestigious institution in Canada, so stop being a fopdoodle. Having a good social life is important, but too much of anything including partying is not conducive to your grades. Your parents are spending 40,000$ a year on tuition alone so that you get the best education in the country. Make them feel proud instead of making them feel their money is being wasted. After four years, you want to graduate with something more than just a piece of paper that says you went to university.'

I could sense him getting irritated. He was neither used to taking so much criticism nor critiquing others, so it was natural for him to have snapped at me, 'Devansh, seriously. You are the one talking about parents and making them proud. They sent you to Canada as a staunch vegetarian and a virgin. You have eaten everything from goose intestines to crabs to venison to female pussy of every color. What the fuck are you smoking, bro? I fucked up freshman year, man. A lot of people do. Cut me some slack here...'

Before he could finish saying what he wanted to, Lydia piped up, 'Guys, we need to avoid getting personal here. None of us are here to malign your behavior or character. Rather than getting aggressive at a person, begin your sentences with "I feel" rather than accusing anyone because accusations lead to slinging mud at one another instead of constructive feedback. Don't let the dialogue get murky. Andre, why don't you go next?' I saw Sam's gaze shifting from me and fixating on the laptop screen.

Since the laptop was facing Sam, I could only hear Andre speak, 'Dear Sam, I want the best for you. As your well-wisher and favorite wingman, I want to be able to recollect our stories from university even when I become a father. I want to tell my children about the good old Uncle Sam. I have lived so many great moments at university with you, and I look forward to many more. I don't want you to become a figment of my imagination. Sam should not be the guy I once knew in school. Your ability to calmly deal with the toughest situations inspires us. But I feel that you need to get your priorities correct. My grades have suffered too, and as a result, I quit the fraternity. I am not telling you to do the same. Do whatever you have to, but make some more time for studying. We are all here to help you. Cut down on watching soccer or picking up blondes if that is a distraction. Time management is a very crucial skill to survive in this country. In India, life might be laid back. But the most important advice that I can give you here is time management. There are apps on your phone you can download, or you could get a timetable planner. Being a bit organized will make a huge difference...a huge difference. Trust me.'

On seeing Sam quietly absorb what Andre had to say without arguing back, Lydia asked Sonia to proceed with her yellow letter. Sonia gave what I would call a very emotional and powerful speech. We could feel every word she said, 'Sam. I love you. We all do. Remember when I needed relationship advice and I called you up at 2:00 am at night because I didn't how to sort out my fight with Keanu? I was crying on the phone, and you walked all the way to my residence with my favorite cookies from Metro. Last year, when I had fever and was worried about having to sit again for my midterms, you took care of me like a child, dealing with all my tantrums. You made sure I was drinking hot broth and taking my medicines. You would take me to the doctor and sit with me for hours so that I wouldn't feel lonely and depressed. I need you again. I need you to look after yourself so that I don't feel scared to ask you for help in the future. I need you to be there for me at 2:00 am or 4:00 am. So take control of your life rather than having a *laissez-faire* approach. Learn to say no. Even if you have to say no to us, don't hesitate. There is a lot of power in this two-letter word. It will help you work your attitude and let you focus on yourself before doing things for others.'

Without making any eye contact with Andre or Sonia, Sam sheepishly looked at the floor and said, 'Studying long hours or time management has not been my forte. But I will try my best to consider your suggestions. Like I said, my fraternity has also given me a warning about my falling grades. People like me work best with a carrot and stick policy. Maybe I needed that figurative stick to pull my socks up. Also, I am going to try and say no more frequently. I have realized that my constant effort to keep others happy and not saying no when I should is hampering my growth trajectory.'

'I think we are finally making some progress here. Manny, why don't you go next?' asked Lydia.

'I want to convey my thoughts through a song that I think is apt. I have written the lyrics of the song in my letter, so Lydia, if you can hold the lyrics up for me.' He adjusted the chords on his guitar. The song chosen by Manny was *Because I got high* by Afroman, and he strummed the strings of his guitar to create the tune of the song.

Manny yelled, 'I was gonna clean my room until I got high

I was gonna get up and find the broom but then I got high

My room is still messed up and I know why

Yeah, hey

'Cause I got high

Because I got high

Because I got high

I was gonna go to class before I got high

I could have cheated and I could have passed but I got high

I am taking it next semester and I know why

Yeah, hey

'Cause I got high

Because I got high

Because I got high...'

'The moral of the song is stop getting high on weed, alcohol, girls, or any kind of drugs. Get high on life, man,' quipped Manny.

We all gave Manny an applause for his mellifluous voice and artistic performance, though I hoped that Sam focused more on the message that Manny was trying to convey to him. 'Nigel, you are the last one left. Go for it,' said Lydia.

'I can feel that Sam has had enough of this and wants this to get over as quickly as possible, so I have kept mine short and sour. Therefore, I want him to read it, as I don't have much to say,' said Nigel, handing Sam his green letter.

Sam opened the letter and looked at it. Then he read it out loudly for all of us with a smile. Nigel seemed to have articulated Sam's state of mind as succinctly as he could. He served it to Sam exactly how he liked it.

'Just try harder, and you will pass with flying colors,

And if you don't, just remember, this too shall pass.'

'Well, I guess you guys are done now. Where are the pizzas? I am starving,' beamed Sam.

'The pizzas are coming in hot and ready,' said Sonia, switching on the TV, 'And today all of us are going to watch soccer with you and cheer for your team. Which one is Arsenal though?'

Sonia, Ryan, and I had sociology as one of our majors in university, so we had decided to enroll in a course together on 'Gender, Politics and Society', which was taught by Professor Ronald Contreras. Dr Contreras was a leading researcher and sociologist who made the lectures very interesting by encouraging active participation in class. Born to Dominican parents, he grew up in a poor Dominican enclave in New York's south Bronx. His perspectives were making waves in academia, because most of the ethnographic research in his field was previously done by privileged White men. His life trajectory grasped a lot of attention because he admitted to dealing in crack cocaine as a teenager owing to the dearth of opportunities and absence of positive role models in his marginalized neighborhood. Contreras had utilized his contacts from his formative years and churned his experiences to write a book called *The Stickup Kids*, which was widely acclaimed. His lecture slides were minimalistic, so we had to take a lot of lecture notes. We were learning about the different waves of feminism and how gender evolved to be treated as a fluid concept rather than being looked at through the binary lens of male and female.

'Can anyone tell me why we have separate washrooms for men and women in public spaces? We don't have separate washrooms for boys and girls at home. Why do you think we have them in public places?'

I thought hard but could not find a logical answer. I wondered how I accepted this practice in society so naturally without ever questioning its purpose. Why did men and women need separate washrooms in public spaces? There are so many things in society that we accept without questioning because they appear to be deeply ingrained into the fabric of the society. We are accustomed to it from a young age. I have always considered public washrooms to be unassuming places – necessary but not worth pondering over. I couldn't think of any biological reason for men and women to have separate washrooms at public places. What was the politics behind it?

Valerie, a Greek geek, who always sat in the first row raised her hand to answer, 'Because men can stand and urinate in urinals. Women need to sit and can't use the urinals to pee.'

'But men don't use urinals at home to urinate. The action of standing and urinating is just one of the ways men practice gender. They could use seats like women or stand inside a cubical. There is no need to have separate washrooms for this reason. Anyone else?'

Sonia raised her hand.

The professor asked her to answer.

'Maybe it was used to prevent sexual practices in public spaces. Couples or homeless people who were looking for private places to have sex might use public toilets for sexual gratification. Since this would be socially unacceptable, probably that is why the government made it mandatory to have different washrooms for people of different sexes,' said Sonia.

'That is a unique way to look at it, but you would be surprised to know how much homosexual activity goes on inside public washrooms anyway. Also, there are a lot of public places like parks, parking lots, etc., where people can have sex without being seen. Also, gender-neutral washrooms are being constructed now in the Western world. The University of Toronto even has few of them on student residences and is building more on the Mississauga campus. The origin of having separate washrooms for men and women has very little to do with preventing sexual activity in public places,' replied the professor.

'Does anyone else want to try?'

Nobody raised their hand this time. The whole class looked blankly at him. He had a knack for making the material interesting.

The professor eventually answered his own question, 'The practice of having washrooms segregated by gender originated in North America in the 1920s. By creating a binary of male and female options, the law aimed to marginalize people who identify as transgenders. Transgenders have challenged the idea that a person's gender and their biological sex at birth are one and the same in the case of everyone. By creating a binary of sex-segregated washrooms, transgenders were forced to declare their sex in public places and practice gender in ways that were congruent with the sex they chose to identify with. Sex-segregated washrooms emerged mostly in the Victorian era. Prior to that, public facilities in Western nations were male only, which was an active way to discriminate against women. By not having the right of access to sanitation, women were indirectly coerced to stay at home. Women were constantly reminded that the public sphere was largely a male domain, and their roles were primarily limited to staying indoors and taking care of their homes and children. The laws reflected the degree of patriarchy and sexist thoughts prevalent in society.'

At that point, I raised my hand to contribute towards the discussion. 'Successive governments in India have failed to sensitize people about the needs of the transgender community despite honoring their accomplishments for the very cause. Last year, I was reading this article about how Akkai Padmashali, who is a trans right activist, was conferred with the second highest civilian award by the state government. She was ironically humiliated for using the washroom in the state legislative assembly just before she was to meet the law minister. Despite the supreme court ruling, transgender people in India have long been denied basic rights like the right to own property, the right to marry, or the right to claim a formal identity through a passport or any other government identification.'

'Yes, Devansh, I have heard about that case too. My colleague from India told me,' said Dr. Contreras.

'Once all of you graduate and go out there in the real world, you will realize that 95% of the problems in life trickle down to money and sex; by sex, I mean both fornication and your physical identification,' he continued.

I had just received my second important lesson in university:

95% of the problems in life trickle down to money and sex.

Location: Whitney Hall student residence

'Please don't cry. The authorities are looking into it. They have already informed campus police, and if required, they are going to pass the matter on to Toronto police. Everything will be okay. I have just spoken to the Don on duty,' said Nigel who was consoling Lydia by hugging her.

Lydia had just been a victim of voyeurism. As the washrooms in Whitney Hall were shared by the whole floor and were gender-inclusive, they were used by boys, girls, and students who identified with the third gender. Lydia had seen a cell phone emerge over her shower cubicle. She screamed out loud as soon as she saw it, and it was then that the voyeur ran away. Sonia, who was showering in the cubicle next to her, quickly wore her towel and went to check on her.

'I have no idea how long the person had been recording me. I am very scared. The last thing I can deal with at this point is a naked video of me going viral,' said Lydia sobbing loudly.

'Whitney Hall has always been such an inclusive environment. I could never imagine there would be such a violation of trust, and people would engage in pusillanimous conduct like this. The most difficult part to accept is that these people are living amongst us. I feel like I am going to be suspicious of every student I meet in this residence now,' said Sonia who was shivering in fright.

'This gender-inclusive washroom stuff is bullshit. Who the fuck even came up with this policy? These guys need to roll back this policy as soon as possible. And next year, Sonia, we are going to move in together somewhere else. You don't have to stay on campus anymore,' said Keanu. I had never seen Keanu so angry before. All of us had gotten to know him well, as he joined us occasionally for dinners at Chinatown or came clubbing with us. Sonia and Keanu were in a serious relationship now, so I could imagine what Keanu must be going through. Even though he vented out his frustration at gender-inclusive washrooms, this was not the time to politically correct him.

'Just got a text from the Don on duty. The police is here on site and is going to investigate it. They might come to this room for further questioning,' said Lydia, addressing all of us and Sonia in particular.

'Lydia, here, drink some water. You are going to feel better. Let me buy some food and drinks from the cafeteria for you both. You haven't eaten anything since the incident. Eating something will make you feel better,' said Andre.

'That is a good idea, Andre. If Manny was not at film school right now, he would probably impersonate Liam Neeson from the movie *Taken*. Do you guys remember that scene? "I don't know who you are. I don't know what you want. If you are looking for ransom, I can tell you I don't have money. But what I do have are a very particular set of skills, skills I have acquired over a very long career, skills that make me a nightmare for people like you..." and then he would probably modify the dialogue and be like, "If you let go of the video recording, that will be the end of it, but if you don't, I will find you and I will castrate you",' I said, trying to lighten the mood.

'Yeah, I would probably castrate this fucker if I found him,' said Keanu.

'Whipped cream is a great innovation, let us use it for this asshole's castration. The next time anyone even hits on you at a bar, I am going to castrate him on the spot. I am going to carry a knife and whipped cream with me all the time from now,' said Nigel with enough dry wit and humor to allow it to circumvent the farcical pitfall of its subject matter.

There was a loud knock on the dormitory's door.

'I think it is the campus police. We might have to leave for a while if they want to question the girls personally,' I said.

'Holy shit! There is weed in my drawer,' said Sonia.

'Don't worry about that. At this point, they wouldn't dare to search your room. You girls have been wronged. The whole staff of residence is with you. Devansh, go open it,' whispered Nigel.

I opened the door to find a short, fat gentleman with bulging eyes accompanied by a young girl who was a UofT student.

'Hi! We are from the Varsity. We heard that the girls who live in this room had recently faced voyeurism. Is it possible to speak to them?' said the plum gentleman.

Sonia got furious on hearing this. 'You guys have no shame, do you? Please leave,' she said and was about to slam the door on their faces when I stopped her.

'I think this is not an appropriate time. Sorry about her behavior but they won't be giving any interviews on this matter,' I said and closed the door in the most polite way I could. The Varsity was the official student newspaper of the University of Toronto and was published weekly on all three campuses.

Lydia was fuming now, 'How the fuck did the news reach them? What the hell is going on here?' she said as soon as the door closed.

'Maybe someone from residence tipped them off,' said Nigel.

'Or it could be the same bastards who did this in the first place,' said Lydia.

'I don't think we should jump to conclusions. The director of University College may have informed them about this incident to raise awareness about this issue. They might be considering changes in policy, so they would want the students to know what induced them to bring about these changes. Hence, the media attention,' I said.

'Well, I guess the practical application of gender-inclusive washrooms is not a viable option on college campuses where people are not mature enough to behave appropriately. Or, maybe these washrooms are not a good idea in environments where people know each other very well and can therefore do creepy stuff to girls. I think these washrooms should just be limited to public places like shopping malls, restaurants, and parks where people don't know each other. I have a feeling, whoever did this must have noticed us using the shower at a particular time every day. This looks premeditated to me,' said Sonia.

Andre knocked on the door and came with a bottle of Sprite and some white chocolate chip cookies that he purchased from the cafeteria.

'There are a lot of policemen in the halls. They are knocking on doors and asking students if they saw anything. Lydia was fortunate to see the camera and raise the alarm. So much police presence and a proactive approach by the residence staff may deter the perpetrator from spreading the footage or misuse it in any way. Just imagine the consequences if Lydia hadn't seen it. By the way, I spoke to Sam, as I was surprised he didn't come here after seeing the messages on our WhatsApp group. He had a very important lecture followed by a tutorial. He said he will be here as soon as it gets over. I am glad he is finally taking school more seriously now. Attending all his lectures and tutorials. Looks like he is finally turning a new leaf,' said Andre.

I wryly thought about the politics behind public toilets. One would never assume that the conception and enforcement of laws that segregated people on the basis of sex for using public washrooms were so malignant in nature. Now that those malicious intentions were recognized and positive changes were being brought about in society, there were people who were creating obstacles to this social progress. One could also argue about the constantly changing definition of privacy over time. In every era, privacy acquires a new meaning depending on what is acceptable to people and considered normative. One's privacy has been breached or not is decided by mores prevalent in that society. For example, in many poor countries of Africa and Asia, it is common practice in rural areas to defecate and perform essential biological functions in the open. Internet and mobile phones have reached some places before proper sanitation facilities. Who was responsible for the plight of those rural women? Could they ever expect media attention or police action when their rights had been breached?

Ryan had kept quiet all this while. He was only listening to what the others were saying. Finally, he got up from his chair and said, 'Whoever did this will have to pay for it. I might not know his name now and will probably take some time to find out. But rest assured, I am going to get to the bottom of this.'

'The police are already investigating this. If they find something, they will surely let the girls know,' said Nigel.

'Fuck the police, man. As someone who studies criminology, let me tell you an important fact. Has anyone heard of the crime funnel? For 1,000 crimes committed, a lot of them are not even detected; out of the ones that are detected, a lot of them are not reported. Statistically, only about a third of the crimes committed are reported to the police. Furthermore, most reported crimes are not solved by the police. Going by the statistics, there is only a 10% chance of an offender being prosecuted and convicted by the court and that too after a long drawn labyrinthine judicial process. Unfortunately, public distrust of the police and the limited resources of the criminal justice system make it difficult to get justice in the world out there. The police are not going to spend a lot of time investigating this matter. Things don't get serious for them until there is a sexual assault on campus,' Ryan said.

'But how will you find the person or people responsible for this by yourself?' I asked.

'Don't ask me that question because I cannot reveal how I am going to do it. But trust the veracity of the information when I have it. It might take me some time, but you guys will know about the culprit soon.' Revulsion and anger swept through Ryan, strengthening his resolve.

'Well, we can give them to the police once you find out who the perpetrators are,' said Keanu.

'No, I cannot reveal my sources or anything about how I found their names. The police won't take my word without any evidence, and I won't be allowed to give them any evidence. I cannot elaborate much on this and sorry for being so evasive. Let us just say, some people will be getting their hands dirty, but that is the only way we will find out about the miscreants,' said Ryan.

Two weeks had passed since the horrific incident with Lydia and Sonia. As Ryan had predicted, the police had reached an inconclusive investigation. The story was covered in the Varsity and had gained widespread attention on campus. The incident was condemned by the highest authorities at University College, and the newspaper article cited the director of UC changing the unisex washroom policies on student residences. The article covered the viewpoint of different students who alleged to have felt unsafe after the incident. The only silver lining in this whole episode was the fact that the article did not have a mention of Lydia as a victim. The article probably would have mentioned her name if Sonia or she had given the interview that day.

Lydia, Manny, Sam, Andre, and I were eating lunch at the Morrison hall. All of us had lectures later in the day and were scheduled to pull off a late night study session at the Robarts Library. Nigel and Sonia had the afternoon off, so they went to a new shisha place that had recently opened on Yonge Street. Keanu had found the place and had asked Sonia to invite all of us, but we were busy with lectures and readings.

Location: Howard Ferguson dining hall at Morrison

'The lamb curry has been made well today,' said Sam digging into his food.

'Yeah it tastes nice. What do you think, Andre?' I asked.

'It is good, but wait till you try my mother's recipe. Her food veritably tastes wayyyyyy better,' he said, emphasizing on the word 'way'.

'Yeah, I bet her jerk chicken would be even better than the ones they make here especially since she was born and brought up in Jamaica,' I inferred.

'I have so many essays due next week. Looks like all my time will be spent at either the Gerstein or Robarts Library. What happened to me really unnerved me, and I couldn't focus on school for a week after that. I am really behind on my readings,' wailed Lydia.

Ryan walked inside Morrison Hall carrying his shoulder bag. We had assumed he was in his criminology lecture that ran from 1:00 to 3:00 pm. That is why he probably didn't make it for lunch at Morrison. In a hurried motion, he opened his bag's zipper and took out a piece of paper and put it at the centre of the table.

Being as laconic as possible, he spoke with a stoic face, 'These are their names.'

There were two names written on the paper: Govind Puri and Alvaro Paz. Beside their names, their majors were written. They both were biology students.

Lydia stopped in the middle of eating her beef pasta. 'This guy Govind, he is such a creep. I know him too well. He had asked me for my number twice, and I had refused him on one occasion and made some excuse the other time. I don't know who the other guy is though,' she said.

'I have met this guy too in one of the Bollywood nights on campus organized by the Indian society. He came across as very weird. Especially his behavior around women was obnoxious. All I remember him telling me was that he was from Punjab. I even got a friend request from him on Facebook, but I didn't accept that,' I said.

'Well, I am looking up the other guy Alvaro Paz on Facebook. Yeah, I think I found him. I got five mutual friends with this guy, so it has to be him,' said Manny turning the phone towards Lydia and me.

'Yeah, it is him. Because the other guy in his profile picture is Govind. Just look at those cunts grinning nastily. They can't even hide their vicious smiles in front of the camera,' I said.

'But how did you find this out, Ryan?' asked Sam who was clueless about Ryan's condition of keeping his sources anonymous because he was not present in the room with us when Ryan had announced to find out who the culprits were.

'Doesn't matter. The pivotal question is how we are going to teach them a lesson. I have the perfect plan,' said Ryan.

'Let us beat the shit out of them,' said Manny who was always ready to flex and finesse his muscular physique.

'Yeah and since there are so many of us, we can file a complaint against them attacking us first. That way, we are not going to have any trouble with the campus police. Also, we will let the duo know why we beat them up. I don't think they would have any moral grounds to go complain after that,' said Sam.

'No, we don't need to use any violence. We are going to give them a taste of their own medicine. Remember the prank I played with you, Sam, when we were roommates last year? I want to do the same thing to them but in front of a professor and a hundred and fifty students,' said Ryan.

'What! No way. That would be sick,' said Sam.

'Fill me in on this prank,' said Lydia.

'Basically, I am going to put this small boombox speaker under his seat, and this speaker will be connected to my phone. Just have patience and listen to what I play,' said Ryan.

'When do you want to do it?' asked Manny.

'They have a biology lecture that starts at 3:00 pm. All of you guys need to miss your lectures or whatever you have planned after lunch. First, we need to teach them a lesson. Especially Govind, since he was the main culprit,' said Ryan.

So we headed towards the Sidney Smith building where Govind's biology lecture was about to start. The lecture hall was almost full of students.

'There he is,' whispered Lydia as she spotted him in his white Canada Goose winter jacket and pompadour hairstyle.

'Lydia, he should not be seeing you. Why don't you go and sit in the last bench? Devansh, since you have met him before, I want you to go up to him and keep him distracted. Just make small talk. Sam, I have connected the speakers to my phone. Open his bag after he has taken out his laptop or books. While Devansh is talking to him, I want you to slide this thing into his bag and make sure he doesn't notice anything,' glozed Ryan.

'Look, Alvaro is there too. He is sitting right next to Govind. These sitting ducks have no clue about what is going to hit them. We should sit not more than three rows behind them so that your phone's Bluetooth does not disconnect from the speaker,' said Manny.

'Cool. Let us roll guys,' said Ryan as Sam and I left on our missions to plant the speaker.

'Hey, Govind. I remember you from the Diwali event of the Indian society. Had no clue you were in this course too,' I said.

'Hey! I am sorry I forgot your name, but I remember your face. I have never seen you before in any biology classes. Didn't know you were majoring in biology,' said Govind.

'No, I am not majoring in biology. I thought of doing a minor in biology, so I have come to audit the lecture today. If I like it, I might take this course in the summer,' I said.

'By the way, this is my friend Alvaro,' said Govind, introducing me to Alvaro. As I shook his hand, I noticed Sam bent down to put the speaker inside Govind's bag, which was under his chair. To make it look natural, Sam decided to sit next to Govind in an empty seat. I shook Alvaro's hand and then told him that I was going back to find a seat because the professor was about to commence the lecture. Sam signaled with his thumb that the job was done successfully. I left the fourth row to go sit next to Ryan and Manny.

Unlike Indian colleges, there was no attendance taken in Canadian universities. You were considered an adult, and the onus was on the student to attend lectures and make the most of his or her time at university. If you were smart enough to do well in exams even after not attending any lectures, nobody could stop you from passing the course due to the lack in attendance. Another advantage of attending a public university in the West was that you could attend any lecture from any program. Obviously, one couldn't give exams and get a degree, but public universities didn't stop anyone from acquiring knowledge. In my astronomy lecture last year, there was an old man around seventy years old diligently taking notes, as he was curious to learn more about our galaxy. Even though our intentions of being present in the biology lecture were not as noble as learning about the human body, the policy of easy access to lecture rooms for any individual made it possible for all of us to seamlessly blend in the classroom.

At sharply ten minutes past three, the professor began the lecture which was standard procedure at UofT. Lectures began ten minutes after the scheduled time so that students had enough time to commute from one lecture to another if they had consecutive classes.

The professor began the lecture in a bromidic fashion, 'Well, congratulations, everybody has survived the midterms, including the TAs who recently have been let out of their entombments with lots of exam pages. So, those are rolling along and everybody is still awake, so that is good. Okay, so we have now officially entered the last part of the course. Now a bit of housekeeping - readings will now be read, hopefully. Okay, so that is not useful...books, books. Now is a good time to actually go and start reading those books, and again if you are not up to all of them, some recommended chapters have been posted on the online portal. Pay attention to those. Now, let's begin with the lecture today. So, to inaugurate the last part of this course and the fact that it is starting off with lectures on sexual behavior, it has to start off with a stupid obligatory sex joke. Okay, so the Martians come to Earth. They turn out to be great guys. They are really terrific, and they get along very well with Earthlings. All of them like each other a lot, and they are all becoming great friends. They pass their hours learning about each other's planets. What is the weather like there? What are movies like here? What are pyramids? Everyone is getting along terrifically, and eventually, the Earthlings and the Martians get around to asking the question that everybody is really interested in, which is how do you folks go about reproducing? So the Martians are going to go first. A big space is cleared out, and the Martians jump in together and stand on top of each other's heads, their noses flash different colors and steam comes out of various orifices and out pops a new little Martian. So now it's the human's turn. So a willing couple is found, and some space is cleared out. And the couple goes at it, and they finish the whole thing with a sweaty mess at the end. After the couple had finished, the Martians loved the way humans reproduce but had one question. Where is the new human? And the humans said, "Oh! That takes nine months." The Martians reply, "Well, if it takes you guys nine months to make a new human, then why were they in such a rush at the end?"'

He was about to continue speaking when Ryan touched the screen on his phone. There were loud moaning sounds that went off from the speaker in Govind's bag. It was as if the couple that the professor was talking about was making love in class. 'Yeah it feels so good, it feels so good, aaaaaaaaaaahh. Does that feel good? Yeah. Ah ah aaha ah ah ah *loud breathing* ah ah aha ah oh fuck! Oh my god! That cock is so big! Oh yeah *sound of sucking tits*.'

The whole classroom burst into laughter. Everyone's gaze was eventually focused towards the epicentre of the noise, which was Govind. His face turned red out of embarrassment. He had no clue about the origin of the noise and felt the floor give way beneath him. Ryan had played a pornographic video of Mia Khalifa on his phone.

The professor shouted, 'Whoever it is, stop it.'

The porn star's voice from the boombox went, 'Don't stop, don't stop...I want you to go harder.'

By now, the angry professor had reached the fourth row. Govind picked up his bag and opened it. He was searching for the source of noise when the professor walked towards him and pressed his laptop screen down to close it, assuming Govind was playing the pornographic clip on his laptop. At the same moment, Ryan turned off the video on his phone, which made it seem like the video was being controlled from the laptop. To his dismay, Govind found the speaker in his bag and took it out.

Scared out of his wits, he stuttered, 'Professor, I have no idea how this speaker got here. This isn't mine,' he said.

The professor seized the Bluetooth speaker. 'I have to confiscate this. Please give me your name and student number. This incident will be reported to the university, and your speaker will be given to the campus police. I am calling them now.'

Govind pleaded with the professor to believe him. 'I swear this isn't mine. I have no idea how this got inside my bag,' said Govind.

'Well, I am going to have to report what I found. You can save all your explanations for the dean,' said the professor tetchily.

I turned back to watch Lydia gloating with joy. I would be recording a video of Govind if I was her right now. For someone who was secretly recording a girl in her shower cubicle, this prank paid him back him with interest. Aghast to see his friend with rheumy eyes, Alvaro came to Govind's rescue.

'Professor, I know Govind very well. This isn't his speaker. Looks like someone in the class has played a prank,' said Alvaro in a desperate attempt to exculpate his friend, but the professor refused to listen.

I bet such a shocking incident never happened in his twenty-five years of teaching human sexual behavior. He knew he couldn't let this slip away. The campus police arrived seven minutes after they were summoned by the professor. Govind was escorted out of the class. His head was lowered in shame as he sauntered out of the class with the look of disbelief in his eyes. He knew he'd been had, but he didn't know how. Ryan cackled nastily, and he had the same evil smile on his face that Govind had on his profile picture. Lydia posted the whole incident on the 'UofT Confession' page along with her first name so that Govind knows why he was made the target of this vindictive plot. In the end, all we lost was a Bluetooth speaker worth 25$, but that was a small price to pay in order to teach Govind a big lesson.

Year 3 Semester I

The summers in Toronto were accompanied by elongated evenings and a lot of rooftop patios that resonated with blissed up crowds. After finishing our second year at university, Sam and I decided to stay back in Toronto for the summer to experience the beautiful Canadian sun and escape the hot, sultry heat of India. After a long academic year, we needed a break from studying and some international work experience on our resumes, so we both took up summer jobs in technical sales that paid us minimum wage. We spent the summer selling internet and home phone packages for a telecommunication company at a Costco location, and our weekends were spent at rooftop bars, live music venues, open air concerts, or scavenging out the popular eateries and food festivals that pop their heads all over the city. Lydia and Andre had found summer internships, which were most likely going to materialize into full-time job offers after university. Nigel was learning the ropes under his father in his family-owned transport business. Manny was taking summer courses to accelerate his acting program whereas Sonia and Ryan had joined a coaching centre to prepare for their LSAT. They were both planning to go to good law schools after university and required high LSAT scores in addition to high cumulative grade point averages at UofT.

'Summer is all in bloom, summer is ending soon,' read Lydia's Facebook status. Just like all good things that come to end, so did the summer break. We had now officially entered our third year at university. During the summer, a new student residence called Parkside was aggressively being promoted and marketed on social media and on college campuses. Parkside, a private luxury student accommodation was opening its door for the 2015-2016 intake. Being a private residence meant it was not affiliated to any one university and was accepting students from all institutions including film schools and language schools. This student housing had been designed to accommodate uber luxurious studios, an arcade room for table tennis, pool, foosball, community kitchens, an unlimited dining program, a 24-hour fitness centre, huge study spaces, and a summer patio for barbecues. In other words, we could envision ourselves living the high life. As it was a new accommodation, the management was giving an attractive discount to entice students and their parents, who wanted their children to live comfortably.

Ryan and I were roommates this year, as we had several debate competitions lined up and thought it would be a good idea to live together so that we could work on our speeches. Sam decided that it would be academically beneficial for him to move out of his fraternity and therefore got a suite with Andre, where they had private single rooms and shared a washroom just like Ryan and me. Sonia and Keanu booked a couple's studio on the penthouse floor of Parkside. Manny, Nigel, and Lydia booked a three-people suite on the penthouse floor too and shared one huge washroom amongst the three of them. Finally, we were all going to be under one roof. Due to a slight delay in the construction and renovation work of the student accommodation, the Parkside management was accommodating all students in a hotel nearby called Eaton Chelsea. When you have so many young students living together in a hotel, there is a lot of testosterone and estrogen seeking action. When there is a lot of testosterone and estrogen, there is bound to be a lot of parties, alcohol, sex, drugs, and drama. The Parkside community had made the hotel one big fuck fest. Students from UofT, Ryerson, OCAD, George Brown, and other institutions were getting to know one another through both implicit and explicit sexual behavior.

The student accommodation had a Facebook group where there were more than three hundred members. However, a group of around thirty students who partied excessively and got along very well had formed a WhatsApp group so that they could make instant plans and communicate within themselves without having to discuss everything in front of all residents. The eight of us and Keanu were also part of this group. Arham and Edgar, two students from Ryerson who we enjoyed hanging out with, went out nearly five nights a week, and they had suggested (by posting a message on the WhatsApp group) that we all go to a nightclub called Cube. Coincidentally, the eight of us were even planning to try out a new club, and Cube was one of the clubs on our mind.

Cube was an upcoming club which had hosted several big names in the last two years and was a force to be reckoned with in the nightlife arena of Toronto. From the pictures online, Cube looked like another glossy club anchored on Queen and its reputation to be unique seemed to be outstripped by its populist vibes. Lengthy, tapered counters stretched across the length and breadth of the club. The interiors sparkled in jet black and had a mirrored coating to give a notion of dabbling through a chic pool of dark chocolate. LED screens behind the DJ booth provided constant video entertainment and created a nice ambience, championing the versatility it was conceived to project. Adjoining the dance floor were grey leather booths that jarred with the club's lustrous decadence.

Out of all the students who received Arham and Edgar's message in the Parkside WhatsApp group, 26 of them showed up. I had my eyes set on this one blonde called Nicole Stasi in particular. She had expressive eyes that were capable of seducing the most loyal of men on Earth. She was a professional dancer in her final year of George Brown College and had the ideal body of a ballet dancer with a slender figure, a good turnout from the hips, and medium-sized breasts. I had been using push pull pick-up tactics with her from the time we had met at one of the icebreaker events organized by Parkside. I was trying to establish a romantic sexual connection with her by teasing her playfully and sexually. I was socko in creating that playful-romantic vibe, and she had realized that I was not here to be just friends. Funnily enough, Sam had taken a shine on her too, and this was the first time I found myself wrestling emotionally with the bro code. We had always helped each other in the field, and now we were pitted against each other over the same girl. But one and a half years of pickup and two years of friendship had made us mature enough to talk it out like adults. Girls have a very strong sixth sense and can easily tell when things are not well between two boys who are quarreling over them. Sam and I didn't want it to come to that point where we ruin both of our chances by quarreling over a girl's attention inside the club. Nothing is a more disastrous than that, as both men lose their chance with the girl and her friends forever. So it was mutually decided that Sam would sacrifice his chances with Nicole, and I would return the favor if such a situation arose in the future. However, he could obviously try for her if I failed at my attempt to sleep with her and gave him the clearance from my side.

We reached the club by 11:00 pm. We had booked two private booths exclusively for Parkside residents. I made sure that I was in the same booth as her, so I could start using my pick-up skills without wasting any time. Sam, Andre, Ryan, Manny, and I had decided to peacock with our scarves. In addition to my scarf, I was wearing a round neck varsity jacket that I had purchased from H&M, and I slung a thick gold chain that had a huge sparkling square pendant. I called this chain 'Insidious'. That chain intrigued a lot of people and served as a hook for girls by giving them a reference point to start a conversation with me.

Those days, Sam and I were religiously following a pick-up artist who had gained a lot of fame in a short span of time. His alias was Deepak Wayne, and he operated out of Berlin. Deepak was an Indian male who had spent all his life in India before moving to Germany and learning pick-up. As someone who had a strong Indian accent and was a visible minority, his game was transferable to a lot of Brown men who wanted to seduce White women. He professed that brown Indian men operated from a position of significant disadvantage due to racial and cultural stereotypes and therefore required a stronger game to get the same results as White or Black men. As a sociologist, I analyzed his views through the theory of intersectionality, which states how the intersection of race, gender, sexuality, and class contributes to a certain type of systemic discrimination and oppression experienced by an individual. According to Deepak Wayne, Brown men had to slightly tweak their game to accentuate their personality and presence in order to acclimatize to Western standards. For example, Asian men and Brown men were comparatively shorter than their Black and White counterparts on average. Therefore, he advised his followers and students to buy elevator shoes, which gave them an extra two to three inches of height while they approached women.

A waitress arrived at the table with complimentary drinks that came with the private booth. As soon as we had a little alcohol inside our systems, some of us chose to escape to the dance floor. Keanu pulled Sonia to the centre of the room, where two different groups were having a dance face off. Sam and Manny careered off to approach girls and wing each other. Since Nicole was still sitting on the couch, I saw this as a good opportunity to pull off one of the NLP routines called the cube because we were in Cube.

'Hey, Nicole, are you planning to hit the dance floor?' I asked.

'Yeah, in a bit. You know I spent the whole afternoon yesterday trying to google how you did that magic trick with my cell phone. I still couldn't find it. I really loved the trick, though it was also scary. I mean someone with a bad intention could really misuse it to hack my phone,' said Nicole.

'Just like I hacked your phone using open innovation, what if I told you I could hack your mind? Have you heard of the cube test before?'

'No, what is it? How do you do all this stuff?' she asked excitedly.

'Basically, I am going to ask you a few questions, and based on your replies, I am going to tell you stuff that only you or people very close to you know about you,' I said maintaining strong eye contact and modulating my voice.

'All right. I am ready,' she said mawkishly, though her eyes belied her words.

'Give me your hand,' I said purposely including Kino while doing the cube test. I was trying to get her comfortable with my touch under the pretense of the cube test. Deepak Wayne emphasized that having a reason behind touching a girl removes awkwardness from the interaction.

'Okay. Now, imagine you are driving through a desert in your car, and suddenly, you stop your car because you see an oasis. Now, you are sitting in your car and from your car you see a cube,' I said, holding her hand with one of my hands and using the index finger of my other hand to gently touch her skin and indicate the movement of the car down to her knuckles. Then I circled the back of her palm so that she could picture an oasis before letting go of her hand.

'You can put down your hand now,' I said.

'Now, remember the cube that you saw from your car. What is the size of this cube that you see?' I asked.

'Ummm, it is a small cube. Maybe the size of this table,' replied Nicole.

'Okay. What is the color of this cube?'

'It is blue...no, I want it to be red. I will go with red,' she replied.

'Is this cube transparent or opaque? Like can you see through it or not?'

'The cube is transparent,' she said.

'Final question. Now I want you to imagine a ladder in this desert beside the cube. How is this ladder placed? Is it vertical or horizontal?' I asked.

'The ladder is leaning against the cube. Like in a climbing position. But what does all this mean?' she said, using her hands to show a leaning ladder against a glass of mixed spirits.

'I know all this seems confusing at this moment, but I am going to deconstruct every answer one by one so that you know what all this means. In the process, I am going to reveal certain things about you that only people who are very close to you know about you, and now I am one of those people too,' I said playfully. 'So the first thing you said was that the cube was small. Now, the size of the cube is a reflection of the size of your ego. This means you have a small ego. You don't take things to your heart, and you are very good at moving on. You forgive people who have wronged you in any way rather than holding a grudge. So having a small ego is a good thing.'

'Hmmm, you are kind of right. I am a forgiving person, and I don't like keeping beef even if it is the other person's fault,' she said.

'Now, the color of the cube you imagined was red. According to Chinese tradition, red is a very auspicious color. It signifies happiness and joy. You are the type of person who doesn't seek happiness in materialistic goods. You are content with whatever you get in life. You find happiness in friends and family and value the bond you share with them,' I said, confidently looking into her eyes, though I knew pretty well that everything I said was bullshit. I had memorized a few cold reading routines like scam artists do for different colors and had got more confident and better by using it on girls over a period of time. I was so smooth in my narration that she was buying every word that I was saying.

'The next thing you said was that the cube was transparent. Remember, the cube is a reflection of your ego. In other words, it is a reflection of you. Therefore, this means that you have a transparent nature, which is supercalifragilisticexpialidocious. You are not double faced. You are not about being pretentious. Whatever is going on in your heart or mind is what you reveal to the outside world. Also, you are an honest girl, as you like to maintain complete transparency in all your dealings and interactions,' I said, knowing very well that everyone likes to hear their own praise from another person's mouth. Had I said the same things without the context of the cube test, she would just consider me another guy who was hitting on her.

'So far you have been very accurate. And what does the ladder mean?' she asked irresistibly.

'The ladder is an indication of your goals in life. The fact that your ladder is vertical and leaning against the cube is a very good sign. This means that you know what you want in life and that you are aware that you have to work your way to the top to achieve it. Unlike most students who are still figuring it all out, you know what you want to achieve and have your eyes set on your goal. However, you are not maximizing your potential. All you need to do now is start working harder and start climbing that ladder of life. Your rewards are waiting on top.'

'Wow! You are correct. I am actually not giving my 100% towards my goals. I do procrastinate quite a bit. This stuff is insane. How did you do this, Devansh?' she exclaimed.

'I told you. This is strong stuff. Only people who are close to you would know these things about you,' I replied. Obviously, I couldn't tell her that she was just another gullible girl, and all that I had just told her was rehearsed and practiced numerous times to perfection. I knew how to modulate my voice and when to change my expressions. The whole drill was part of my muscle memory.

'But what if I said the ladder was horizontal instead of vertical?' she asked.

'Well, the fact that you didn't choose that justifies what I told you. You have your goals set out for you. That is why you didn't imagine your ladder to be horizontal. This test is designed to make you answer in a way so that your thoughts correlate with your inner self,' I gave another mendacious explanation. I knew how to manipulate every answer to give a positive reply or a reply where the subject would agree with me. For example, it is human nature to feel that you are not maximizing your potential or one could get better results if they worked harder.

While I was making conversation with Nicole, Andre came to me with a vodka shot. I used this opportunity to ask Nicole to excuse me for a while. My push pull routine was still at work. I had just impressed her, and I could sense that she was having a good time with me and wanted me to stay. But Deepak Wayne's golden words reverberated in my brain. Always keep the girl confused and do the unexpected. Leave her alone when she desires you, and pull her towards you when she is least expecting you.

'Why are you not sarging this meat market, man? Holy shit! You are hammered as fuck,' I told Andre after we were at an inaudible distance from Nicole.

'Today, I am not in the mood to smash pussy. All I want to do is drink.' And then he went on a maudlin rambling of Martin Luther King Jr's famous speech that he modified in his drunken state. 'In a sense, we have come to our nation's capital to cash a check. When the architects of our republic wrote the magnificent words of our Constitution and the Declaration of Independence, they were signing a promissory note to which every Canadian was to fall heir. This note was a promise that all men, yes, Black men as well as White men, would be guaranteed unalienable rights of drinking alcohol. It is obvious today that Canada has defaulted on this promissory note insofar as her citizens of color are concerned. Instead of honoring this obligation, Canada has given the Negro people a bad check, a check which has come back marked insufficient funds,' said Andre pulling out his debit card and struggling to stand straight.

'Fuck, you actually finished your debit card balance on booze?'

'Yeah, 283$. Nigel and I went all in today. I want to go home and crash now,' he replied.

'Okay. We will leave soon. Lydia and Ryan are dancing there. Go to them while I check on the others,' I said.

I waded through the crowds to find Sam and Manny grinding a pair of White girls who had natural black hair. Manny's girl looked so petite compared to him. Sonia and

Keanu were dancing at the other end of the club. Sonia seemed like she was having a great time. Keanu brought a lot of joy in her life. Sonia looked like she had left all her stress and worries behind. A free spirit that could dance until dawn if Keanu was by her side. She always told us how much she cared for him and loved him. I approached Sam and told him that we should leave in half an hour since Andre was piss drunk and wanted to go to sleep. The girl whom Sam was grinding turned around and gave me a dirty stare as if I was here to pull him away from her and spoil her night. After conveying what I had to say, I went back to Nicole. I saw that she had left the booth and was on the dance floor with her friends. So I went up to her, and as soon as she saw me, I whisked her away with a sharp pull. She was a bit shocked initially but didn't protest. Her friends were taken aback by the move, but when they didn't see her resisting, they let us be.

'My friends must be jealous of you right now. You stole me from them,' teased Nicole.

'Nicole, attraction is the most natural thing that can happen between a man and a woman. I took a shine on you ever since I saw you at the ice breaker event held by the Parkside staff. At this moment, I won't make false promises to you but what I can promise you is a good laugh,' I said, lowering my voice and holding her by her waist. I was using the progressive escalation technique of Deepak Wayne. Start with touching less sensitive areas like the waist and slowly turn up the heat. She smiled and lowered her eyes without saying anything. By not removing my hands and continuing to slowly sway to the music, I was quick to note her behavior as another indicator of interest. Therefore, I decided to progress to a level two escalation. I tilted her face upwards so that we made eye contact, and then I shifted my gaze between her eyes and her lips to increase the tension between us. By shifting gears, I had created the ideal atmosphere to go in for the smooch. The final act of closure was following the kissing routine contrived by Wayne.

'I have a thought in my mind. Do you know what it is?'

'No. What is it?' she asked the question that I wanted her to ask.

'I was wondering what it would be like to feel your lips with my lips,' I said and moved in to smooch her. After kissing me for one minute, she pulled back.

'You are a good kisser,' she said and moved in to kiss me again. I kissed her passionately and slowly moved down to her neck to give her a hickey. She held me tightly, and I could feel she was enjoying the moment.

'My friends and I are planning to go back to the hotel. We are going to play *Cards against Humanity* and order some food from China Town. Why don't you join us?' I said. *Cards against Humanity* was a popular board game, and it became even better if you involved alcohol while playing it.

'Okay. Let me tell my friends that I am going with you and will be seeing them at the hotel,' she said.

Manny had already left for the hotel with the girl he was grinding in the club. The girl who was with Sam was from Parkside, so she easily agreed to come back with us. Andre and Nigel were already waiting outside. Ryan, Lydia, Keanu, Sonia, Nicole, and I hailed a large taxi back to Parkside. Andre, Nigel, Sam, and his newly found nocturnal companion took another normal four-seater cab back to the hotel, as our cab was full and could not accommodate anyone else. It was decided that we would be playing the board game in Sonia's room. Everyone went up to their rooms to bring whatever alcohol they had. I told Nicole to come with me, as the game belonged to me and I would need help carrying alcohol to Sonia's room. On the way to my room, we happened to cross Manny's room and heard the sound of a girl moaning inside. Nicole giggled and looked at me. I pretended like I didn't know whose room that was. I knew I had to act as normal and calm as I could. I had planned to seduce her inside my room. I knew I had a small window of opportunity because things would get difficult once we reached Sonia's room, as everyone would be there. Should I kiss her as soon as we enter my room? Should I excuse myself to use the washroom while she sits on my bed and gets comfortable in my room? Should I ask her if she wants to cuddle? Fuck all of this, let me use one of Deepak's tried and tested routines.

I inserted my room card to enter my room. 'Jeez, you have a pretty tidy room. I am impressed. I have seen some guys keeping their rooms so messy. One of my friends had mold growing in his dishes,' said Nicole.

'I like to keep my room clean. I believe in feng shui. If a room is clean, it gives positive energy and leads to good results in whatever you do.' There was not even a modicum of truth in that statement. The only time I cleaned my room is before I went out at night with the hope of coming back with a one-night stand.

'There is my game. Why don't you sit down? I need to use the washroom. I will be back in a bit,' I said, giving her time to get comfortable with her surroundings. I had successfully completed the first step of my plan. The next step was to seed the idea of sex inside her. I was arranging my wallet inside the washroom by taking out my condom and room card from the side pocket hole of my wallet and putting it in the cash pocket with the dollar bills. One of the ways Deepak Wayne used with women was to pretend that he lost something and was looking for it in his wallet. Then he would act as if he was searching for it and take out cash, cards, etc., one by one from his wallet and ask the girl to hold it while he continued searching for his lost item. The girl would think that she was helping Deepak find his lost item by holding on to his clutter while he continued searching. At that moment, Deepak would take out his condom and give it to the girl with a look of indifference as if it was normative to have condoms in wallets. Only after making her hold the condom, he would pretend to have found his lost item.

I took a deep breath and exited the washroom.

'Hey, Nicole, do you remember where I put my room card? I cannot seem to find it. I don't want to be locked out of my hotel room after coming back from Sonia's room,' I said.

'I thought you kept it in your wallet. Didn't you?' she said surprisingly.

'Wait, let me check again. Could you hold my stuff while I empty my wallet? It has so many cards,' I said.

'Sure,' she said assiduously.

So, I took out five bills of 20$ and pretended to search inside. Then I took out my UofT ID card, debit card, credit card, and Ontario ID and gave everything to her. After that, I took out a condom and placed it in her hand while I continued to look down as if I was still searching for my room card. I could see her smirk through my peripheral vision, though I pretended not to react.

'Ah, found it. It was behind this 50$ bill; I can take back my stuff now,' I said. She handed me the cash and the cards from her right hand. I purposely took time to arrange the cards in my wallet. Now, all she had in her hand was my condom, and I made sure she holds it for a while before I neatly arrange my cash and cards.

'Now give me the condom. We are going to need it,' I said.

'What! No...let's take this slowly,' she said in a shocked voice, not expecting me to make a move. 'I think you are a really nice guy. I don't want this to be a one night thing where we go our separate ways the next morning. I feel we should get to know each other better. Don't you think so?' she said. I was well equipped to deal with all her obstacles. Deepak taught his followers that men should always handle rejections positively with a smile. A girl should never know that her refusal affected you. Once she senses that, it becomes very hard to sleep with her. So I acted like I didn't care and quickly added humor into the conversation to keep a playful vibe. It is always a bad idea to push for sex. One should never come across as desperate and needy. Also, it was necessary to keep a playful vibe to take the pressure off the girl.

'Talking about taking things slow, I will penetrate you very slowly when you are ready to do it. I am a man, and I will escalate things sexually with you in the future. I don't want to lie to you, but I am not here to be just your friend. Friend reminds me, my friends are waiting for us. Let us go,' I had successfully handled her rejection with a memorized script as well as quickly changed the topic so that she doesn't get a chance to raise objections to what I planned to do in future.

The North American University Debating Championship (NAUDC) is the most prestigious university debating competition to be held in North America. It is held annually by either a Canadian or an American University and only debate teams from institutions in either Canada or USA are allowed to participate in the competition. In 2015, the iteration was held at New York University. Ryan and I were representing University of Toronto's Hart House debate team at this competition, and we had prepared extensively for it. New York University, as its name indicates, is located in New York, which is a three-hour flight from Toronto. As the host, members of NYU were judging the competition and were not allowed to participate. The debates were held in the British Parliamentary format where each debate consisted of four teams, and each team has two speakers. There are two teams on each side of the debate, but even those two teams compete against each other. One side consisted of Opening Government and Closing Government whereas the teams on other side were Opening Opposition and Closing Opposition. Each debate had a specific topic which was announced fifteen minutes prior to the beginning of the debate, giving all teams fifteen minutes to prepare their speeches. During this time, no team was allowed to use any electronic devices to aid them in preparation. They could only consult their teammate or the notes they had made in advance on popular notions.

The tournament was held over a period of three days from 2nd November to 4th November. After successive rounds of intense debating, Ryan and I just managed to scrape through to the finals. We were the only Canadian team out of the four teams that would be facing off in the finals. The other three teams were Harvard, Yale, and John Hopkins

University. There was a lot of chatter about the Yale debaters – Ritika Mookerjee and Kyle Hietala – winning the cup, as they had been hot favorites throughout the tournament. Finally, the time came when the motion for the final was to be announced. We were Opening Opposition, which meant that we would have to rebut the points made by Opening Government which was Harvard University.

The topic of the debate was: This house would allow the use of racial profiling by police forces.

According to the first speaker, communities that were based on racial lines were the source of most crimes or the place where crime happened the most. He supported his statement by giving examples of ethnic enclaves like the Pakistani community in England and the Black neighborhoods in Detroit. The speaker from Harvard went on to emphasize how political correctness was undermining the ability of the police force to stop criminals. Political correctness, according to him, was stopping policemen from acting in the best interest of the people, even though it was statistically proven how people belonging to certain races were more likely to commit offences. Lastly, he talked about the impact of racial profiling by laying down what he considered were three benefits of racial profiling. The ability of police force to deal with crime with all available information allowed them to be more flexible and deal with crime more appropriately. Secondly, he stated how racial profiling benefitted minorities by protecting them against crime. Thirdly, he demonstrated how positive racial profiling allowed government to zero in on high crime areas and run awareness campaign against crime in those areas. He ended the speech by saying how positive racial profiling allowed police personnel to float like butterflies and sting like bees (paraphrased version of a seven-minute speech).

'Now, I would like to call upon the leader of opposition, Ryan Principi, to open the case for the opposition. Hear, hear,' said the speaker as Ryan arose from his seat.

'Ladies and Gentlemen. It is quite clear that the proposition's system is racism. It is deleterious to the police system, and it is completely illegitimate and unjustified, so we are very happy to oppose the motion today. Let us be very clear on our stance. We think it is very important that the police do not judge people based on their biological traits like age, gender, and race. They should have the same treatment for everyone irrespective of religion, race, caste, or creed unless, of course, someone is very closely matching the description of the suspect, and even in that case, they should proceed very carefully by explaining why they have stopped a particular person. Just because they are looking for a Black suspect does not give them substantial ground to stop any young Black man in a Jamaican neighborhood where plenty of people would be young and Black. We think that proposition have three burdens in this debate. First is to show that this measure is legitimate and justified. Second, they need to show it is effective, and that is the only one they addressed in the opening speech. Thirdly, they need to show that there are no wider harms that outweigh the benefits, if there are any benefits.

So we come to you with a three-point case. According to our team, this measure is illegitimate, ineffective and actively causes racial tension. Our first point is about how this is an illegitimate measure. They need to show us why it is legitimate to target someone because of their race. They need to show why it is legitimate to target someone who may be innocent and search them. Because sometimes even if a measure is effective, if it is not legitimate, if it is racist, ladies and gentlemen, it is fundamentally against the principles of our constitution. Since they haven't addressed the principle of legitimacy, it means that none of their case stands anyway. In terms of how they are framing profiling, they assume it is something that is going to be very easy. If you found out that a particular criminal is Black, you find that Black criminal and you search him or her. That is not the case, ladies and gentlemen. It's like stopping and searching loads of people of that color. That is what profiling is. Racial profiling like this culminates in house raids when police barge into a house in the middle of the night and arrest people because of their race.

Now let us look at the substantive case. First, they told us that race is a reason for crime. First of all, we think it is absurd, and there are many social issues especially with Black communities in America. These social causes bring them down and degrade them in society which makes them feel they are treated unfairly and instills a feeling in them that they need to get back at the state by committing a crime. The proposition ignored the sociological reasons why people who belong to marginalized racial communities have higher rates of crime. So it is not justified to collectively punish all Black people in America by searching them just because they are people of color. Secondly, they were telling us why this measure will be effective. We have quite a few responses to that. For instance, their example about Germany. We would like to ask them how many people were stopped and searched in the first place, how many people were arrested in the first place before the law got to these two perpetrators. Thirdly, they told us how innocent minorities in the USA will not be targeted again under their model of racial profiling. We would like to ask them, "How are you going to find that one particular Black person who apparently committed that stabbing without searching loads more because you think that it is more likely they did that?"

Secondly, what profiling people on the basis of their race does is that it can perpetuate offences. The reaction of the society towards an individual who is regularly profiled or searched can result in the individual being more prone to actually commit offences. According to a lot of experts on gang membership, if a person is confronted by the police several times, society comes to a conclusion that there might be flaws in the character of that person or that person is into illegal activities. As a result, the person starts getting viewed as a criminal, and all other forms of identification are subsumed in the background. This identification of a person as a criminal may even result in the person being ostracized by the members of his community. Therefore, constantly being rebuked or condemned by the members of the society makes it difficult to participate in the cultural, economic, and social activities of mainstream society, thereby making the supposedly deviant person seek peers who have similar interactions or have experienced harassment from the police. These groups of people are at a higher risk to flout laws in the future. Also, by delineating racial minorities as a cause of most crimes, the proposition has tried to smear the debate by choosing to ignore the role of the state that is responsible for the impoverished conditions of the minority population.

According to the theory of social disorganization, the causes of crimes in ethnic enclaves could be attributed to the poor conditions of those neighborhoods. The neighborhoods of ethnic minorities are characterized by poor dysfunctional institutions that fail to provide social support and infrastructure required to achieve success. The social institutions are not equipped in meeting the educational, health, and religious requirements of the youth which lead them in the wrong direction. Financially disadvantaged neighborhoods lack the social control that is required to make sure that its minority residents follow the norms of the society. This problem is exacerbated by blocked opportunities, forcing people of color to find illegal ways to gain upward social mobility. Therefore, racial profiling would not solve the problem of crimes committed by Black, Latino, or Pakistani men as mentioned in proposition's case because the root of the problem is not race but inadequate funding and government support.

Furthermore, we think that racial profiling undermines the police's role. They are there to protect people. They are there to make people feel safe and comfortable. But what racial profiling does is treat someone in an undignified and unfair manner like you feel when you are leaving a restaurant, and you feel that they are more likely to pick on you; you don't feel safe, you don't feel that they are on your side. By doing this, the police is actively imposing an identity, and this is not the police's role. By targeting an individual because of their race, the police would be alienating the minority communities who are more likely to resent men in uniform rather than respect them. As a result, this would even thwart noble efforts of community policing where people would lose faith in the police force which is meant to aid them. As a result, people stop reporting crimes. People are not trusting the police when the police go to them and are hiding facts about the criminal because they might think, "Oh, no! The police might actually target me." This is why, in South Africa, where majority of the police is White, the darkest skin-colored people in Cape Town are targeted unfairly. For these reasons, I am proud to oppose.'

After Ryan made his case, the speaker called upon the second debater from Harvard to conclude the case for Opening Government. The second debater started his speech by rebutting some of the claims made by Ryan in his speech. He mentioned how racial profiling did not lead to negative stereotyping because racial stereotypes existed in society much before the racial profiling law was introduced. He further countered Ryan's view of racial profiling leading to the unjustified search of many innocents by saying, 'Just because something is difficult doesn't mean we don't do it. People are searched at airports all the time, and we don't find something on every person, yet everyone continues to use airports.' After finishing his rebuttals, he came to the substantive part of his speech where he put forward two new points for why his case was relevant. I was carefully noting them down, as I knew I had to rebut both the points. His first point described how racial profiling was useful in preventing international crime, as people constantly moved across borders, and countries had discrepancies in the capabilities of their police forces. He continued to emphasize the importance of racial profiling in preventing international crime and protecting the victims of the crime. According to him, countries had an obligation to their own people and also to people who cross borders to reside in a particular country. He exemplified his argument by mentioning how countries that implement racial profiling have managed to decrease the amount of crime without causing any racial tension. The second point he advanced was about how racial profiling could save the law enforcement a lot of money. He explained this point by showing how it becomes easier for police personnel to know which locales to search based on the profile of a person, which in turn leads to fewer resources being consumed. According to him, it led to a faster tracking down of leads. Also, by saving money here, the government could spend more money on community initiatives, pension programs, police salaries, and other needs that are normally not given importance. He concluded by characterizing Ryan's whole speech as an exercise in floccinaucinihilipilification. He condemned certain minority groups and the opposition (Ryan and I) for protesting against a law made by elected representatives and therefore disrespecting the law as well as the efforts that policemen make by putting their life on the line.

The speaker brought the house in order, 'I would like to thank the speaker for his speech. Now, I would like to call upon the deputy leader of opposition to deliver the next speech of the round.' I walked nervously towards the dais. I could feel my heart impound because of the tension in the air. Our whole case depended on how I delivered my speech. We had gotten so close to that trophy, and I fretted at the thought of it slipping away now. The following is my speech as it was delivered at the North American University Debating Championship.

'*Madam Speaker, we would like to thank the proposition for their wonderful anecdotes and bedtime stories, but I think it is time for them to wake up. There was no actual engagement by the proposition on legitimacy. There was nothing on the rights and responsibilities of the police force. First, I am going to rebut the points that were made by proposition in their last speech. According to the proposition, racial profiling does not lead to stereotyping people or negative stereotypes because they said that those stereotypes existed in society much before the racial profiling law was introduced. They also said that racial profiling prevents international crime and protects the victims of racially motivated crimes, and that is why they think the measure is effective and does not create racial tension. We on the opposition believe that racial profiling undermines due process and is therefore illegitimate. There is no better example of racial profiling and the tension it creates than what happened with Michael Brown in Ferguson, Missouri, and is continuing to happen today. The streets of Ferguson were boiling with protests after the killing of Michael Brown by the hands of a police officer. That protest was the product of gradual frustration, struggle, and resentment that people had been facing from their police department. At the time of Michael Brown's incident, Fergusson's population was 67% Black, but only three of the city's sixty-three police officers were Black. Black people in Fergusson make up 86% of the people who were stopped by police that year and 92% of the people who were searched by police that year. While the people in the city were busy protesting, it was appalling to see the mayor of the city publicly announce on television that residents of Fergusson believed there was no racial divide in their city. The opposition seems to be as oblivious today as the mayor of Fergusson was when people took to the streets to voice their concerns. We have to focus on the series of small injustices that go under the radar but breed that distrust in the first place, and that is why practices like racial profiling are illegitimate and ineffective and even counter-productive for the police force that implements it.*

Secondly, the proposition stated how racial profiling could save the police department a lot of money, and countries that do have racial profiling have managed to reduce the amount of crime that has been committed. I think this argument is completely flawed and a gross misrepresentation of the actual scenario. This rebuttal also brings me to my first point of positive matter. Racial profiling is costlier than traditional police methods because concentrating on minorities disproportionately does not yield better returns on the investment of law enforcement resources. Also, when police officials in USA used race or ethnicity as a parameter, they did not get better returns on their enforcement efforts that they were expecting. Instead, their use of traditional police methods against criminals did a better job and did not sweep a high number of innocent people under the law enforcement's net. Therefore, using actionable intelligence and data is a more economical and time-saving method than racial profiling. Race and ethnicity are very poor predictors of behavior. In fact, innocent people who have been targeted on the basis of race have sued the police department for millions of dollars which has burnt a hole in the pockets of those police forces. Furthermore, let us look at the social costs. A recent report in Spain revealed how people who are targeted because of their racial appearance experience a very different kind of reality. So profiling sends a very clear message that if you are not conforming to heteronormative standards, you are dangerous and must be controlled. They stop you, and the onus is on you to prove your innocence. An individual's body bears the shadow of permanent suspicion. Worst still, criminals from other groups may act with impunity knowing that the probability of them being caught are slim. Dan Osborne, who committed a vehicular attack in the UK, killing one and injuring nine, was a Caucasian male.

Lastly, racial profiling disenfranchises an individual and alienates them from the economic, political, and civic affairs of their society. The individual feels violated, and it is a violation of their personhood. Racial profiling causes targeted groups to be incarcerated at rates that are disproportionate to their offending rates. Incarceration has a negative consequence on employment and income. To make matters worse, these effects are compounded beyond the individual to affect the family members of the incarcerated person. The family members of the incarcerated person suffer due to a loss in income and employment-related benefits. They have to bear the strains of parenting, social stigma, and the emotional toll of having an absent family member. Arab employers in Windsor, Ontario, have reportedly discriminated against Arab job candidates in favor of Canadian or white-skinned candidates because they do not want goods that they are transporting to the United States to be delayed at the borders. From the use of slave patrols to lynching to legal segregation and in modern iterations like stop and frisk, racial profiling has long been used to maintain White authority by singling out the presence and behavior of people of color – especially African Americans. Furthermore, if we are to believe that just because it is a limited resources environment and attention can be encapsulated by the virtue of how one looks, then criminals or terrorists who belong to minority groups could easily adapt their modus operandi. They could radicalize or recruit people who look White or belong to the majority community and who subscribe to their beliefs and use them to commit crime or terrorist attacks...was merely an attempt to strawman us. If Jim Crow was in this room tonight, he would be nodding his head to everything that the proposition has said so far because he agrees with them. The speaker from the proposition said how minority groups and the opposition tonight were disrespecting the law and the efforts of policemen by protesting against racial profiling because the law was made by elected representatives. I would like to remind him that St. Augustine said that an unjust law was no law at all, which means that people have the right to protest and demonstrate against a law that curtails their civil rights. The proponents of racial profiling are lucky that people are only protesting peacefully and not breaking any laws by getting violent. Remember, if you vote government tonight, you will be voting for a structural setup that enables institutions to cement discriminatory practices in nonchalant ways. Therefore, Madam Speaker, we beg to oppose.'

I ended my speech to a thunderous round of applause. I was not half expecting this kind of a reaction. As sociology and criminology majors, Ryan and I had learnt quite a bit about race, discrimination, and policing. Maybe that is why what we said appealed to the audience. My speech was followed by members of Closing Government and Closing Opposition, which were Yale and John Hopkins respectively. The speakers from Yale did a spectacular job in driving home their points. Just like UofT, Yale had also won the North American University Debating Championship five times and were very likely to seize the trophy this time too. The speakers from John Hopkins had a very solid case for Closing Opposition. It was going to be a very tough call for the judges. Ryan was confident that Harvard was not winning it this year because we had done a good job at shredding their weak arguments. It was either Yale or John Hopkins. The time to declare the results had come. After an intense discussion of fifteen minutes, the Chief Adjudicator showed up to disclose the results of the finals.

'The winner of NAUDC 2015 is *deliberately paused for effect* Opening Opposition Hart House. Give a huge round of applause for Ryan Principi and Devansh Gupta from the University of Toronto.' I couldn't believe the words that came out of his mouth. Time seemed to come to a halt, and I sat frozen, kvelling in my chair. We had beaten Harvard. We had even beaten Yale, setting an eximious record for UofT's Hart House debate society of winning the NAUDC more times than any other university.

Year 3 Semester II

Location: Parkside Cafeteria

January 2016

Within the first month of 2016, UofT was hit by a huge scandal. The fleeting Christmas break was followed by a new semester and a new year. The new year didn't just bring back the students to university, it brought to the forefront the workings of the mysterious secret society at UofT. A video whose origin could not be traced was being widely circulated on all possible social media platforms like Snapchat, WhatsApp, and Facebook (though Facebook eventually took it down), creating a stir in the student community and giving birth to many speculations about 'Episkopon', which was a secret society at Trinity College in the University of Toronto that has been active since 1858. As a Trinity student, I had a vague idea of its existence, but it had never piqued my curiosity until this video had surfaced. The video showed a female professor at UofT who was sleeping in lingerie presumably after an intense session of sex, and on her bedside table was a specific key that only members of Episkopon possess. Beside the key, there was a used condom filled with sperm which the person who was filming the video had zoomed in to indicate what had transpired between them.

The female professor in the video was identified as Brenna Keatinge. She was a tenured professor at the University of Toronto. Her LinkedIn bio read: *My areas of expertise include urban issues, municipal governance, housing and gentrification, social inequality and environment sustainability. In my spare time, I play the flute and sing in choir, practice yoga, meditation and hoop dancing. I am also a scotch connoisseur!* 😉 She had a very beautiful face and a gorgeous figure. If there was a prettier professor than her at UofT, I had yet to see her. Her pictures blew my mind, and I seemed to have a visceral inclination to stalk more of her social media profiles, but at the same time, I was feeling bad for her. Not only did Episkopon beguile her but also demonstrated how one could get away with immoral and unethical behavior. Professor Keatinge was held captive of her own actions. If she identified the culprit and initiated proceedings against him for sharing a video of her in a compromised position, she would be the first person to lose her job for sleeping with a student. The university's policy bars any sexual relationship between a student and a professor because of a conflict of interest and the unfair advantages a student might get because of that relationship. Losing a high six-figure job and being barred from teaching at any university is not something one could come to terms with easily. Secondly, it would be difficult for her to prove the guilt of the student who belonged to Episkopon, since she was sleeping while he filmed her, and the culprit had used proxy servers to make the source of the video untraceable. The culprit could very well deny filming her or having any allegiance to Episkopon.

The viral video clip had garnered intense attention and was a hot topic of discussion throughout the university corridors. People who didn't belong to Trinity were taking a keen interest in Episkopon and asking questions to know more about it. People oblivious to the existence of a secret society on campus were suddenly surfing the net to read as much as they could about it. I decided to do my own research about this society, as I had a sociology course on research methods which required me to carry out a qualitative research study by interviewing a sample group of people, but I knew I had very slim chances of accessing this coveted society. Nonetheless, it was all very intriguing, and I wanted to know more about this subculture.

Based on the material available online, Episkopon had three annual public gatherings which were called readings. Investigative journalists have often drawn comparisons between Episkopon and Yale's mysterious Skull and Bones society, which boasts George W. Bush among its alumni as well as numerous politicians, corporate leaders, and supreme court judges. The leader of UofT's Episkopon society is called a Scribe. The position of the Scribe was known to be held by Bill Graham, the renowned minister of foreign affairs and national defense. One of Canada's most famous poets Archibald Lampman was also a Scribe during his days at Trinity. Having such distinguished alumni legitimized the secret society in the eyes of successive batches of incoming students, who aspire to become a member of the group. Unlike other societies, Episkopon is deeply immersed in the pride of tradition with members wearing black gowns, holding secret meetings, keeping meeting minutes, and maintaining original paintings at Episkopon's archives.

The members of Episkopon wore silver-colored keys around their neck as part of tradition. It is like an ID card with each key carrying a unique number. The Scribe wears the biggest key, marking his special status and position in the group. It is said that the color of the Scribe's key is golden. The number on the key of the Scribe is always 58, which is a reference to the year Episkopon was founded - 1858 - as a satirical newspaper. The female branch of Episkopon was founded in 1899. During the three annual readings, the members publicly satirize the everyday activities and events of Trinity through a wide range of puns, innuendos, jokes, rhymes, and songs delivered mostly by the Scribe. There is a skull present during all the readings of the secret society, because the skull represents the spirit of the Venerable Father (or Mother) Episkopon.

Episkopon uses the code words 'ice cream socials' to announce its annual readings. As a Trin student, I was privy to this information because an upper-year student had told me this during lunch at Strachan Hall when I had joined the university three years ago. There are several posters or notices around campus whenever a reading of Episkopon is about to happen. The sociologist inside me started making sense of all this. As I read more about this, I understood how this group evolved within a normative structure that was composed of privileged straight White men and why it was considered elitist to belong to this group. Membership in this group enabled an individual to gain power through this social structure. It was a mistake to view Episkopon as just a group of individuals. Episkopon was structured to be a deeply impended institution, one that facilitates groupthink and was exempt of criticism from its members as well as disconnected from the harmful repercussions of its iniquities. With the rising focus on equity issues, both male and female branches of Episkopon created an opt-out policy where an individual had the right to opt out from being mentioned in the readings. However, members were reluctant to exercise the use of this policy because they worried about being ostracized or facing the stigma that came with it.

As UofT evolved to echo the cosmopolitan city of Toronto around it, Episkopon seemed to have adapted its traditions by launching venomous tirades against their peers by publicly humiliating them for being unhealthy, calling out homosexual behavior, mocking students trapped in financial debt and those who were unable to uphold Trinity traditions. The critics of this society considered it to have reached a saturation point and become anachronistic while others were of the opinion that it was restructuring itself to accommodate hazing and alcohol-induced behavior.

The Trinity College Council voted unanimously to ban Episkopon in 1992 after the secret society refused to consider and comply with the recommendations proposed by the task force. A student suicide in 1985 that was allegedly linked to Episkopon brought the secret society under the lens of the Trinity Council. In 2008, a student suffered serious head injuries after tripping and falling down a hill during an initiation ritual of the secret society. In my opinion, banning did not have any negative effect on the secret society because all their activities were carried out in complete secrecy, and even their annual readings took place in the dark outside the property of the university. Also, it is difficult to ban a group that culminates in existence only when members of that group congregate together. In this case, they always congregate in secret and don't even publicize their recruitment process. If Episkopon wants you as a member, it finds a way to reach out to you. A newspaper editor once posted an article about his experience of trying to deconstruct the functioning of Episkopon. The editor had managed to secure the @utoronto.ca email ID of a member and had requested the member for an interview only to get the following response.

Those who know do not speak. Those who speak do not know.

NTSM,

Him

The NTSM stood for *Notandi Sunt Tibi Mores* which means 'Your ways are being noted'.

There were rumors that a second-year student from Trin was planning to create a group called 'Episkopositive' to create awareness against the misogynistic practices prevalent inside Episkopon. Apparently, he was planning to pitch Episkopositive as an inclusive alternative to the Finance Committee for seeking grants. He believed that Trin students deserved an inclusive and safe environment, where people would only be told positive things and not be subjected to caustic comments for deviating from the norm. Even though his intentions were noble, I doubted whether he would actually succeed in delegitimizing Episkopon's place within Trinity, as some of the most privileged and powerful people were known to be its members and alumni. Also, a club where people are told only positive and nice things was not likely to receive a lot of buy-in, as the world is quite a ruthless place. Ultimately, people tend to be attracted to things that mirror their reality.

'I still can't believe how people can stoop so low. This guy has literally double fucked the professor. Not only did he fuck her in bed but also fucked her life up. She cannot complain against him, rat him out, or even leave the job of a tenured professor so easily,' I said while everyone sat down with their lunch around me.

'Just imagine what this lady must be going through right now. Imagine the shame when she goes to take her lectures. What sort of disgusting animal could do this?' said Sonia angrily.

Andre acidly chimed in, 'Well, the professor is no saint either. I mean she knows what she was doing was wrong. Who knows if she has slept with students in the past as well? I fucking respect this guy. This guy is the god of pick-up. I mean we thought we were the ones on a seductive spree. But there is so much to learn from this guy. I would love to be under his wing.'

'Amen to that,' said Sam.

'I can't believe you guys are actually glorifying such behavior. I agree that the professor was wrong, but what this guy did is unpardonable. Who in their right mind videotapes a professor in lingerie after seducing her and then broadcasts it on every available online platform? Moreover, zooming in on that used condom was just disgusting,' said Ryan brusquely.

'When the professor is so smoking hot, I would fuck her. Maybe making a video of it and getting it viral was part of this secret group's intention. Maybe they were making some kind of a statement like Episkopon is alive and lives until this day,' said Manny.

'What a way to make a statement about your group. I wonder how their female branch is though. Are they known to indulge in such sort of crass behavior?' asked Lydia.

'Well, they took down the board which had the name of former female Scribes in solidarity with the male group after the male branch was banned by the Trinity Council,' I replied spontaneously like some knowledgeable member of the group. As someone who had read a lot about Episkopon, this information was fresh in my memory, as it had recently percolated my brain.

'Why are students buying into this anyway? A bit of hazing and over-consumption of alcohol goes on in fraternities and sororities too. I mean if you don't do it now, then when you will ever get an opportunity to do it again in life, because adulting does not permit late nights and ludicrous behavior. But this is just crossing the line. Lydia and I were blenched after a random camera popped up on our shower cubicle. My heart goes out to Professor Keatinge. I wish I could hug her right now,' said Sonia.

Nigel harangued Sonia, 'You are comparing two very different incidents, Sonia. What happened to you and Lydia was uncalled for. I mean you didn't invite it on yourselves. But this lady is a UofT professor. She should have known better. Why would a beautiful and intelligent professor like her sleep with a student in the first place? I am sure she was aware of the risks. I mean it could cost a person her job.'

'True says,' said Andre ruefully.

'Lydia, I always thought our fraternities and sororities went overboard at times. If I knew this is how shit goes down at Episkopon, I would have never rushed Lambda Chi. Instead, I would have tried to enroll myself at this organization,' said Sam.

'Well, I belong to University College so I wouldn't be eligible to join the female branch at Episkopon. And I am glad we don't have this elitist secret society at UC. People at UC are much more grounded. I feel a lot of students at Trin are pompous snobs because of traditions that go on at your college and the privileged backgrounds they come from,' replied Lydia.

'Four of your best friends are from Trin. If the adage *You are a product of the company you keep* is true, then you too are a pompous snob by now.'

Lydia threw up her hands in vexation, 'I can't argue with you.'

February 2016

Have you, the reader, ever heard of Punta Cana before? You might have if you have lived in North America all your life. I had never heard of it until it was collectively decided by Andre, Manny, Nigel, and Ryan that we would be spending a substantial part of our reading-week break at the resort town. We had booked an all-inclusive resort called Occidental Punta Cana at the La Costa del Coco, which is popularly known as the Coconut Coast. Punta Cana was located on the eastern coast of Dominican Republic, which had tropical weather all year round and was a paradise for tourists like us who wanted a break from the cold, dry weather in Toronto. Getting a cheap, all-inclusive deal meant that we could feast and drink with no restrictions without having to worry about a steadily increasing bill. As Keanu had plans with his family of going to Vancouver, he could not join us, which meant that Sonia and Lydia would be roommates again after a long time.

We landed at the Punta Cana International Airport and took our pre-booked airport shuttle to the resort. As we drove along the stretch of beaches, I was amazed to see the abundance of picture-perfect palm trees swaying in the warm ocean breeze. I could dub this place as 'The Land of Palm Trees'. On one hand, this whole place had a very touristy vibe, but on the other hand, it had an alarming presence of security guards and tall resort walls with barbed wires. I could deduce this to be an indication of a high crime rate which reflected the socioeconomic inequality present in the Dominican Republic. The economy of Punta Cana heavily relied on tourism, and the government could not afford tourists being targeted, because that would give Punta Cana a bad reputation and negatively affect the flow of business.

We arrived at the hotel to be greeted by a host of cheerful staff members who were carrying welcome drinks for us. The margaritas did feel refreshing in the northern tropical sun. A brief interaction with the local staff imbibed us with the knowledge that English was not their forte, so we knew we would be required to download an English-to-Spanish dictionary on our phones to navigate our short stay here. The Occidental Punta Cana was a beachfront hotel with casual Spanish-style rooms. The hotel boasted of ten restaurants and three swimming pools in addition to a spa. Having direct access to the beach saved us from booking expensive cab rides. I was marveled by the fine white sand of the El Cortecito Beach and the crystal-clear turquoise waters of this idyllic enclave. The opportunity to indulge in myriad water sports like windsurfing, kayaking, snorkeling, water jet skis, and deep-sea diving made it a haven for tourists seeking out adventure. Our days began with a massive spread at breakfast and ended with drinks at discos or sundowners by the sea.

On our last day, the eight of us went sailing at noon. The girls were flaunting their bright-colored bikinis. Looking at Sonia's body, I could only think how lucky Keanu was to tap that on a regular basis. Her parents would have kicked her out of the house if they saw her like that. According to her, the Muslim community at her mosque would have disowned her if they had any inkling of her real self.

'Hey, Sonia, you are looking so hot. How about I send a beautiful picture to your parents?' I joked, taking out my cellphone while she stood at the northernmost tip of our private yacht.

'Before you send my pictures to my parents, you would find yourself drowning without a life jacket in the ocean,' she cattishly replied.

'I know how to swim.'

'So do the sting rays and the sharks,' she sneered.

'Shots fired...oooo,' screamed Sam enjoying the light banter between Sonia and me.

'Devansh, my parents would be pretty mad if you sent them this picture, but if I happen to tell your parents about all the debauchery and the girls that you have slept with, I reckon it would be impossible for you to go back to India,' said Sonia. 'Imagine if I told Nicole about the pick-up stuff you guys are into, your booty calls at Parkside would come to a halt.' Nicole and I had gone out several times after we had met at the Cube last semester, and I had fucked her numerous times after my first failed attempt at the hotel.

'I know you aren't going to be so mean, Sonia. You know I love you,' I said in an affable tone.

'But Nicole was quite a slow cooker, eh?' said Andre, referring to a pick-up terminology which meant that a girl has not rejected you but will take her time before she trusts you enough to let her seduce you.

'Yeah, she was. I mean for the first few dates she only let me see and feel her philosopher's stones. It took me a month to open her chamber of secrets and release my prisoner of Azkaban,' I said, drawing an analogy between *Harry Potter* and sex. Andre laughed uncontrollably on hearing that.

'But the best part about slow cookers like Nicole is that once you have opened their chamber of secrets, they keep coming again and again for your prisoner of Azkaban,' said Andre, which was true because I didn't find any resistance after I had fucked her once. She longed for my dick and was dominating in bed.

We were soon joined by Nigel who emerged from the cabin of the yacht with an open bottle of beer. He looked calm and reserved. After taking a sip from the bottle, he said that he wanted to share something with all of us.

'Guys, I have to tell you all something...*pause*...I just got off the phone with Hannah, and we have mutually decided to break up. I am not in a relationship with her anymore,' he said. I was surprised to see how he had managed to maintain an emotionless face while delivering this news as if it did not affect him at all. He seemed unaltered and unmoved looking into the vast expanse of the ocean, even though his relationship just went kerflooey.

Manny proceeded warily like an endangered animal, 'Sorry to hear that, Nigel, but how did it happen so suddenly? I mean she was over at Parkside just two weeks ago, and everything seemed fine.'

'We felt like we were growing apart. Long-distance relationships come with their own struggles. The added stress of university compounds the problem when you can't meet each other so often. Also, you are spending a significant part of your day with other people, and as a result, conversations with your significant other get pretty monotonous and artificial, you know. That is when long-distance relationships start masquerading as genuine relationships, devoid of the facts that are necessary to determine if it will swim or sink.'

'I think you guys should definitely talk it out again once you are back in Canada. I hope I am not prying into your private life, but there is nothing that cannot be worked out. Hannah is a wonderful girl. Don't let her go,' said Lydia.

'I have thought this through. I don't think Hannah and I are going to get back. Things have been a bit rough recently. I think we both don't see the relationship progressing and were letting things boil within us which was mentally not good for us. When you boil something for long, it will break or burst. I kind of saw it coming.'

'Is it okay if I hug you?' asked Sonia. This was the first time I had witnessed Sonia asking for permission before hugging any of us. Nigel gave a faint smile. I felt that he was maintaining a solid exterior but was broken from within. He had been dating Hannah for almost four years, and breaking up with her from a yacht in the Atlantic Ocean was definitely not how he had envisioned their future. Sonia went over to hug him, and he reciprocated the action. She understood Nigel the best and could empathize with his feelings better than any of us.

'Nigel, I think you should definitely meet her once after we return to Canada. You know, you are on a boat in the Dominican, and she is back home in Canada, and things often get heated up on the phone. Take her out for coffee once you are back and discuss things face to face. I am sure when you guys are sitting across the table and talking with calm minds, it is going to be completely different. Trust me on this one,' said Ryan.

Nigel pointed at the water around us, 'Ryan, do you see the changing tides in the ocean? Relationships are like these tides – they ebb and flood with time. When the tide is high, every moment is rejoiced and full of love and passion. But when the tide is low, it is necessary to accept it and live with it. Sand trickles out of your hand if you hold on to it forcefully. Life's most important lessons can be learnt from nature.'

What Nigel said made sense to me. 'I agree with Nigel. Just like one cherishes the similarities in a relationship, it is also important to accept the differences.'

'But you guys have been together for almost four years, and have strong feelings for each other. It's not easy to let go of those feelings,' said Sam with the full emotions of an Indian man.

'Certain feelings are like your sister's vagina, Sam. You know where they are, but they are best left unfelt,' countered Andre.

'We can count on you to take something like feelings and make it sound as dirty as that,' said Lydia.

'I think this topic is exhausting. Let us treat it as water under the bridge. How about we drink to celebrate my single bachelor life? In four years, I seemed to have forgotten what it was like to be single. It seems like I put a huge load off my chest. I am not calling Hannah a load, but what I mean is that it feels different. I am very relaxed and light-headed now,' said Nigel.

'That is my boy. We are going to make your last night in Punta Cana count. I believe, in order to live the university life to its highest potential, one should refrain from nesting during these four years. Nigel, I am confident you won't regret your decision. Being single is actually a boon in university,' said Andre.

'If by highest potential, you mean tricking women into bed with you, I am sorry, but I beg to differ,' retorted Sonia darkly.

In order to prevent another debate on relationships, I quickly changed the topic. 'Well, there needs to be a happy ending to this relationship. How about we set Nigel up for a *nuru* massage tonight?'

'Devansh, what a brilliant idea!' said Andre.

'What is a *nuru* massage?' asked Lydia innocently. She didn't have the smallest hint of how adventurous and innovative people could get with massages.

'Manny, would you like to do the honors and explain what a *nuru* massage is to Lydia?' I said. The girls were oblivious to the fact that all the boys except Nigel had purchased a *nuru* massage yesterday. They had assumed that we had gone to a regular spa for a full body massage. Since Nigel was a loyal boyfriend, he had bailed on us, but there was nothing stopping him now.

'A *nuru* massage is an erotic massage technique that originated in Japan. In this technique, a nude masseuse slides and rubs her body against the client's body when both of them are naked and smothered with an odorless, colorless gel. *Nuru* massages are finished with a happy ending which you must know is terminology for a handjob. It is great for physical and mental relaxation,' said Manny.

'I don't think I need a happy ending, but yeah, a *nuru* massage would be great,' said Nigel.

'Also, there is a crazy party at our hotel tonight. Everyone should focus on winging Nigel. Remember, Nigel, you have to hunt to kill. Smash the hottest pussy in Punta Canta,' said Ryan as he got up to get the pack of beers.

'Well, it is settled then. I am going to scuba dive now. Anybody wanna join me?' asked Manny sarcastically as he stood up to change into his diving paraphernalia. He knew very well that nobody other than him was a certified scuba diver, and he had dived at various locations over the years. As someone who was pursuing acting, he was training to learn a new skill every few months. He had taken short courses on horse riding, scuba diving, and martial arts. It was a good thing that he wasn't seeking to work in the Indian film industry. Otherwise, he would also need to learn dancing.

I looked at Manny get fully dressed as he stood on the swim platform of the yacht, wearing his diving mask, diving suit, fins, and other equipment necessary to help him survive under water. By the time he finished his dive and came back, the sun had started to set on the Atlantic Ocean. The sunset looked like a postcard one could send home as the turquoise blue water added a contrasting flare to the deep oranges of the sky. There is something spectacular, magical about the fading sun that enhances all five human senses at the same time. The colored flavor of the landscape heightened the palette of the sun. All of us looked as the sunset touched our souls and took our breath away. The transition from day to night reflected how nature embodied the human spirits. It reminded all of us, and especially Nigel, that the only thing constant in life is change. The only way to make sense of change is to sway with it, because the people who survive are not always the most robust or the cleverest but the ones most adaptable to change.

Location: University of Toronto Mississauga, Mississauga

One of the most anticipated pub nights at the Mississauga campus of UofT was Sex Pub. *The Medium*, which is the student newspaper for UTM, had written extensively about the success of the annual event. As students who attended the downtown campus, we had never visited the Mississauga campus, but this event was infamous for high levels of alcohol drinking and grinding bodies on the packed dance floor. I definitely couldn't give it a miss and didn't find it difficult to sell it to my squad. However, Sonia bailed on us, as she preferred to stay at Parkside with Keanu and spend the night studying. Manny was home in Brampton visiting his mother and sister. It was the last pub night on campus before the final exams started. Therefore, we decided to go all out without any inhibitions, and I personally took the responsibility of purchasing the tickets for everyone.

Sex Pub was organized by the Sexual Education and Peer Counselling Centre (S.E.C.) at the Blind DuckPub in UTM. The motive behind organizing the event was to give students a safe environment to express themselves without any judgments and stimulate dialogue around the conventionally taboo subject of sex. Every year the event was completely sold off due to its popularity. In a gesture to raise awareness against sexual assault and rape, the S.E.C. decided to donate the proceedings from the ticket sales to the Sexual Assault and Rape Crisis Centre of Peel. In some way, this made me feel good because I convinced myself that I was participating in a noble cause rather than going there only to satiate my animalistic desires. The Facebook page for Sex Pub had a description which mentioned that the organizers had arranged for jelly-wrestling and a sex-doll competition during the night. The page even mentioned a burlesque show by a group called 'Hips Don't Lie Dance Company'. There were arrangements for a photo booth and a bed inside the pub. Even though sex was prohibited on the bed, I could imagine students getting pretty wild with the kinky handcuffs and other sex toys made available.

The six of us (Ryan, Nigel, Sam, Lydia, Andre, and I) took the inter-campus shuttle bus from Hart House to reach UTM for the event. There was a long queue outside the pub. I mentally saluted the spirit of the boys who had come to the event shirtless, naked from waist up. As it was a clothing optional event (only genitals needed to be covered), it meant that they were eligible to enter the pub, but I would not risk standing in the queue bare chested in negative eight degree Celsius temperature. Either they were too stingy to spend 2$ on coat check or they believed hypothermia was a hoax perpetrated by Kim Jong Un. Blind Duck was surprisingly more capacious than I thought it would be. The organizers strategically removed the partition in the middle to make use of the adjacent room for the various activities advertised during the event. They had a huge bar that served both alcohol and bubble tea. This was the first time I had seen bubble tea being served inside a pub, but the disproportionately large Asian population on the Mississauga campus justified the business decision.

After feeling the vibes of the pub, we took some *jäger* shots to kick off the night. The Blind Duck even had special blowjob shots for the occasion. After taking four rounds of shots, Nigel and Lydia hit the dance floor while Sam, Andre, Ryan, and I began sarging for hot girls. I noticed a group of eye candies near the stage where the burlesque show would take place. A group of three girls wearing thongs were making their presence felt on the dance floor. Who could resist watching young athletic bodies in sexy thongs?

'That is where I need to be, guys,' I said, pointing to the girls wearing thongs.

'Holy fuck! I can't wait to experiment some Real Social Dynamics on them,' said Andre. Andre, Sam, Manny, Ryan, and I were watching videos and had even bought some online video lessons from a company called Real Social Dynamics. RSD was founded in Los Angeles in 2002 by pick-up artists who went by the name of Tyler and Papa. Tyler and Papa were former students of Mystery and had branched off to perpetuate their own brand of pick-up. They took pride in teaching a different form of pick-up and referred to their company as the gold standard in the pick-up industry. As we were curious to learn new material, we decided to channel all our energies towards RSD. I had even enrolled in a summer bootcamp that RSD was organizing in Toronto.

'I am joining you on this one, Andre,' said Sam in an excited voice.

'Best of luck. You guys go ahead. Two is a company, but three will become a crowd, so you guys give it a shot,' I said as Andre and Sam got charged up to approach the girls. The girls were fringed by a lot of thirsty male students who were approaching them. Nobody had achieved success in foraying into the group yet. I wanted to observe if the stuff taught by Real Social Dynamics would actually work on this tough set.

Andre took the lead whereas Sam became the wing. He confidently approached the least attractive girl in the group and hooked her in a conversation. Soon, he introduced Sam to the girl. I thought his next move would be to get that girl to introduce him to her attractive friends without mentioning it directly, because that is how RSD instructors functioned. I wasn't wrong. The girl introduced Andre and Sam to her other two friends. After a brief conversation, the most attractive blonde in the group said something and took the other two away. I could see the look of dismal rejection on Sam's face while the duo walked back towards me.

'RSD didn't work, eh?' I asked as they came back dejected.

'The blonde was a bitch. Her friend had caught the bait, but the White bitch spoilt the game,' said Andre. 'Sam, you had to take care of the obstacle.'

'Hey! Don't blame it on me. RSD isn't for club game. It is appropriate for day game in places like malls, parks, and grocery stores,' said Sam.

'I am going for the blonde. She is playing hard to get, but the fun is in the challenge. I am not experimenting with RSD because it is clearly a loser in club settings. I am going to play it safe with Mystery's old-school method. Let me try the gay routine,' I said.

'Are you sure you wanna go with the gay routine? This bitch is rude as fuck. She won't take kindly when you eventually tell her the truth,' cautioned Andre.

'Stop acting like a cantankerous old man, Andre. Just because you got rejected doesn't mean that I would experience the same fate. If there is anything that a girl trusts more than her best friend in a nightclub, it is a gay man,' I winked.

'Okay! Best of luck to you. I am going on a grinding spree with Ryan and Sam,' said Andre.

I walked up to the group which had changed location after Andre's and Sam's approach. They had moved towards the right side of the stage from the left side. The biggest obstacle in the group was the blonde, and I knew that I should directly approach her instead of following Andre's footsteps. She seemed to be the boss in that group, dominating her other two subjects. For some reason, I could see her being dominated in bed. The hottest of girls take the toughest of tests, but once you jump all the hurdles, the rewards are very satisfying.

'You would be so mine if I wasn't gay!' I purred after walking up to her. Mystery vouched for this line. It could make any girl laugh. In my experience, it worked nine out of ten times. She laughed uncontrollably, and her cold hauteur deserted her now. Then she told her friends what I had just told her. They laughed with her, no longer perceiving me as a threat trying to break into their group.

'What is your name?' she asked me.

'My name is Devansh. What is yours?' I asked.

'Devan? Is that how you pronounce it?'

'No, it is Devansh. You can call me Dave,' I said.

'Dave is easier. I am Daria,' she said.

'So, you are Russian. *Previet,*' I greeted her in Russian, exhausting one out of the only five words that I possessed in my Russian lexicon.

'Wow! You are a smart guy. A lot of people here can't tell my origin from my name, even though Daria is a very common name in Russia. Where are you from?' she asked.

'I am from the land where Yoga was born,' I smiled.

'India! You know Shahrukh Khan? I love watching Indian movies. Even my mother watches them. She likes Raj Kapoor. He was very popular in the Soviet Union,' she said.

I was somewhat nonplussed on hearing that, 'I know Shahrukh Khan very well. He danced at my sister's wedding.'

'Really? I love him. I wish I could see him dance live too,' she said.

'I am just joking. Even if I sold both my kidneys and lungs, I couldn't afford him for a performance at a wedding, but yeah, every Indian has heard of him or seen his movies. I have a picture with him though,' I said taking out my phone and preparing for Neil Strauss' photo routine. According to Neil Strauss, pictures conveyed more than words and were a great way to tell a girl everything about yourself and demonstrate a high social value in her eyes. The photo routine consisted of keeping five or six different photographs in a separate folder that you could show to a girl on your phone. Every photo must be accompanied by a short description. Every picture should be based in a different setting and address a specific character trait. For example, he advised his followers to keep one picture with a group of friends and that group should include attractive girls. This shows that a person is socially acceptable, fun and has attractive friends. The moment a girl sees you with other attractive girls, she is more likely to trust you and desire you. The second picture was me delivering a classroom presentation in a suit. I told Daria how I had been chosen by my peers to deliver a presentation for one of my sociology courses. The goal was to convey the idea that I was an eloquent speaker who was confident to address a room full of people. The third picture was me playing cricket. I told her how I had been playing the sport since a young age. It conveyed the idea that I was not all about studying but also cared about physical activities and fitness. The fourth picture was me with Shahrukh Khan back in India. I told her how my father had arranged a meeting for me with him at a cricket match that his team was playing in Kolkata. Getting access to celebrities was a way of showing that I was influential. The fifth picture was me eating pizza at the Grosvenor House Hotel in London, UK. This showed that I could afford to eat at expensive places and was very well travelled.

My experience with Russian girls had taught me that like India, Russia wasn't a very rich country, and only people belonging to rich families could afford to study at universities like UofT. Also, they were old school in the way where they expected men to be very chivalrous and take the lead when it came to choosing restaurants to eat or opening the door of the car for them on formal dates. How much money a guy had and whether he could take care of her financial and emotional needs mattered to Russian girls a lot. They were submissive to their boyfriends as opposed to the feministic approach of girls in Canada. Therefore, the picture routine was bound to work on a girl like Daria.

I was having a good time with Daria when Nigel approached us. He was shirtless, and I could see Daria's friends ogling his ripped physique and chiseled back.

'Where is your shirt, dude?' I asked.

'I opened it. It was too hot for a shirt in here,' he replied in a manner which was enough for me to understand what he was implying. I introduced him as my best friend to Daria and her skimpily clothed friends. I could see them exchanging glances, as they seemed to be very impressed by his bare body. He was exactly the chocolate dessert which girls like them had come to taste here. After introducing Nigel to the girls, I continued my conversation with Daria while he spoke to her friends. Even though Nigel didn't have any pick-up skills, his body was working for him. I teased Daria playfully as she divulged into the intricate details of her life. I learnt how she came to Canada five years ago to study in high school. She joined a private school in grade eleven and was now a third-year student studying management at UTM.

The DJ made an announcement that the burlesque show was about to begin soon. It was a tantalizing show that incorporated sensual dance, acting, and sexuality. The hand-bedazzled costumes of the performers studded with crystals and complemented by ruby red shoes added to the saccharine music. There were performers of all shapes and sizes to foster a body positive atmosphere. It played the role of a stimulator in enhancing sexual desires in a room that was already steaming with old and new couples waiting to jump in bed. While keeping it sexual and risqué, the aim of the performers was to tease the audience. In the midst of this show, I found the right blandishment for Daria and made out with her. She pulled back and asked me hesitantly if I was gay. I convinced her that I was gay but was experimenting with women on the advice of one of my friends. After that, the ease with which she let me kiss her made me feel that I could escalate things further.

After the show ended, I led her to the bed placed inside the pub, so that we could get even more intimate while kissing each other. On my way to bed, I saw Lydia in a suspended position against the wall with her legs wrapped around an Asian guy's thighs and the boy's hands were cupping her butt as they were passionately kissing. I had never seen Lydia being so intimate with a guy in public, but everyone had left their inhibitions outside the door. Sam and Andre were grinding a girl each. I saw Sam turn the girl around and finger her through her thong. An S.E.C. volunteer came up to Daria and me and asked us if we wanted our photos taken as we lay on the bed. We agreed and I told him to take one picture as we kissed each other. As I lay cuddled with her on the bed, I began seeding ideas of sex using NLP techniques. The aim was to plant the idea of sex at her place without directly mentioning it. I started kissing her sweet spots like her earlobe and caressed her inner thighs. She closed her eyes. Then, I took her to the bar to get us a few *jägerbomb* shots when I realized that the club was about to close in fifteen minutes as it was 2:45 am.

So I excused myself to go check on the others. Coincidentally, Sam and Andre were looking for me as well. They told me that they had got the numbers of the girls they had been grinding and would be meeting them soon. They congratulated me when I told them about my progress with Daria. Sam informed me that Lydia had left with the Korean guy I had earlier spotted her with. She messaged Sam that she would meet us at the UTM shuttle bus stop to take the morning bus back to the downtown campus. We saw Nigel dancing with Daria's friend and asked him what his plans were. He had been invited by Daria's friend for drinks, and we all knew where that was going. Ryan was the only one who was nowhere to be found. Eventually, we found him in the smoking zone. He had met some girls who were the epitome of beauty in the pub and built a strong rapport with them. They had invited him to a Chinese restaurant called Mandarin that was open 24 hours in Mississauga. Since Nigel and I were going with Daria and her friend, Sam and Andre decided to join Ryan and the girls he had befriended. The group of girls whom Ryan had befriended were definitely a 9 or a 9.5, and I could see why he would invest so much time on them. He knew they were slow cookers and wouldn't be up for a one-night stand. I admired his patience, ingenuity, and pick-up skills. He was in '*The Game*' to grow every day.

I left with Nigel and the girls to a student residence called Roy Ivor. Roy Ivor was an upper-year student residence on the Mississauga campus. As we entered the residence, Daria told her friend that she has to show me her high school album in her room and that we would be joining them for drinks in a while. She even offered to bring her stock of Russian vodka to her friend's room. Just like guys, girls have their unspoken codes too. It was pretty obvious that her statement was a hint for her friend to take Nigel to her room so that she could take me to hers. I hoped Nigel wasn't flustered about what was going on and got the hint like me. Though I expected him to catch the bait, I was a little unsure of his social intelligence, since this was the first time he would be getting laid with a girl since he broke up with Hannah.

'So high school album is your safe word for sex,' I said, breaking the awkward silence as the both of us walked towards her room.

She blushed, 'What else could I say in front of you and your friend?'

Once we were inside her room, the obvious happened. In two hours, we had two intense sessions of hot sex. By the end of it, I felt Sex Pub had quenched my thirst more than I had expected it to. As I lay beside Daria, I wondered how Nigel and Lydia were doing with their one-night stands. We had planned to regroup at 6:00 am at the shuttle bus stop in the IB building. So I told Daria that I had to leave soon and took her number. Unlike White girls in the West who don't expect anything after a one-night stand, Daria made me promise that I would text her and we would meet again. I promised her I would and confessed that I was never gay but only did what I did because I saw her rejecting a lot of guys. She didn't get angry on hearing that and said that she knew it after the way I kissed her the first time. She was a goddess in bed, and I wanted to see her again. I reached the bus stop to find Ryan, Andre, and Sam already waiting. They were kind enough to get Chinese takeaway for Nigel, Lydia, and me because they knew we had not eaten anything since dinner. Lydia arrived shortly to be followed by Nigel.

'Dude, congratulations! For finally breaking the dry spell. I told you relationships were overrated. You are young and desirable,' said Andre when Nigel had just walked in completing his stride of pride.

'How was it? Was it the same girl in a black dress that you were chatting with?' asked Lydia.

Nigel nodded, 'The sex was okay. She was nothing like Hannah though. On a scale of one to ten, I would rate the experience a six.'

'You need to get over Hannah now...FUCK! FUCK FUCK FUCK! Oh my God, look at that...it's Harvey!' screamed Lydia.

'Who?' asked Nigel.

'Harvey from *Suits*. I am getting a picture, folks!' said Lydia as she dashed in his direction.

'Yeah, even Mike is there,' I said, pointing to the person standing ten feet away from Harvey.

'What are they doing at UTM at this time?' asked Sam.

'Probably shooting an early morning scene before the campus gets busy,' said Ryan.

'Makes sense. Maybe UTM buildings were apt for the kind of locations they were looking for. Let us go take pictures with them. We are not going to get this great an opportunity again,' said Sam.

'I had no idea *Suits* was shot in Canada. I always thought that was New York,' said Nigel.

'It is shot in downtown Toronto. Just a few blocks from our campus,' I said.

We walked up to Mike, since Lydia was already chatting and taking selfies with Harvey. She was obsessed with everything about Harvey from his sharp jawline to his hairstyle.

Ryan addressed Mike with his real name. 'Mr Adams, we love your work in *Suits*. Could we all have a picture with you?'

'Sure!' said Patrick Adams (who plays Mike Ross on *Suits*).

Nigel whispered, 'I don't care about having a picture with this guy. Let me click it while you all can pose comfortably.'

'So do all of you go to school here?' asked Patrick Adams after Nigel took the picture. It wasn't every day that a celebrity took interest in our lives.

'Yes, but the downtown campus,' said Ryan.

'What are you studying?' asked Patrick Adams.

'I am doing a double major in sociology and criminology. My goal is to get into a good law school like Harvard or Yale,' said Ryan.

'Wow! That is great. I hope *Suits* didn't inspire you to become a lawyer, because trust me, what you see on our show is very far from reality. A lawyer's life isn't as thrilling as that,' said Mike with a semblance of congeniality. Lydia came running towards Mike for a selfie. She had had her fan moment with Harvey.

'Thank you so much for the picture. Best of luck for your shoot,' Lydia thanked Mike.

'Thank you,' replied Mike.

'Low-key, if you don't mind me asking you this - Are the rumors between Meghan Markle and Prince Harry true? I have read about it, but I don't know what to believe,' said Lydia.

Mike answered, 'I can neither confirm nor deny any details of her private life without her consent. However, the honorable gentleman in question does have a flamboyant past. Now, you would have to excuse me. I have to get back to work.' Mike had answered Lydia's question without actually answering it. Maybe playing a lawyer on screen had made him adept at the craft of diplomacy. He seemed to have perfected the art of lawyering people.

Until today, I don't know whether Mike had to instantly get back to work or if Lydia's question made him flee the spot. Regardless, I knew I would cherish this moment for a long time and was very eager to share this news with my family. On the way back home in the shuttle bus, I indulged in the pan-fried noodles that my friends had bought from Mandarin while visualizing my next meeting with Daria Apelsinova.

Summer 2k16

We had completed our third year at university. It was summer 2016, and I decided to stay back for the summer in Toronto again but this time for summer school. I wanted to take one credit over the summer so that I could reduce my course load over the next year. I knew that my final year would be very intense and challenging, because I would have to juggle between my course work and applications for graduate school. Therefore, summer school would help reduce the stress. After studying at the top institution in Canada, the goal was to get into the top graduate school in the UK. Just like me, Sam was not going back to India for the summer vacations. He had only taken three credits during the year instead of five, so he was lagging in terms of credits. His approach of taking minimum credits was helping him because his GPA shot up considerably, but at the same time, taking summer courses to make up credits was expensive when you are living in a city like Toronto. The only silver lining in this situation was that the minimum lease at Parkside was for twelve months instead of eight months like other residences, so we didn't have to bother about shifting accommodations over the summer.

I had been seeing Daria on a weekly basis ever since we met at the UTM pub last semester. The sex was great, and it was fun to wantonly seduce her. It helped me study better too, breaking the monotony of lectures and readings. In order to spice up things and explore our sexuality further, I proposed that both of us visit a water themed adult playground called Oasis Aqualounge in downtown Toronto. Oasis was located just beside Parkside. It had a large gated fence to obstruct the view from the school on the opposite side of the street. A string of visiting couples as well as single men and women always spiked my curiosity. I had never experienced an adult playground before. I wanted to experience what it would be like to play with all the leather gear and equipment in a sex dungeon. Could I actually have sex in their heated swimming pool while other people were present in it? How do people enjoy the pain in something as painful as BDSM? Fortunately for me, Daria was quick to jump on the bandwagon, as the idea resonated well with her. She had never been to a sex club before and thought it would be a good experience that would help her dismantle the shame that comes with nudity in public.

We visited Oasis Aqualounge on a Monday afternoon, because they had student discounts every Monday. After buying the couple's pass at the entrance, Daria and I entered the clothing optional club. The Oasis Aqualounge was a beautifully restored 19th century house with no hint of frippery and had three floors and a basement. The first space that we found ourselves in when we entered was the bar area that was playing loud music while nude men and women sipped fancy cocktails. I was astounded by how comfortable people could be with nudity in public spaces. Nobody seemed like they cared about being watched. I held Daria's hand, and we went to check out the poolside patio. There were around ten people in the pool. Some of them were enjoying the warm water whereas one couple was kissing. I overheard a patron telling her friend that the management took strong measures to ensure that the pool always remained disinfected. Contrary to what I had imagined, Oasis Aqualounge was very clean and hygienic even after being a sex club. After viewing the pool, we went upstairs to the locker room to secure our belongings and get undressed. Daria and I were now only wearing the complimentary towels we had been given at the entrance to cover our genitals. Standing in towels, we discussed where to begin. Suddenly, we could hear someone being spanked loudly, which was accompanied by the painful cries of a woman. For a moment, I forgot we were in a sex club and thought that a poor lady was in distress. We followed the sound to be led into the sex dungeon which was on the same floor as the locker room.

Upon entering the sex dungeon with our towels clad to our bodies, I saw a young White girl tied to a cross. The BDSM cross was in the shape of an X. Her hands were chained to the cross while her limbs were spread open and tied too. She was facing forward while a man, who was very large and obese and much older than her, was playing the dominant. He had a sex flogger in his hand, and he was whipping her boobs with it while she cried in pain. He whipped her several times on both her boobs as she endured the pain. They seemed like regulars because she wanted him to continue the flogging. I must admit that seeing her being flogged so hard was nerve-wracking for me. I scanned the room to see two bondage couches, a small massage table, a restrain kit, and other sex paraphernalia hanging from the hooks on the wall. The black leathern furniture set a particular atmosphere to the dimly lit dungeon. Other than the furniture, there were some nude and semi-nude male bystanders who were watching the White couple. I could see one of them reach out for his dick as the fat man began to eat his girl's pussy while she was tied to the cross.

I turned towards Daria and said, 'I want to fuck you right here, right now...but in the ass.'

'Have you ever had anal sex before?' she asked.

'No, never, but I want to try,' I replied.

'I have had it once with my ex-boyfriend in Moscow. It is painful,' she said.

'But we have come to experiment, haven't we?'

'Fine. Let us give it a try, but please use lube,' she said. The next task was to pick furniture that was ergonomically sound for anal sex and gave me the freedom to handcuff Daria. I chose the small massage table that was located around eight feet from the cross and looked ideal for anal sex. I opened my towel and placed it on the table and then asked her to lie down on it with her back facing the ceiling. She opened her towel and took the submissive position. Then I cuffed both her hands as she stood bending forward on the table. I went to the storage box of equipment and brought a spanking paddle with me. Since it was my first time in a dungeon, I didn't want to try the floggers or the cane because they seemed like they belonged in the hands of more experienced swingers. Our efforts for targeted pleasure garnered the attention of the crowd, and by now, I could see a lot of heads turn in our direction. A new show awaited them. I felt conscious about my nakedness at first when so many people were staring at us, but then I managed to overcome that feeling by telling myself, 'This is what I have come here for. This is a judgement-free and safe environment meant to stifle the stigma that accompanies consensual sexual activity.'

I caressed her right butt cheek with my left hand. Then I removed my hand so that she doesn't feel my touch. Waiting for me to do something, she tried to look back, but the cuffs prevented her from turning around. It is then when I spanked her right butt cheek with the paddle that looked like a thin table tennis bat. She shrieked in pain. Next, I spanked her left butt with that paddle. I kept on alternating between her right and left butt cheeks for five minutes. By now, I had spanked her around forty times. Her ass was crimson red. Red seemed to be rightly known as the color of passion and love. I whispered in her ear to say the following words loudly the next time I spanked her, 'I am your slut, sir.' I spanked her hard with my bare hands, and she repeated those words like a parrot. Spanking a girl in front of a live audience and being called sir gave me a kink. Spanking was one of my sexual predilections, and I was enraptured by the sight of her red ass. I told Daria that I would be increasing the intensity of the spanks.

She replied 'Yes, sir' in a submissive tone.

The next few spanks with the spanking paddle were very severe. I was surprised that she was stoic enough to bear it. After another minute, she told me that the spanks were hurting her, so I was impelled to lower the intensity of the motion. I went behind her and was fully erect by now. I kept her in suspense while I put durex on my medium length. She was slightly nervous. Without any warning, I entered her from behind. She cried out in surprise. I pulled my dick out and then put a generous amount of lube in her butt hole and slowly rubbed it with my fingers. Once her butt hole and crack were well lubricated, I spread her cheeks and slid my throbbing cock inside her. I grabbed her by her hair, disheveling it, and went as deep inside her anus as I could. Keeping my dick inside her and holding on to her hair, I started fucking her with my full vigor. My dick was inside her while I made small back and forth motions. She winced in pain. This was the first time I was fucking a girl in the ass, and I felt much tighter sensations than what I had felt while having vaginal sex. After a while, her pain subsided, and she started moaning out of pleasure. As soon as I felt that she was enjoying the sex, I decided to take the head of my dick out of her ass rim. In order to tease her, I was sliding my dick on her butt crack.

'Don't stop, please fuck me, sir,' she begged, maintaining the submissive role.

I slowed down the thrust, and now I was inserting my gentleman sausage inside her ass and then taking it out completely. I was enjoying every single thrust while she craved that I go harder. I was enjoying being in control. After ten minutes of fucking her, I stopped and untied her cuffs. She sat on the floor, naked and tired, slightly sweating from the forehead. I sat on the massage table with my legs hanging towards her. The crowd intensely looked on to see what we would do next.

I turned around and asked the bystanders, 'Wasn't she great?'

Some of the men shifted their gaze out of awkwardness as if they weren't watching. One of them replied 'Yes, she was' and laughed back at me.

I turned towards Daria and asked her to massage my foot. I was experiencing a spasm in my foot due to the contraction of muscles during sex. She put a towel over her shoulders and started massaging my foot. I sat back and enjoyed the unprofessional foot massage. After getting my foot massaged and recuperating the lost energy from all the spanking and anal sex, I suggested that we go up to the play area where only couples or women were allowed, and solo men were restricted. However, I wanted to lead her there with a leash. So I took a leash off the hook and tied it around her neck.

'I want you to be my sex slave. Follow me,' I said as I held her by the leash.

'Yes, sir.'

We went upstairs and entered the play area. One of the rooms had two huge mattresses built on a raised platform. One of the mattresses was occupied by a couple who were getting it on doggy style. So I held the leash and took Daria to the other mattress.

'Now it is my turn to please you,' I said, undoing her leash.

I inserted two fingers inside the pink puffy vagina and her glistening flesh parted, making way for my fingers. I kept stroking her with my fingers, tracing short trails back and forth. The incessant fingering stiffened her clit, and the clit pushed out between her labia. By now her pussy was wet and swollen. I took my fingers out and went down on her with my tongue, stimulating her clit. Until now, I had only received oral sex from girls. This was the first time I was giving oral sex and that too without a dental dam. She squealed as I did circular and sideways motions with my tongue and pressed my face against her pussy, thereby stimulating her clit further with my nose. The squeals became long gasps of 'Aaah...aah...aaaah' as her vagina and ass clenched with joy. She writhed and pressed herself down against me. After working on her pussy for some time, she came hard spasming as waves of pleasure seized her entire torso while her moan could probably be heard in the hallway outside. I almost gagged at the amount of cum flowing from her. I grabbed both her luscious creamy orbs and pressed them while our teeth clacked against each other as I laid claim to her mouth.

'Now, I am going to fuck you and then come inside your mouth,' I whispered coquettishly.

I wore a new condom and removed the used one that was still stuck on my erect dick. I took some of the complimentary lube available and applied copious amount of it around the entrance of her sex. Then I rammed my dick into her swollen cunt. My man meat was inside her wet cavern, and I was stroking her hard. I traced my fingers along her décolletage as her nipples stiffened at the tip. She lifted her right boob to her lips and nipped the tip of her ovoid, flirting with me through her lashes. I wanted to change positions and asked her to come on top. The cowgirl is my favorite sex position. Every inch of me was invigorated as she moved her hips up and down and caught on to my rhythm. I continued to slam my cock inside her, and the sound of flesh banging against flesh filled the room. She bit her bottom lip as she was riding my cock. Amplified pleasure swelled within me. I knew I would cum soon, so I asked her to suck my dick. She got off and used one of her hands to play with my balls while the other hand seized my cock at its base, preparing it for a good suck. In order to tease me, she licked up my shaft, tracing a bulging vein and smiled naughtily at me. The vein was beating fiercely. 'Suck it, Daria, before I cum.' She thrust my dick against her tonsils and purred throatily. I closed my eyes as I enjoyed the warm feeling around my dick and finished with my load inside her mouth. I made sure she swallowed every drop of it.

After making her swallow my load, I suggested that we buy some cocktails and chill in the jacuzzi. The jacuzzi was located on the ground floor next to the shower and sauna rooms. Luckily, it wasn't very crowded, so we found a comfortable spot. After an intense session of sex, the jacuzzi was a sweet paradise. We had a great laugh while I kept cracking dirty jokes in between. We sipped on our cocktails, made out, and kept a playful vibe. The upscale interiors of the sex club and the warm ass of my Russian blonde against my crotch made me feel like a hedonist. As Mondays were student days at the Oasis, there were a lot of millennials around us. While some of them seemed to be immersed in this libertine culture, others were slowly treading this lascivious terrain. I felt blessed to have been introduced to the world of pick-up artists at the right time. If it wasn't for *The Game* and the subculture of pick-up artists, I would have never scored a beautiful chick like Daria. I would probably be one of the many voyeurs in this playground who were titillated when they watched other people have sex.

'Babe, I want you to make me scream in the pool,' said Daria after we had spent an hour in the jacuzzi.

'The pool is so crowded, babe. Aren't we better off in the jacuzzi here? I am allowed to fuck you here too,' I said.

'I know, but I want you to finger me in front of the whole crowd. I have never done anything sexual in a swimming pool. I have thrown all my inhibitions outside the window. This is something I will remember for a long time,' she said.

'Okay. Let me finish my drink first,' I replied and kissed her on the lips. She wrapped her hands around my neck and started making out with me. I could taste her flavor in my mouth.

'Devansh, I have never told you this, but I have a twin sister,' she said, breaking the kiss.

'Really? Do you girls have the same sexual appetite too?'

'Stop it.'

'I am just curious *laughing*. What does she do?' I asked.

'She is studying arts at the University of British Columbia in Vancouver.'

'Are you identical twins?'

'Yes,' she said. I wondered what it would be like to have a threesome with twins. I wish I could make that proposal to Daria, but I didn't want to bite that bullet and vitiate the sexual chemistry we had created.

'Well, let's take this twin swimming,' I said as we exited the jacuzzi to go towards the pool patio.

We paced across the patio to get inside the swimming pool because the cool breeze against our naked wet skin made us feel cold. I felt relieved as I entered the warm waters of the pool. Being naked around naked people inside a pool was a new experience. Daria wrapped her hands and legs around me to show her affection and stay afloat. She seemed so light because of the buoyancy of the water. If we were outside the pool, I wouldn't be able to lift her above the ground and finger her at the same time. The pool was filled with students and young adults unwinding, discussing politics, playing catch, or making out.

'I am going to finger you so hard that everybody will stop what they are doing to look at you moan,' I said.

'Bring it on, baby,' she whispered in my ear. I slid my middle finger inside her pussy and went wild with the fingering. She moaned like she has never moaned before with me. Every single eyeball in the vicinity gaped at our sexual fecundity. Few boys in the crowd cheered us on, as they were enjoying the show. I wanted to hit her G spot now. So I went two inches inside her vagina and curved my fingers around her pubic bone. I was now accessing her clitoris internally, and she screamed her lungs out. Once I was finished fingering her, we headed to the locker room to change into our clothes. Oasis Aqualounge will be clearly etched in our memories for a long time.

Location: Cabana Pool Bar

Date: 1st July 2016

Canada Day is officially a federal statutory holiday in Canada, because it celebrates the anniversary of the Constitution Act that came into effect on 1st July 1867. Canada came into existence on that day, and that is why it was an official government holiday. For us, it was a cause for celebration because it meant no lectures. None of us really cared about the significance of the Act or which colonies came together to form Canada on that day. In 2016, 1st July was a Friday, and that meant we could kick off our weekend early. The weather was predicted to be moderately hot, and everyone was looking forward to a bright sunny weekend. A bright sunny day screamed an outdoor party, preferably at a poolside bar. That is how we zeroed in on Cabana Pool Bar and booked our tickets in advance. Girls could enter for free before 3:00 pm, so we thought of reaching there by 2:00 pm to queue up for the Canada Day party. I had purchased red denims from H&M especially for this day and used one of my white Hollister t-shirts to delve into the theme.

We arrived at the Cabana Pool bar to join a massive line of people eager to enter the premises that was located on the Toronto waterfront. The red and white colors of the Canadian flag were aptly reflected in the attire of the revelers who had descended down to the waterfront area to party. The Cabana Pool Bar was one of the premier properties of the entertainment bourgeois Ink Entertainment, which was owned by a man called Charles. Lydia and Sonia entered the property for free whereas Nigel, Sam, Manny, Ryan, Andre, and I had to get the bar codes on our tickets scanned in order to enter. The Cabana Pool Bar encompassed a huge area that had white umbrellas and tables, chaise loungers, and pure white cabanas. There were red party balloons all over the venue to match the aesthetics for the occasion. Even the cocktail waitresses were directed to wear red and white to show their solidarity with the theme of the party. In fitting with the indulgent theme, Cabana had a myriad menu of frozen cocktails, popular wines and beer as well as a catered menu from Canada's leading hospitality company Oliver and Bonacini. We ordered a number of dishes on the menu which ran the gamut from chicken wings to supreme fries to gourmet burgers. The best item on the menu was the freshly cut fries with parmesan and truffle oil. Hot models were frolicking in the water, but we were strapped to our cabanas mainlining the fries because they were so deliciously good.

The Cabana Pool Bar was high on energy and had a very cool vibe. The venue played the latest hit songs of the year. Majority of the crowd was in the age range of 20-30. The Canada Day event was completely sold off, and there were an estimated two thousand people at the venue. The view from the waterfront was breathtaking. Lydia wanted a photograph against the backdrop of the city's skyline and asked me to be in the picture with her. We asked a stranger to take our picture, and he readily obliged in his Arab accent.

'I want to seize these moments forever. I just realized that this time next year nothing will be the same,' said Lydia, looking at the yachts in the water.

'What do you mean?' I asked flustered. She held me by the elbow.

'What I mean is that all of us will be in different parts of the world. All the fun that we have when we are together will come to an end. You know, the parties, all this drinking and eating and going to new places. This is probably the last summer where we all are together. By next year June, all of us would have graduated. You are planning to go to graduate school in the UK. Sonia and Ryan are applying for law school. Manny will be going to LA to pursue his career as an actor. I feel my whole life would experience some kind of a paradigm shift. No matter how expensive and greasy campus food is, I can still digest it with all of you around me. I don't want to take these moments for granted anymore. Even if I make new friends, it won't be like this.... It will never be the same,' asserted Lydia.

I didn't know what to tell her. It dawned on me for the first time that this beautiful journey would end soon. It was 1st July today, and we would have graduated by this time next year. I avoided looking at her because I was feeling emotional too. I knew what she said was correct. Most of us had graduate school or a new country to look forward to. But she was staring at the monotonous office routine of nine to five.

'We are fortunate to live in the era of uber-fast technology. All of us will still be just a Skype call or a text message away. It won't be the same as meeting or chilling every day, but adulting is a necessary evil. I wish we could all work our way around it, but...let's cross that bridge when we get there. They must be expecting us in the pool now. Let us go change into our swimming costumes,' I said in an effort to console her.

Lydia and Sonia were looking stunning in their bikinis. They were giving all the other girls a run for their money. We played a game where Sonia and Lydia were respectively sitting on the shoulders of Nigel and Manny, and they had to unbalance one another by pushing their rival into the water. Although it looked like all the work had to be done by the girls, Nigel and Manny were the ones doing the heavy lifting here. They had to balance the girl who was sitting on their shoulders and also carry her weight until she succeeded in pushing off her rival in the pool. I offered to be the referee to ensure nobody used any unfair means. Once we were done with the fun and games, we changed into our clothes and entered the club that was attached to the Cabana Pool Bar and owned by the same company that owned Cabana. This venue called Rebel was part of the same complex and people who had bought tickets for Cabana could enter Rebel without any additional fee.

The Rebel was a mega entertainment complex which boasted of 45,000 square feet of space and claimed to be the largest nightclub in Toronto. Rebel had installed the most advanced LED technology in the world to create a visually striking platform for the revelers and headliners that visit the establishment. The theatrical lighting and the unparalleled video production transported us to a marvelous, multi-dimensional universe that matured throughout the night. We headed upstairs to a room called the Purple Room to buy some drinks. Manny and Nigel were getting hammered tonight as they purchased one drink after another. Ryan advised them to slow down on the alcohol consumption since it was only 11:00 pm, but his advice fell on deaf ears. We were all dancing in a circle when a brown-skinned man approached Sonia for a dance. She politely refused by telling him she had a boyfriend. He left us and returned after ten minutes with two of his friends. They were standing behind Sonia and looked as if they were talking about her. Another guy from that group got behind Sonia and grabbed her by the waist. He was about to grind her when she turned around and pushed him away.

'Put your hands away. I am not going to dance with you,' she snapped out irascibly.

'Come on. It is just a dance,' he said and grabbed her hands. Manny got furious on seeing this and slapped the guy in the face.

'Stay away, you cunt. She said no,' said Manny. By now, the Brown guy who had approached Sonia earlier came to the rescue of his friend and punched Manny on his face. Considering Manny's huge size and muscular brawn, it was not a good idea to mess with him, but the male ego supersedes rational thinking. After seeing Manny being smote on the face, Nigel punched the Brown guy several times, and they got into a terrible scuffle. Manny recuperated from the punch and joined Nigel in beating up the guy. Sensing the gravity of the situation, Andre, Ryan, and I went to disengage the conflict and separate the three of them. Sam had taken Sonia and Lydia away from the location of the brawl so that they don't get harmed by any of the men. By now, the guy who had misbehaved with Sonia and was punched by Manny came back with a beer bottle that had deliberately been broken to make it work like a scimitar. Engaging in a fist fight is one thing and handling an assailant with a dangerous weapon like a broken bottle is another task. Fortunately, he was stopped in time by the bouncers. Another bouncer had pinned Nigel to the ground while we separated Manny and the guy he was in tussles with. Needless to say, we were all asked to leave the premises, and the guy with broken bottle was kept in custody until the police arrived. After being thrown out of the club, we hailed two cabs and went home to Parkside. Nobody spoke a word in the cab that I was in until we reached Parkside.

Location: Parkside Cafeteria

We were the only ones sitting in the empty cafeteria discussing the incident that had just transpired inside the club. University life isn't complete unless you get into a brawl at a club or a bar. We had witnessed several brawls before, and the root cause of it always involved a woman. Today, we were at the epicentre of a nightclub brawl that had no rules. From headbutts to a kick in the groin or an attack with a weapon like a broken beer bottle was all fair game.

'No wonder Brown men have such a nasty reputation in the West. Sometimes, I actually feel ashamed of the color of my skin. How hard is it to understand that no means no?' raged Sam. This was the Indian Samridh Lakhanpal speaking and not the Canadian Sam.

Ryan said, 'Yeah, but I told Nigel and Manny not to drink so much. Manny shouldn't have punched that asshole no matter what. We have dealt with creeps before too, but fighting is not a solution unless you are physically assaulted. If the bouncer didn't stop that guy with the broken bottle, this could have gone down fatally.'

'I am sorry about my alcohol-induced behavior. I should have known better. When the guy grabbed Sonia's hand after she said no...that was the last straw for me,' said Manny.

'I think we should all go to bed and discuss this tomorrow. It has been an eventful day,' said Sonia as she rose to leave.

'Well, I am going to bounce as well. Good night, guys,' said Lydia as she followed Sonia out of the cafeteria. I assumed they had some girl talk to do.

'These Brown fucks literally took the piss. Fuck them,' sniggered Nigel after the girls had left for their rooms.

'You are right. They actually did take the piss, and now I am going to make the whole of Parkside drink my piss tomorrow. You see the ketchup dispenser there? I am going to take a leak inside it. Let everyone drink my concoction of ketchup and urine with alcohol tomorrow,' said Manny as he walked towards the large ketchup dispenser that was placed on a counter between the serving stations and the dining area. The Parkside cafeteria had two large dispensers for ketchup and mustard sauce that students used to garnish their food.

'Don't be silly, we all use ketchup,' said Andre.

I tried my best to refrain Manny, 'Stop being a dick, dude.'

To our surprise, Nigel joined Manny in his uncouth adventure. 'Manny, while you piss in the ketchup dispenser, I am going to masturbate in the mustard dispenser. Let all residents of Parkside taste a specimen of my cum. Listen guys, I am officially creating a new kind of sauce that will go by the name of lite Mayo-mustard. I am sure no one can tell the difference between lite mayo and cum unless they taste it,' laughed Nigel. I thought Nigel was joking until he picked up the mustard dispenser and took it to a corner. Then, with his back towards us, we heard his fly go down. From where I was sitting, I could actually see his hands move in a way as if he was stroking his dick.

'Are you guys for real? What the fuck do you think you guys are doing?' screamed Ryan. I had never seen Ryan raise his voice so much.

'Peeing inside a shitload of ketchup,' replied Manny.

Ryan looked at Sam, 'Dude, aren't you going to say anything?' he asked.

'Like always, I only have one word for this - unbelievable. But I have an awesome idea where Parkside and all its residents actually feel the heat of this. There should be an anonymous mass dispersion of this information, and then we sit back and enjoy the stir that will follow,' said Sam.

'How will we do this?' asked Manny coming back to the table after he emptied his bladder. Nigel was still engaged in the act of masturbation. I wondered if I would ever be able to eat ketchup or mustard at Parkside again even after they have changed these containers. The thought of sperm-infused mustard and urinated ketchup disturbed my mind.

Sam continued, 'Tomorrow, once everyone is done with their breakfast and lunch and a significant proportion of ketchup and mustard has been consumed, we submit a post on UofT confession page and tell everyone about what these guys did without naming them. By submitting a post to UofT confession page, our identities would never be revealed.' Confession pages are pages on social networking websites that allow students to express their feelings, thoughts, deeds, or problems anonymously, as the posts are directed to the administrator who then posts it by using a general handle.

'Son of a bitch. You are way smarter than I thought you were,' said Manny giving Sam a high-five.

'And you are way more drunk than I thought you were,' said Andre.

Breakfast started late on the weekends compared to weekdays. There was a standard breakfast of eggs, omelette, bacon strips, hash brown, and potatoes. Most of the people took ketchup with their hash browns and potatoes. Some even liked their omelettes with tomato sauce. Every time someone used the ketchup dispenser, we smirked silently at each other. Sonia and Lydia pressed us hard to tell them why we were exchanging glances among ourselves, but nobody told them anything. We only warmed them against using the ketchup and mustard. Coincidentally, the lunch menu on that day included veg and non-veg hot dogs. It is human tendency to put ketchup and mustard on hotdogs because no one likes a sausage dry. Manny and Nigel had just hit the jackpot. They couldn't wait for lunch to get over and break the news on the internet. A lot of people who skipped eating any of those sauces for breakfast fell prey at lunch with their hot dogs. Now, it was the right time to send the post to UofT confession page. The post created by Manny read as follows:

Friday night, when my friends and I got back to the Parkside residence drunk as fuck, we thought it would be funny for one of us to urinate in the ketchup dispenser and the other to jerk off in the mustard dispenser. For all those who enjoyed the ketchup and mustard with their hotdogs for lunch or with their food for breakfast, you can thank us in this post, and if you didn't like what you ate, we are sorry that are actions were in bad taste ☺☺.

Needless to say, the post spread like forest fire throughout all UofT residences. The management of Parkside was notified and took cognizance of the whole incident. When we went downstairs for dinner, we could see the management installing CCTV cameras in the cafeteria. All residents received an email saying that the management is probing into the incident, and the sauce dispensers had been changed. They even assured all residents that dispensers would not be accessible outside eating hours, and if any resident had any information about the culprits, they could come down to the office and report it. I could sense the frustration among the residents. A lot of people didn't feel like coming down for dinner. I talked to some of the residents by claiming to sympathize with the people who had eaten the impure sauces, only to learn how much anger and spite they had towards the people responsible for such distasteful behavior. I listened with concealed rapture without letting my true emotions betray me.

Location: John M. Kelly Library

August 2016, before the summer school exams.

The final-exam season for summer school was around the corner. So all of us except Manny were huddled up around a huge table with our lecture notes and books inside the Kelly Library near the Kelly Café. It was ironic because Kelly Library was the main library at St. Michael's college, which was Manny's college before he decided to drop out of UofT. As UofT students, we were eligible to use any of the forty-four libraries on campus, and this time we chose Kelly Library to experience a change of environment. The Kelly Library's collection mostly comprised of books in the disciplines of humanities and social sciences with a specialization in history, media studies, philosophy, Celtic history, Canadian history, Medieval history, and English literature. The theological collection was made up of a gamut of sub-disciplines like patristics, early and medieval church history, Thomism, liturgical renewal, and Catholic missions. There was a large suite of public computers for the patrons.

It was spacious, well organized, and well maintained by the staff. I respected the cleanliness and organizational skills of the staff at UofT even more when I was pursuing my master's at the London School of Economics, because LSE had only one library and that too was infested with rats.

'Dude, check this out. Bitcoin has touched 600$. Now is the time to sell it, Sam,' I said when we interrupted our study session for a coffee break.

'How much did you guys buy it at?' asked Nigel.

'12$,' I replied.

'Holy fuck! You guys are already getting a return of 5,000%. That is fucking insane. I should have listened to you guys when you told us about it in freshman year,' said Andre.

'Bitcoin is created on blockchain technology, and blockchain is the technology of the future. It is here to stay, and fortunately, Canada is one of the pioneering nations in the use of blockchain technology. A major cryptocurrency called Ethereum has two Canadians as its founding members,' I elaborated on the subject.

'You Indians are geniuses in either finance or IT. I will come to you guys when I draw my financial plan after college,' said Ryan with zany energy.

'And, surprisingly, cryptocurrencies require knowledge of both finance and technology. Actually, fintech is one of the fastest growing areas for venture capitalists,' I said, demonstrating my acute knowledge about the latest trends of the markets.

'Yeah, but don't book your profits now,' said Sam, using financial lingo which meant don't sell your Bitcoins now. 'Trust me and hold onto to your investments. This is just the beginning of growth. Bitcoin has not even begun to boom.'

'Why do you say that?' I asked, disheartened by his response. Sam had bought 500 Bitcoins when they were selling for 12$. At 600$ a Bitcoin, his investments were worth 300,000$. To put that money into perspective, he could easily fund his entire undergraduate tuition fees and living expenses in Canada as an international student for four years. Or buy a one-bedroom apartment in midtown Toronto. I couldn't believe my ears when he refused to sell at such a high profit margin.

Sam replied, 'I am saying this because I have been studying the crypto market ever since I decided to invest in Bitcoin. One of the famous quotes of Peter Lynch is "Know what you own and know why you own it". I know Bitcoin inside out, and I own them because I am in the game for long. A good investor does not let his emotions dictate his decisions. Don't sell your cattle to the highest bidder. Instead, invest in them so that one day you can own your own dairy farm.'

'But where else will you get returns of 5,000%? In the stock market, a 10-12% return is considered great. You are never going to get returns of 5,000% anywhere else. Something that you bought for 12$ is priced at 600$ and you want to risk holding it. People are going to speculate, and Bitcoin prices might crash anytime. I think you are getting greedy now,' I pursed my lips in disagreement.

Sam said, 'What if I told you 5,000% is just peanuts? I know it sounds like an incredible return, something that is unheard of in the world of investments. But trust me on this one. Bitcoin is a game changer. Its price is going to go through the roof. It has not even reached half of its potential. The big bulls haven't entered the market yet, and it hasn't caught the attention of the world now. Once money starts pouring in, it is going to be the star investment of this decade.'

'I think you are an idiot for not selling at this point. I am selling all my investments in Bitcoin. It's going to be enough to make up for the extra money I had to spend on summer school and create a small financial pool for graduate school in the UK,' I said.

'I guess time is the best teacher. Only time will tell who is right and who is wrong,' said Sam in a calm tone. He didn't get agitated at being called an idiot or tried to justify his decision. He always knew how to compose himself and stay relaxed. I could see him make his familiar I-know-it-all face. He seemed so cocksure about his research on Bitcoins that my confidence began to waiver. But I decided to play it by the book and sell all the Bitcoins in my account. Anyone with decent knowledge about how the markets work would agree with me that it was not a wrong decision to sell my investment in Bitcoins when I am getting returns of 5,000%.

Sonia brought up her favorite topic of politics, sensing an interminable debate, 'Time is not only the best teacher, it is also the best healer. For instance, look at the American presidential elections. If Americans end up choosing Trump as their president, their country would take a lot of time to recover from all the damage he would have caused.'

'As a matter of fact, if you consider the options Americans have, Trump would be the better man for the job. I don't really think Hillary should be the president after all the things she and her husband have done. For instance, she deleted and acid washed thousands of emails that she accessed from a private server in violation of a congressional subpoena. As First Lady, she defended her husband Bill Clinton when he accused Monika Lewinsky of lying about having sex with him. As secretary of state, she signed one of the worst nuclear deals with Iran which has made Israel and the world more susceptible than ever,' I replied in Donald Trump's defense.

'Devansh, you want Trump to be the next president? He is racist, xenophobic and disrespects women. How can someone call for banning a whole religion from the United States?' said Sonia. Being a Muslim, she felt targeted and threatened by his comments.

'His statements have been misrepresented and misunderstood. If you hear what he said, he called for banning Muslims from seven Islamic nations until better screening mechanisms are developed in those countries. And he is the only candidate who is self-funded. Corporate lobbies have been known to exercise complete control on former presidents in return for funding them. No wonder America is in nineteen trillion dollars of debt. Hillary is entirely funded by the corporates and would end up working for the 1% like former presidents have. This would further increase inequality in America,' I said.

'I don't support Trump, but I hate the guts of that bitch even more. Trump is right about her. She is crooked as fuck and deserves to be locked up because what she did with those emails is a crime,' said Lydia giving her opinion on the American election, even though she knew zilch about politics in general. She was more of the type to consume her news from unverified sources on WhatsApp and Twitter.

'Let us go up to the quiet zone. It is getting too crowded in here. It is going to be difficult to focus in this hubbub,' said Nigel.

'I agree,' said Ryan.

'I will join you guys in half an hour. I am on the last page of my essay,' I said as the others started packing their notes and books. Once they left for the quiet zone upstairs, I diligently started penning down the conclusion of my essay. In the process, I happened to drop my pen on the floor and reached below my table to pick it up. The pen was still out of my reach, so I got down from my chair and knelt on the floor so that it would come within my grasp. What I saw next froze my nuts. Right below the centre of the table, lying on the floor was a key. It was no ordinary key. It was the same key that had surfaced in the video where an Episkopon member had allegedly had sex with Professor Keatinge, and the key made headlines on her bedside table. The reason I knew that it was the same key from the video was because every Episkopon member has a unique number inscribed on his or her key. The digits matched, and the design was identical. The keys of Episkopon members are not designed like standard keys. They have large bows in the shape of a ring to allow members to wear them around their necks. I was scared as I held on to the key. Different questions and thoughts sprang to my mind. What was this key doing under the table at a library of St. Michael's College? Then it struck me that only students who go to Trinity can join Episkopon. Holy fuck! Does this key belong to one of my friends who was just studying here? Lydia, Sonia, and Nigel went to University College, so that eliminated suspicion from them. That left Sam, Andre, and Ryan, as all three of them went to Trinity. This put me in a dilemma because I couldn't share this information with any of them now. I couldn't fathom how an Episkopon member had been among us all this while without giving away his identity. Moreover, this guy was responsible for the scandal that had rocked the whole university. I started perspiring excessively and felt rigid and dry like a pair of shoes that have become so stiff that it was impossible to force your feet inside them. What do I do now? Is there a way to trace the owner of this key so that his identity remains concealed? I couldn't risk putting him in any trouble. Do I just throw the key away and pretend that I know nothing about it and carry on with my life? But, at the same time, I couldn't rest peacefully without finding out which friend of mine was part of this elite secret society. So I hatched a plan and prayed for it to work.

I decided that I would take a picture of the lower portion of the key so that the identification number on the key is not revealed. Then I would send the picture on our WhatsApp group with a casual message saying that if anyone happened to drop their key, they could let me know; otherwise, I would be submitting it at the front desk of the library as a lost item. I had a strong hunch that the owner of the key would respond immediately on seeing this message and take the necessary steps to retrieve the key in the fear that I would submit it to the staff at the Kelly Library. That key was infamous all over Toronto, if not Canada, as a lot of news channels had picked up on the trending video that had created a ruckus because of the unethical practices of professors at institutions of higher studies. I am sure the owner of the renowned key would value it too much to lose it as well as jeopardize losing the respect that he must have earned at Episkopon after the incident. So I crafted the following message and put it on our WhatsApp group with the picture of the lower portion of the key:

Hey guys, I found a key on the floor below the table where we were studying. If anyone of you happen to have lost or misplaced your key, let me know and I will bring it up with me. If not, then I am submitting it as a lost item to the front desk.

Now all I had to do was be patient and wait. But my heart began to start racing, and a feeling of nervousness gripped my stomach. Time seemed to come to a screeching halt like a fast-moving car on the highway. The sensation of frozen time arose as a byproduct of suspense, as I nervously looked at the screen of my iPhone. I could only hope that things would go the way I had planned. I fretted at the thought of Episkopon breathing down my neck. The feeling of anxiety made me check my phone every two minutes, hoping someone would reply in the affirmative. Only Lydia and Sonia had seen the message, and there was no reply from any of them. The first person to reply was Nigel who said that the key did not belong to him. The next person who replied was Ryan. Ryan kept his reply short and succinct: 'Not mine'. Sam and Andre were the only ones who hadn't read the message until now, and I was anxiously waiting for their reply. After the longest ten minutes of my life, I checked to see whether they had seen my message, and I saw that both of them had. Blood pounded in my ears, and my heart heavily thudded against my chest. Fifteen minutes had elapsed, and still, there was no reply from any of them. Neither Sam nor Andre had physically approached me to ask for the key either. I began to think that I was doubting my friends for no reason, as none of them would indulge in such a grotesque act. It was possible that someone had got a duplicate key made after the video of Episkopon went viral. So I got back to work on my essay and thought of keeping that key to show it to Manny when I met him. I would pretend to be the real owner of the key just to see if he would believe me, since I went to Trinity and was therefore eligible to join Episkopon.

As I was working on my essay, I felt a heavy pat on my shoulder which startled me. I turned around swiftly.

'I believe you found something that is mine. Could I have it back?'

'What the fuck! You snake! So all this while you were in Episk...' he hushed me up before I could complete my sentence.

'Dropping my key was a reckless mistake. But I need you to promise me something. You can never tell anyone what you know or saw. By anyone, I mean your closest friends or your family. I was planning to take this secret to my grave with me, but I cannot force you to take the same oath. However, I request that you don't utter a word about it until we all have graduated. It would not only jeopardize my education but also taint the secret society forever if my identity gets out and especially someone like me who slept with a professor and put the aftermath of the incident online...*pause*.... I did that only because it guaranteed that I would become the Scribe, which as you know is the leader of Episkopon,' he said. I could feel the blood drain from my face.

I gathered myself before I spoke, 'Don't worry. I am going to erase everything from my conscience. I am going to purge this key and your association with it from my memory. Every brain cell that remembers anything that transpired in the last fifteen minutes could be considered dead. Rest assured. In retrospect, I still cannot believe how innocently you reacted when we were discussing this for the first time when the news had broken out. You are a better actor than even Manny,' I said.

'Fuck! You have no idea how tensed I was. I will always owe you for this. If this key had gotten into the wrong hands and if the authorities had decided to check the CCTV cameras, there would be a massive fucking inquiry into all of us who go to Trinity. You are a true friend, Devansh. This mistake could not only scathe my reputation but also jolt my career path.'

'I don't remember what mistake you are talking about,' I said, returning him the key with a wink.

Year 4 Semester I

We had made it to the home stretch. It was our last year at university, and by now, I was well acquainted with UofT's cornucopia of magnificent resources, world-class faculty, and its diverse student body, which translated into an international network. Either I knew somebody or had a friend in every major country in the world ranging from the USA, China, South Korea, Australia, Spain, France, Kenya, Mexico, and even Azerbaijan. By fourth year, one knows the ins and outs of navigating university, and someone who still hasn't figured it out by now, probably never will. I was capable of curating a survival guide for UofT if a hot froshie had asked me to make one for her. By my final year, we had become accustomed to the smaller class sizes and were adept at the art of saving money on food, transportation, and partying. By the time one hacks university life, you realize that it was almost time to move out, because others were waiting to fill in your shoes.

Everyone except Sonia and Keanu had moved out of the Parkside student residence, because Parkside had made a steep increase in its accommodation price. Since Sonia and Keanu were sharing a studio, Parkside was still economical for them. The rest of us had shifted to another private accommodation called Tartu on Bloor Street which was a stone's throw away from campus. Lydia volunteered at the university mentorship program which was open to fourth year students who wanted to mentor a small group of incoming freshers. She had always been an average student, so initiatives like this were a good way of building her resume. Sam was elected as the treasurer of his fraternity. He had been dedicated to his fraternity for three long years and had gained the trust of all his brothers. Moreover, as an economics major with sound investments in Bitcoin, he had gained a credible status to look after the fraternity's finances. He would have unanimously been voted the president because of his popularity if he ran for that office, but he shrugged off that responsibility due to his academic commitments.

Location: University of Toronto, Varsity Stadium

The stage was set for the big game. It was the week before Thanksgiving, and UofT was playing an intercollegiate football game against the University of Waterloo. The winner of this game would be competing against Laurier University in the finals. Manny, Ryan, Sam, Andre, and I joined the assemblage of around 5,000 students who had come together to watch this high-stake game at the Varsity Centre in UofT. Nigel was in the UofT football team, which was known as the Toronto Varsity Blues. We had come here to support him and be in solidarity with our school. The atmosphere in the stadium provided an incongruous immersive edge that comes from the right combination of music, imagery, cheerleaders, and a sense of agency that football games are known for. The weather was ideal for the players as well as the spectators on the stand. Blaring music blasted through the speakers as the UofT band slowly strutted in with their fight song. The cheerleaders succeeded in titillating the audience with their flips and well-practiced gymnastic moves. To add to this maelstrom of enthusiasm, there were thousands of froshies with their blue thunder sticks. The whole stadium was bleeding blue in support of the home team.

The referee blew the whistle, and the game began. In the first drive of the game, the Blues drove down the field but could only manage a field goal. In Waterloo's ensuing drive, quarterback Best Iriah was sacked 2.5 yards from the goal line, and the Waterloo Warriors opted to take the intentional safety to give the Blues an early 5-0 lead. In American football, a sack occurs when a quarterback or another offensive player acting as a passer is tackled behind the line of scrimmage. Performing a sack was advantageous for the Blues, as the Warriors lost a down and the line of scrimmage retreated several yards. After the Blues were forced to punt, Warriors scored a field goal to make the score 5-3. In the second quarter, the Warriors tacked on another field goal to take a 6-5 lead. Nigel, being the quarterback for the Blues, decided to take his offence down the field and completed it with a 39-yard touchdown pass to receiver Michael Jacobsen for the first touchdown of the game. The Warriors then came right back in the ensuing drive to score their first touchdown of the game, taking a 13-12 lead. With time winding down for the first half, the Blues marched down the field in their next drive but were intercepted by the Waterloo defense. This gave way to half-time, which was to last for about twelve minutes just like they do in NFL games.

The players went off the field to their respective camps. The Blues were playing under the tutelage of Coach Greg Gary, who was boosting the morale of the players as they were lagging 13-12 from Waterloo. The organizers distributed some freebies during the interval, which included some snacks for the students who fervently supported their school teams. The small number of Waterloo supporters were seated at quite a distance from our benches. This year, the organizers had added a new entertainment feature in the interval called the kiss cam. The kiss cam is a social pastime that takes place during sporting events in Canada and the USA. A kiss cam camera scans the crowd and selects a couple who is shown on the jumbotron screen in the arena. Once their live video is displayed, the audience cheers the couple on the screen to kiss.

The camera focused on two freshmen who did not seem to be in a relationship but just happened to be sitting together. The crowd rooted for them to kiss. At first, both of them hesitated and refrained from even looking at each other. Then the boy was seen saying something to the girl. She smiled and looked down. Then he put his arm around her shoulder and kissed her on the cheek. The audience was unsatisfied and booed the couple because they wanted to see a proper kiss. After this debacle, the kiss cam locked in on a couple that seemed like they were in a romantic relationship, as the boy had his arm around her and the girl had one of her hands on his lap. On closer look, I felt my jaw drop to the floor. The boy on the screen was Keanu, and the girl he was cozied up against was not his girlfriend Sonia. Andre and I looked at each other in total disbelief. Sam, Ryan, and Manny were taken aback as well. Keanu too seemed to be in shock, as he didn't expect to be put in a spot in front of a crowd of 5,000 people with a girl who was his side chick. However, the girl he was sitting with had no qualms about publicly displaying her affection and moved in to kiss Keanu. We watched with bated breath while the crowd cheered them on. Keanu reluctantly gave in for the kiss, though he broke it off as soon as he could. He looked nervous and fucked from his face. He was cheating on Sonia and had managed to lie low all this while, but his cover was blown in one of the most unsuspecting places on campus. What were the odds of that happening? I wondered if we had come to watch *The Hunger Games* instead of a football game, because today the odds were definitely not in his favor.

'That rat bastard,' said Manny, clenching his teeth.

'Who the fuck is that girl? How could he do this with Sonia? She loves him so much, and he is fucking around behind her back,' said Ryan who was as aghast as Manny. I could feel emotion in every single word that came out of his mouth. It was as if Keanu was cheating on him.

'Guys, the important thing is that Sonia needs to know this. But this is a sensitive matter, so I suggest that we wait until the game is done so that we can decide on how we want to tell her and who should be dropping the bomb,' I said.

'Look at Nigel. I think he saw that too. He is staring in Keanu's direction, and his face has turned red. I bet Keanu had no idea that Nigel is playing today's game. Even if he knew about Nigel, he didn't expect his ignoble affair to be showcased on the big screen,' said Andre.

'I am sure he won't risk staying any longer. He is going to weasel out of the stadium like a rodent,' said Manny.

Andre continued, 'That is going to make it easier for us to find out about this girl he is with. I think Keanu is lying to this girl just like he is lying to Sonia. It is obvious that he hasn't told this girl about Sonia. Now it all makes sense.

Remember how he deactivated his Facebook ID over the summer? He gave a vague reply about taking time off from social media when we asked him about it. That is because he had several pictures with Sonia on Facebook. Even his profile picture had Sonia in it. Well, I guess he has been double timing Sonia for a while now.'

Sam recovered from a state of silent disbelief, 'Andre, since this girl with Keanu is Black, I think you should go and check if Keanu is still there or not. If he has left, go to her and make up some bullshit that you are the president of the African society and represent the voice of Black students on campus or make something up about "Black lives matter" and go talk to her. Find out her name and whatever information you can from her.'

'Alright, I will try if Keanu doesn't take her with him. Regardless, I can take her picture and ask my friends in the Jamaican and Caribbean societies if they know her,' said Andre as he took out his mobile phone from his jean's pocket. His cell phone would double up for a spy cam and abet his cause of espionage.

As soon as Andre left to snoop around, the game resumed. I noticed that Nigel had a very angry, scornful look on his face. After watching Keanu on the screen indulge in infidelity and invidious behavior, Nigel was bound to react like we did. In the third quarter, Waterloo sacked Nigel and forced the fumble, and on the first play, made a 39-yard pass down the field. The Warriors made it to first and goal on the one-yard line, but the Blues' defense came up big, forcing Waterloo to settle for a field goal. On the ensuing Toronto drive, the Blues' offence went two and out. During the Blues' punting play on third down, the snap went over the kicker's head and was recovered by the Waterloo Warriors to give them the ball on Toronto's 22-yard line. There was a noticeable change in Nigel's game as he could be seen getting very aggressive. Maybe he was channeling the anger that was borne from Keanu's episode into the game. I didn't blame him. The thought of Keanu cheating on Sonia disturbed me so much that I could not enjoy the game as a spectator. Nigel, on the other hand, had to perform for his team.

Fortunately, his anger brought out his best performance in the season so far.

'Hey, I managed to get a hold of the girl. I told her that I belonged to the Caribbean society and that our society was holding a Caribana party to celebrate the success of Black students on campus and I would like her to come for it. She was welcome to bring her friends to it as well. I found out that her name was Stephanie Mukena, and she is an international student from Kinshasa, Congo. She is in her third year studying Equity Studies at Victoria College,' said Andre after coming back to the stands.

'That is quite a lot of information you got on her. I am assuming Keanu has left, and that is why you were able to approach her. Did you manage to get a picture of her while you were there?' I asked.

'Yeah, I took one before approaching her. Got her side face. She is rachet as fuck. God knows why Keanu would tap something so unprepossessing when he has Sonia,' replied Andre.

'I think you guys should let me handle this. I am going to tell Sonia everything but only after the game is over,' said Ryan.

'The Toronto Blues are leading. It is good to get into the minds of the Warriors now. I am going to start a cheer, and I want all of you to repeat it so that all the Blues fans here pick it up,' lurched Sam.

'Go for it,' said Manny.

'Waterloo, smells like poo...Waterloo, smells like poo,' jeered Sam, and we followed with promptitude. Soon, the entire stand echoed the chorus, and it spread like a wave throughout the arena.

The Blues' defense succeeded again with defensive back Karan Thukral making an interception which stopped the Warriors from scoring. After these momentum shifting plays by the defense, the floodgates opened for the Blues in the fourth quarter. It started with a game high 79-yard pass from

Nigel to receiver Solomon Lupo. From then, the Blues never looked back, with Nigel scoring three more touchdowns and running back Gokce Can Ertem, making a one-yard run for the final touchdown of the game, ending it with a harrowing score of 57-26. Nigel had led the Blues to a clinching victory as they made it to the finals. Interviewers from the student newspaper rushed to get a byte from him, but he ignored everyone and went towards the locker room. He did not take part in the team celebrations either. The music started pumping again, and the UofT cheerleaders were performing with renewed vigor as the crowd rejoiced.

When we met him after the game, he seemed very disturbed from Keanu's incident. He had won one of the most crucial games of the intercollegiate tournament, but he wasn't elated as one would expect him to be.

'Have you guys told her yet?' asked Nigel.

'No, but we are going to,' replied Ryan.

'The worst part is that they live together. I feel so bad for her. My team is going to the Fox and Fiddle Pub to celebrate the win, but I don't feel like joining them. I think we should inform Sonia now and provide her with any support she needs,' said Nigel.

'Yeah, you are right. Keanu is probably at Parkside, so it won't be a good idea to go back to Parkside now. I don't want a repeat of the Rebel brawl,' said Ryan.

'Okay,' agreed Nigel.

Ryan mustered up all his courage together before dialing Sonia's number. He put the call on loudspeaker so that we all could hear.

'Hey Sonia! What's up?' asked Ryan.

'Nothing much. Just running a few errands. It's laundry day today,' she replied.

'Is Keanu with you?'

'No, he has gone down to the cafeteria to get food for me.'

'By the way, I am curious. Did Keanu go to the football game today?' asked Ryan.

'Obviously not. I would have been there too if he had gone for the match. I had asked him yesterday when Nigel invited me, but he said he didn't like watching football. And honestly, I still don't understand the rules, so we bailed. But why do you ask?' replied Sonia.

'Sonia, what I am about to tell you is going to hurt you, but I need you to stay strong. Keanu did come for the game today. All of us saw him, but the issue was in the way we spotted him. In the interval, they had a kiss cam focusing on random couples. You know how kiss cams work, right? Unfortunately for him, the kiss cam spotted him with another girl whom we found out is a third-year student, Stephanie Mukena. It looked like he has been seeing her for a while now, and she had no hesitations in kissing him. I am sorry to be the messenger of such devastating news, but we all thought that it was imperative you know this,' said Ryan. There was an uncanny, eerie silence on the other end.

'Are you still there?' asked Ryan.

'Yes,' she replied in a melancholic tone. Her voice cracked like she was almost in tears.

'I am sorry,' apologized Ryan again before Sonia hung up the phone.

From what I gathered later, an ugly spat transpired at Parkside soon after Ryan's call. Based on Sonia's account, she threw orange juice on Keanu's face, and it turned his white t-shirt into an electric orange color. He apologized profusely when she confronted him, but all his efforts were in vain. Keanu Barrage was barraged with buckets of hate and abuses. I have seen what Sonia is capable of when she gets extremely mad, so I am sure that Keanu wasn't spared for his impetuosity. Needless to say, they broke up and Sonia had notified Parkside that she would be moving out to seek alternate living arrangements. Fortunately, there was a vacant room at our residence in Tartu that she could lease. Sports play a pivotal role in our society in the integration of social classes, races, gender, and cultures. Who knew it was even capable of disintegrating relationships between lovers?

On 8th October, 2016, I turned 22. It was going to be my last birthday at the University of Toronto and also my last birthday in Canada. So I wanted to celebrate it in a big way. This was the first time I had begun planning for my birthday a month ago. This birthday was also special because I had invited Afifah for it, as my friends insisted on meeting her. I had never made my friends meet her, knowing she would not approve of the alcohol or the way we rated women or maneuvered them into bed. But I was being persistently pressurized from both sides. Afifah was eager to meet my friends as much as they were curious to meet her. So I cautiously found a middle ground where I chose an Indian restaurant in Mississauga that did not serve alcohol. As a Pakistani, I thought she would relate to Indian food, and the commute would also be convenient for her because the Gurulukhsmi Restaurant was located near her house in Mississauga. A day before my birthday on 7th October, 2016, the world saw a video clip released by the Washington Post about how Donald Trump bragged about grabbing women by the pussy. So I thought that I should send out my invite in a way I assumed Donald Trump would write it.

I would like to invite you all to a restaurant; it is a great restaurant, it really is. It is the finest Indian restaurant out there, and I have talked to people, lots of people actually, and they all agree with what I think. Their ratings would have tanked if they didn't do a great job at feeding people. Their ratings beat every restaurant out there, and they even have the best waitresses. Some of the most beautiful waitresses in any Indian restaurant you have ever seen. And I love waitresses. Nobody respects Indian waitresses more than I do, even though they take our part-time jobs. I want everyone to be at the Gurulukshmi Restaurant at 1:00 pm for lunch, and believe me, I am going to make you pay for your food. It is going to be huuuge.

To cap off my birthday celebrations, we were going to a Drake concert. The plan was to drop Afifah home after lunch and meet my friends at the Air Canada Centre in downtown Toronto. My favorite singer was performing in

Toronto on my birthday, and there was no way I was going to miss it even if I had to watch it from nosebleeds. Fortunately for me, my parents offered to buy me a concert ticket as a birthday gift. It took a while to sink in that I would be watching Drake live. According to me, Drake was the biggest living artist in the world.

My birthday gaiety began a night before. The plan was to party my way into my birthday. It was a booze-fueled night as we got sloshed on every spirit available at the Liquor Control Board of Ontario (LCBO). It was a treat to get pickled in martinis and vodka coke as the liquor bottles coquettishly smiled back at us. Our living room at Tartu had turned into a drinking den. The in-house spirit infusion experiments were crazy. Manny was in charge of the music, and he would have kept us on our feet until the wee hours of the morning with his sick playlist that he had concocted over the years if it wasn't for the legal poison we were drinking down like water. Like every year, Andre gifted me a birthday joint which contained the finest quality of grass in Toronto. Sam had brought me a champagne bottle that he popped open at midnight only to bespatter copious amounts of it. By 1 am, we were all hungry, so we headed to the Shark Club on Dundas Square. We indulged in food porn that consisted of Korean chicken wings, mini sliders, double cheese nachos, and quesadillas. We came back home by 3:00 am and headed off to our beds, because we had to get up and reach the Gurulukshmi Restaurant on time.

Location: Gurulukshmi Restaurant, Mississauga

The Gurulukshmi Restaurant was an authentic South Indian restaurant that only served vegetarian food. The intimate décor made it a gem for casual elegant dining. It had a sizeable Caucasian population for a vegetarian Indian restaurant, showing that it was a favorite with the locals. All the servers were Brown and were communicating amongst themselves in either Telugu or Tamil from what I reckoned. I could never tell the difference between the two languages. We arrived at 1:03 pm and had a table reserved for nine. Afifah had texted me saying she was running twenty minutes late.

'What are *dosas*?' enquired Nigel going through the menu.

'*Dosa* is a fermented, thin and papery, crusty crepe-like dish made from rice batter. It looks like what the gentleman on that table is eating there,' said Sam, pointing at the food that was being consumed on the table next to us. 'You can choose what stuffing you want inside it.'

'What do you recommend?' asked Nigel.

'Since it is your first time trying *dosa*, I suggest you try the plain one without any stuffing,' said Manny. Being a Brampton boy, he grew up around Indian restaurants and knew the likes and dislikes of White folks at ethnic Indian restaurants.

'I think I am going to stick with the Indian bread and potatoes. How do you pronounce this again?' asked Ryan who was only looking at the English translations.

'*Parathas*,' I said, leaning in to see his menu. Sonia wasn't much of a *dosa* fan, so she ordered *idlis* which are another South Indian delicacy. Sam and I went for the Mysore *dosa* whereas Lydia and Andre opted for the cheese *dosa*. Manny chose the *rawa* onion *dosa*. We had just finished placing our orders when Afifah walked inside the restaurant. Afifah was wearing a red cocktail dress that featured a keyhole detailing on a turtle neckline with a side train on the waist. She paired the ensemble with black strappy heels, silver earrings, and pretty accessories. This was her boldest look ever that I had seen. Her lips were bright red, and her makeup was glowing which made her eyes shimmer and her brow look fleek. She wore her hair in a low ponytail to display her accessories and elegant high neckline. Lydia rolled her eyes and gave me a look of approval. She seemed to be blown to smithereens by Afifah's beautiful face and sexy outfit.

'Hey Afifah, you look gorgeous,' I said.

'Happy birthday, Devansh,' she said hugging me. She had purchased a cake for me that she was holding in her hands. It explained why she was late.

'You shouldn't have bothered to bring this. But I am glad you came,' I said.

'I wouldn't miss your birthday for anything.'

'Everyone, as you may have already guessed, this is Afifah.' She met everyone individually and shook their hands before being seated.

'Devansh was telling us that your parents are from Pakistan. My mother is from Pakistan too,' said Sonia, trying to break the ice with her.

'Wow, which part of Pakistan is she from? My parents are from Karachi,' said Afifah.

Sonia replied, 'My mother grew up in Lahore. And my father is from Saudi Arabia. They met in Saudi when my mother was working there.'

'Let her order first and then you guys can carry on bonding,' I said as everyone except her had already placed their food orders. She ordered the *Chettinad Dosa* which was the signature *dosa*. She didn't have to refer to the menu, and it was then that we found out that she had come here before. The *Chettinad Dosa* comprised of a mixture of red chillies, herbs, and spices that were spread on the *dosa*.

'I cracked up laughing when I saw your invitation to this place. It seemed like you actually got that message drafted by Trump,' she said after placing her order.

'I am sure you have seen the video that surfaced yesterday. This guy has crossed every level of scumbaggery in politics. I doubt if there is any global leader who has made such lewd and reprehensible comments like Trump has made during his campaign. After this, I don't know if he stands any chance of winning the White House,' said Nigel.

Afifah went on a rant about Trump, 'As a Muslim, I wouldn't want him to ever become president. He wants to ban an entire religion from the United States because of the actions of a few people. Muslims like me would never want to visit a country that is capable of electing an Islamophobe like Trump as their president. He sounds like a retard when he says things like, "I love the uneducated people, or I love the Blacks." What kind of presidential candidate speaks like that? Why can't he speak a more inclusive language and be like, "I love all Americans."?'

Lydia joined in the roast, 'When Trump says that he loves the Blacks, I think he is a referring to a family of White people whose last name is Black like Lewis Black or Lucas Black from the *Fast & Furious* movies.'

As the discussion shifted gears to be centered around Black people, Andre felt a need to say something, 'As a Black Canadian, I feel that the hegemony of media houses like the CNN and BBC is responsible in propagating a rhetoric that is responsible for polarizing society and pushing the interest of White supremacy. Their deliberate portrayal of Muslims and Blacks as dangerous and unsavory feed into the narrative of right-wing politicians and conservatives.'

The food arrived as we continued with our discussion on American politics which was accompanied by some fun raillery, laughter, and teachable moments. Breaking bread with friends on a special occasion like a birthday resulted in a boisterous meal. I felt an immense sense of gratitude when I looked around the table and saw our plates filled with good food and the chairs filled with great friends. The constant stress of midterms and assignments had forced me to eat on the run, and my meals had become a reflex of just shoving something down my throat to stave off hunger. I was eating mindfully and peacefully after ages because I could feel and smell every grain that went inside my body. Once we were done with the meal, Afifah set out the cake and lit the candles for me. I had told the others before reaching this South Indian restaurant that I wanted to spend some private time with Afifah, so I would meet them directly at the Air Canada Centre for Drake's concert at 5:00 pm. Therefore, everyone except Afifah and me left for Air Canada Centre after I cut the cake.

'How did you like the cake?' Afifah asked me as I took a small serving of it. It was just the two of us now, and I had planned this moment because I wanted to tell her how I felt about her and that I secretly crushed on her since I had first seen her.

'I like the Oreo flavor. Where did you get it from?'

'Demetres,' she replied.

I thought this was the right moment to tell her how I felt about her. I was overanxious and already feeling the nerves, even though I had rehearsed what I wanted to tell her many times. I felt like I would stutter if I opened my mouth now. Who would believe that someone like me who has been practicing pick-up for almost three years and has slept with more than thirty girls would be nervous to confess his feelings to a virgin girl?

'Listen Afifah...I want to tell you something; actually, I have wanted to tell you this for a while now...ummm...the thing is...' I said as she furrowed her brows to listen keenly to what I had to say.

'Basically, what I am about to tell you might sound unsettling because we have been such good friends all these years. I was pondering about how to tell you this and whether it would be appropriate or not, but then I realized that attraction is the most natural thing that could pan out between a boy and a girl. When I saw you for the first time ever, I took a shine on you, and as we got to know each other, I realized that you are the kind of girl I would want to grow old with, and I know this sounds crazy, but I am comfortable with my manhood to put it out there.' I felt naked from inside. I realized it was so much easier to get naked with a stranger than it was to reveal your feelings for someone you cared about. She looked me in the eye and held my hand from across the table.

'Devansh, I have never made it evident, but I kind of knew that you had feelings for me. I appreciate you telling me this, and I think you are the most genuine guy I know. It takes a lot of courage to be so vulnerable. But...' she paused.

'You knew that I liked you?'

'Girls are intuitive when it comes to matters like this. And I deliberated on this, thinking you would ask me out someday. But I don't think things will work out between us. I know how people always find a way to make it work in soap operas televised in India and Pakistan, but in the real world, we need to take into account a lot of external factors we can't control. When I say external factors, I mean things like religion, cultural differences, and our different upbringing.'

'You are going to graduate from the best university in Canada next year. I am surprised you are still measuring the viability of relationships through the narrow conduit of religious and cultural factors when we belong to a generation that is so integrated and accepting of these socially constructed differences,' I said.

'It is not that I discriminate against anyone based on their religion or culture. I have been brought up in a way to respect my parents' wishes. They have given me everything I have, including my life, and I owe them. According to my parents, I can only marry a Muslim. They wanted to get me engaged after my undergraduate studies were over, but when my father found out that I was very keen on pursuing a master's in management, he allowed me to pursue it without any questions. I promised him that I would get married after my master's was over to whomever he wanted. My grandfather chose my father for my mother, and my father will choose my groom. I have been brought up with these values. Not only are you not Muslim but also an Indian. We don't have a future, so there is no point in getting into a relationship,' she said. Impulsively, I withdrew the hand she was holding.

'It was important that we had this conversation. I might not agree with the way you rationalize your decision, but I respect our differences. I hope we could still continue to be friends and put this behind us,' I said.

'Thank god! I was so scared I would never see you again. I would never want to lose a friend like you.'

'Since we are done here, let me book an Uber so that I can drop you home first and then go downtown for the concert,' I said.

'Sure. Thank you for the lift. I could bus it too if you are getting late.'

'Not at all. I will make it on time.'

So I dropped Afifah to her place and then met up with the gang at the Air Canada Centre. We knew Drake would give a great concert, because it was his last show of the Summer Sixteen Tour, and he would pay homage to the city he is always repping. Future preceded Drake to fire up the crowd and get them ready for the man whom everyone had come to watch. Future's blustery performance traded off in nuance for gruff exhortations. Drake, however, won the audience with his abrupt magical entry that was met with a frenzied crowd and a delirious applause. Something alchemical happens when fans join Drake to hurl out the lyrics of his songs which focus on internal ructions, animosities, trust issues, and his love life. In addition to the music, the concert had awe-inspiring visuals. The ambience was enhanced with fire and sparks that accentuated the stage, and large balloons descended on wires from above, illuminating the whole arena. The balloons first emerged during *Hotline Bling* and bounced up and down, undulating like waves and glowing like a canopy of fireflies. Another reason why fans relate to Drake is because he invokes nationalist pride by making his love for Canada and Toronto really evident. He was carrying a Canadian flag with him and even wore a Blue Jays jersey that he gave to a fan in the first row. When he performed on the hit song *Hold on, we are going home*, he stepped on a platform that raised him over the crowd so that he could get near his fans and personally cater to them by shouting out what they were wearing. As a hip-hop phenomenon, he has umpteen rhymes about money, women, marijuana, and Hennessey, but his effusive love for Torontonians and his ease of showmanship are unparalleled. This is what lets him seduce his audience. He ended the concert with a satisfying closure, proving that he was a consummate entertainer who performs with bravura. It was no coincidence that Drake was on top of the 6ix, and the 6ix felt on top of this world.

Location: Tim Hortons on Bay Street

Our final exams for the fall semester were going to begin in a week. Sonia, Ryan, Manny, Sam, and I had come down with our laptops and study material to the Tim Hortons on Bay Street to pull an all-night study session. Sonia, Ryan, and I had planned to indulge in generous amounts of caffeine and finish our group assignment by morning because it was due at 3:00 pm the next day. The three of us had to take a course on classical sociological theory, as it was a mandatory prerequisite to complete the sociology major or specialist. As part of the course, we had to get into groups of three to write an essay that was worth 40% of the total grade, so it was necessary that we got it right. Sam and Manny were working on their individual assignments under tight deadlines. It was going to be a long, tedious night, and only affordable coffee and doughnuts were going to get us through it.

Just like football is ubiquitous in Texas, Tim Hortons is ubiquitous in Canada. For Canadians, Tim Hortons is synonymous for fresh coffee and is seen by many as an indispensable thread in the social fabric of Canada. Over the last few decades, the brand cultivated its image to become the cornerstone of national identity. A store, which opened with very humble beginnings at one location in Hamilton, grew into a corporate giant with 4,800 stores, making it a testament of the affection people had for it. Other than affordable prices, Tim Hortons vouchsafed students like us with free Wi-Fi and a space which was open around the clock. As patrons, we were partaking in something more exalted than merely exchanging money for coffee; we were indulging in something local and ceremonial. We were being sold an indelible vision.

'Which course is this assignment for?' asked Manny.

'It is on classical sociological theory. This is one of the toughest courses on the program because the readings are very arduous,' answered Ryan.

'What is classical sociological theory about?' pressed Manny again.

Ryan answered, 'The course explores and analyzes some of the most important theories in the discipline of sociology from luminaries that include Marx, Durkheim, Weber, and Simmel, to mention few of the important figures. For this assignment, we have to choose any one theory that was created by these people and apply it on a contemporary issue.'

'And what contemporary issue have you guys chosen?' asked Sam.

Ryan answered, 'We have decided to write our essay on ISIS, and we are going to analyze it through Durkheim's theory of functionalism. According to the theory of functionalism, our society is made up of different social institutions, and each institution is designed to perform a particular function. An institution is relevant only until it performs a function, and it starts to decay when it no longer serves the needs of societies. According to Durkheim, disorganization in our social structure leads to change because societal components must reorganize themselves to fill the void that has been created and regain order.'

'I have managed to draft quite a bit of the introduction on which you and Sonia can build the analysis. I was working on it yesterday so that we could save time today,' I told Ryan as I started working on citations.

'Devansh, you are a savior. Please put it in on OneDrive so that both Ryan and I can have a look and edit it,' said Sonia.

'Sure.'

The document that I sent them contained the following work:

All nations, big or small, are susceptible to and have been victims of despicable acts of terror, with branches of terrorism spawning its poison on the entire human race. Out of the various terror groups and organizations that have inflicted scars on the human civilization, the Islamic State of Iraq and al-Sham (ISIS) has been one such group that has carried out operations on a massive scale by systematically organizing itself. Currently, every major newspaper, magazine, or television news channel has an article, report, or headline dedicated to its heinous crimes. As a result of the incessant media attention, which ISIS has garnered over the past year, it has always been in the limelight. This constant media attention stemmed our group's interest on this topic, and we decided to investigate the struggle for power in the Middle East and the repercussions of the mayhem that ensued in Iraq and manifested itself on a global platform.

The activities of ISIS have a significant impact on the policies of different countries, thereby influencing world dynamics, because they serve as a potential threat to the rulers in their neighboring vicinity as well as create uncertainties for the countries that advance their support to the Muslim countries who are neighbors of ISIS-occupied territory. Unlike the Taliban regime that had lost its foothold in Afghanistan after the US intervention, consequently depriving it of its ability to train terrorists because of inadequate camps, ISIS took control over large chunks of land when the US decided to withdraw its troops in 2011. Access to the most vital resource that is land, enabled it to cultivate highly skilled operatives because their commandoes had the space to setup highly functional training camps. These developments create a pyramid of hurdles for the various governments because a certain cohort of individuals have been drawn to this radical organization and want to advance their cause. They have beheaded various journalists, aid workers, and foreign nationals and uploaded videos of their brutal killings. All videos have carefully been articulated by shaving the captive's head and placing the prisoner in a Guantanamo bay-type outfit. These acts have been orchestrated to distinguish them from other terror organizations and establish themselves in the eyes of the world as a separate state.

Having perceived the threat from ISIS as imminent and grave, it is imperative that the international community addresses it with a sense of solidarity. This is only possible if the state of ambiguity and abstruseness of the international community to arrive at a stipulated definition of terrorism is resolved. Without a concrete definition, 'the term is open to politicized manipulation, conjecture and polemical interpretation' (Lawless 2007:147-148). Vanquishing the surge of violent extremism is the only way to attain peace and harmony, which the world seeks at large.

'That is quite an impressive synopsis on ISIS. It is going to be very helpful to us for building our analysis,' said Ryan.

Sonia had a suggestion after reading my synopsis, 'I was wondering if you want to change the theory of analysis to Marx's conflict theory. As you guys know, conflict theory posits that since resources in society are limited and the competition for resources is inevitable, society will always be in a state of conflict. Marx is not saying that conflict is good or bad, but it is an unavoidable aspect of society and helps explain why society functions the way it does. Conflict theory can be used to look at the extremism and war in ISIS-occupied territories.'

Ryan replied, 'Yes, that makes sense. Conflict theory could explain the turmoil in Iraq and Syria, but I think we should stick to functionalism for now, since we all have extensively read on that for this essay.'

'By the way, are you guys done with your law school applications?' I asked Sonia and Ryan.

'I have finished my applications to Yale, Harvard, Stanford, and Berkley. The only application left is that of the University of Chicago,' said Ryan.

Even I am done with all my applications. I have obviously applied to UofT Law. The other applications I have made are to Osgoode, Queens, and Mcgill. Queens is my safe option here. I am pretty confident that I will get into McGill and Osgoode. UofT looks tricky, as I fucked up my midterms after my breakup with Keanu. I submitted them in October, as some of the deadlines were in November,' said Sonia.

Ryan had a stellar CGPA of 3.92 and an LSAT score of 176. He was the only person I knew who was capable of cracking all the law schools on his list. Sonia had a CGPA of 3.7 at the time of her application, but her LSAT score was 167. She had a very high CGPA for a UofT student, but her chances at UofT Law looked bleak to me even with these scores, since UofT was very selective.

Sonia asked the same question back to me, 'How are your applications for UK coming along?'

'I have started writing my personal statement. I am applying to only four universities in the UK - University College London, Imperial College London, the London School of Economics and Political Science, and Oxford. I didn't want to apply to Oxford, as I don't think I would be able to adjust in such a small quiet town after having lived in cities all my life. But the professor who wrote my recommendation letter was very unhappy when he found out that I wasn't applying there. Being an alumni of Oxford himself, he wants me to go there and also believes that I have a solid GPA for getting in,' I said.

'When do you plan to submit them?' asked Sonia.

'I should be done with them by the end of December. I will submit all my applications once the final grades for this semester are out by January,' I said.

So we got back on the grind. For the next two hours, all of us worked with intense concentration on our tasks like carriage-pulling horses fitted with blinkers to avoid distraction. I thought of taking a break, as I was really craving one of those Boston cream doughnuts. I knew I needed one of those bad boys to refuel me. The Boston cream doughnuts were gooey and had the perfect blend of cakey goodness mashed up with a sugary glaze of chocolate. Ryan had asked me to bring him a medium French vanilla coffee whereas the rest of them had collectively asked me for a box of ten Timbits. I could buy food and coffee for all of us and yet the total bill was under 10$. Such value for money was only possible at this Canadian chain.

As I got back with everyone's order, Manny burst out into a loud gasp as we caught him staring at his laptop screen.

'Fuck, fuck, fuck, fuck, fuck. Holy crap. This cannot be true.' Manny was so loud that the cashier gave us all a dirty look.

'What happened?' I asked concerned. Until then, I thought the news was bad.

'I just got a letter from the office of Christopher McQuarrie. The email states that Mr McQuarrie and his casting director saw my work in the student film *What will you sacrifice for success?*, which we had filmed for one of our courses, and they found it visually arresting. As a result, he would like to consider me for a prominent role in his upcoming movie and wants me to come for an audition and screen test to Los Angeles in three weeks. He has also offered to pay for my air fare and hotel stay,' said an elated Manny. Canada had long been a northern talent farm for Hollywood directors and producers. Furthermore, the weaker Canadian dollar and tax incentives allow Hollywood producers to get way more worth for their money in Canada as compared to the US.

'Wow, congratulations! This is such great news,' said Sam.

'Congratulations, Manny. This is crazy. I am sure you are going to crack the audition,' said Ryan.

'Hey, rock me an autograph now because I know that once you are famous, it is going to be hard to get a hold of you,' I exclaimed.

Manny said, 'This email has been lying in my inbox since yesterday. I decided to clear the clutter by removing some old emails when I saw this. I cannot wait to share this news with my mother and Victoria. I feel this news might confound them though. Let me reply to their email first before they decide to change their minds or think I am not interested.'

'On this happy occasion, I would like to share some good news with all of you guys. I know I should have shared this news earlier, but we wanted to be sure about it before spilling the beans,' said Sonia.

'I think we know what this news is,' said Ryan.

'I am pretty sure you don't.'

'You are seeing someone, aren't you?'

'For fucks' sake, how did you know that?' asked a stupefied Sonia.

'It was pretty evident from the constant text messages you have been getting lately. Also, you have been smiling a lot when you are on your phone these days. I don't need to know rocket science to do the math here,' said Ryan.

'Stop being a wuss and tell us who it is,' asked Sam doggedly.

'I am dating Nigel,' said Sonia. There was a short pause on the table as everyone stared coldly at Sonia's face. Ryan stopped slurping his coffee and froze with his cup to the mouth.

'Son of a bitch. He has been dating you right under our noses, and I didn't get even the slightest hint from him,' said Ryan.

'Hey, hotshot. You are not as smart as you think you are,' said Sonia, looking at Ryan.

'I am happy for you guys,' said Manny as he got up to give Sonia a hug. 'Do Andre and Lydia know about this?'

'No, I will tell them soon.'

'So, how did it start?' I asked

'We both came out of relationships with people whom we thought were meant to be. I was a bit hesitant at first when Nigel asked me out, because I didn't want it to feel like a rebound. But then I realized that the best relationships are those where there is complete trust and transparency, and as they say "Friendship is the purest form of love". There was something inside me which told me that being with someone who likes me and whom I have known for such a long time would be the right decision. So, eventually, I agreed to go out with him, and that is how it all began,' replied Sonia.

'You are right. There is nothing more behooving than falling in love with a friend whom you trust more than yourself even if they belong to a culture and religion that are different from yours,' I said as the thought of being rejected by Afifah zapped my mind.

Year 4 Semester II

Winter Semester, February 2017

I woke up at 8:00 am on a Sunday to fourteen missed calls from Sam on my phone. Our midterms were starting from the next day, and I planned to hit the Robarts Library after taking a shower and eating breakfast. On seeing the long list of missed calls from Sam, I knew something was not right. Unless it was an emergency, he would have never called me more than two or three times. Since we lived in the same unit, I decided to brush my teeth and go knock on his door to check what the matter was, but there was no reply. I felt the soft panic that would increase or fade away depending on what I did next. Maybe he had received some devastating news from his family in India and wanted to share it with me. I called him back, and what he told me sent a chill down my spine. Just like one cannot stop the dawn ebbing its gradual way into daylight, one cannot stop a harbinger of bad news. I sat in thunderstruck silence as the magnitude of what had prevailed percolated through subsequent membranes to be absorbed by my brain. I was told by Sam that Manny was severely burnt and was admitted in the burn unit of the Brampton Civic Hospital.

Once I accepted the grim reality of what had transpired, I knocked on Ryan, Andre, and Nigel's door to wake them up and told them that Manny was severely injured and was admitted in the hospital. We took the first cab to Brampton in order to be near Manny and his family and help them out in whatever way we could. Sam and Lydia were waiting on the ground floor of the hospital for us, as they only allowed two people per patient in the visitor's area outside the operation theatres, which were located on the third floor. Continuous calls by Sam on Lydia's phone had woken her up and so she could revert Sam's call before any of us. That is how she was already here to support Manny's mother and sister.

'How did this happen?' I asked them the burning question.

Lydia answered in a breathless spiel, 'Based on what Manny's sister Victoria told me, the fire started around 2:00 am in the morning when only she and Manny were at home, as their mother Parveen was working a night shift. The authorities haven't officially declared the source of the fire, but she is confident that it started from the oven, as she had forgotten that she was cooking bacon in it. Manny was fast asleep by then, and she was also in bed. There was an oil bottle in the kitchen which probably exploded as they woke up with the sound of a loud explosion. The fire alarms went off soon, and that is when she rushed towards the kitchen. Fire started to spread quickly from one unit to the next, engulfing the bottom half of the house. By then, Manny and his sister knew that things had spiraled out of their hands and so they scudded out of the front door in their night suits, taking only their winter coats and mobile phones. They were safely outside the house when Manny realized that he had forgotten his cat Nunu, who was trapped in his room, as he had closed his bedroom door before fleeing the house. In a desperate attempt to save his cat, he went inside, but by then, the flames had found their way between the walls up into the attic. The conflagration raged uncontrollably as Victoria and her neighbors watched from outside. Before going to save Nunu, Manny had given Victoria his phone and told her to call Sam and apprise him with the situation. Going inside a burning house proved to be a fatal mistake because he didn't return with Nunu. Firefighters donning breathing apparatus cut through the wooden front door and went upstairs to find him lying unconscious on the floor.'

'What is the status now?' asked Andre.

'He is currently undergoing an escharotomy operation so that they can release the pressure of the inelastic tissue on his body, which would help restore circulation as well as enable them to remove dead skin. His mother and sister have been here since 3:00 am, and I reached here soon after Victoria called me. I don't think there is much left of their house. Other than that, we have to wait for any further news from them,' replied Sam.

For the next two hours, we waited in numbed silence for the outcome of the operation. Being a single mother, Manny often talked about the sacrifices his mother made to give him and his sister a good life in Canada. I was thinking about the pain and agony she would be experiencing on seeing her son suffer such a severe burn. We were not prepared to embrace the immeasurable loss that we were possibly staring at.

Shortly after, Victoria as well as her mother Parveen Teji came out of the elevator. Parveen had tears rolling down her cheeks whereas Victoria was holding medical documents in her hands. Lydia rushed to comfort Parveen while we asked Victoria about Manny's condition.

'The surgeries were successful, but the doctor says he is still critical. They also had to amputate two of his fingers because of the severity of the burns. The doctors say that more than 60% of his body is burnt, and the areas include the left side of his face and neck, his legs, arms, abdomen, back and buttocks,' said Victoria as she broke down into tears. '40% of those burns are third-degree burns.'

'Don't worry, he is a strong guy. He will fight it out,' I said.

Victoria sobbed, 'It is all my fault. I forgot the bacon in the oven, and the grease from the bacon must have caused the fire. Also, I should have stopped him from going back inside for Nunu. If he hadn't gone inside again, he would be fine now.'

'When can we visit him?' asked Andre, comforting her.

'The visiting hours will resume at 4:00 pm. You guys could go in turns. Sam, I would like to thank you and Lydia so much for reaching the hospital as soon as you could. In fact, I appreciate all of you coming here and standing with us in this difficult time when you have your midterms coming up. I am sorry for disturbing all of you. And Sam, Manny said you would be the only person who would be awake at

2:00 am in the morning, so that is why he gave me his phone and told me to call you before he went inside to get our cat,' said Victoria.

'Don't mention it. It wasn't trouble at all, and we all will get through this. Have you figured out anything about where you and your mother will be staying until you get things sorted with your house?' asked Sam.

Her mother Parveen answered for Victoria, 'Unfortunately, the fire landed in a window of time when I had cancelled my insurance until I could afford it again. So the insurance company will not give us any compensation. We have lost everything. All the possessions that we currently own are the clothes that we wear on our body. My daughter and I will have to find a shelter until we figure out a plan to get our lives on track. Honestly, I don't care about any of the stuff that we have lost. The only thing I want from God is good health and a long life for my son.'

'Mrs Teji, we will help you to relocate to a shelter. I am going to visit a couple of shelters and explain your situation to them. Don't worry, we will find something for you and Victoria. You must be exhausted and emotionally drained. Why don't you have something to eat or drink while we sort out your accommodation?' said Andre.

'I will come with you,' said Nigel.

'Thank you so much, son. I want to go to see what is left of our house. If you boys could arrange a place in a shelter for us, we would be highly obliged. At this point, I cannot afford to spend on getting a rented accommodation, because we need to save every penny to build our house back,' said Parveen.

It was decided that Victoria was staying back in the hospital with Lydia and Sonia whereas Andre and Nigel were going to look for shelters that would accommodate the Teji family. The rest of us were accompanying Parveen to see what was left of her house that she had bought after struggling in Canada for years.

We reached Darras Court to find the media clicking pictures of the burnt house and covering the tragic episode from last night. The house had become a complete wreckage. An incinerated bicycle sat in the garage. The charred remains of their home stood in the pale afternoon light like a skeleton. The wrath of the fire had destroyed everything. Pieces of glass littered around the broken windowpanes, and metal pieces lay blackened and twisted on the floor. The roof that had been their shelter in every snowstorm was ash. Under it, they had lived and loved. Parveen explained how the roofs of her house employed a style called mansard, which folds down over two floors and had abetted the fire to spread quickly. Black dust hung in the air and invaded our lungs as we walked around the burned house. Parveen ran her fingers over the ashes of her book collection. I wasn't sure what she was expecting to feel by touching the remains, some tangibility of her lost possessions perhaps.

'Mrs Teji, I think you should talk to the media and tell them about your situation. They want to interview you,' I said.

'Yeah, but I have lost everything. What good will talking to them do now other than giving them a story for their evening news? I don't want everyone watching the news to know my plight. It will be ignominious,' said Parveen.

'The reason I am telling you to talk to the media is because I think the people ought to know everything about what happened. I have something in mind that will alleviate your troubles, and I have a good feeling that it will work. But in order for my plan to work, the whole community will have to come together, as I am planning to setup a fundraiser that will help you rebuild this house. But first, I need a credible newspaper article that will strengthen your case,' I explained.

She hesitated a bit but agreed to give the interview. While she was giving the interview, I looked around to see if I could find Nunu or her dead body anywhere. Unable to find any trace of her, my hunch was that she was a waif now just like the hundreds of pets who were homeless in the streets of New York after 9/11. After spending some more time in the house, we grabbed some food on the way for everyone and went back to the hospital, as the visiting hours for the patients would begin soon. Nigel had called to tell us that Andre and he had found a shelter that would accommodate Parveen and Victoria until they could save enough to move out.

Location: Brampton Civic Hospital

The first people to visit Manny in the ICU were his mother and sister. My emotions were in flux as I fretted at the thought of entering the ICU. After learning about the intensity of the burn, I could see his career as an actor vaporize in front of my eyes. For an actor, the most valuable asset is his appearance. After losing two fingers and receiving burns on more than 60% of his body, it was not possible for him to pursue acting professionally. I was thinking about something to tell him that would cheer him up when I saw Victoria coming out of the elevator. She was lugubrious, as she couldn't bear the pain of seeing her brother battling for his life.

'He will be fine, Victoria. He will get the courage to fight only if you are mentally strong. Did the doctors say anything?' asked Sonia.

Victoria wiped her tears, 'It is very painful to see him like this. Fifteen hours ago, he was a happy and healthy young boy, and now nothing makes sense. Yesterday, the nurses had placed an intravenous line in his left arm, because burn victims are in immediate need of fluids. Apparently, a molten tar-like substance dripped from the ceiling, which resulted in his back burning. During the operation, the surgeons used a material called Integra Dermal Regeneration Template which is used on patients suffering with severe burns. In this process, the wound is first cleaned and a sheet of integra is laid on top. The doctors then wait for a week for the material to grow in. New capillaries actually weave their way up into the material. Finally, an extremely thin layer of the patient's skin is grafted on top and allowed to heal. They are keeping him in a highly sedated condition. If he survives, they say he might lose certain sensations like light, touch, and temperature differentiation and would need to be alert about his external environment.'

By then, Parveen had also returned after seeing Manny. Sam and I were the next people to visit Manny, so we took the visitor's passes from Parveen and Victoria.

Before entering the ICU, the head nurse made us wear protective clothing so that we don't transmit any infection to the patient. Upon entering Manny's unit, we saw a burn bed which he was being monitored on. A burn bed is different from other hospital beds. The purpose of the burn bed is to distribute the weight of the patient in a way so that no single point of contact on the bed is pressed harder than any other point. Manny was in an air chamber burn bed which prevented the formation of bed sores and ensured that the patient's skin was kept dry in a comfortable and controlled warm air atmosphere. The burn bed prevented friction against painful burn wounds, and it even permitted easier nursing care. We walked up to Manny's bedside. His upper lips were swollen all the way into his nostrils. His right arm, burnt around the elbow, was in a splint to keep the elbow extended and prevent a contracture from forming. A foley catheter was carefully slipped through his urethra and attached to a bag calibrated to measure his urine output. EKG sensors were clipped to his chest, and a pulse oximeter capped one of his toes. An endotracheal tube made it possible for him to speak.

'Hey, Manny, your cat is missing you. It is waiting for you to get well soon and come back home,' I said with watery eyes. He looked like a roasted pig. I didn't have the courage to look him in the eyes for long.

'I, I...I want to...live. I don't want to die now,' he said.

'You are going to be fine,' said Sam.

'Show me a mirror,' said Manny. Sam and I immediately exchanged silent looks upon hearing that request. As a burn victim, Manny was prohibited from being shown a mirror because seeing his burnt face could psychologically injure him.

'We are not allowed to bring mirrors inside the ICU. The hospital authorities don't allow it,' I said.

'Show me the selfie camera on your phones,' he said. I understood that his mind was still very alert.

'We aren't allowed anything inside. Not even our phones,' I lied.

'Devansh, please take care of Victoria,' said Manny. I couldn't bear it any longer. I wasn't able to keep it together emotionally. I turned around so that he couldn't see me sobbing.

'Nothing is going to happen to you,' I said and exited the ICU. I couldn't see him suffering and battling for his life. The emotional baggage was much heavier than anything I could carry. I ran sniveling down the stairs instead of waiting for the elevator. Maybe I was running away from the fear of the inevitable.

The stairs led me to the lobby of the hospital where everyone was waiting. From my eyes, they could tell that I had been crying. Lydia walked up to me to hug me and tried to console me. I held her tightly. Unable to hold back my tears, I broke down in her arms. Through informal mechanisms of social control, society reinforces the notion that men are not supposed to cry. It is a sign of weakness and was something only females did. But I feel it is necessary for all of us to let our emotions flow freely.

Once everyone had visited Manny, we decided to head back home to study whatever we could for our midterms tomorrow. Nigel did not have a midterm the next day, so he offered to stay back longer with Victoria and Parveen. It was already 6:00 pm by the time we reached home. Not only did I feel unprepared to give the midterm tomorrow, I found it difficult to study. Every time I tried to focus on my notes, the images of Manny lying on the hospital bed with tubes and wires came before me. I knew I would bomb the midterm, but the question was how badly. It was a fourth-year management course on 'operations', and I breezed through most of the lecture slides due to the lack of time.

The next day I gave the worst midterm of my academic career, but strangely, I didn't care about it. I was worried about Manny and rushed to the hospital to get the latest updates from his family. As our midterm was in the second half of the day, Andre and I were the last ones to reach the hospital. We arrived at the hospital to witness what looked like an argument between Parveen and Victoria. As we were standing at quite a distance from them, we couldn't hear the exchange of words, but it looked like a heated discussion. The discussion ended with Parveen breaking into tears and going upstairs while Victoria went back to her seat looking equally miserable.

After a little hesitation, we decided to approach Victoria to find out what the matter was. We wanted to know if everything was alright with Manny, because it was strange for a mother and daughter to argue at this critical hour.

'Hey Victoria, is everything alright? Your mother looked very upset,' said Lydia.

'The doctors said that Manny has lost a lot of blood and would require immediate blood transfusion. They have kept him on a ventilator because his condition has deteriorated from yesterday. Now, Manny's blood group is AB negative, which is a very rare blood group, and the hospital does not have it. Coincidentally, as his twin sister, I am the only one in the family to have the same blood group as Manny. My mother wants me to donate my blood, but I told her that I won't, and I have my reasons for it which I cannot tell her, because she is very religious and would be very hurt to find out the truth,' said Victoria.

'Your mother is right. What could be a bigger reason than saving your brother's life?' said Sonia in a fit of impotent rage.

'Sonia, please don't talk like that. We have to respect her personal choice even if we disagree with it,' interrupted

Ryan as he held her, knowing how aggressive Sonia could get. He was also aware of the fact that we couldn't cross boundaries, as we were only Manny's friends and not his biological family.

'There is a bigger reason than saving my brother's life, Sonia. You might not agree with me, but I can share my reason with all of you without the fear of any negative repercussions. The reason I cannot donate my blood is because I have submitted myself to God. I am opposed to any medical practice that violates my scripture, like blood transfusion. I cannot donate or accept blood because of the scriptural admonition against the donation or consumption of blood. According to the books of Leviticus and Deuteronomy, blood is not to be poured out but returned to God as it were. No one can fight the will of God. I know this doesn't make sense to you now, but it will when His voice will reach you. Following God's will is more important to me than donating blood to Emmanuel,' said Victoria with a lilt in her voice.

'What scriptures are you talking about? Jesus never forbade blood transfusions. I am a Christian and have studied the Bible too,' said Lydia.

'According to our interpretation of Bible, Jesus is not God. God is greater than him because he created Jesus. Also, I am not an orthodox Christian like you or Emmanuel. I am a Jehovah's Witness,' enunciated Victoria, voicing the sentiment of her cult. Now I understood why she could not reveal her reason to her mother. I was confident that she had managed to keep this secret from Manny too.

'What is a Jehovah's Witness?' asked Lydia. Sonia, Ryan, and I already knew the answer, as we had studied about their subculture in one of our sociology classes.

I answered the question on behalf of Victoria, 'Witness of Jehovah is a millenarian restorationist Christian denomination that holds beliefs distinct from mainstream Christianity. They base their beliefs on the texts of the Bible but ignore mere human speculations and religious creeds. They abstain from celebrating festivals like Christmas and

Easter because they believe these festivals are based on pagan customs and religions. They point out how Jesus never asked his followers to celebrate his birthday. Similarly, they refrain from joining the military or politics. Also, they lacerate the use of blood transfusions even if their own life is in danger.'

For the next two hours, we waited in anxious silence for Parveen to come back with some news about Manny. This was a stressful time for all of us, as it was happening in the middle of midterms. We were torn between studying and being there for Manny. I opened my laptop to skim through some notes and readings for the next day's exam. Parveen finally came back to the lobby. She was silent like a lobotomized potato. Victoria was asking her questions about Manny, but she just stared coldly at her face.

'Mom, how is Emmanuel? What are the doctors saying?'

'He is no more. He died of multiple organ failures due to an excessive loss of blood. But it was you who pulled the plug off that ventilator,' said Parveen as she looked mechanically at Victoria, exhibiting no signs of any emotion.

It took some time to dawn on me that Manny was no longer amongst us. His body must be lying on some stretcher, devoid of the warmth of life. His cold, listless body was in sync with the wails of his friends and family who had prayed for a different outcome. The boundary that separated life and death seemed to be thin, bleak, and easily permeable. However, no one who has ever crossed that boundary has managed to return. I will never hear his voice again. Never again see the smile that was so comforting. A young man who died before he had lived. Manny was in a languid sleep where he didn't need any alarms to wake up. But he had left me wide awake. I had a sort of an epiphany, and it was then that I got my third lesson before graduating:

Stop taking time for granted. Getting out of bed hail and hearty is a blessing that we don't realize until the day when getting out seems difficult. I know that all my troubles will never fade away, but I wouldn't wish them away. Those troubles are a reminder that I am alive. There are moments that I take for granted thinking there is a lot of time before I die. The average human life span is 72.6 years. Manny had lived only 22 of those years. He was dead before he was fully born. Maybe he would have lived longer if Victoria had donated her blood. I was angry at her, but I also forgave her. Most people who think that they have been wronged by someone live with feelings of revenge, hate, or wanting justice. In the real world, justice is often elusive. The person who has wronged you has nothing to give you. Only you can give them something, i.e., forgiveness.

Full battery charged = 100% life = 72.6 years [avg. human life]

70% charge left. By the time one graduates 30% life is already over. Manny's battery was over before graduating.

We came back to the library to study for our midterms. The midterm madness did not even allow us to mourn for Manny properly. I tried hard to focus on my readings, but I couldn't study at all. The last words that Manny spoke to me echoed in my mind, 'Take care of Victoria.' I remembered the fundraiser that I had planned to start for Manny's family. The interview that Parveen had given on my insistence was already printed and available online. So I asked Lydia and Andre for help in drafting a nice message for the fundraiser that I was going to start online on GoFundMe. We had kept a target of 32,000$ for the Teji family. In order to get the ball rolling, the seven of us contributed 100$ each in the hopes that people who knew him or anyone in his family would shower their generosity. The pitch for the fundraiser drafted by Lydia, Andre, and me was the following:

RISING FROM THE ASHES

One of our friends, Emmanuel Teji, had a major house fire that led to his painful demise while rendering his mother and sister homeless. The only possessions that his mother and his sister own are the clothes that they are wearing on their bodies. As a single mother, Emmanuel's mother had undertaken a lot of hardships to purchase her house, and unfortunately, the fire struck at a window of time when she could not afford insurance. In this hour of need, the greatest gift for them would be to live in their own house as no amount of compensation would be able to replace the loss that has left them bereft.... They are willing to take any expression of support that you are willing to give –from blessings for a brighter tomorrow to small amounts of monetary donations. Your donations could be even as little as the price of a coffee. We would highly appreciate if you helped us spread the word. Keep them in your prayers and keep your family close. God bless you. If you want to reach out to Emmanuel's family, their email is parveen.teji@canadacartage.ca.

After writing the message, we attached the newspaper article with Parveen's interview and posted it on GoFundMe. We also posted the fundraiser's link on our Facebook profiles. As I couldn't get back to studying, I knew I would fare badly on the midterm if I sat for it. So I decided to fake an illness and get a doctor's note made the next day to postpone my midterm. As a result, I was sitting at the doctor's clinic at UofT, waiting for my turn to see a doctor instead of appearing for my midterm. In the last few years, the only memories I had of visiting the health centre on campus for a doctor's appointment was for an STI test. If a student would be missing a midterm or an exam, he had to get a special form filled by the doctor and pay money to get that form filled, because that service was not included in the student health insurance. I knew a lot of students who faked illnesses during midterms or exams so that they could reappear for it at a later date, and I was confident that the doctors could tell when a student genuinely had a stomach ache and when the student was lying to avoid a test. However, they turned a blind eye as long as money was exchanging hands. The students benefitted as much as the doctors did. The noble profession was no longer so noble.

Location: A funeral home in Brampton

Parveen had organized a viewing, or as some would call 'a wake', for Manny and had invited all of us so that we could mourn his death. A viewing is an informal gathering of friends and family which gives mourners an opportunity to share their grief, provide pastoral support to one another, and say goodbye to the deceased on a personal level. In order to lower her burden, all of us decided to get a food item each and offered to help with the cleanup too. As Manny was fond of mulled wine, Victoria had arranged it for the guests. A big picture of Manny was framed and kept on a table.

When I met Praveen, she hugged me and said, 'Thanks for helping out with the food and fundraising. We are blessed to have people like you in our lives.'

'Actually, I had something to give you,' I said, taking out a paper from my pocket. 'These are the account details for the GoFundMe campaign. We have already managed to raise 30,000$ out of our total target of 32,000$. You can update your bank information and claim the amount. I was surprised that we could achieve 94% of our goal in just two weeks. The whole community has been extremely kind. Manny was a good son, a good friend, and I believe this is the result of his karma.' Parveen was very happy after learning about the success of the fundraiser.

'I am eternally grateful for this. The money will be very useful in getting our lives sorted and will also help me with rebuilding my house. We can finally move out of our shelter and find a place on rent,' said Parveen.

'I am glad we could help.'

'By the way, what are your plans after graduation?' she asked.

'Recently, I have got offers from several universities in the UK. I have chosen to accept my offer from the London School of Economics and Political Science, as their management department is pretty good.'

'Congratulations! I wish you the very best in your future endeavors. Few days ago, we heard back from the office of Christopher McQuarrie. They were asking for Manny's contact details, because they had tried to reach him and weren't aware of his death. They told me that Mr. McQuarrie was very impressed with his audition and wanted to offer him a role. I apprised them with the situation, but I couldn't sleep peacefully that night. All he ever wanted was to be an actor,' said Parveen. I felt hollow from inside. Until two weeks ago, I had only read about death in textbooks or newspapers. For the first time ever, I had seen death and felt it again when Parveen told me how eager they were to sign a contract with Manny.

After finishing my conversation with Parveen, I glanced around the room and noticed some people paying their respects in front of Manny's portrait before helping themselves with some light snacks. Sam was seated near the food counter, sipping a glass of warm mulled wine. Ontario was cold in March and so mulled wine was ideal considering the weather outside. I thought of sharing the news of Manny's acting offer with all my friends. Even though the news was heartbreaking for them, they were proud of Manny for cracking the audition and receiving an offer from one of the most distinguished directors of Hollywood.

While I was chatting with my friends, Victoria walked up to me and said, 'Could I speak to you privately for a minute?'

'Sure,' I said and moved away where nobody could hear us.

'I know you are angry with me because you haven't spoken to me since Manny's death. Just like my mother, even you think that I was responsible for Manny's death, don't you?' said Victoria.

'I wouldn't go so far as to blame Manny's death on you...*silence*...I think that he could have been alive today if you had given him blood, but I am not angry anymore. I am not in your shoes, so I understand that I shouldn't judge you for your decisions. You had your reasons, and I came to terms with the fact that our perspectives on this incident will be different. I don't know if what I am about to say will make a difference to you, but I will always be there for you,' I said.

Victoria replied, 'If Emmanuel was alive, he would have wanted us to be friends. I am sure that he is looking upon us from a place of comfort and eternal bliss.'

'Amen to that.'

CONVOCATION DAY

The time had come to graduate. I couldn't believe that today would be the last day I could call myself a student at UofT. I was soon going to be an alumnus. Six weeks ago in April, I had given my last exam, and now I stood on the threshold of completing an important chapter of university life. After putting down my pen for the last exam, I felt like I had said adieu to all the stresses of life. I had avoided thinking about a lot of important questions due to the work at school, and these questions now came back to flood my mind. I did everything that was expected of me. I was graduating with a CGPA of 3.65 and had a standing offer from one of the best universities in the UK. But there was something that still made me feel that my time at UofT was not over. I didn't feel ready to leave this place. Uoft had checked my ego, showing me that I had to work hard to enjoy every success in life. It constantly challenged my beliefs and outlook on life. It pushed me out of my comfort zone every day; and though I detested it on some days, I wouldn't want it any other way. If I hadn't been forced to push my limits, I would be the same person that I was on the first day of university. The person who was graduating from UofT could think critically, write better, debate more confidently, earn higher, eat meat (which opened my eyes to many tasty cuisines that I would earlier dismiss as disgusting without even trying it), and fend pussy on a constant basis.

On the day of my convocation, I woke up excited for the big moment. I knew I had to look my best, so I went for a clean shave and a haircut to a Black barber joint called

Onyx, which gave me a sexy fade. My parents and my sister had arrived from India a day before to witness my convocation. The convocation ceremony was from 4:00 to 6:00 pm, but the university required the graduands to reach an hour early so that they could pick up their convocation regalia and be made to stand in the order in which their names would be called out. After that, all graduands made the historic walk around King's College Circle to be finally seated in their designated spots inside the Convocation Hall.

I arrived on campus with my family to see the Convocation Plaza decked out in celebratory blue and white, which was the university's official color. There was a sea of smiling faces, cheers, and students in black graduation robes with their families, taking selfies on the front campus lawn. At UofT, every college has a separate convocation ceremony. The convocation ceremony that I was attending was for Trinity College. I met up with Ryan and Andre who were graduating with me and entered the building where the convocation gowns were being handed out. Sam was graduating at the fall convocation ceremonies that would be held in November, as he was two credits short which he was completing over the summer. Sonia, Lydia, and Nigel were graduating four days after us at the University College Convocation. However, they were all coming to meet us after our convocation ceremony to celebrate this joyous moment with us. Also, today was my last day in Toronto, so they wanted to meet me before I left for a family vacation to the Canadian Rockies. After collecting our convocation regalia, all the graduands were taken to a room where the convocation marshals began arranging us in order. Once we were standing in the correct order, the head marshal came in to deliver a speech about how we were going to embody the moment which we were all waiting for. His job was to ensure that the ceremony took place smoothly and all the students knew what to do. We listened as the head marshal began his speech:

Today, the University of Toronto is formally recognizing your hard work, your accomplishments, your perseverance, and your dedication. This is a very important milestone in your life. Each of *you as a member of the graduating class of 2017 is joining an extraordinary family of University of Toronto alumni. As soon to be graduates, you have had the privilege of consuming knowledge that has evolved over thousands of years. Today is your day. Often in life, we get caught up with the stress of work or social responsibilities, and we forget to sit back and enjoy all that we have accomplished. Today is that day where you can forget all your worries and celebrate everything that you have accomplished during your time at university, because you deserve it and also because that diploma is very expensive (sarcastically)... *blah blah blah*.... I want to remind you of certain key points for the convocation ceremony. In order to maintain the decorum of this event, you are not allowed to leave unless the ceremony is officially over and you are told that you can leave. Some people choose not to shake hands with the chief guest, the President, the Chancellor and other dignitaries on stage, as they are not comfortable with handshakes. Don't worry, they will not mind it. Lastly, don't forget to return your gowns after the ceremony is over and you have finished taking pictures and making Snapchat stories in it. Today is your moment. Congratulations, and I wish you all success in whatever you pursue next.*

After the speech by the head marshal, the graduate procession left for the famous traditional walk around King's College Circle from the marshalling area to the front doors of the Convocation Hall. The procession was led by a Trinity staff member who was carrying a gonfalon that identified the college participating in that day's convocation. The banner captured an expression of pride and accomplishment that would enhance our storied ceremony. As I entered the Convocation Hall, I remembered the comical announcement that Andre and Sam had made during an astronomy course in freshman year. Once we were seated inside the domed rotunda and were waiting for the dignitaries to arrive, I could see my family waving to me from the seats below. The Convocation Hall seemed to be the metaphorical and physical centre of the University of Toronto, and its radial structure seemed to anchor a newly rationalized campus layout. A large glass oculus allowed natural lighting into the centre of the hall below.

Everyone stood up and welcomed the dignitaries and the professors as they entered the Convocation Hall. The chief guest speaker for our convocation ceremony was the Mayor of Toronto, John Tory. I looked at the other end of the Convocation Hall where Andre was seated. He was chatting up some random girl with a cadaverous face sitting next to him. From his expression, I could tell that he was in game mode and was going for her number. A mature student who was graduating with us was breastfeeding her baby during the convocation ceremony. The fact that this was possible was an indication of how progressive Canada was as a country. I couldn't imagine this happening back in India. The speakers spoke in consecutive succession, but there was one piece of advice that ringed with me and that came from the President of UofT, Meric Gertler. He told us that we were graduating at a very exciting time and that we would be entering a world which has way more opportunities compared to the time when he graduated. He told us to always maintain contact with the professors who taught us and the friends we had made during our journey at UofT no matter what we did or where we went in life.

Once the speeches ended, the master of ceremony began calling the name of the students so that they could come on stage to be felicitated. The diploma was handed to the students by the staff members once they shook hands on stage and came down from the podium. When my name was called out, I could hear Andre and Ryan cheering loudly from the crowd. The feeling of holding that diploma in your hands is a feeling I cannot express in words. For those who argue that there is no need of attending convocation when you could just get your diploma mailed at home, I would beg to differ. The sense of pride and accomplishment stays with you forever. As soon as the last person got his diploma and the ceremony ended, the whole room burst into a delirious applause. The class of 2017 had made it.

We walked out of the Convocation Hall to take part in the requisite photo-taking and family hugging on the Convocation Plaza lawn. The bells in the soldier's tower were ringing like they did every time a convocation ceremony took place. Andre took a family picture for me, and I returned the favor to him. The Convocation Plaza had a photo booth with myriad props to take pictures with family and friends. My mother was fascinated with the props and insisted I take several pictures with her. She kissed me on the cheek which made the 22-year-old me slightly embarrassed. My parents had met my friends before when they had come to Canada for a vacation, and I had met Andre's parents and Ryan's mother too. But our families had never met before, so we introduced them and left them to socialize while we went to meet Sonia, Sam, Nigel, and Lydia who had reached after the convocation ceremony was over, because graduating students usually get two tickets per person which are utilized by family members.

'Congratulations! You made it,' said Sonia and Lydia in unison.

'Thank you. It is your turn next,' I replied.

'Congratulations,' said Nigel to the three of us.

'Why couldn't you fucks wait for me to graduate?' joked Sam.

'Because we couldn't afford to waste money on taking summer courses for two years like your lazy dumb ass,' replied Ryan.

'Also, who wouldn't want to graduate on time if they got accepted into Yale Law School?' said Andre who was referring to Ryan's admission at Yale. Ryan had made us all proud by getting offers from America's top-tier law schools like Harvard, Yale, and Stanford. He had chosen to go to Yale after considering all his options. Sonia had accepted her invitation to Osgoode Law School at York University. She had received offers from Queen, McGill, and Osgoode. UofT had put her on a waitlist but eventually rejected her. She chose Osgoode so that she could be near Nigel in Toronto.

Sam shot back at Andre, 'In my defense, I more than made up the money that I invested on taking summer classes with the meteoric rise of Bitcoin. As of today, the value of

Bitcoin is 2,617$. I just need to sell ten Bitcoins to make up the extra money spent on my tuition and living expenses.'

'Are you for real?' I asked stumped as I had sold all my investments last year when Bitcoin was around 600$, because I expected it to crash.

'Yes, I told you selling your investments would be a mistake. You should have held on to it for longer. Not only would it have covered your entire cost for graduate school, but you could have also afforded a down payment for your first apartment,' said Sam.

'Well, now that I look at the crypto markets, I concede that I was wrong and you were right about Bitcoin,' I said.

'Which places in the Rockies are you visiting? Since Canada is celebrating its 150th year, I heard they are offering free transportation for tourists in Banff,' said Lydia.

'I am going to Calgary, Banff, Jasper, and Edmonton. We leave tomorrow morning. The picturesque mountains, beautiful wildlife, and alpine lakes make it one of the prettiest places on Earth. I badly need this holiday before I begin graduate school,' I said.

'Are you two lovebirds planning to go somewhere before Sonia begins law school?' Andre asked Sonia and Nigel. They had been dating for seven months now.

'We were planning a small skiing trip to Blue Mountains, but I am unsure about the dates. My father has made sure that I am constantly occupied with work at our transportation company. I am made to grind harder than a domesticated donkey,' said Nigel.

'After looking at all of you go places like graduate school or working in a family business like Nigel or starting a good-paying job like Andre, I feel so lost. I have no idea what I am going to do with my English degree. I feel like I am more confused than I was when I began university. I had come here to find answers, and I thought that reaching the finish line and getting a UofT degree would fix everything in life,' said Lydia.

'I don't know if this will make sense to you, but it is okay to not have everything figured out by 22. University might not have given you all the answers that you were looking for, but I can see that it has changed you as a person. You are not the same girl I met four years ago, and I guess that is what should matter. University challenges you and makes you evolve as a person unless you show resistance to all kinds of change or refuse to come out of your dorm room,' said Ryan.

'Yeah, you are right. I think I got a little demoralized after seeing you guys have a concrete plan,' said Lydia.

'Where do you all want to go for dinner?' Sonia asked sonorously.

'Since it is our last meal together, I suggest we go to either Boston Pizza or the Big Smoke Burger,' said Nigel.

'If our parents were not coming, I would have voted for Big Smoke Burger, but since our families are coming along, I think we should go to Boston Pizza. It is classier than Big Smoke Burger and appropriate for this occasion,' I said.

'I haven't tried Boston Pizza before, so I am up for it. I think we should return our gowns without dawdling more time,' said Ryan.

'Yeah, I don't want them to charge a fine on my online account for not returning the gown,' said Andre.

Finishing university was a bittersweet experience. On the cab ride to Boston Pizza, I became nostalgic as I saw all the bars, pubs, restaurants, and cafés that I had spent so much time in. Leaving Toronto was hard because I loved it, but at the same time, I was looking forward to living the British dream. I knew I couldn't hold on to UofT and keep reminiscing in the past, because change is inevitable. As much as I was excited to go to a new city and make new friends, I feared I would evanesce out of the lives of the friends that I made in Toronto. I knew I would face a few difficulties in the beginning as I transitioned to a new place and gave up an ensconced lifestyle. I wasn't worried about the extremely high costs of living in Central London, I was concerned about the psychic cost of leaving Toronto. The only reason I had turned down my offer from Oxford University was because I couldn't untether myself from an urban lifestyle. As a young man, I prioritized seedy bars and bartenders in an urban sprawl over a small quaint town in the countryside even if it had the most prestigious university in the world. On the positive side, I was eager to try out my pick-up skills in what pick-up artists call 'the toughest city in the world', because London was known to embody the most talented, beautiful, and richest girls in the world. Getting laid was not difficult in London, but getting laid with the nines and the tens in the British capital was not a piece of cake. We had a wonderful feast at Boston Pizza, where I had to pretend being a vegetarian to bamboozle my family, even though I craved chicken.

On my way to the airport next morning, I received a phone call from Afifah who congratulated me on graduating and wished me good luck for my future. She said she would miss me and told me to stay in touch with her. Scurrying to catch the plane, I let the airport in Toronto swallow me and spit me out in the province of Alberta where I spent the next two weeks exploring the Canadian Rockies before returning to India to apply for my UK student visa.

Niagara Falls

Note to the reader: Now that I have taken you through a nostalgic flashback of my university years, I think you have a better context for the text message that I received from Afifah at my reunion which read:

Devansh, I need your help. Please meet me on Wednesday. It is very important, and I feel you are the only person who can help me now...

Since I was in Canada primarily for the reunion, my schedule over the next few days involved meeting some friends who were not part of my main group. On Wednesday evening, I was leaving for Niagara Falls for three days before coming back to Toronto on Saturday in order to catch my flight to London, as I had report to work on Monday. So I gave Afifah a confirmation for lunch on Wednesday and suggested that we go to a board-game café called Snakes and Lattes, which was located downtown on Bloor Street. Her medium of communication indicated that whatever she wanted to say was not something she was comfortable sharing over a phone call. That night, I kept tossing in bed, as I worried about Afifah's situation.

Location: Snakes and Latte

I entered the café at our scheduled time. To my surprise, Afifah was already waiting for me on a table near the entrance, so I could spot her as soon as I entered the cozy, energy-radiating space decorated with couches and chairs. She had a glass of iced latte on her table, which was only half full indicating that she reached the place much before the scheduled time, which was very unlike her. I could not recall a meeting between us where she had reached before me. It was suggestive of an urgency that was deep and raucous. Just like I was surprised to see her waiting for me, she was surprised to see me with a large piece of luggage.

'What is that luggage for?' she asked me as I warmly hugged her.

'I am leaving for Niagara today at 5:00 pm, so I thought I would directly go after meeting you.'

'Oh! It is the best time of the year to visit Niagara. They have fireworks during the summer for the huge influx of tourists that visit the Falls. Maybe you will be lucky to experience a grand display of crackers,' she said. Her demeanor lacked a certain verve, and she sounded like an empty catechism of words.

'I squeezed in this trip, as I have many memories of the Falls with my friends and family and I want to revisit those memories, because I am not coming back to Canada anytime soon,' I said.

'They have a good collection of board games here. I wonder how I didn't know about this concept café. When I was looking up this place online, I found that they have quite a few outlets in the GTA,' she said.

'I haven't come here much either. It is my second time here. I came here once during university and I liked it, so that is why I suggested that we meet here. Also, it is very close to my Airbnb,' I replied, settling down on the table. Snakes and Latte employed a concept where patrons were expected to hock their mobile phones, MacBooks, and Wi-Fi for old-fashioned board games. For 5$ a person, customers could play any game in the store. The store had board games for all ages and from all time periods. Their collection ranged from ancient games like chess to classics like Monopoly and Clue as well as recently created games like Catan. The baristas at Snakes and Latte struck a balance between serving customers and acting as their tutorial leaders whenever patrons needed help in understanding the rules or clarifying them.

'Is there any game you have in mind?' she asked. I would have preferred to play chess with her just to gauge the current status of her skills and see if her game had improved or deteriorated ever since we had played our last game in the chess society. However, I was aware of the stilted nature of the conversation that was going to unfold once the small talk was over; hence, I didn't want to choose a game that would take a toll on our cognitive capacities.

'I am okay with whatever you want to play,' I replied. She smiled demurely and went to the rack of board games to fetch a game for us. After pondering indecisively at the myriad options available, she came back with a game called 'Guess who'.

'Do you know how to play this?' asked Afifah.

'Yes. Basically, both of us pick a card each, and we have to guess the person on each other's card by using questions that can only be answered in a yes or no.'

'That is correct. I used to play this game with my sister when we were children. However, we were disappointed at the lack of female characters in this game, so we wrote a scathing yet unassailably logical letter to the company complaining about the lack of balance between the number of male and female cards. I heard that they eventually launched a more feminist version of the game when a lot of people brought this discrepancy to their notice, but I have never played the newer version of the game,' said Afifah.

We were having fun as we locked horns over guessing each other's card. After two rounds of the game, we summoned one of the baristas to place our order for food. Afifah ordered clafoutis, which was a flan-like cake originally from Limousin, France, courtesy of the French background of the owners. I ordered a buffalo chicken wrap, and we decided to share a plate of tacos for starters. We continued playing, and she was giving me tough competition, as our scores were tied. Our food arrived, so we decided to halt our game and continue with another board game after our meal was over.

'Let us dig in. I am super hungry,' I said. She reached for the tacos, and I knew that it would be appropriate to slowly initiate the conversation she wanted to have with me.

'Now, we can discuss the message that you sent me. I was deeply worried when I read your text. What is the matter?' I enquired.

'My family is considering a marital proposal for me and is adamant to take me to Pakistan with them. The boy is a relative of one of my relatives. But I don't feel prepared for marriage right now, and I can't see myself married to a boy who has never lived in the West and is unfamiliar with how life outside Pakistan is,' replied Afifah.

'But you had a strong conviction about marrying a boy your parents chose for you. He is a Pakistani, and I am sure they have chosen a Muslim for you. Wasn't that what you always wanted?' I asked a loaded question.

'I was wrong to have viewed marriage through the axiom of religion, and I have no qualms about admitting that. I never thought that they would choose a boy all the way from Pakistan. Even though he has an MBA degree from the Lahore University of Management Sciences, I don't think we would ever be compatible. Moreover, he sounds more excited about moving to Canada than marrying me. I have a hunch that he is only marrying me for the Canadian passport, but my parents don't agree and are emotionally blackmailing me for this arranged marriage,' said Afifah. From where I was sitting, it looked more like a forced marriage than an arranged marriage. Forced marriages are often conducted under the façade of arranged marriages and result in pernicious effects on the people who enter this union. These kinds of marriages were a funny concept to me because all your life you are instructed to be cautious of strangers and suddenly you are asked to sleep with one.

'I understand that you are in a very difficult situation, but I am flustered on how I could be of any help in this case,' I said.

'The reason I am telling you this is because I know the type of feelings you harbored for me, but I could not never reciprocate those same feelings for you, because I was bogged down by a lot of hierarchies. But today I don't want to mince my words and tell you that I want to be with you. Take me to

London with you. I am carrying my passport and some cash on me,' she said. Nobody had ever declared their feelings so guilelessly and innocently to me like she did. However, adhering to her request was akin to opening a Pandora's box.

'Afifah...*pause*...I am not sure if you realize the impracticality of the suggestion you are making to me. Moving to another country, let alone another continent, cannot be impulsively decided over lunch. What you are asking of me is unreasonable.'

'Don't worry, I won't burden you. I am going to work and do whatever you ask of me. All I want is to be with you,' she said. I was overwhelmed to hear this. I looked down. My gaze traced the thick wooden legs of the table, the sinuous curves of its corners, and the gleam of its shiny, camel-brown surface.

'It is not about being a burden. I have a huge studio in Central London that can accommodate another person, and my job pays me enough to buy groceries for the both of us. But you want me to abet you in eloping to another country!' I said, emphasizing on the word 'eloping'. I sounded like a person to whom a unique and coveted privilege had been offered.

'Elopements don't have to be an exclusively late night, spontaneous rendezvous to Paris,' she said curtly.

'What about your family when they find out that you have left the country with a boy whom you knew from university? They don't know anything about me. There are going to be so many questions, and they would be seeking so many answers.'

'I haven't thought about all that. For now, I have run away from home, and I don't wish to go back and be coerced into marrying a guy against my wishes. Tell me something honestly, Devansh, didn't you always desire me at university? Now that I want to be with you, you are unsure about us.'

'Trust me, there is nothing more I have wanted than to be in a relationship with you. But I never imagined that the proposition of being with you would entail so many caveats. The purpose of me coming to Canada was a reunion with my friends. In a few hours, I am boarding a bus to Niagara Falls and suddenly you ask me if I could take you with me to London. How do you expect me to make such a big decision?'

'Then take me to Niagara with you for now. Please don't ask me to go home. We can figure things out there, and this way you will have more time to consider taking me to London. You are my only hope,' she pleaded.

'...*pause*...All right, come with me to the Falls. I hope the bus is not full, and we can find a seat for you,' I said. It took me some time to absorb the ramifications of this commitment. Afifah dug into her cake while I laid my eyes on the large wrap lying in front of me. She looked content. The whole conversation started to feel too surreal and magical to be true. I didn't feel like I was living in the now. But I didn't want to share the decision to take Afifah with me to Niagara with anyone. People would already start predicting outcomes and judging her to the extreme, as the primal mind is accustomed to see the negative before the positive.

'I guess we would have to shop for some basic supplies for you in Niagara. You don't have anything on you other than your passport and money,' I said taking the first bite of my wrap.

'I would be needing some clothes. I didn't take anything before coming here because my family was at home. They would be suspicious if they saw me carrying anything other than my purse. I didn't want to ring any alarm bells. Also, I was unsure of how you would react when I told you that I wanted to run away from home,' she replied.

'They are going to report your absence to the police when you don't come back home tonight. I don't want police officers showing up at our hotel in Niagara looking for you,' I said.

'Don't worry about that. I am going to take out my sim card and turn off my phone so that they cannot trace me. Also, I am going on my own free will, and I am old enough to make my decisions. Legally, they cannot force me to go back to my parents' house.'

'Yes, but you are forgetting that you would need to present your identification on the bus to Niagara. Also, they will be checking your ID at the hotel. We cannot use your passport because then they can easily trace you,' I said.

'So, what do I do now?' she asked.

'There are many shops downtown that make fake identification cards. We will have to visit one of those before we go to the bus station. They won't take long to create a new ID for you. The last time I visited one of these seedy places was in freshman year when my roommate Andre wanted a counterfeit ID so he could drink booze before being of legal age,' I said. I never thought I would need to revisit one of those establishments again.

We finished eating our lunch and split the bill. Then I looked online to find the closest shop that made fake ID cards. Luckily, we found one on Bloor Street itself. Afifah and I headed for the store where Afifah purchased a new identification card and now she would be travelling under a new alias: Saima Khan. The person who was printing out the fake identification gave me a dirty look as if I was a kingpin of a gang who coaxed innocent girls into making counterfeit identification cards and carry out nefarious activities. I wanted to get out of the place as soon as I could, as this place gave me bad vibes. After paying for her counterfeit identification, we went to the bus station on Bay Street. Afifah enquired for the availability of seats on the bus that we were expected to board, and as her luck would have it, there were three seats left.

As we began our journey on the bus, I began to reflect philosophically on life. I have often heard self-proclaimed clairvoyants tell me that life is about the journey and not the destination. This journey with Afifah was turning out to be like the journey of life. It was full of surprises just like life is.

However, the human mind is accustomed to a set of habits and routines and is comfortable with repetitiveness and familiarity. This sudden plan of experimentation and exploration shook me from the inside. I know that university was meant to prepare us for the world outside, but the structured microcosm of the schooling system didn't prepare students to make the most important decisions of life. For now, I thought I should just be a good friend to her. William Shakespeare had once said, 'A friend is one who knows you as you are, understands where you have been, accepts what you have become and still, gently allows you to grow.'

I was gawking at all the mansions that came after the bus crossed Burlington. The beautiful, rolling country with the many vineyards ensorcelled me and made me crave for a sweet glass of ice wine. However, I knew that Afifah wouldn't approve of me drinking alcohol, even though she wouldn't express her feelings in words. It took me a while to realize that I was already considerate about what she felt and thought. The bus dropped us off at the Niagara Falls bus station, and we took a cab from there to the Crowne Plaza hotel where I had a booking. At the lobby of the hotel, I asked the jocund receptionist assisting us with check-in to change my booking to a room with a double bed. At this stage, I was very uncomfortable to share my bed with her, and I knew she would be equally uncomfortable to sleep next to me. I knew I was sharing a room with a girl who had never even kissed a guy before. Things were already very awkward for her.

The Crowne Plaza hotel had 234 guestrooms, so upgrading the room to a room with a double bed was not difficult. The hotel sat steps away from the Niagara Falls and was revered for its legacy of service and elegance. The hotel was part of a huge entertainment complex that featured indoor connections to the Fallsview Indoor Waterpark and Casino Niagara. At the ground level, the hotel had a shopping concourse with souvenir and chocolate shops. It also had its very own Starbucks café situated in the lobby. We freshened up in the room, rested for a bit and then went out to explore the nightlife in Niagara.

Nothing spells nightlife in Niagara more than Clifton Hill. Clifton Hill is a street in Niagara Falls that is chock full of attractions that range from fun houses, a wax museum, bowling alleys, miniature golf courses, scary houses to a buffet of restaurants. Even though most tourist attractions close by evening in Niagara, one place that does not roll the red carpet even after midnight is Clifton Hill. As we made our way towards the tourist promenade, we walked past the broad walk where we could see the magnificent beauty of Niagara Falls. The sunlight gleamed at the cascade waterfalls with its aqua-colored water jumping out at the bevy of people who stood by the railings, capturing the awe-inspiring views on their electronic devices. We were visiting Niagara Falls in the peak summer season, and the whole town felt like a tourist mecca.

We reached Clifton Hill, which was replete with opportunities to enjoy the splendor of the festive street.

'I have never been to a scary house before. Could we try it out?' asked Afifah meekly.

'Seriously? You have not been to one even on Halloween?' I asked back.

'As a child, I was always scared to try it.'

'Trust me, I have been to the scary house in Canada's Wonderland. You guys don't make it scary enough. At least, I didn't find it scary when I went there. It is a waste of time,' I said, trying to persuade her to change her mind. I genuinely felt it was too childish.

'Please, I don't want to do it alone,' she said in a beautiful whisper. I couldn't refuse her now. She reeked of a childlike innocence, and I felt an instant desire to protect all her needs and wants.. The depth with which I could feel her desires and the intensity of the attachment that was developing between us was becoming evident to me.

'Sure, if you want to dive right into a Halloween nightmare,' I said in jest.

We purchased our tickets and entered the haunted house. She was concentrating on the sounds and the staff members who were planted to scare us. I was concentrating on her. On several occasions, she yanked on tightly to my arm. I could feel her nails dig into my skin. I did my best to protect her from the wrath of Dracula and his goons. As a woman, she needed to feel protected even if it was a small gesture like putting my hand on her back. The point of those gestures was to make her feel emotionally secure. Whether or not a woman is consciously aware that we are only a pandemic or a natural disaster away from death, she still feels more attracted to a man who can make her feel secure under any circumstance. Like most women, Afifah had an innate need to be made to feel safe.

'Hope you won't have trouble sleeping tonight,' I said after we came out of the ghost house.

'How do you not feel scared?' she asked.

'Because I know they aren't ghosts and they are not allowed to harm guests. Technically, they are more worried about our safety than we are worried about our own. I have done much scarier and longer versions of this concept in India. This was a very mild version built for kids. Let us grab something to eat and then go back to the hotel so that we can start the day early tomorrow.'

The next morning, we woke up to a bright and sunny day. After eating breakfast, we went to the Fallsview Mall, which was located inside the Fallsview Casino Resort, so that Afifah could purchase a few essential clothing and hygiene items for herself. She had left Toronto with just her passport, her cell phone, and 2,000$ in cash that she had saved by working summer jobs. I wondered about the current status of her family. She had left a letter on her desk informing her parents that she was running away from the tyranny imposed by their set of rules, whereby she was not allowed to answer back, think for herself, or marry someone she wanted. She was tired of following the norms in her house, even though she was groomed as a child to abide by those norms. Her refusal to comply with their wishes resulted in her being accused of bringing shame upon the family. Why does the onus of upholding culture, tradition, and the family's honor fall upon the woman?

Upon reaching the Fallsview Mall, the first store we entered was Sirens. Afifah bought some plain tees and dark-washed skinny jeans that would go with tops of any color. She was a clever shopper and knew how to budget her expenses. From the next store, she bought panties and socks. To cap off her shopping list, we went to Shoppers Drug Mart where she bought products for personal hygiene. One of the essential items on that list was a toothbrush, because the toothbrushes available in our hotel were low quality and she personally didn't find them reusable. I had chaperoned her throughout her shopping spree until she had bought everything she needed. Once she had finished shopping for her needs, I decided to take her to a store called Pepper Palace which was located in the same mall and sold some of the spiciest hot sauces in the world. Some of their sauces were so spicy that one had to sign a waiver before being allowed to sample them. However, if you are an addict of hot sauces, then this place was your drug dealer. Since Afifah hadn't come here before, she was oblivious to how uncontrollably hot these sauces were. I decided to use her ignorance to lure her into the sampling process. I told her that she should sample the Flashbang, which had a spice index of 3.5 million Scoville. I made her believe that the employees make customers sign the waiver as a formality whereas in reality the sauces were not very hot. She signed the waiver in an unsuspecting manner and took me on my word. The capsaicin from the mind-numbingly hot chili sauce stimulated the receptors in her mouth. The searing pain felt across her tongue brought tears to her eyes, and she made a frantic cry for water. She darted out of the store like an arrow to find something cool to depolarize the extreme pain of spice in her mouth. You could call it coincidence or a premeditated business idea, but right near Pepper Palace, there is an ice cream store that helped Afifah cool down the heat in her mouth.

'How are you feeling now?' I laughed uncontrollably at her.

'Why would you do such a thing? What have I done to you to deserve this?' she asked indignantly.

'You are going to avoid spice for a long time now.'

'I don't know what I would have done if there was no ice cream store close by.'

'You are never going to trust me with food again after this,' I continued as she ate more of the ice cream to subside the effect of the sauce.

'When I told you that I want to be with you, I opened myself up to pain and vulnerability. I don't mind you burning my mouth again, as long as you never burn my heart. I will never recuperate from the nauseating pain that burn will cause,' she said with bleary eyes. It was a pretty powerful thing to say to someone else, and in a way, a pure expression of what it can mean to accept someone unconditionally. I felt a telluric current through my entire body.

'Why would you open yourself to pain for me? Shouldn't you look after your comfort first?' I asked.

'There would be something wrong in me if I wasn't ready to do that. True love will be painful. True love should be painful.' This was the first time she used the word 'love'. Even though she didn't explicitly tell me that she loved me, she indicated the extents she was willing to go for me. I understood that she was trying to tell me that I should disabuse my mind of a fluffy, painless love because that kind of love did not exist. She was talking about the form of pain that involves a continuous worry for your lover's happiness and health. She plowed on, 'The reason I know this is because I have felt this pain before. It hurt when my parents disappointed me. I love them so much. I expected my brother to understand. He disappointed me too. The people I have loved the most have hurt me the most.' There should have been an eleventh commandment: Thou shall not force your children to marry people they don't want to.

'Then why do you trust me so much? No matter how much you try, you will end up getting hurt by me too, even though I have no intentions of ever hurting you. Remember Murphy's Law? Love is not a like robot that can be controlled through computer codes and there will be times when we have bad days.'

'I knew you were someone I would want in my life even on those bad days. I would rather have my bad days with you than good days with someone else,' said Afifah. I swallowed the lump in my throat that resulted from her words.

No visit to the Fallsview Casino Resort is complete if one hasn't tried his or her hand at gambling. I am not advocating betting huge amounts of money, but if you have come this far, it is harmless to try your luck with a few dollars at the slot machine just to get the feel of the *belle époque* theme of the complex. I felt a strong urge to play roulette, even though gambling is something I have consciously stayed away from. However, today I looked forward to my duel with Lady Luck because Afifah was beside me. As a religious Muslim, she always held herself back from entering establishments that involved activities like gambling, smoking, and drinking. But she gave a slow burdened smile when I told her of my desire to gamble. Even though she didn't look happy with the idea, she didn't show any resistance. Just like I had accommodated her request to go inside the scary house, she was accompanying me now. Maybe these adjustments meant something more than what they looked like on the surface. We were behaving like couples who sacrifice for each other in a relationship.

The environment inside the casino was structured to induce consumer spending. Dim lights, soothing music, and the maze at passages led people back to the slot machines. The whole floor was devoid of clocks and windows so that the gamblers would not realize how long they have been losing money. Cheap alcohol was being poured down by beautiful young women, and oxygen was being pumped in the room to make people stay awake. In addition to all this, there was a constant symphony of bells and sirens to make it seem like someone was winning all the time. Everything was fabricated to seduce the gamblers. Being completely aware of the semantics of the trade, I sat down at the roulette table and placed my bets. Afifah sat patiently trying to figure out the game as well as the odds of someone winning. After taking a short tour of the casino floor, she realized that the odds of every game were stacked in favor of the casino. I gambled unabashedly for the next three hours and came off the table winning 360$ using a strategy of small outside bets and doubling the next bet whenever I lost. Before I ended up losing the newly minted bank, I thought it would be best to cash out the money and treat us both to a wonderful dinner at a premium steakhouse.

According to my itinerary, on Friday, I had planned to take a boat tour to get a close and personal experience of the Falls. Afifah gladly agreed, as she had done the boat tour only from the American side. Before purchasing our tickets, we stopped at a viewing point to capture a selfie with the Horseshoe Falls, which is one of the three falls that constitute Niagara Falls. As we hadn't booked the boat ride in advance, we had to wait in a long queue due to the high demand during the summer months. We experienced a prolonged wait of two hours, which made me regret not having purchased the tickets online. We started at the top of the escarpment and then took a ride down the new funicular, which brought us to the docking area on the Niagara River. The staff provided us with bright red biodegradable ponchos before boarding to protect us from getting wet. We boarded the state-of-the-art double decker catamaran, which carries on the legacy of Canada's most iconic visitor experience. On the Canadian side, the tour was called Hornblower whereas it was referred to as The Maid of the Mist on the American side. The customers had an option to avail an audio guide which could be used in eight different languages, telling people interesting facts about the history of the Falls.

Upon boarding the boat, Afifah and I gathered around the front edge of the railing with the intention to get the best view of the waterfalls. The boat sailed through the turbulent waters, drenching the poncho-clad passengers on board. As the boat approached the base of the falls, we could feel a lingering sense of danger by seeing the force with which the water flowed down. 3,160 tons of water flows down the Niagara Falls every second. To put this quantity into perspective, the amount of water that flows down in one minute is enough to fill seventy Olympic-size swimming pools. Huge drops of water pelted us from head to toe. The wind began as a gentle breeze but soon became a gale-like windstorm, strong enough to make us reach out for some support. The boat took us all into the mist and furor of the falls. We could tell that the boat engines were genuinely struggling to keep the boat where it was. The water churned and broiled violently as I looked down at it. It is only when you reach the base of the falls that you realize how petite, weak, and temporary you are against the force of nature. We staggered at the power of the water and its inherent twisting currents. We were below the brink of something magnificent.

The boat took a slow turn to head back towards the dock. The mist, the roar of the water, and the magnetic pull they seem to exert on you as you look at them is not something man could replicate even after so much progress in science and technology. One cannot simply get the true experience anywhere else, not even at the closest viewing point to the Falls. A rainbow arched its multi-colored hues from, seemingly, the Canada shore to the American side. It was a spectacular site which aggrandized the magnificence of the natural wonder. As the boat left the falls behind, I looked at Afifah who was clicking pictures on her cell phone. Her skin was like silk over glass, and she radiated an inner beauty that made those billboard princesses look as fake as they were. Both her eyes held a coruscate gleam that made them shine like stars, resting behind the soft cushion of her lips. Her cheeks were naturally blush, capable of swallowing galaxies, and one would assume she had them rouged. Age was not touching her aura anytime soon. She was not aware how beautiful she looked against the background of the waterfalls. It seemed as if God used his own palette to create such a visual delight, because painting such aesthetics was even beyond the realm of Picasso. As she smiled, the rays of colors from every end of the spectrum went running in all directions, looking for an untouched canvas on which to leave a mark.

The boat ride lasted for around 20-25 minutes. As we got off the boat, I felt something strangely odd, as I was seeing her use her phone after two days.

'I hope you are using your phone for only taking pictures and have not put the sim card back. Otherwise, the cops are going to trace us down. I am sure your folks have filed a missing complaint for you,' I said.

'Don't worry. I remember your instructions. The sim card is not inside the phone. I just put the sim inside for a brief fifteen minutes this morning to speak with my friend Kashia. I have always shared everything with her, and I thought about updating her with my whereabouts,' she casually replied.

'You did what!'

'It was a brief call. I took out the sim as soon as I finished speaking with her.'

'Holy shit! We have to check out of the hotel right now. We cannot stay at the same place anymore.'

'Why?' asked Afifah.

'Because you committed the biggest blunder you could. It doesn't matter that you put your sim away after finishing the phone call. The police use a software for tracing phones that work on the principles of triangulation. They obviously know where we are if your phone was on trace. If we are lucky, they may not have been able to pinpoint the exact location, but it gives them a range with around 70-80% accuracy.'

'How do you know this?'

'Crime TV shows.'

We maneuvered to get ahead of the disembarking crowd of people and rushed in the direction of our hotel. Panic-stricken and flabbergasted by the sudden turn of events, we were both nervous about the consequences that were to follow. Until a minute ago, everything was hunky-dory, and we were swarmed with joy in the company of one of the seven natural wonders of the world. Now every emotion seemed fleeting, every thought gave way to a new one. Should I end this game of cat and mouse and tell her to go back to her parents? Should I try convincing her parents that their daughter's happiness was more important than catering to societal or religious expectations? Expecting the police to already be present at our hotel, we cautiously entered the humongous lobby and tried to lie as low as we could. We approached the reception to find out if there were any enquiries for us, because the police would have spoken at the front desk if they had come here.

'Hi, could you check if anyone has come looking for us or left a message?' I asked the receptionist. Afifah grasped my hand tightly, as she was tensed to the brim.

'Just a minute, sir. Could you help me with your room number?'

'403.'

'Not that I see anything on my system. I can ask my colleagues, as I just started my shift ten minutes ago.'

'That won't be necessary. We would like to check out early due to a change of plans. We are going to pack our suitcase and come down in five minutes.'

'Sure, that will not be a problem. I will be here to help you whenever you are ready, and we hope you have enjoyed your stay with us,' said the receptionist. I didn't bother to hear him out completely. I was relieved that there were no enquiries, and I turned around to go upstairs and pack my suitcase and whatever stuff Afifah had bought the day before. Caught unaware and unguarded, I received a bare-fisted punch on the left side of my face that left my teeth rattling. I lost my balance and slumped on my stomach.

'Bastard, don't ever come near my sister again,' said the person who punched me. I couldn't put a face to this voice as I was lying on my stomach, but the words from his mouth didn't leave any doubt as to who this guy was. It was Abdullah Javed, Afifah's brother. A shrill cry escaped Afifah's mouth, and she started crying.

'I will slap you too, if you don't come back home with us right now. Ammi has found such a nice boy for you, and you want to elope with a *kafir*?' snarled her brother and kicked me hard as I tried to slowly get up. Feeling a sense of acute pain, I groveled on the floor to get out of his immediate vicinity. I went from being a bastard to a *kafir* in a shorter span of time than what it takes to make a packet of instant noodles. I guess being a bastard wasn't illegitimate enough for him. Even illegitimacy needed to have a religious connotation.

'Stop hitting him. He is only helping me out. You should have stood up for me. As a brother, you were not there when I needed you the most,' Afifah raised her voice. Before the argument could escalate any further, her brother was pinned down by a police officer. Afifah's distant relative was in the police force, and he was privy to any inside information on this case. He had informed Afifah's family about her location and her conversation with Kashia in the morning. Kashia spurted out all the information like a parrot when Abdullah threatened her on the phone. Afifah's family had left for Niagara as soon as they got the update from their cop relative. Had Abdullah not assaulted me, the police would not be forced to interfere in the way that they did unless Afifah personally filed a complaint to seek restraining orders. Seeing the ensuing commotion and the paranoid guests, the hotel staff came to my rescue and helped me get on my feet.

After watching Abdullah pinned to the floor, Afifah's mother got furious and threatened her with a pointed finger, 'End all of this right now and come home with us, Afifah. This is the last warning we are giving you. Look at what is happening to Abdullah because of you. Think about the honor of our family.' Guilt was a mandatory weapon that is available in the arsenal of every Brown parent, and they use it incisively when all their efforts fail to bear fruit. She was evoking sentiments of guilt by construing Afifah's actions with besmirching the honor of their family and community. Afifah's father was busy placating the police officer who had pinned Abdullah to the floor and was now cuffing him. The second police officer from the Niagara police department interjected Afifah's mother to settle the dispute. Afifah clarified that she had run from home out of her own will. She dismissed all suspicions of being trafficked or lured by me to do illegal activities. She explained how her counterfeit ID was a coy to deceive the authorities in the incriminating witch hunt that would follow in her absence. After being equipped with the complete facts, the officers asked Afifah's parents to stay away from their daughter; otherwise, the police would be liable to take action against them.

'Sir, are you okay?' I was asked by one of the officers.

'Do you want to press charges against the individual who assaulted you?'

'No, let him go. However, I don't want any of these people near us, and I promise that Afifah will not use her fake ID again.' Afifah's parents gave me dirty, scornful looks from a distance. Until today, I cannot erase their cold, blood red eyes from my memory. Those eyes were a manifestation of the boiling anger, frustration, hate, and spite that they harbored for me. Those looks were sufficient to kill all my instincts. The police escorted the trio out of the hotel and my sight. Afifah comforted me and put up a strong exterior, though I knew she was torn inside.

'I am sorry on behalf of my whole family.'

'I am not letting you go back home to those people again,' I said. She kept shtum but gave me a tight hug. This was the first time I had given her an affirmative response with respect to letting her stay with me. She was conditioned to expect rejection from her loved ones. After a long time, she found support from someone whom she had kept her hopes on.

'I had already made my choice long back. I don't know how you will keep me, but I know that I will be safe.'

'I need to put some ice. Let us go back to our room,' I said, embarrassed at the whole episode that had played out in the hotel's lobby. We were the subject of everyone's gaze, including children who were scandalized by seeing me assaulted and police officers stomping in a place that was supposed to be their holiday destination. If there was anything more humiliating for a man than being beaten up, it was being beaten up in public. Just the other day, we were discussing how love was meant to be painful. Little did I know that I would experience it so soon and that pain would be physical.

Afifah inquired, 'Could I ask you something if you don't mind?'

'Sure.'

'Why didn't you press charges against my brother for assaulting you?' she asked with a sense of disbelief.

'Because I knew that would mean pressing charges against you. After all, he is your family. Even though he was wrong, your heart would ache to know that he would have to see the inside of a lockup. You wouldn't sleep peacefully at night wondering how disturbed he would be. The pain you must be feeling because of your family abandoning you is not something I can obliterate. It is a type of pain that can only heal with time. The least I could do is take away the pain that could result from my actions,' I said.

'You care about me so much! I wish I had never turned you down when you asked me out in university. Well, I can experience what I missed out in university when we go to London.'

'We are not going to London. I am cancelling my flight for Saturday.'

Chapter 12

'What! Why?' asked Afifah.

'Because even if I take you to London with me, you cannot stay there for more than six months without a working visa. Also, I don't want to leave you alone in Canada without finding a permanent solution for you.'

'Do you have a plan in mind?'

'No. But at the moment, this is what I think is the right thing to do. I need to defer my return to London for now. Meanwhile, this would give you enough time to see if any of your relatives would help you with long-term accommodation until you can find a job and be financially independent.'

'Yes, I could give it a shot. Though I doubt anyone would risk helping me now, because that would mean irking my parents. All of a sudden, I feel like a stock that has crashed and lost all its value because of a negative piece of news. No relative would want to invest in me no matter how strong my fundamentals are. Overnight, I have become a penny stock,' said Afifah.

'Don't worry, I am going to make sure that everyone knows you are still a blue-chip stock,' I retorted using financial lingo and dry wit in a way that would allow me to circumvent the feeling of opprobrium in her subject matter.

'I know that we are in an unusual situation, but how would you define our relationship? We haven't been on planned dates or formally asked each other out. I can't even call myself your girlfriend considering the way I imposed myself on you so that you would take me to Niagara. However, we have passed the stage of being just friends. What exactly are we?' she addressed the elephant in the room as I inserted the key card to enter our room.

'We have never actually discussed being in a relationship, so yeah, I cannot call myself your boyfriend either. But does a relationship need to have a name for it to be legitimate? You mean more to me than what the words "friend" or "girlfriend" could ever encapsulate. I don't know if there is a word in the English language that could describe our current relationship status, but the mere absence of such a word makes the relationship special. I have not explicitly said yes, and you have never expected a no, and this shows that some relations don't have a name, but they have emotions, feelings, and stories hidden in them.'

'You should be a part-time motivational speaker. I would pay to listen to you,' she said, trying to flatter me.

'While I cancel my ticket to London, why don't you look up for a cheap Airbnb on your phone, since our stay at this hotel ends tomorrow. Try finding an Airbnb that is not more than 50$ a night, because we need to account for every penny that we spend from now. I don't know how long this situation is going to last, and we cannot exhaust our funds.'

By knowing where to look, how to use the search parameters and digging a bit deeper, Afifah found us an accommodation that was within our budget. The room was equipped with the bare minimum, and we got what 49$ a night could get someone during the summers in Niagara. The host reluctantly offered us a breakfast of milk and cereals, as guests expected breakfast at a place that was called Air Bed and Breakfast (BnB). I didn't blame him for cutting corners, as he had to make his business sustainable with whatever little he earned. Our new accommodation was a long walk from the centre of the town and the Falls. However, our priority for now was saving money. But considering that this Airbnb was near a grocery store and provided us with a roof over our heads, I would call it a good deal.

Both of us mutually decided that we would live within a budget of 100$ a day and avoid any frivolous expenditures. 49$ were already being spent each day on accommodation, so we had a total of 51$ between us to spend every day. As a result, I decided to draw a list of all the free things we could do in Niagara. I wanted to save every penny so that we had enough to buy lunch and dinner. I was surprised to see the numerous things that one could do for free in a small place like Niagara that enticed tourists from all over the world. We were so accustomed to spending money that we had developed a myopic vision, which prevented us from experiencing the myriad things that were always available at no cost. It is true that the best experiences of life don't cost money. A very famous travel blogger had once told me that few years from when you visit a place, you will not remember the food you ate or the hotels you stayed in but what will make the place memorable will be the experiences. I jotted down some of the free places that we planned to visit over the next week. Our itinerary covered the hiking trails at Niagara Glen and Heartland Forest. The Niagara Parks Botanical Gardens was another popular recommendation. Dufferin Islands, Hershey's Chocolate World, Niagara Falls History Museum, winery hopping, and the Niagara River Gorge Hike were some of the other places that made it to our list.

We began the list with the hiking trail at Niagara Glen, which was a popular trail with hiking fanatics. The rhythmic stepping combined with the sweeping vistas placed me effortlessly in a meditative state. Afifah too mentioned entering a trance at one point, lost in the beauty of the creek in front of us. The trail was lightly blazed with red paint and small rock cairns as it weaved across open ledges. We stopped at the ledges and gaped at the stream of water that flowed beneath us. I found myself noticing trees, mossy rocks, fungi, and a horde of insects – things I didn't give much thought to in daily life. It was both exhausting and liberating at the same time, and after experiencing the steep climb upwards, I was convinced that we could finish the trail only because we were both young and healthy.

We wanted to take a break before our next exhaustive hike, so we spent the following day at the Niagara Parks Botanical Gardens. A couple, who were also visiting the gardens, were generous enough to give us a ride. The

Botanical Gardens spawned an area of 99 acres and featured a wide variety of flora arranged taxonomically and kept in a meticulous condition. As an exhibition of plant life, the garden contained 2,400 roses in bloom. In addition to the roses, the large arboretum composed a collection of fur, elm, maple, and pine alongside many other trees and woody plants. Afifah took a strong fascination to the Dorothy Perkin's rambler rose and asked me to take her selfie with the large matt pink flowers. The plants that caught my eye were the phlox and the white hydrangeas. In the middle of the park was a Butterfly Conservatory, which hosted 2,000 butterflies in a lush, climate-controlled environment. As I envisioned the complex life cycle of a butterfly, I realized how complex our lives had become.

On the third day of our daily excursions, we went winery hopping. We wanted to see the vineyards at our own leisure, so we rented two bikes instead of taking one of the many tourist-laden winery tours. In order to discover the wines that reflect the unique terroirs of Niagara, we started our trip with a family estate winery. The owner was a German man whose forefathers had emigrated from Germany; and hence, his winery specialized in Riesling wines. He told us how the weather and soil in the Niagara region created the ideal environment for artisanal wine venues and vine growth. The owner went on to enlighten us about the wine spittooning process where he taught us the correct way to sniff, taste, and spit wine into a spittoon, which sat on the tasting counters. We were amazed to know that he owned the oldest vinifera plantings in Canada.

After thanking him for his hospitality, we went to visit the Pillitteri Estates Winery. We entered the gift shop of this establishment, which was overcrowded with tourists. So we quickly moved towards the humble tasting rooms which offered a nice breath of fresh air. This tasting room had a tasting counter, a record player, and hill-top views. The tasting room led into an underground wine cellar that was stocked full of wine barrels. Since this winery had a commercial eatery for tourists, we ordered lunch and found seats on the serene patio overlooking the vineyards. Visitors who ordered lunch were offered a complimentary charcuterie pairing after their meal was over. The charcuterie pairing let us taste chocolate, cheese, and crackers with a sample of their wines and even educated us as to which wine went best with which food and why. As Afifah abstained from alcohol, I got double the amount of wine than I was entitled to. If I could ever afford a vineyard, I would like to buy one of these wine estates and retire to spend the rest of my life producing and drinking wine.

The next place on our list was Dufferin Islands. Dufferin Islands were a group of scenic man-made islands enveloped by miniature lakes and trees. A lightly forested series of walking paths marked by creeks gently snaked through the property. The islands were connected through walking bridges, and the governing body had introduced fishes, bird-feeding stations, and bird boxes, which were increasingly popular with the locals. After finding a secluded spot, I unpacked my shoulder bag to take out the picnic sandwiches and iced tea cans that we had purchased from the supermarket. It was Afifah's idea to have a picnic instead of a regular sit-in meal that we had been having every day. We had a peaceful lunch in the company of a Canada goose and her goslings, who socialized in the pond nearby. Our evenings were spent buying groceries and preparing dinner at the Airbnb, and it was during these suppers that I discovered that Afifah was a great cook.

By now, we had become so prudent in cost-effective sightseeing that we planned our trip to the Niagara Falls History Museum on a Thursday, as they had free admission on Thursdays after 5:00 pm. The Niagara Falls History Museum is touted as being the oldest museum in Canada. The museum displayed a smorgasbord of items related to the history of the Falls, and I found the whole experience to be very interactive and informative. The space was designed with the audio-visual ambiance of the historic Battle of Lundy's Lane, which is known to be the bloodiest battle of the 1812 war. Afifah tried on a replica uniform from the war. I participated in hands-on activities that included lifting a real canon ball and feeling the heft of a musket. After getting our goofy silliness out of the way, we proceeded to the community gallery where visitors could learn about the geology, culture, social life, and industry of the region. Finally, we entered the theatre where we witnessed a series of Mocassin Talks that provided us with a thoughtful window to the past by examining how peace and art have been joined together in the education of Aboriginals.

As I walked back through the town past bustling hotels and sleepy dwellings, I found myself grappling with the uncertainty and ambiguity of our current situation. Everything looked blurred; it seemed like I was seeing through smoked glass. I felt like I was in the middle of a game and had no idea what the rules were. I was feeling defeated and sagged like a sail bereft of wind. Astonished to see the various slivers of myself, I was utterly confused about how I should handle Afifah. I felt a sense that I had signed up for something that was beyond the realm of my control. The dissonance between expectation and reality was pestiferous. It is confusing when someone comes back in your life and you expect nothing out of it but suddenly, there, standing in front of you is everything that you have ever desired. The only way to allay my fears was to do something about it instead of procrastinating. I had talked a lot but said very little.

A week had passed by since my unpleasant experience with Afifah's family, contemplating our future course of action. 14th June, 2019, was a big day for Torontonians and Canadian basketball fans as the Toronto Raptors took their first legitimate stab at the NBA championship, being the only Canadian team in the tournament. To view what could be a momentous and historic win for the Raptors, I took Afifah to a local noshery called Casablanca to take in the game live and join the legion of fans who had come to show their solidarity with the team. I feel that most people have the tendency to romanticize the virtue of being at a game. You cannot see all the intricacies that you can see on live TV, especially the replays and the slo-mos. Fun for less than the price of parking at a stadium. I would have preferred to go to a sports bar, but I knew that Afifah would not find it congenial to enter a place reeking of alcohol and an inebriated crowd. The Casablanca was a multi-cuisine restaurant, which served Mediterranean, Italian, and Canadian food along with hookah and the usual pub grub like burgers and wings. The electric atmosphere had become a boon for proprietors, who were reaping the financial benefits tending to the hungry and thirsty basketball fans. I had witnessed the frenzied atmosphere in Toronto when the Raptors had won the third game. The streets had become jammed with rambunctious fans. The size of the crowd continued to swell as the fans chanted, sang, and cried. Champagne corks popped, and people climbed everything in sight from traffic lights to public buses.

We had to reach the Casablanca Restaurant two hours before the game started to secure our seats, because no restaurant was taking reservations considering the high number of walk-in customers. The civic pride at this noshery was palpable. Afifah ordered a smoked meat Italian sandwich whereas I ordered a plate of spicy chicken wings.

The Golden State Warriors were two-time defending champions, so the Raptors knew they had a tough game awaiting them. The two teams went back and forth from the opening tip until the final buzzer. Klay Thompson, of the Golden State Warriors, went down with a knee injury late in the third quarter and left the arena in crutches. However, the Warriors, true to their name, didn't lay down. They threw every punch they had in the bag. Steve Kerr drew up a terrific play, clearing out the far side of the court for a pass over the top that diverted the Raptor's attention just enough for Steph Curry to get a screen and fly open around the arc for a potential game-clinching, legacy defining, three. With Steph Curry's three pointer going awry, the Raptors came clutch securing the NBA championship with a 114-110 win over the Golden State Warriors ending the series 4-2. Kyle Lowry finished with 26 points, seven rebounds, and ten assists to lead the Raptors. The star player of the season and the final's MVP responsible for the Raptors seizing the trophy was Kawhi Leonard. Before this season had begun, no one had expected Kawhi Leonard to emerge as one of the greatest basketball players on Earth. The ensuing victory resulted in an explosion of joy as Canadians waved their flags, high-fived their friends as well as strangers, and surged down the streets in Niagara. A grand display of fireworks went off. I signaled for the cheque, and the hostess brought it along with two fortune cookies.

'I have only seen fortune cookies being given at Chinese restaurants at the end of the meal. It is quite strange that a place like this would also give this too,' said Afifah.

'Maybe they want a good tip,' I winked at her.

'I think they deserve a good tip. I don't think the staff at any of these places have got even a moment's rest. They have been on their feet this whole season, courtesy of the Raptors,' she added.

'Aren't you curious to know what destiny has in store for you?' I asked, pushing the plate of fortune cookies towards her.

'Yes, I like biting into these cookies and reading the aphorisms and prophecies. They have turned out true for me most of the times,' she said, unwrapping one of the cookies. She bit into the fortune cookie and took out the slip of paper with a lot of excitement. The paper read: *Afifah Javed, will you marry me?*

She looked at me to find me down on one knee with a ring that I had hidden in my pocket to surprise her. The staff of the restaurant and the customers who hadn't left to celebrate in the streets coaxed her to say yes.

'Afifah, I have seen the questions in your eyes, and I know what is weighing in your heart. You have chosen me over your cognate bonds. Now I want you to choose us. I want to share my bed, groceries, household chores, and friends with you. Will you be my wife?' I dropped the marriage bomb. She had tears in her eyes. She accepted the ring and let me insert it on her finger, saving me from potential public embarrassment that would have ensued if she had refused my proposal. She was the first girl on whom

I had inserted something peripherally round, which was not my dick.

'I love you, Devansh.'

'I love you too,' I replied.

'How did you manage to plant the proposal note in the fortune cookie?'

'I had called this restaurant yesterday and told them what I had in mind. This morning when I told you that I was going to the bank, I went to a shop and bought you this ring. Don't worry, I am going to get you a proper rock once my parents are on board and are willing to fund our marriage,' I said.

'Will they agree?' she asked the million-dollar question.

'I hope so.'

I belonged to a country that was partitioned on religious grounds, and she belonged to a country that came into existence as a result of that partition. In the subcontinent, interfaith marriages are often fraught with acts in varying degrees of violence because religious boundaries are trespassed. Apart from crossing religious boundaries, we had dared to transcend a more dangerous border – it was guarded by the metaphorical assault rifles of our relatives and the electronic sensors of society. Love was making us cross one of the most militarized borders in the world, and in terms of legitimacy, the only visa we had was hope.

With a faint glimmer of hope, Afifah called her parents and told them about her decision to marry me. They strongly demurred against our marriage and threatened to sever all remaining ties they had with her if she went ahead with her decision. Their words and attitude had made it evident that they were not willing to compromise an inch with their credo. An ultimatum was served, which forbade Afifah from celebrating her differences with me and intimidated her to compromise with the differences she had with the boy her parents loved. She had an equally strong conviction of not submitting even a quarter of an inch to her parent's ultimatum. Afifah's parents had discarded her from their life like she was a pokeroot. Our last hope was convincing my parents. In order for our marriage to materialize, it was imperative that my parents were on board with the plan. It was not financially, logistically, or socially possible to get married after being disowned by both sides of the family. With a deep breath, I called my mother to break the news to her.

The phone rang once.

Twice.

Three times. She picked up the phone on the fourth ring.

'Hello, Devansh, how are you?' answered my mother.

'Hi, Mom. I am good. Is this a good time to talk? I want to discuss something important.'

'Yeah. Is everything okay? You sound tensed,' said my mother.

'I wanted to tell you about a girl. I've known her for almost six years now since I started university. I love her, Mom, but things were complicated, so I didn't share anything with you earlier. But now I want to tell you that I proposed to her and I want to get married to her. Please understand...'

'That was a nice joke. I am your mother. You can't fool me,' she said, cutting me off mid-sentence.

'Mom, I am not joking. I am bloody serious. I proposed to her yesterday. She is a very nice girl. I am confident that you will like her.'

'How is it possible that I have never heard of this girl before if you liked her so much? Do you actually expect me to believe that a girl from your university randomly shows up in London and you propose to marry her?' she said belittling me.

'Mom, I am not in London. I never went back to London. I am still in Niagara Falls,' I said glumly.

'Son, are you on drugs? Wait, I am telling your father to call you,' she said and hung up the phone. I waited patiently for my father to call me. These seven minutes of waiting seemed like the longest seven minutes of my life.

'Hello,' said my father in a stern voice. My father, who had been brought up in an orthodox Marwari household and had tried, to the best of his ability, to give us a liberal upbringing was not pleased.

'Hi, Dad, how are you?' I began with surface level talk.

'Is it true what you just told your mother? She and your sister are listening to this conversation on speaker.'

'Yes, Dad. I would have told you all earlier, but all of this happened very suddenly. I don't know what to say. That is why I didn't go back to London. Her family is not accepting us, and she has nowhere to go unless she agrees to marry the boy they have chosen for her.'

'What is her name?' asked my father.

'Afifah,' I said softly, avoiding saying her whole name, though I knew what the next question would be.

'Afifah what?' he asked. It was very important for Brown parents to figure out the dynamics of religion, race, and caste, and if all the parameters didn't conform to their social norms, they would view us as asymmetrical. Since it was socially unacceptable to ask someone's religion or race, they were trying to find their answers through her last name.

'Afifah Javed,' I said closing my eyes, expecting an explosion on the other side of the phone.

'You want to marry a Muslim?' shrieked my mother before my father could say anything. 'Now I understand why her parents are against the marriage,' she added.

'Yes, Mom, she is a Muslim, but how does that make any difference? Educated people are wise enough not be swayed by bigoted narratives that we see on television or cinema.'

'Are you saying that we are uneducated? Just because you have a few degrees from universities abroad doesn't mean that you have experienced more life than we have.'

'I am not calling anyone uneducated. All I am saying is that her religion should not be viewed as a detrimental factor to our marriage.'

'How will you guys be compatible? You are a Hindu, and she is a Muslim,' my mother pressed on.

'A successful marriage cannot be judged by how compatible we are. It is going to be judged by how we eventually deal with our incompatibilities. Furthermore, belonging to different religions does not make us incompatible,' I said. When she saw that she was not winning this argument, my mother shifted gears.

'But I am sure she eats non-vegetarian food, and they even eat beef during their religious festivals. I am not going to allow all this inside my house. Devansh, we are Hindus. Would you like her bringing the flesh of cows inside our house?' I found it difficult to answer that question with a straight face considering the amount of meat that I had consumed in the last five years without her knowledge.

'Let us not jump the gun here. We haven't yet decided whether we would be living in Canada or coming back to India. Even if we decide to live and work in India after marriage, she will not bring any form of meat inside our house. You will know the type of girl she is when you meet her. She is very respectful and sensitive to other cultures and traditions. She won't do anything that would make you uncomfortable. There are many restaurants where she could go and satisfy her craving for chicken or red meat.'

'What about your family's future? I am telling you she will bring up your children as Muslims. You don't know how clever these girls are. In the beginning, they act all nice and sweet, but they reveal their true colors later on. She will never let your children follow our traditions and values.'

'First of all, if we have children, they are going to be our children and not my children alone. Secondly, Mom, all religions propagate the philosophy of acceptance and love for other human beings. She is willing to leave her family and friends and uproot her entire life, and you are concerned about which God she would make our children follow. Didn't you always tell me that there was only one God? I haven't discussed intricate details with her like the religion that our children will follow, but I am pretty sure she would give them the freedom to embrace the culture they would like to. She has also suffered a lot because of the non-inclusive approach of her parents,' I said. By now, I had begun to get frustrated with the Islamophobic questions, so I decided to counter question her to show them the fallacies in their rhetoric.

'Mom, Dad, instead of insinuating that a Muslim girl cannot make a good wife, why haven't you even asked me one question that would make me feel that you genuinely want to know what kind of a girl Afifah is? Why don't you ask me about her education or what qualities I like in her or how we met instead of focusing on just one aspect of her life.' On hearing that, my parents calmed down a bit but kept raising their doubts. The conversation went on for two hours, and I explained everything in detail from meeting Afifah to our present situation in Niagara and why I did not go back to London. Luckily, my elder sister was empathetic to my situation and saw the whole thing with a broader mind, so she helped me convince my parents to agree to the marriage. My parents asked to speak with their future daughter-in-law, and Afifah's expression throughout the time they spoke to her indicated how nervous she was. However, when she finally put the phone down, she was unperturbed.

After dealing with our family melodrama, the next sequential step was to invite our friends. Owing to the short notice and the sudden nature of this wedding, we wanted to keep the whole affair as small and intimate as we could. This meant inviting people that mattered the most. I arranged a conference call where everyone from my group excluding Ryan was present, since Ryan was overloaded with work. When I broke the news of my decision to marry Afifah and everything that transpired over the last ten days, the news struck them like a bolt of lightning. Initially, their reaction was similar to my mother, as they thought I was joking, but when I showed them that I was still in Niagara Falls and a picture of Afifah's finger with a ring on it, it dawned on them that I was no longer playing. The act of finalizing marriage with a girl whom I had not even kissed was alien to everyone other than Sam, since he was Indian and knew that it was common in arranged marriages, but in this case, even he was bewildered because mine wasn't an arranged marriage. It was going to be an unconventional love marriage. After having slept with so many girls, I didn't believe that love could blossom and thrive without physical intimacy. I told my friends that there was something about Afifah that brought out the best in me. I was a different person around her.

After a discussion with my parents, we came to the conclusion that the wedding would be taking place on the Sunday of next week, which was nine days from now. We did not want to indulge in an elaborate spectacle of conspicuous consumption that is characteristic of the big fat Indian wedding and thought it would be best to get married in a small chapel. This way neither my Hindu nor her Muslim rituals dictated the proceedings of our secular wedding. Since Afifah and I had met for the first time over a game of chess, it was decided that chess would be the theme for the wedding. I requested all my friends to equally share the responsibilities, as Afifah only had her best friend attending the wedding.

Nigel opted to take up the job of arranging the wedding officiant and booking the chapel. Sam was incharge of hiring the photographers and buying the confetti. Andre took the responsibility of ordering and customizing the cake. Sonia was ensuring that there were no hindrances with the bridal makeup, hair, and dry cleaning. Lydia was handling the booking of the bridal bouquet along with other miscellaneous items like a cloth chess mat where everyone could write a message for the bride and groom. I realized how planning a small wedding required so much effort.

(With the desi youth appropriating globalization and the structural changes in urban society by attaching new meanings, I predict that marriage rates will significantly decrease in South Asian countries by 2050, as more couples will choose to enter common law unions or cohabit. I would like to divert off topic for a bit and make another prediction based on current trends. Seeing the socioeconomic progress that has been made by the Indian and the Chinese communities in Canada, I predict that by 2050 Canada will have a prime minister that has Indian or Chinese origins).

The quest to be the best man at my wedding led to an ego clash between Andre and Sam. They both wanted to be my best man and started luring me with bribes. Up until the day of the wedding, I received requests from both of them, sometimes at weird hours through text messages, describing why I should pick one over the other. When the bribes did not work, they played the emotional card by reminding me how our friendship over the years had lasted through thick and thin. Andre made me recall how he had introduced me to *The Game*, which helped me cultivate pick-up skills and enhanced my social calibration. Sam said that I was obliged to him for all the high returns I made from the tips he regularly gave me about the cryptocurrency market. To show how much being my best man means to them, they had both started working on their speeches as well. I was secretly enjoying the attention, and I had told them that they should both be prepared, as I would keep them in suspense until the day of the wedding.

My father had booked several rooms for us and all our guests at the Prince of Wales Hotel located in Niagara-on-the-Lake. This enabled all my friends and Afifah's bridesmaid Kashia to move in on Friday with us and officially begin the wedding celebrations apart from following up on their individual responsibilities. Niagara-on-the-Lake is a quaint old town bordered on both sides with arbor-framed streets, red brick Victorian buildings, lush boulevard gardens, and window boxes overflowing with flowers. It takes around twenty-five minutes to drive from Niagara Falls to visit this historic charm. The reason we had chosen to book a hotel in Niagara-on-the-Lake was because it was close to the chapel where Afifah and I were getting married. Moreover, the Price of Wales Hotel enjoyed a privileged location at the heart of the town and was the only hotel in the region that could give us a taste of English royalty with antique furnishings. The delicious gourmet cuisine as well as the traditional afternoon tea served in Victorian drawing rooms were a significant upgrade for Afifah and me, making us feel special before our big day. I felt an immense sense of pride in the fact that I was staying at a hotel where Queen Elizabeth II as well as the Prince and Princess of Wales had resided on their Canadian tour.

I was getting married the next day. It was my last night as a bachelor. We had barely scraped through completing my wedding preparations, let alone have any time left to plan a stag night due to my abrupt proposal. Therefore, I was drinking with my friends at the hotel bar until the final call. The alcohol was verily helping me calm my nerves, as millions of emotions assaulted me. Giving up singlehood at the young age of twenty-four was tough. I knew my load of responsibilities would increase, and I would have to put the needs of my significant other ahead of me. I could not believe I was the first in the group to take the plunge. As we left the bar, I was the last one to get off the elevator, since my royal suite was on a floor above the rooms of my friends. Slightly tipsy and prepared to crash on my bed, I entered my suite and shut the door with an exaggerated gesture. I opened my shoes without bothering to switch on the light, as I was too lazy to change my clothes. My tired body and my whimsical mind needed the comfort of a soft mattress.

I stopped short of laying claim on my mattress, as an unfamiliar scent entered my nostrils. It was the scent of a heavily cloying perfume. I stood still and smelled harder. Then my eyes adjusted themselves more to the darkness and I saw something in the shape of a leg move on my bed. Terrified, I ran across the length of my suite and switched on the light with a flick of my index finger.

'Don't worry, it is only me,' I heard Afifah's voice. 'Switch off the light, please. I am turning the light of the bedside lamp on.' I tried to catch my breath.

'You scared me!' I said.

'I am sorry,' said Afifah.

'How did you get in?' I asked, walking towards the base of my bed.

'Through the keyhole like Peter Pan,' she giggled. She was wearing one of my shirts that had wrinkles on it and looked two sizes big on her. She sat up on the bed and pulled the blanket over the lower part of her body. The brief delay allowed me to see that she was wearing nothing beneath the shirt other than her panties. Maybe she wanted me to notice that. Her kittenish eyes peered at me. I was seeing a new shade of her that was alarming on many levels.

'How did you manage to make your way inside my room?' I asked again.

'Stop asking stupid questions. I am your fiancée, so getting access to an extra set of keys to your room from the reception wasn't difficult. Besides, it is going to be my room too from tomorrow.'

'But why would you sneak in?'

'Shhhhh...let me do the talking. Come closer...I am here to give you what you have been wanting for a long time. I want you to consummate our relationship now,' she whispered, inexpertly attempting to seduce me. I could sense that she was shivering after she had spoken.

'I know that your values and upbringing forbid you from premarital sex. You don't have to make such compromises for me,' I said holding her hand. A tear rolled down her cheek.

'All these days, I have only thought about myself. I feel guilty for treating you like this. Just because I believe something does not give me the right to ignore the physical needs of a relationship. I am sorry for being selfish,' she said vulnerably. She was prepared to cry any moment. I knew she was not being herself. She was not prepared to lose her virginity but was only willing to have sex for my sake.

'Hey, hey, hey...don't do this. Afifah, men only need a place to have sex, but women need a reason. You will have a reason tomorrow. Trust me, I can wait,' I said. She looked at me with empty emotionless eyes. I felt she could see my soul.

'I am so lucky to be marrying you, Devansh,' she said as she got out the blanket to hug me. I hugged and comforted her, and she ended up in my arms with watery eyes.

'Today is a big day for us. You should get some sleep. Let me take you to your room. First, let me grab your key,' I said and lifted her in the air with both my hands. She had both her arms around my neck as she looked romantically in my eyes. I carried her all the way to her room, hoping no one would be awake at this late hour to spot me carrying my semi-nude fiancée. After tucking her in bed, I came back to my suite and pulled the curtains to look outside at the dimly lit street from the comfort of my chair, eventually falling asleep in it.

The team of hair and make-up artists that were hired began their work at 9:30 am. They further split into three smaller teams. One team catered to my family. The other team catered to my friends who were the groomsmen, and the third team catered to the bride and the girls, which included Kashia, Sonia, and Lydia. Afifah, being the bride, was the last person to get her hair and make-up done so that she could look the freshest as she walked down the aisle. A small photography team arrived with their camera equipment to take pictures and videos of the bride getting ready. They even had a drone to take aerial shots of the moment when Afifah and I would be departing on separate horse carriages for the chapel. It was 1:00 pm, and the wedding ceremony was about to start two hours from now. Everyone other than Afifah was ready. She was busy with her hair and make-up as Kashia helped her cope with all the emotions she was experiencing. She was getting married without her parents' presence, or approval, so it was natural for her to get more emotional than the average bride.

'Man, it is high time you kill the suspense. Please tell everyone that I am going to be your best man,' said Andre, giving Sam a cunning look.

'You better not pick Andre as your best man. I have worked very hard on writing the best man's speech for you. Plus, Andre doesn't deserve to be your best man. You don't want a best man who is thinking about hitting on your bride's maid of honor. Once he gets in Kashia's pants, you will have to clean his crap for the rest of your life,' said Sam.

Nigel broke off their childish feud, 'Before you choose one of these fools to be your best man, let me get one last laugh. To sum it all up, you liked Afifah all through university while you were busy smashing girls you met at bars, libraries, classrooms, and clubs. You confessed your feelings to her, and she did not reciprocate them, and you come back to Toronto for a reunion only to realize that you still like her two years after graduating. You find out that she is being forcefully married, so you take her along with you to Niagara and end up being the person to put a ring on her. Man, you are a dick!'

'You don't have to put it like that,' I said.

'I cannot think of a sophisticated way to call you a dick,' said Nigel.

'Think what you want, but the biggest dick amongst us all and my best man has just arrived. Guys, look behind you,' I said. Nigel, Andre, and Sam turned to see Ryan enter the bar where we were taking the customary pre-wedding drinks that the groom has with his friends. Nigel was pleasantly surprised to see Ryan, but Andre and Sam could see their hopes of being my best man wither away. He had flown in from the United States especially for my wedding and was going back tonight itself, as the place where he was doing his article of clerkship did not give him a leave. He was impeccably groomed and had the stride of a confident lawyer entering a court room.

'Holy shit! I thought you couldn't make it to this wedding,' said Nigel.

'Devansh and I wanted to surprise everyone, so that is why I lied that I would not be coming, but I wouldn't miss his wedding for anything in the world, even though I have to report back to work tomorrow,' said Ryan.

Gutted to see his contention for being my best man slip away, Andre scrambled to say something, 'He might be a lawyer from Yale, but that doesn't mean you should pick him over an investment banker from Rotman like me.'

'He is not only a lawyer from Yale, he is also the guy responsible for the scandal with Professor Keatinge. Remember the key I found in the library? It was the same Episkopon key that surfaced in the scandalous video, and it belonged to Ryan. Told you, he is the biggest dick amongst us all. I desperately wanted to share this with everyone at my wedding because he prohibited me from sharing this information with any of you during school. You know how this shit works, they have to take oaths and all that crap. But now that school is over, I wanted all you guys to know this, so I asked him if I could share this with all of you. He gave me permission on the condition that I make him my best man, so basically, his bribe trumped all your bribes,' I said.

Sam remorsefully said, 'At this point, I don't know whether to believe his miraculous arrival at your wedding, thereby snatching away my chance of being your best man, or the fact that he was getting his dick inside a gorgeous professor while I was chasing sorority girls.'

'What a prick! Never imagined you to be responsible for that shit,' said a shocked Andre.

All of us other than Afifah and her maid of honor left for the Living Water Wayside chapel, the destination of our wedding. The chapel, a short ride from our hotel, was delightfully quaint as it looked like something that was magically teleported from Europe. The inside of this miniature worship place held four short pews as well as one Bible and a guest book. One of the characteristics that made me choose this chapel was that it was known to be the smallest chapel in North America.

Today I was missing Manny terribly. His void was partially filled by his mother and his sister whom I had invited for the wedding. They had come from Brampton with a cousin of Afifah called Aqsa, who had sneaked out of her home under the pretense of doing a group assignment at university. Afifah's cousin Aqsa, who was very fond of Afifah, wasn't allowed to attend the wedding because Afifah's parents had asked all their relatives to boycott the occasion. The photographer took group and solo pictures of all the attendees while his acolyte began to setup the angles to capture the arrival of the bride and her maid of honor. My parents gave Ryan both the wedding rings they had purchased in India, which were designed in the shape of a chess king and queen to emphasize the theme of the wedding. Lydia had arranged headgears for us in the shape of the king and queen pieces on the chess board, which were symbolic of the fact that Afifah was going to be my queen. Lydia even had a headgear for the person officiating our wedding in the shape of the chess bishop, which was also in congruence with the theme of the wedding and was symbolic of a priest. Ryan and Lydia managed to reconcile their mutual uneasiness towards each other at my wedding that had begun two years ago ever since Ryan had rejected Lydia's romantic advances.

It was 2:45 pm, and the ceremony was about to start in 15 minutes. Shortly, Afifah arrived like Cinderella in a horse-drawn carriage along with Kashia. Afifah was carrying an artificial flower bouquet of black and white silk roses, as black and white reflected both the colors of a chess board. My parents and sister were seated inside the chapel whereas Ryan and I waited at the altar as Afifah walked down the aisle escorted by her maid of honor. At 3:00 pm, the officiant began our wedding proceedings with his standard opening remarks. Then he specifically addressed Afifah and me and explained the significance of the vows we were about to exchange. Instead of having amorous readings or votive candles, we had tweaked the order of events to include the speeches of the best man and the maid of honor before exchanging vows, because we weren't throwing a reception due to the limited number of guests. After the speeches finished, it was time to exchange our wedding vows. The wedding vows were as follows:

Devansh: ***Dear Afifah,***

When I first saw you, you seemed to appear out of a fairytale. My focus was on you, consistently, as I tried to decipher who you were and what you studied. Now, as we get married, I look forward to play all my moves in this life of chess with you. After all, the strongest piece on the chess board that ensures the protection of the king is the queen. Also, I promise to comfort you when Pakistan loses its cricket matches against India.

Afifah: ***Dear Devansh,***

*You have been my friend, advisor, confidant, and my biggest challenge. But most importantly, I love you more than anything in the world, and you give me more joy than you can ever imagine. You have made me a better human being, as our love for one another is reflected in the way I live my life. I am truly fortunate to be a part of your family, which from today becomes ours together. I will listen to your advice even if I don't follow it *chuckles*. Also, I promise to never overdraft your bank account.*

After exchanging vows, we exchanged rings.

The officiant made us official, 'I now pronounce you husband and wife,' and told me to kiss the bride. I couldn't move to kiss my beautiful bride. A confused officiant looked at me and repeated the words again assuming that I hadn't heard them. But he had enunciated them clearly the first time, and I had heard him loud. My frozen self was the result of the norms in Indian society where I found it embarrassing to kiss a girl in front of my parents. Indian boys operate with the understanding that parents know that we might be kissing our partners, but that doesn't mean that we can validate their beliefs. Afifah, a child of Pakistani parents, instantly understood the reason of my embarrassment and inaction. Unruffled, she took two steps forward and landed a kiss on my lips. My stiff body made our first kiss awkward, but her telepathic reaction made it the most beautiful moment of the wedding. If this was not true love, then I don't know what love is.

As we walked down the short aisle as a couple, we were showered with confetti. Everyone congratulated us, and the photographers took a plethora of pictures of us with our guests. I was touched to see the funny, cute, and heart-touching messages that people had written on the cloth chess board ordered especially for this exercise. Andre had done a fantabulous job with customizing a grandiose chess-themed cake. The three-tiered cake sat on a stand outside the chapel, and it had become a prime setting for photographs. Customizing the wedding cake was probably the toughest job after choosing the bride's outfit. There were sugar busts of the various chess pieces like knights and elephants. The three layers of sponge was covered in squares of buttermilk and dark chocolate to blend in seamlessly with the theme.

'Let us have a picture of the couple with the cake now,' said my sister in a long drawl.

'We cannot thank all of you enough for your contributions,' I said.

'I have already thought of names for your children,' added my sister, teasing me and Afifah.

'I will take your suggestion if our first born is a girl,' I said thoughtfully. 'Because if it is boy, his name is going to be Emmanuel.'

CPSIA information can be obtained
at www.ICGtesting.com
Printed in the USA
LVHW050130010522
717630LV00004BA/106

9 789354 273995